Keiko Suenobu

LIMIT
2

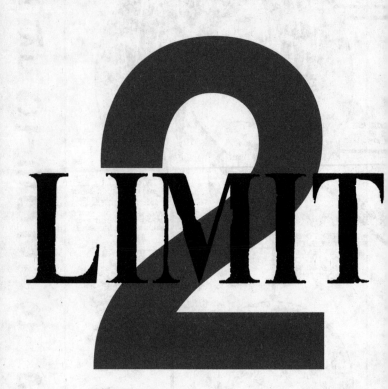

VERTICAL.

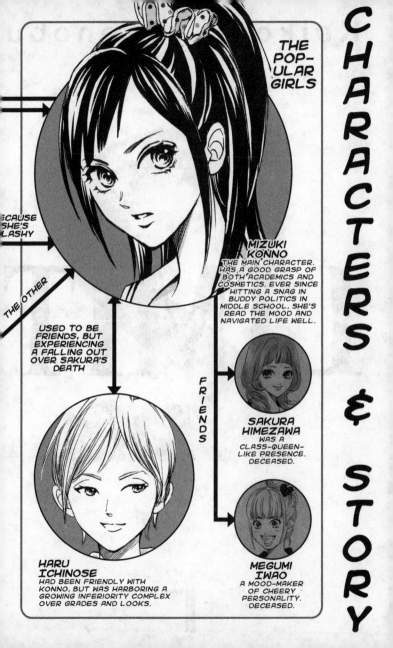

THE POP-ULAR GIRLS

BECAUSE SHE'S FLASHY

THE OTHER

MIZUKI KONNO
THE MAIN CHARACTER. HAS A GOOD GRASP OF BOTH ACADEMICS AND COSMETICS. EVER SINCE HITTING A SNAG IN BUDDY POLITICS IN MIDDLE SCHOOL, SHE'S READ THE MOOD AND NAVIGATED LIFE WELL.

USED TO BE FRIENDS, BUT EXPERIENCING A FALLING OUT OVER SAKURA'S DEATH

FRIENDS

SAKURA HIMEZAWA
WAS A CLASS-QUEEN-LIKE PRESENCE. DECEASED.

HARU ICHINOSE
HAD BEEN FRIENDLY WITH KONNO, BUT WAS HARBORING A GROWING INFERIORITY COMPLEX OVER GRADES AND LOOKS.

MEGUMI IWAO
A MOOD-MAKER OF CHEERY PERSONALITY. DECEASED.

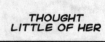

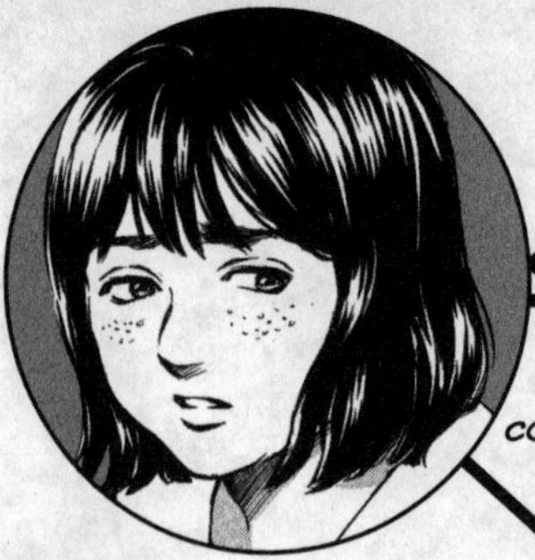

THOUGHT LITTLE OF HER

CAN'T FORGIVE HER

CONTROLS HER HEART

ARISA MORISHIGE
WAS A SUBDUED PRESENCE IN THE CLASS AND WAS BULLIED. AFTER THE ACCIDENT, SHE GETS AHOLD OF THE ONE WEAPON, THE "SCYTHE," AND VENTS HER ANGER.

KONNO HAD BEEN SPENDING HER DAYS AS PART OF THE CLASS'S CORE CLIQUE, AS ONE OF THE STRONG.

BUT THE BUS ACCIDENT THAT OCCURRED ON THE WAY TO AN EXCHANGE CAMP CHANGES EVERYTHING. THERE ARE ONLY A MERE FIVE SURVIVORS, ALL GIRLS. HER PERFECT, ORDINARY LIFE THAT WASN'T EVER SUPPOSED TO CHANGE COMPLETELY CRUMBLES AWAY.

MORISHIGE, WHO HAS SEIZED POWER, IMPOSES A "STATUS SYSTEM" AND REQUIRES KONNO AND HARU TO FIGHT OVER THE MINIMALLY REMAINING FOOD.

KONNO DECLINES BUT MORISHIGE MULISHLY POKES AT HARU'S INFERIORITY COMPLEX. HARU FINALLY SNAPS AND SWINGS THE SHARPENED POINT OF HER RAGE TOWARDS KONNO, AND—?!

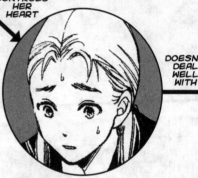

DOESN'T DEAL WELL WITH

CHIKAGE USUI
HAS A DOCILE PERSONALITY AND IS EASILY INFLUENCED BY OTHERS. HAS A LEG INJURY.

NEITHER ACKNOWLEDGES

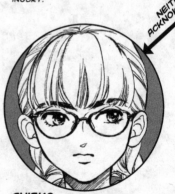

CHIEKO KAMIYA
A CALM, COOL, AND COLLECTED PERSONALITY. HAS AN ABUNDANCE OF KNOWLEDGE REGARDING NATURE AND RESCUE, BUT ALSO HAS A CALLOUS SIDE.

contents

Scene.4 –
That Which Cannot Be Seen, That Which Shall Not Waver

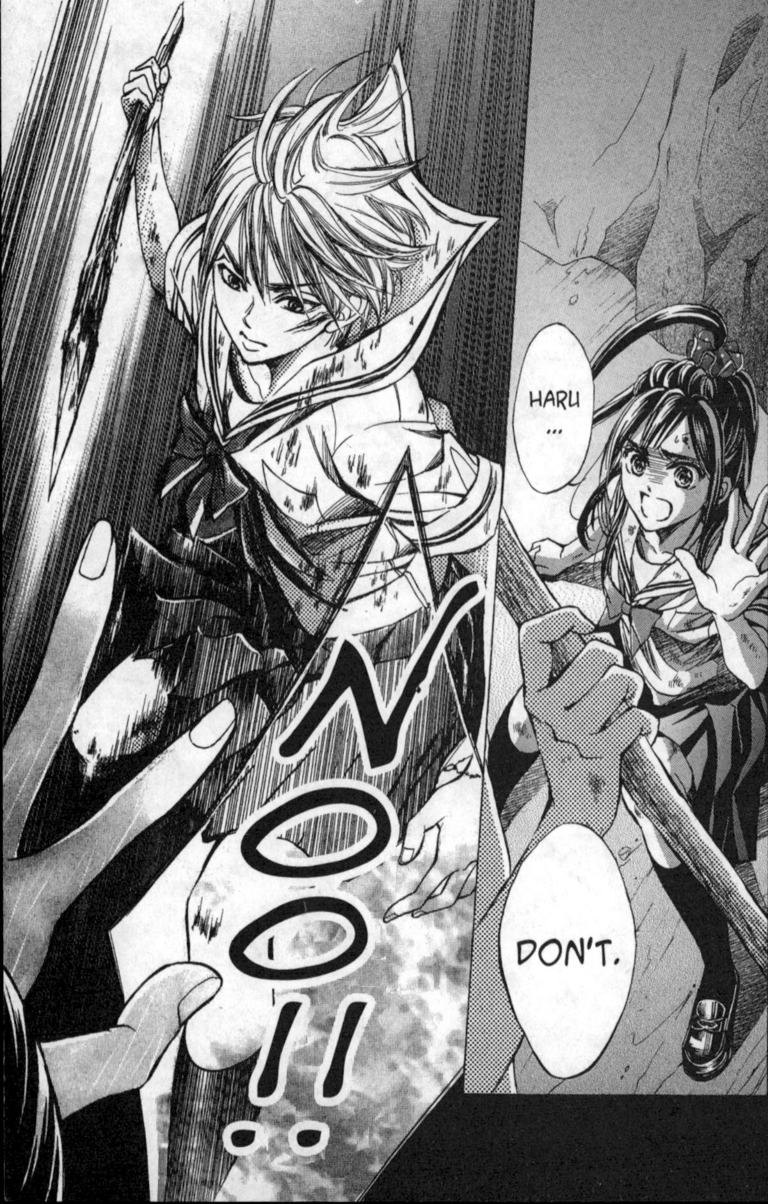
HARU ...
DON'T.
NOOO!!

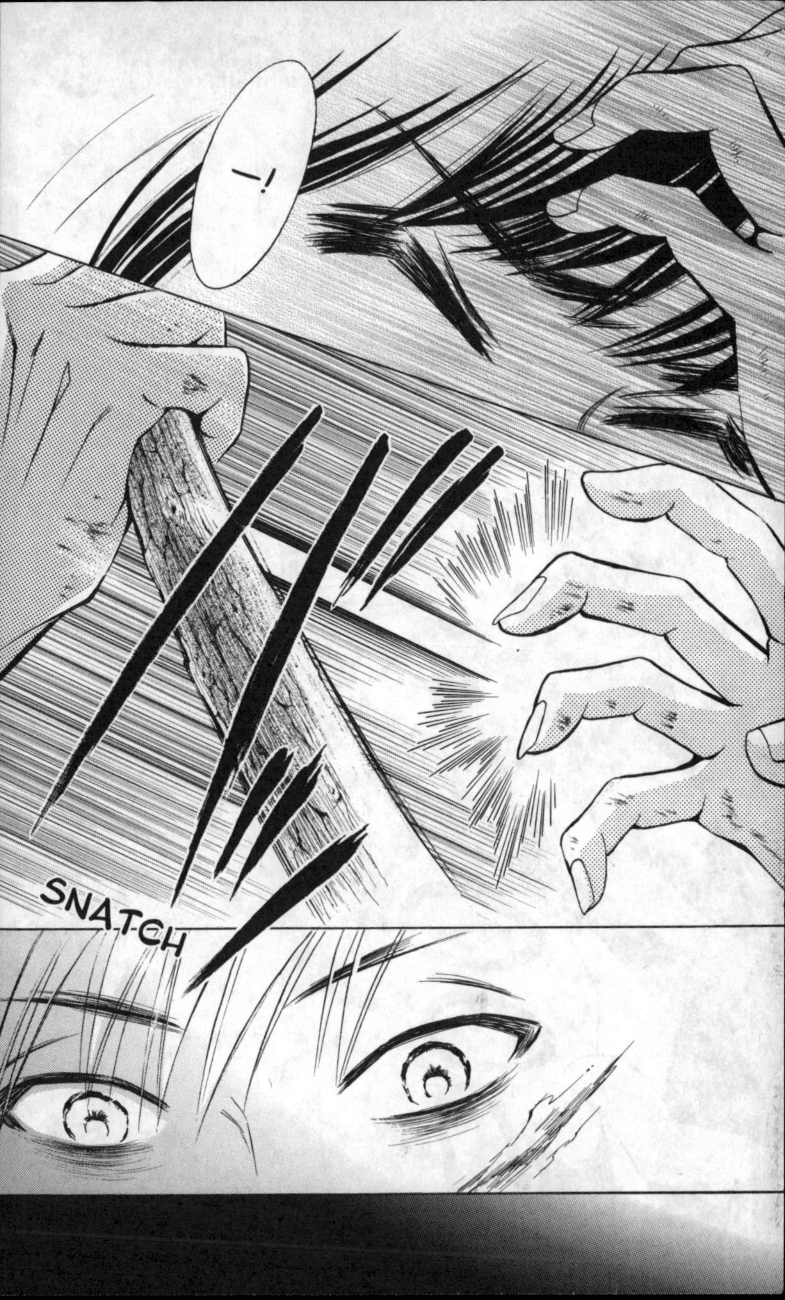
–!
SNATCH

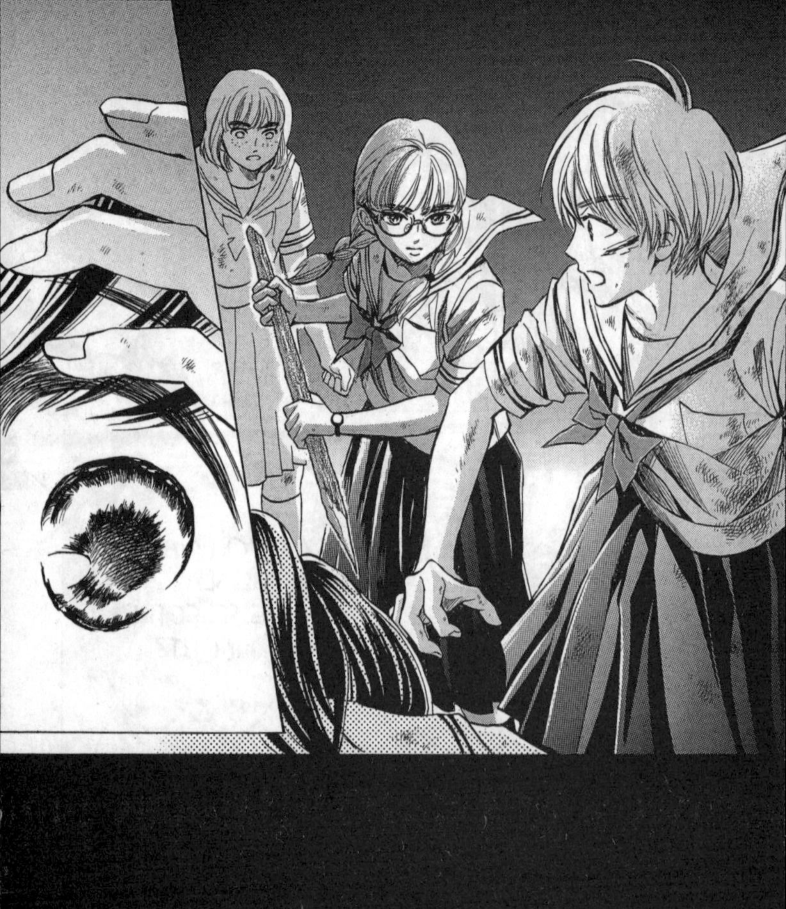

LIMIT

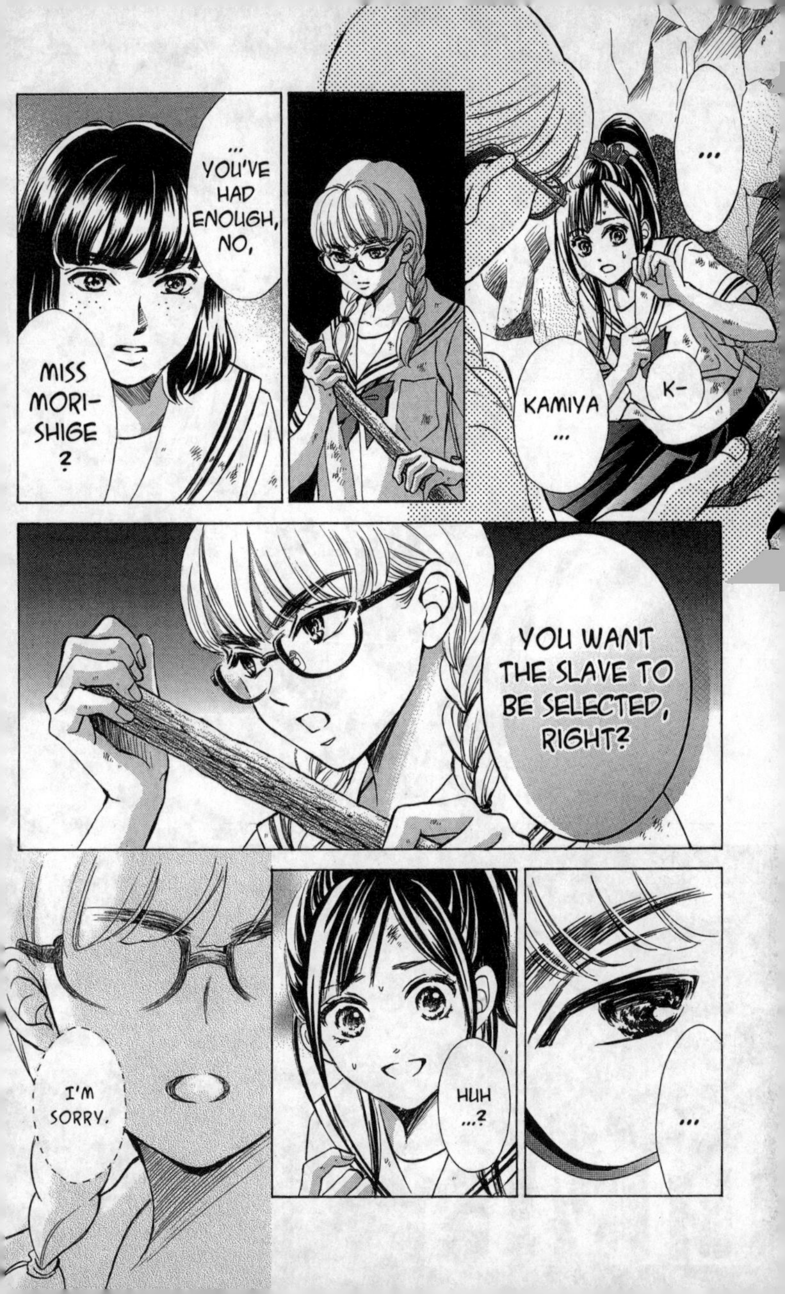
...
K-
KAMIYA ...
... YOU'VE HAD ENOUGH, NO,
MISS MORI-SHIGE ?
YOU WANT THE SLAVE TO BE SELECTED, RIGHT?
...
HUH ...?
I'M SORRY.

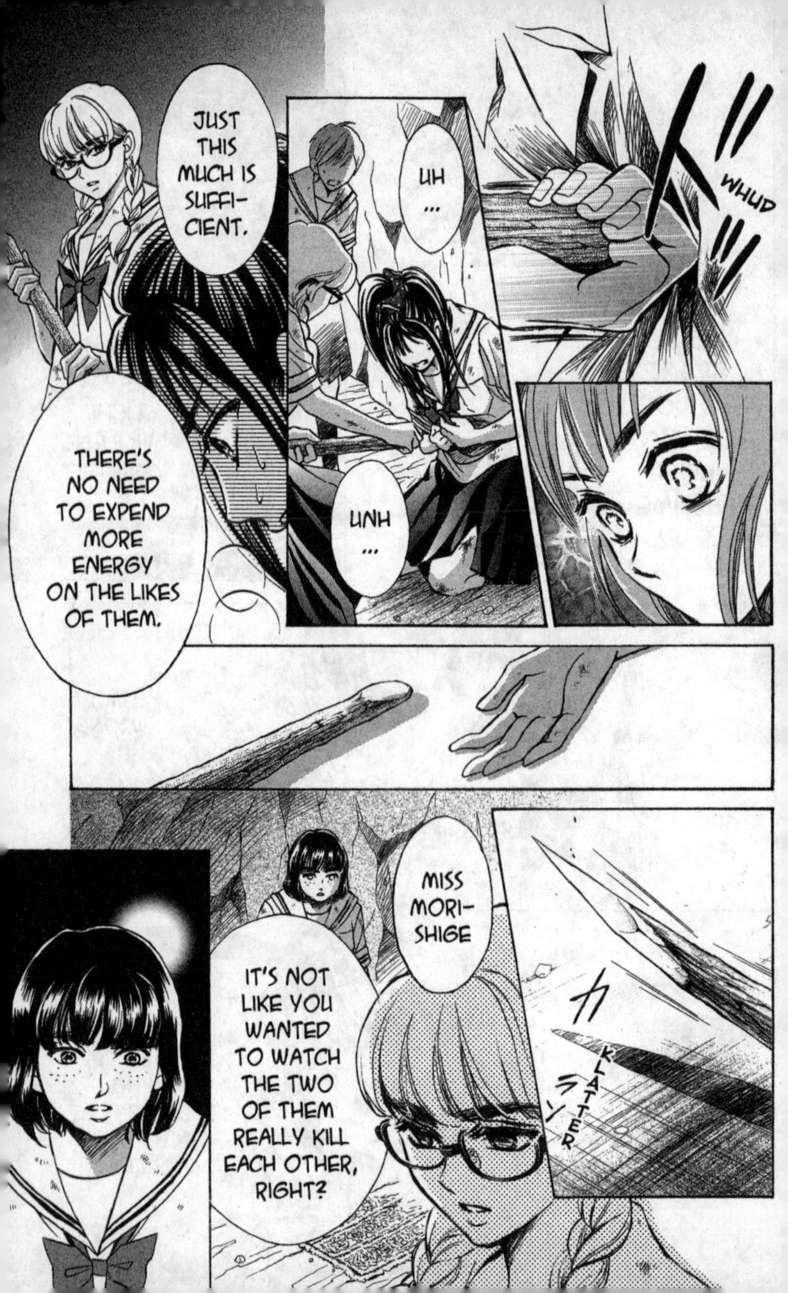
WHUD
UH ...
UNH ...
JUST THIS MUCH IS SUFFICIENT.
THERE'S NO NEED TO EXPEND MORE ENERGY ON THE LIKES OF THEM.
KLATTER
MISS MORISHIGE
IT'S NOT LIKE YOU WANTED TO WATCH THE TWO OF THEM REALLY KILL EACH OTHER, RIGHT?

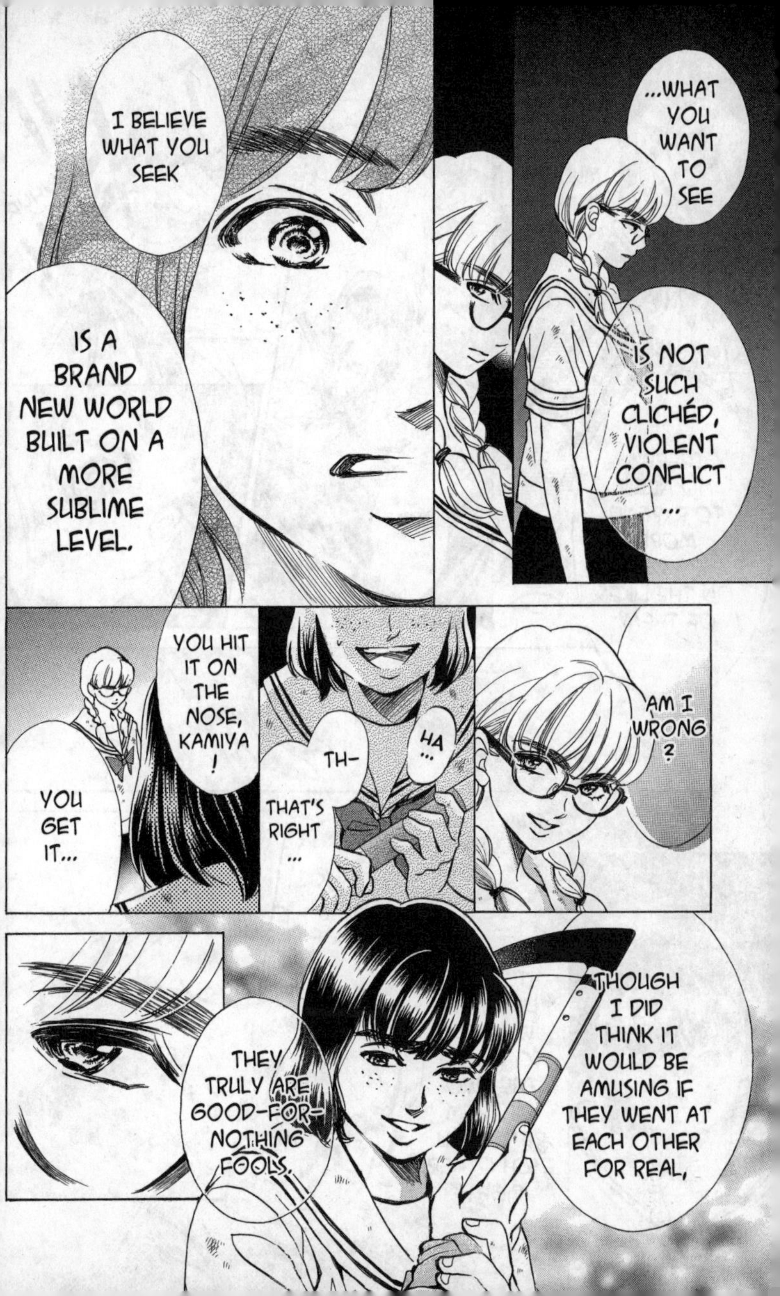
...WHAT YOU WANT TO SEE
IS NOT SUCH CLICHÉD, VIOLENT CONFLICT ...
I BELIEVE WHAT YOU SEEK
IS A BRAND NEW WORLD BUILT ON A MORE SUBLIME LEVEL.
AM I WRONG?
HA ...
TH-
THAT'S RIGHT ...
YOU HIT IT ON THE NOSE, KAMIYA!
YOU GET IT...
THOUGH I DID THINK IT WOULD BE AMUSING IF THEY WENT AT EACH OTHER FOR REAL,
THEY TRULY ARE GOOD-FOR-NOTHING FOOLS.

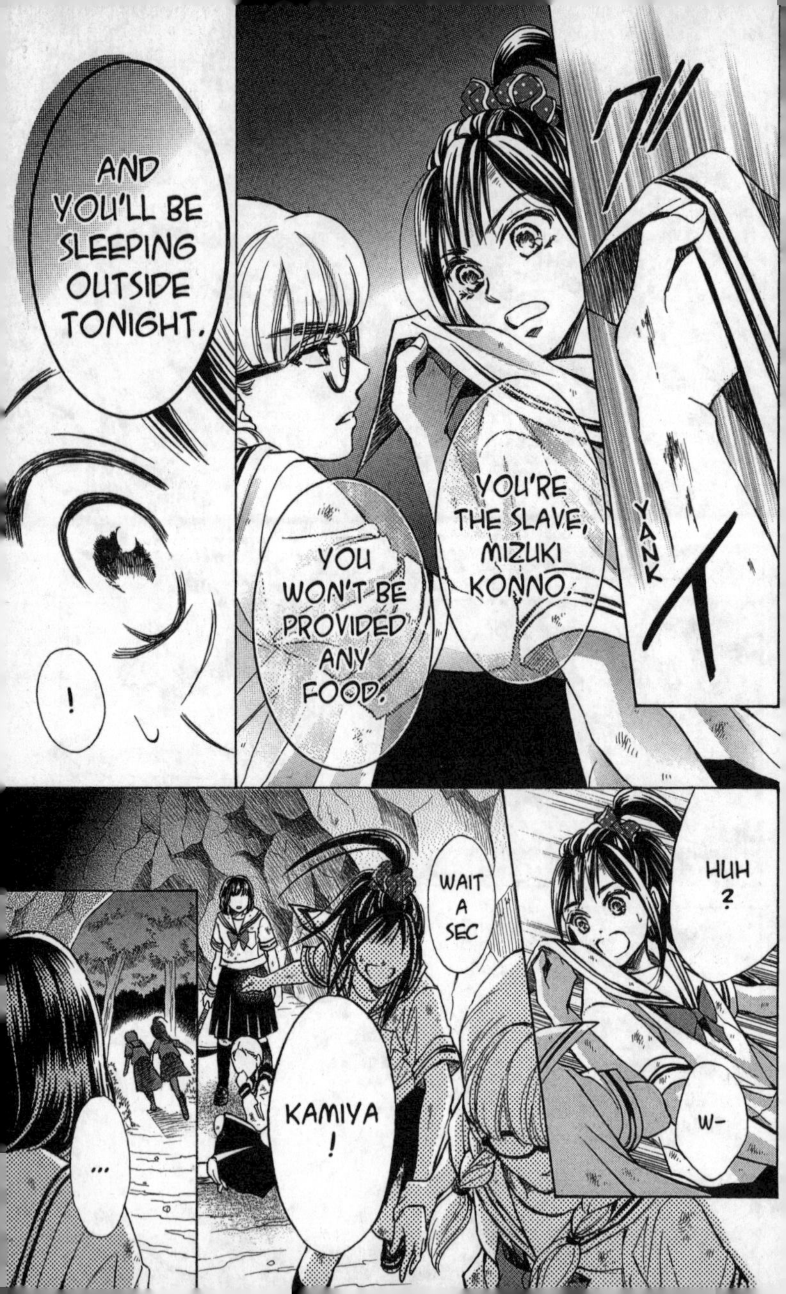
YANK
YOU'RE THE SLAVE, MIZUKI KONNO.
YOU WON'T BE PROVIDED ANY FOOD.
AND YOU'LL BE SLEEPING OUTSIDE TONIGHT.
!
HUH ?
W-
WAIT A SEC
KAMIYA !
...

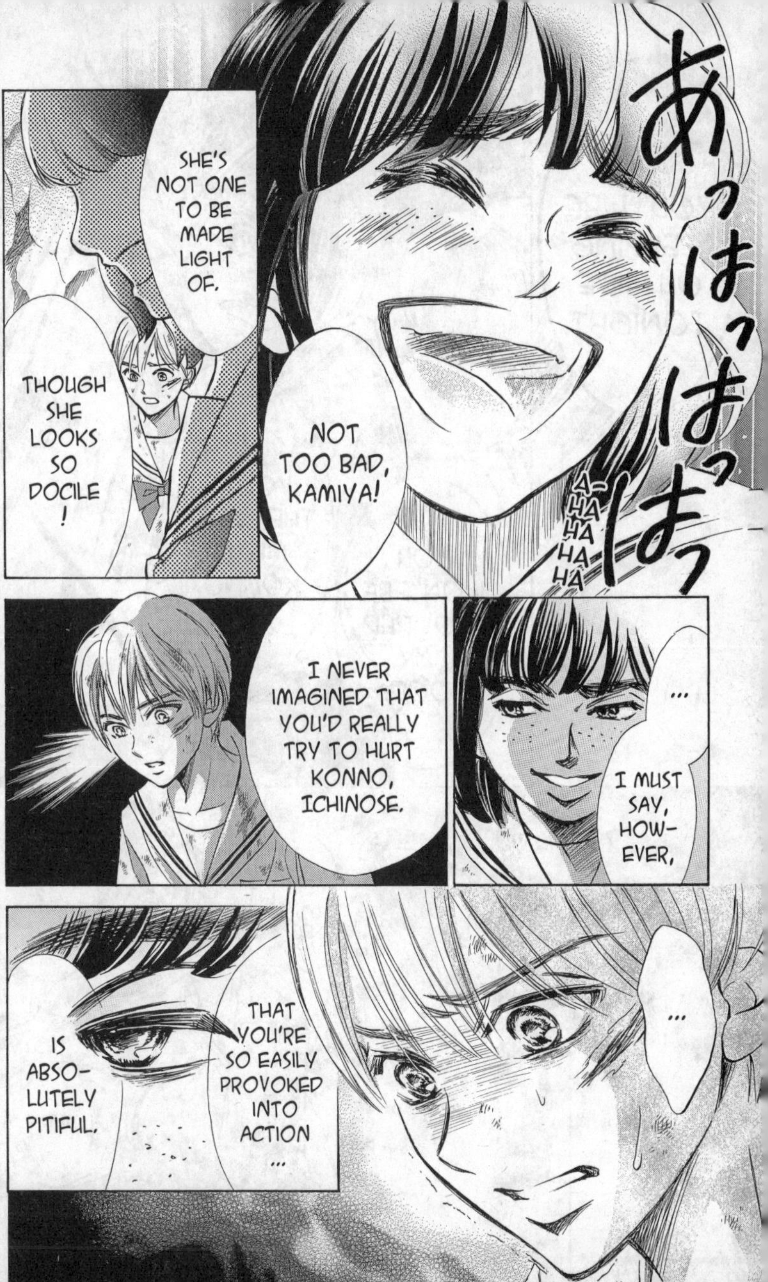
あっはっはっ
A-HA HA HA HA HA
NOT TOO BAD, KAMIYA!
SHE'S NOT ONE TO BE MADE LIGHT OF.
THOUGH SHE LOOKS SO DOCILE!
...
I MUST SAY, HOW-EVER,
I NEVER IMAGINED THAT YOU'D REALLY TRY TO HURT KONNO, ICHINOSE.
...
THAT YOU'RE SO EASILY PROVOKED INTO ACTION ...
IS ABSO-LUTELY PITIFUL.

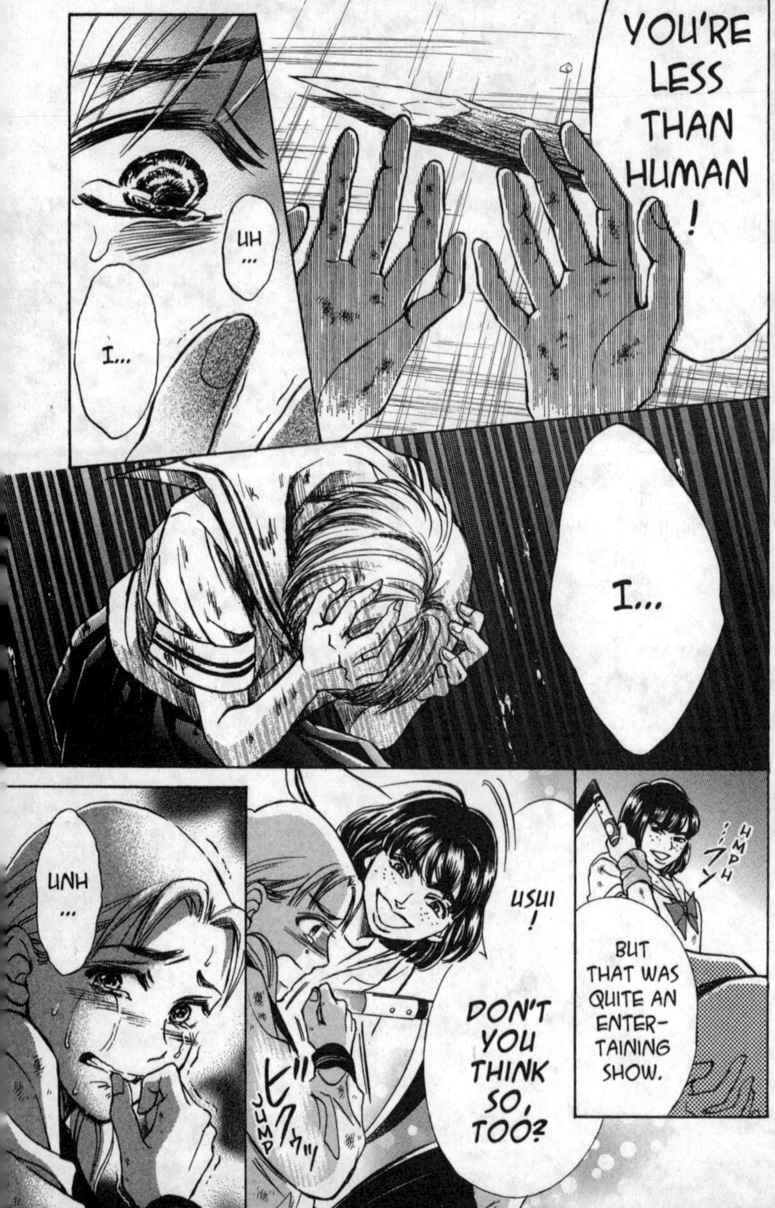
YOU'RE LESS THAN HUMAN!
UH ...
I...
I...
HMPH
BUT THAT WAS QUITE AN ENTER-TAINING SHOW.
USUI!
DON'T YOU THINK SO, TOO?
JUMP
UNH ...

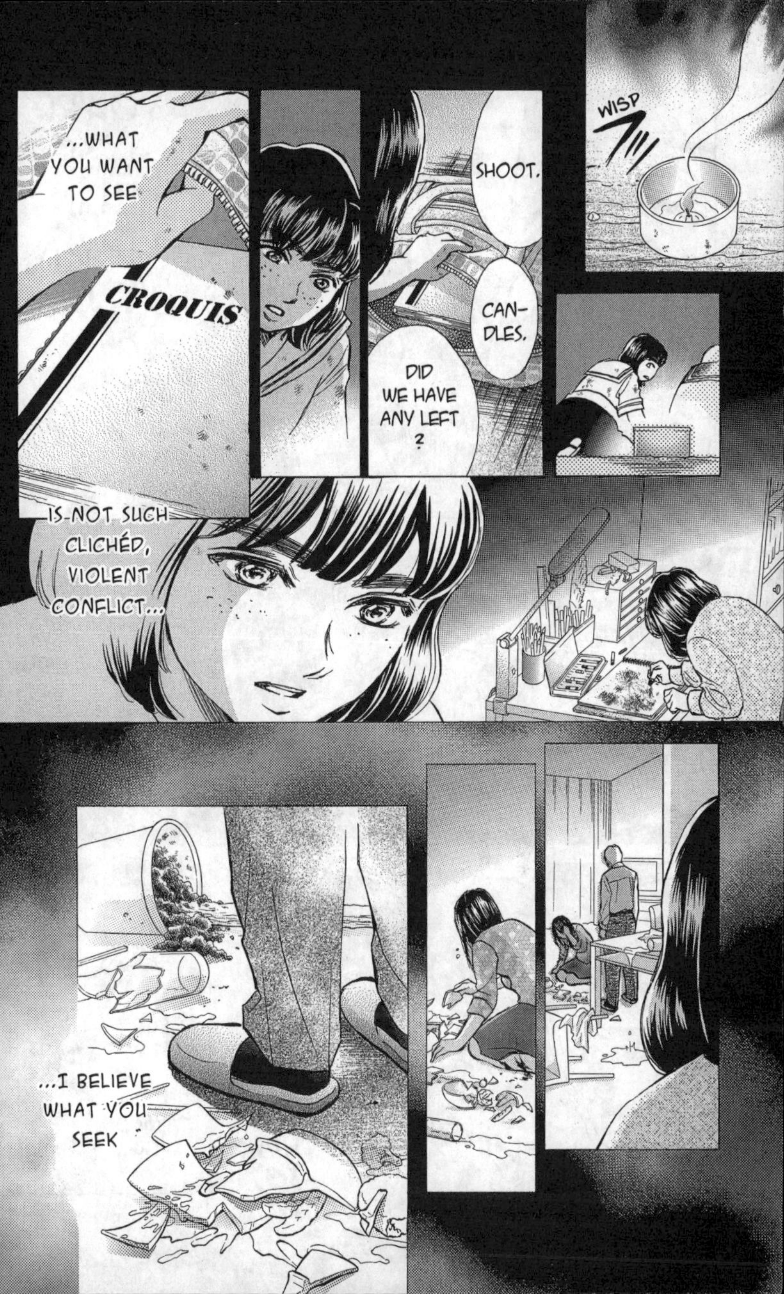
WISP
SHOOT.
CAN-DLES.
DID WE HAVE ANY LEFT?
...WHAT YOU WANT TO SEE
CROQUIS
IS NOT SUCH CLICHÉD, VIOLENT CONFLICT...
...I BELIEVE WHAT YOU SEEK

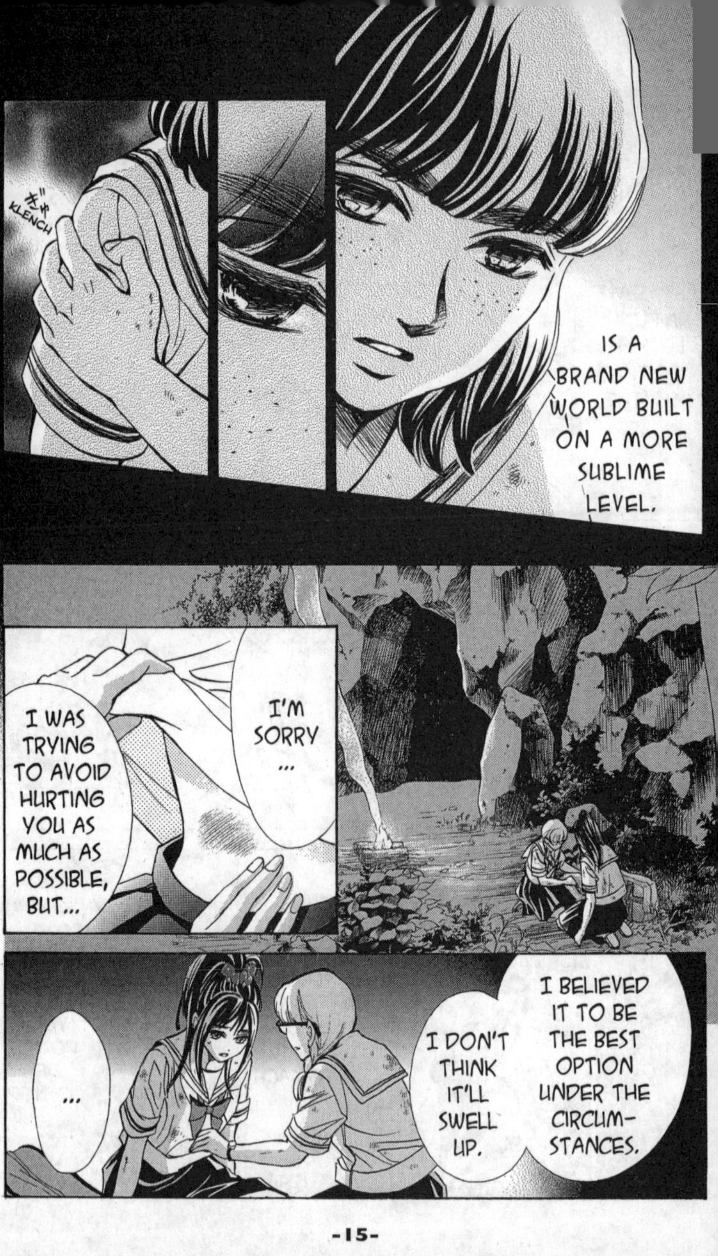
IS A BRAND NEW WORLD BUILT ON A MORE SUBLIME LEVEL.
ぎゅ KLENCH
I'M SORRY ...
I WAS TRYING TO AVOID HURTING YOU AS MUCH AS POSSIBLE, BUT...
I BELIEVED IT TO BE THE BEST OPTION UNDER THE CIRCUM-STANCES.
I DON'T THINK IT'LL SWELL UP.
...

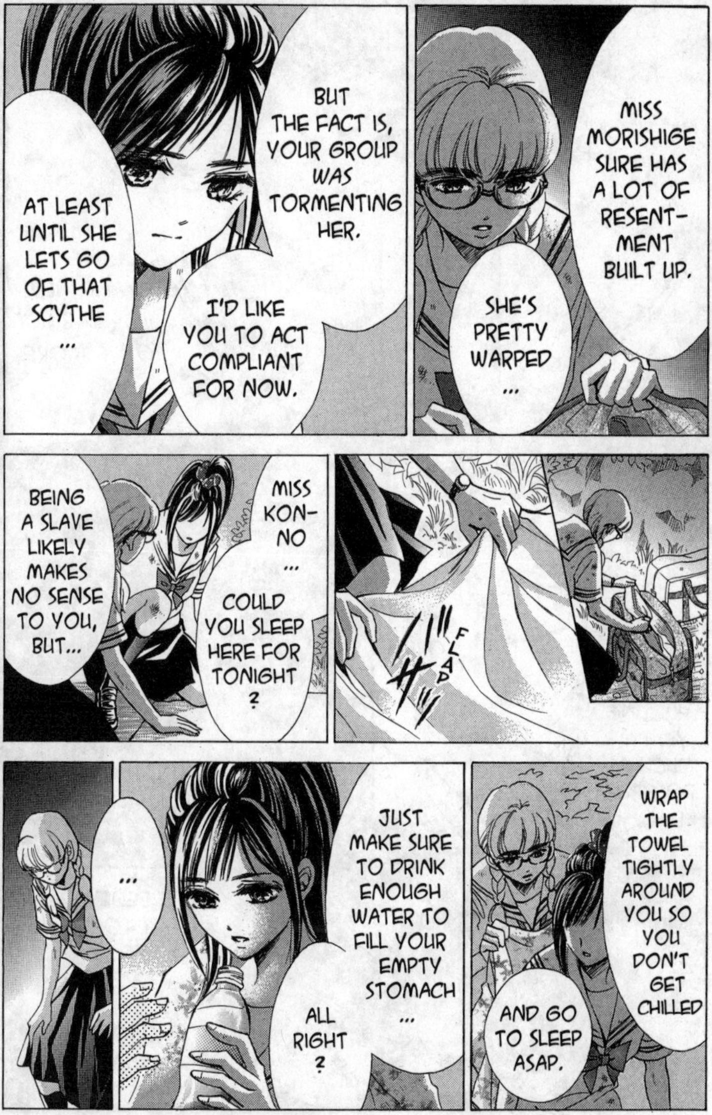
MISS MORISHIGE SURE HAS A LOT OF RESENT-MENT BUILT UP.
SHE'S PRETTY WARPED ...
BUT THE FACT IS, YOUR GROUP WAS TORMENTING HER.
I'D LIKE YOU TO ACT COMPLIANT FOR NOW.
AT LEAST UNTIL SHE LETS GO OF THAT SCYTHE ...
FLAP
MISS KON-NO ...
COULD YOU SLEEP HERE FOR TONIGHT?
BEING A SLAVE LIKELY MAKES NO SENSE TO YOU, BUT...
WRAP THE TOWEL TIGHTLY AROUND YOU SO YOU DON'T GET CHILLED
AND GO TO SLEEP ASAP.
JUST MAKE SURE TO DRINK ENOUGH WATER TO FILL YOUR EMPTY STOMACH ...
ALL RIGHT?
...

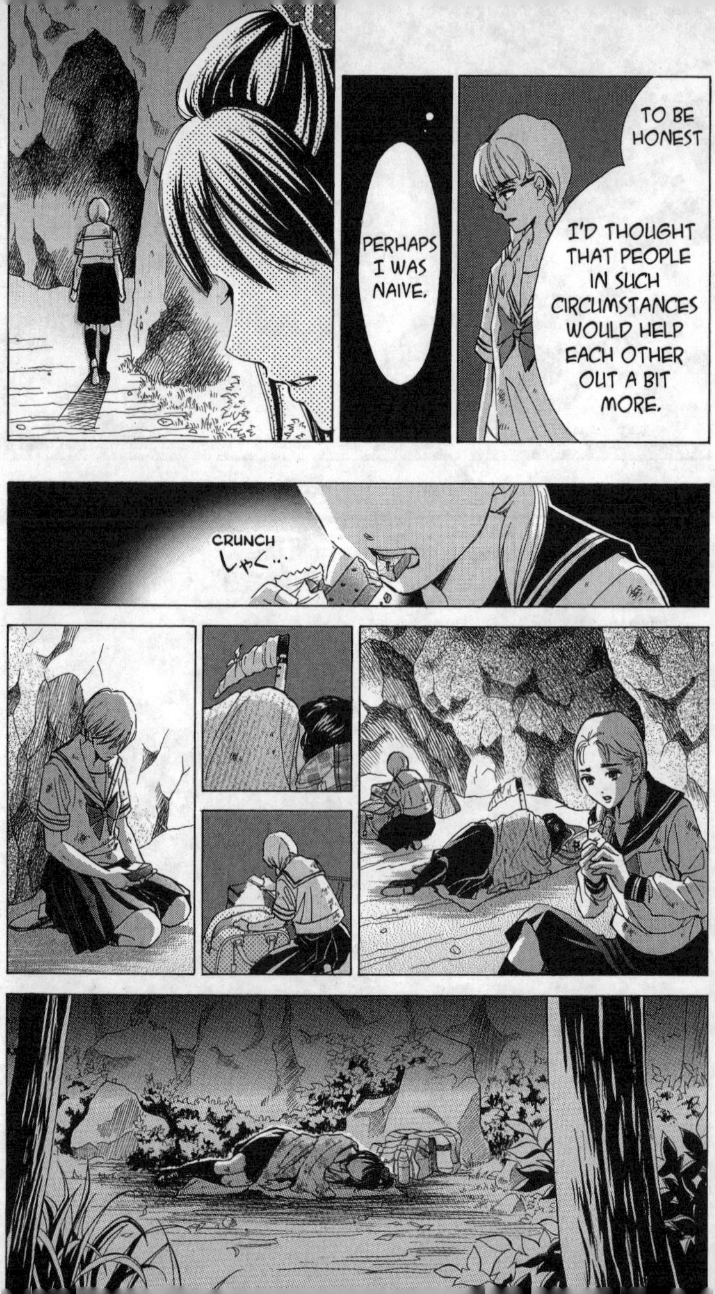
TO BE HONEST
I'D THOUGHT THAT PEOPLE IN SUCH CIRCUMSTANCES WOULD HELP EACH OTHER OUT A BIT MORE.
PERHAPS I WAS NAIVE.
CRUNCH
しゃく…

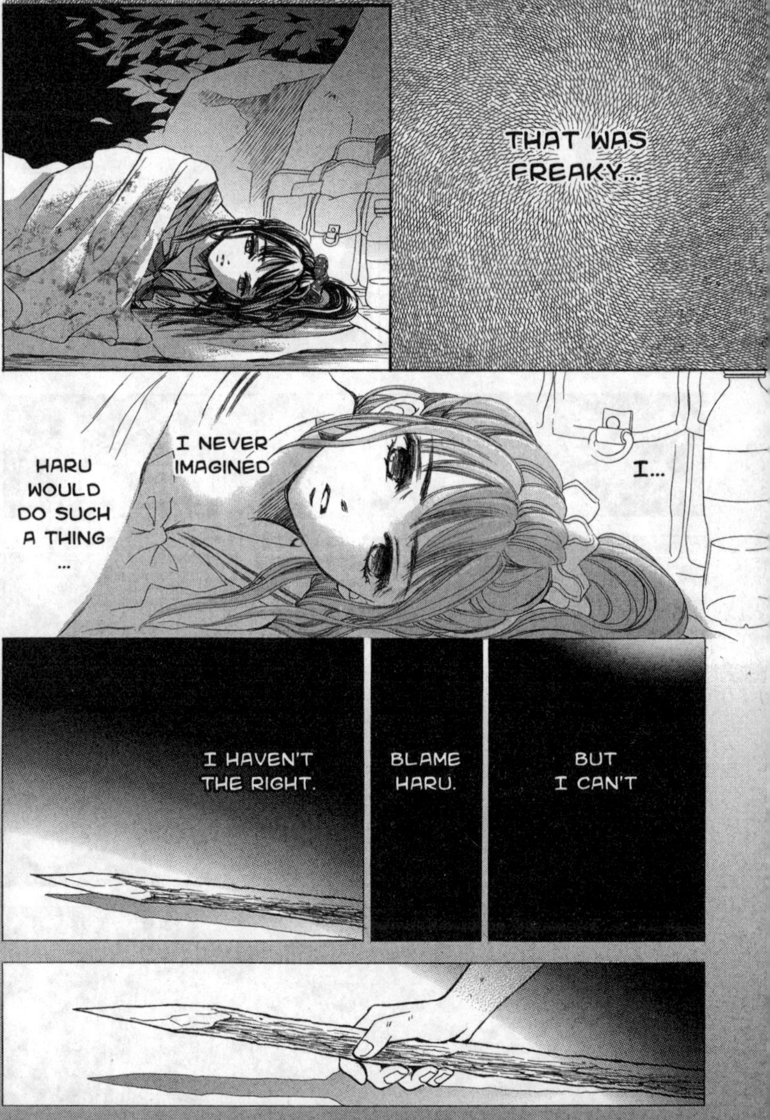
THAT WAS FREAKY...
I...
I NEVER IMAGINED
HARU WOULD DO SUCH A THING ...
BUT I CAN'T
BLAME HARU.
I HAVEN'T THE RIGHT.

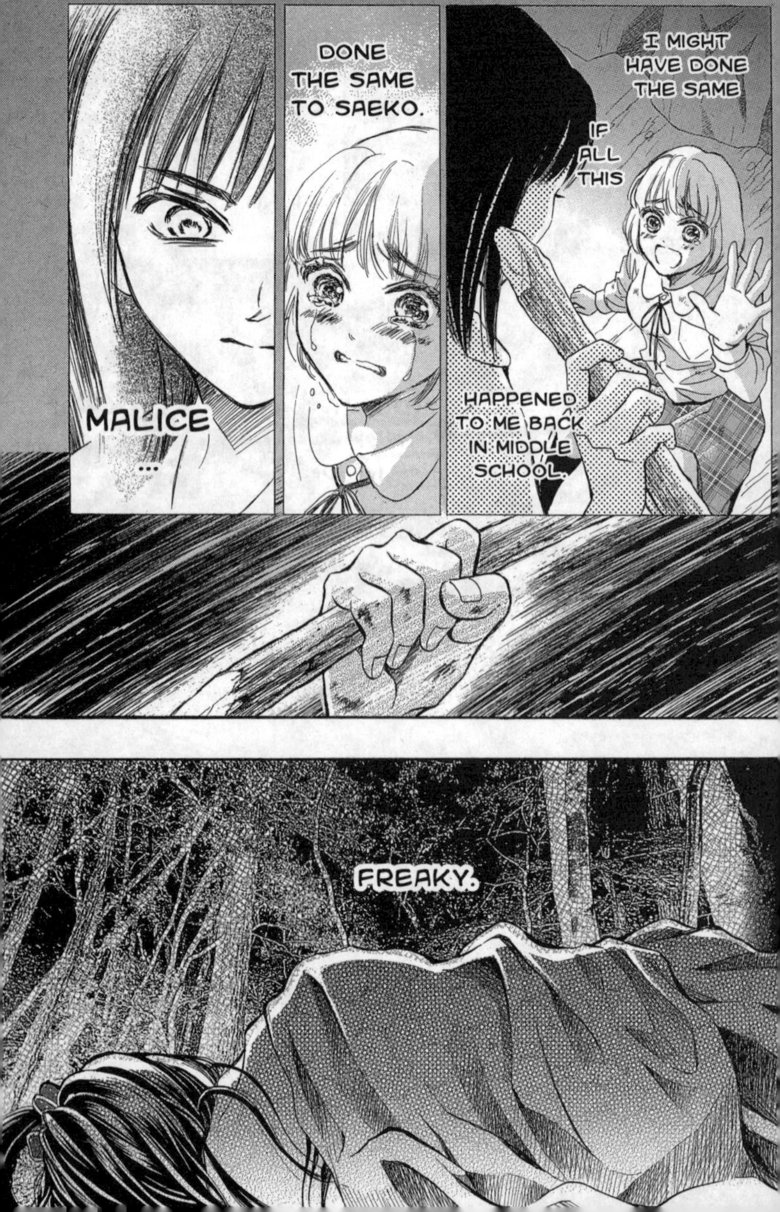
I MIGHT HAVE DONE THE SAME
IF ALL THIS
HAPPENED TO ME BACK IN MIDDLE SCHOOL.
DONE THE SAME TO SAEKO.
MALICE
...
FREAKY.

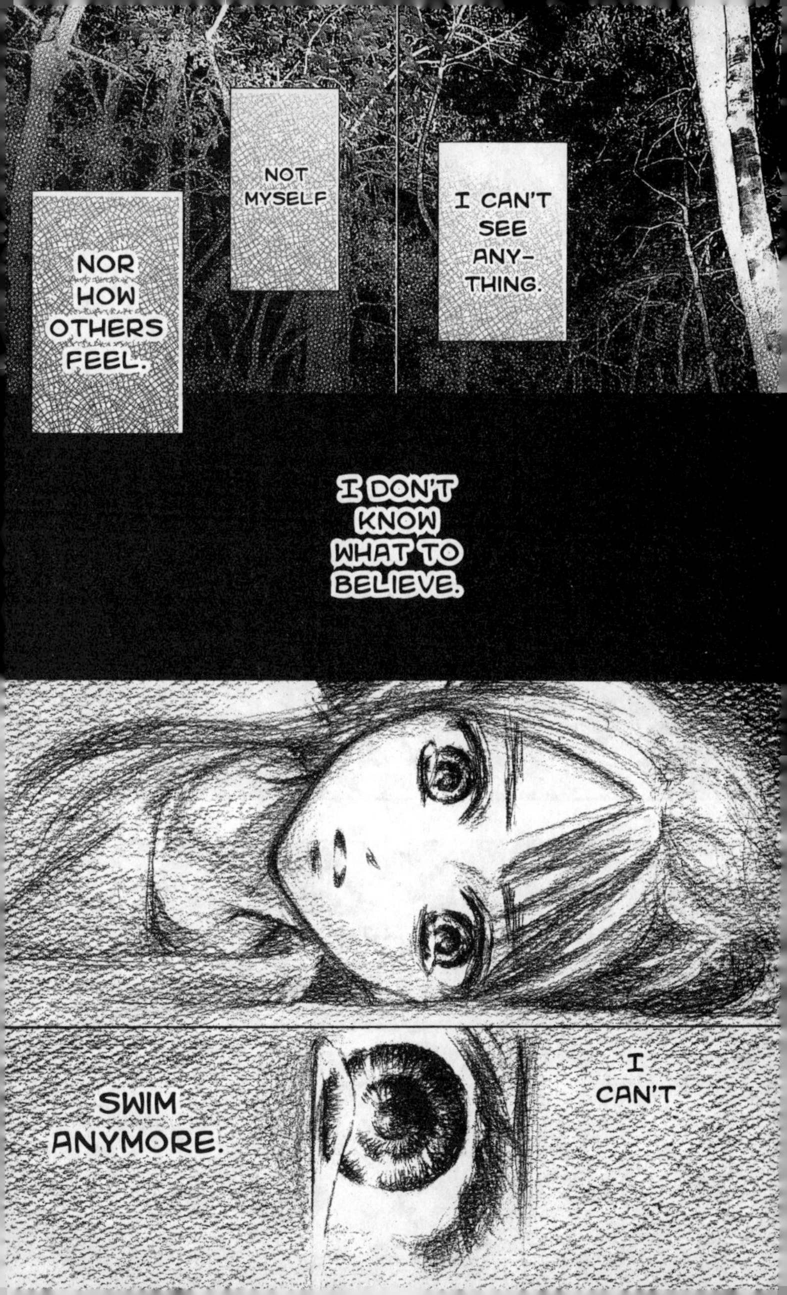
I CAN'T SEE ANY-THING.
NOT MYSELF
NOR HOW OTHERS FEEL.
I DON'T KNOW WHAT TO BELIEVE.
I CAN'T
SWIM ANYMORE.

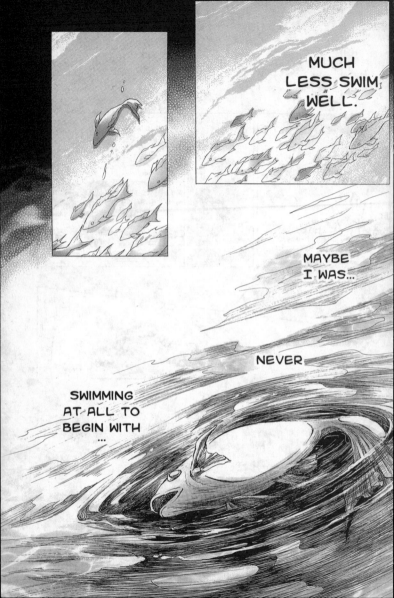

MUCH
LESS SWIM
WELL.

MAYBE
I WAS...

NEVER

SWIMMING
AT ALL TO
BEGIN WITH
...

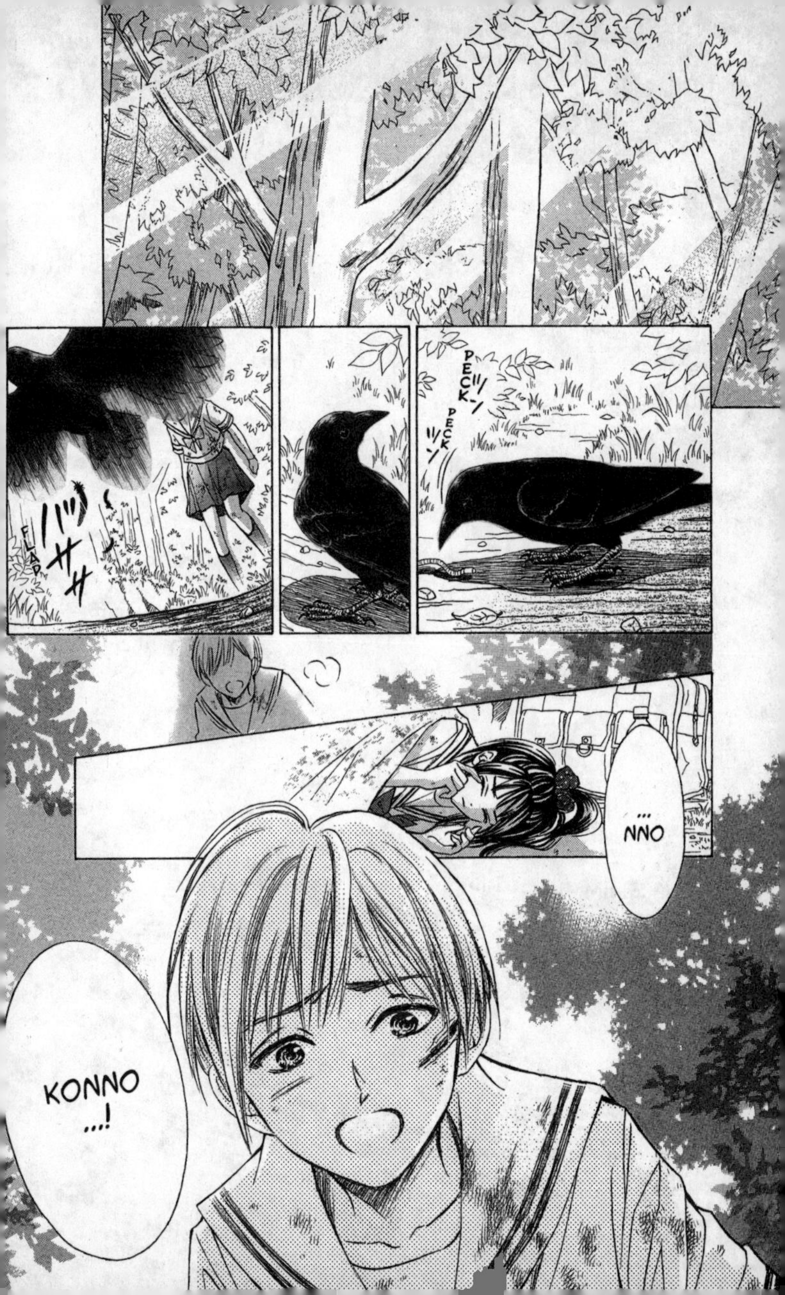
PECK
PECK
FLAP
...NNO
KONNO ...!

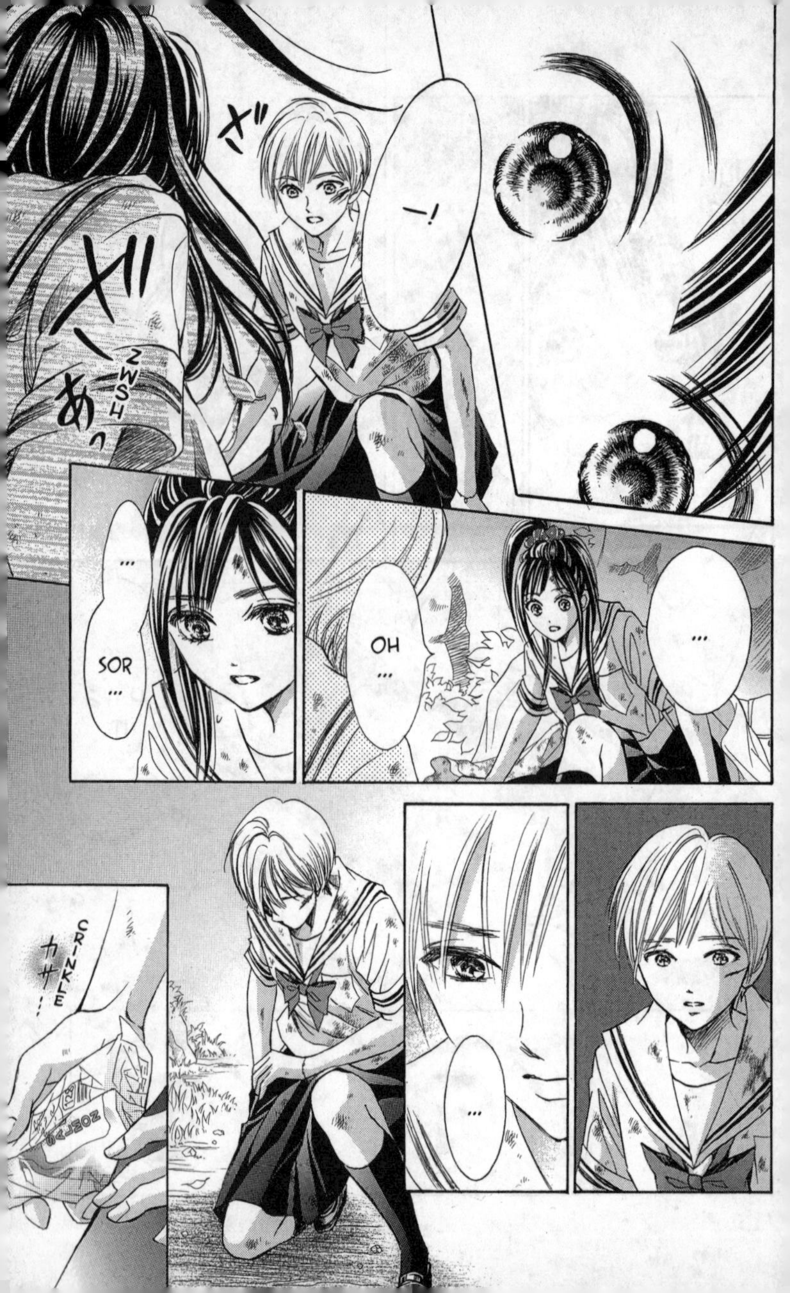

—!
ZWSH
...
OH ...
... SOR ...
...
CRINKLE

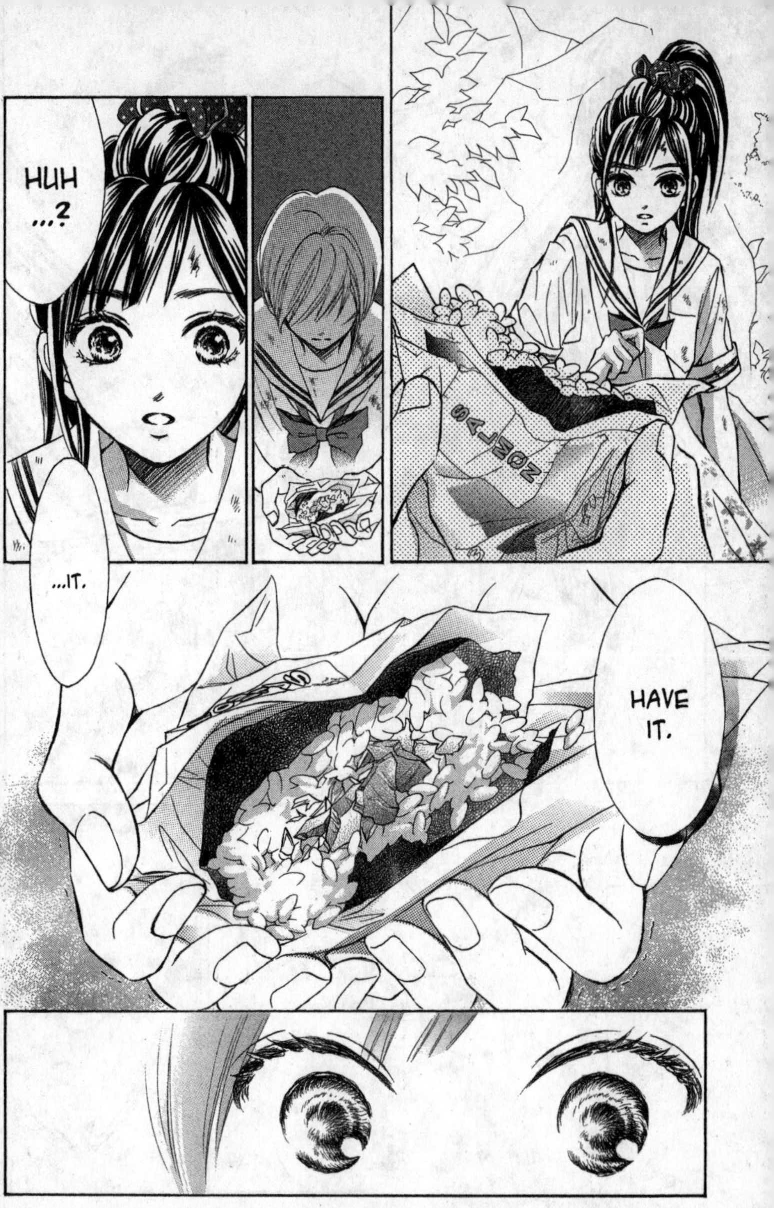
HUH ...?
...IT.
HAVE IT.

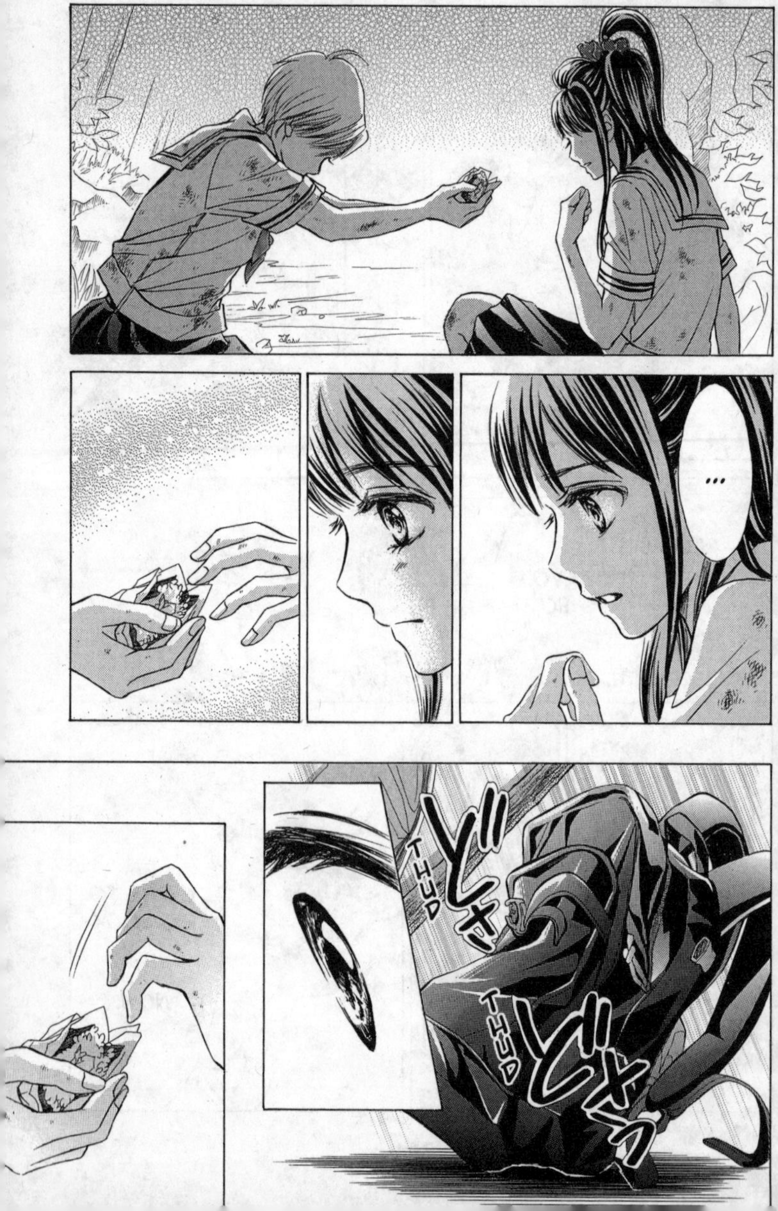
...
THUD
THUD

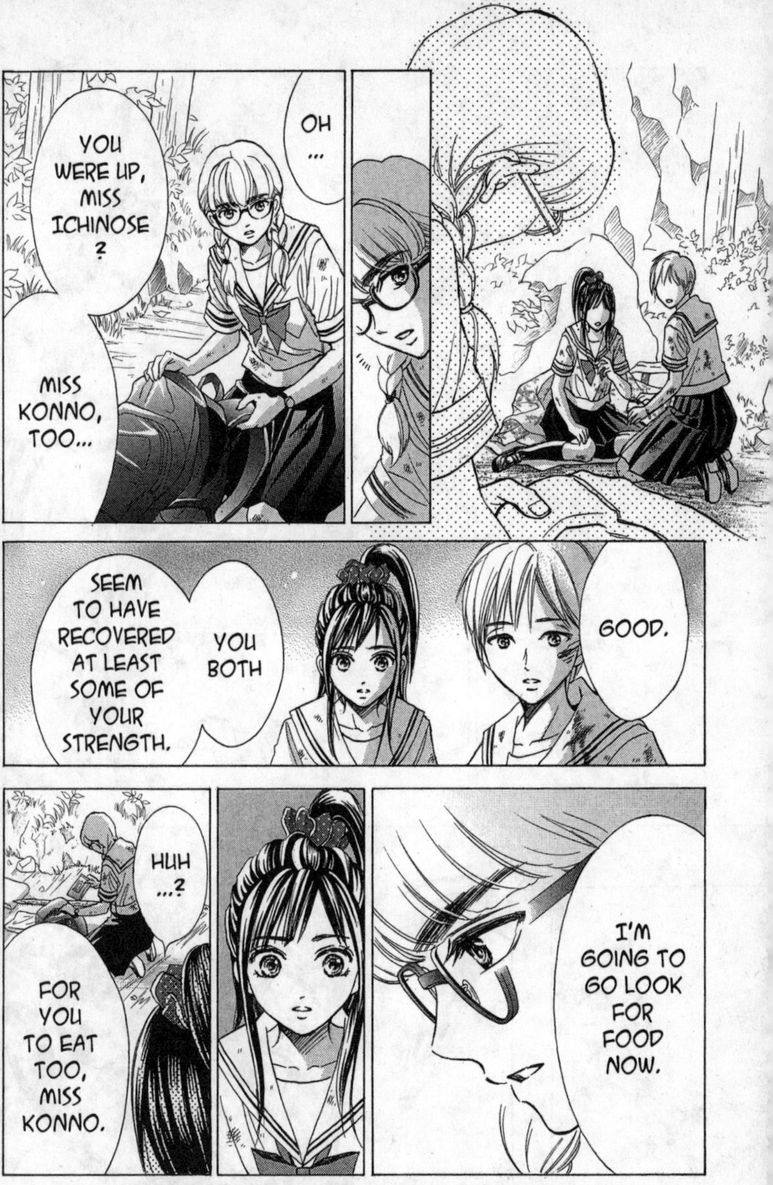
OH ...
YOU WERE UP, MISS ICHINOSE?
MISS KONNO, TOO...
GOOD.
YOU BOTH
SEEM TO HAVE RECOVERED AT LEAST SOME OF YOUR STRENGTH.
I'M GOING TO GO LOOK FOR FOOD NOW.
HUH ...?
FOR YOU TO EAT TOO, MISS KONNO.

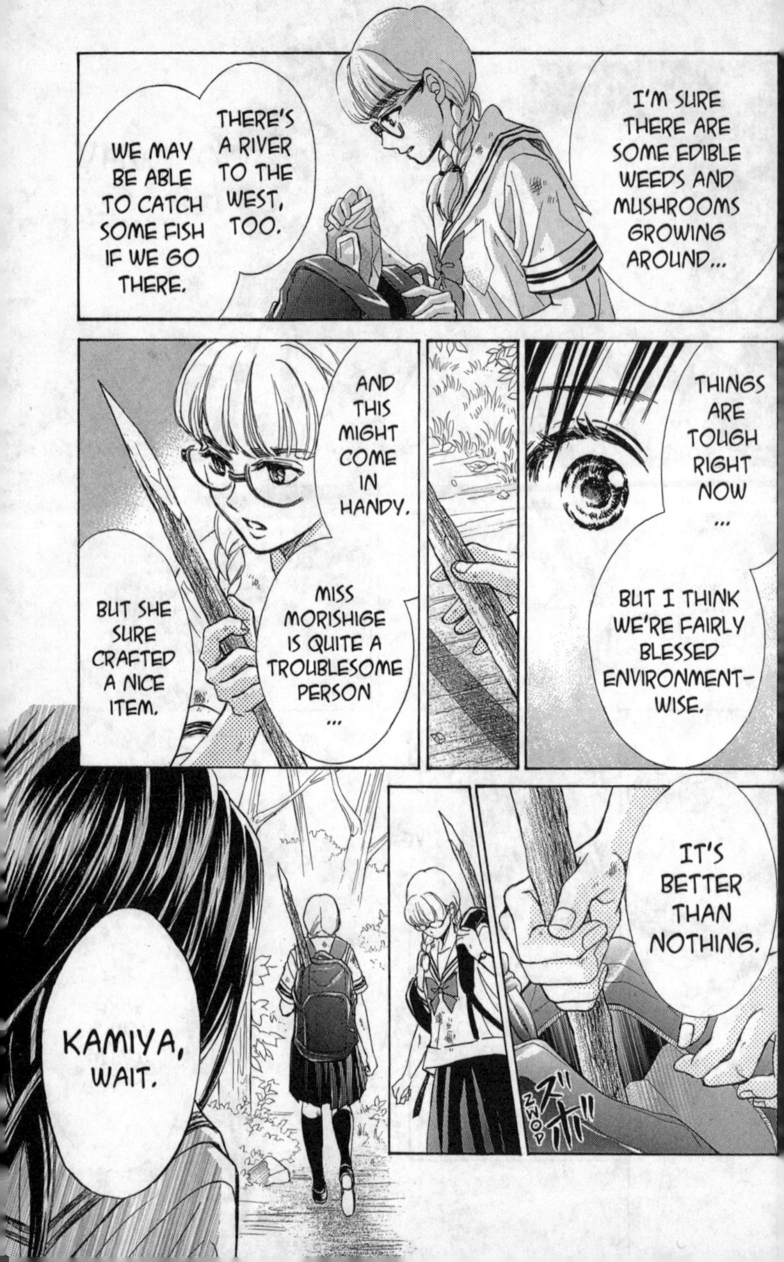
I'M SURE THERE ARE SOME EDIBLE WEEDS AND MUSHROOMS GROWING AROUND...
THERE'S A RIVER TO THE WEST, TOO.
WE MAY BE ABLE TO CATCH SOME FISH IF WE GO THERE.
THINGS ARE TOUGH RIGHT NOW ...
BUT I THINK WE'RE FAIRLY BLESSED ENVIRONMENT-WISE.
AND THIS MIGHT COME IN HANDY.
MISS MORISHIGE IS QUITE A TROUBLESOME PERSON ...
BUT SHE SURE CRAFTED A NICE ITEM.
IT'S BETTER THAN NOTHING.
ZWOP
KAMIYA, WAIT.

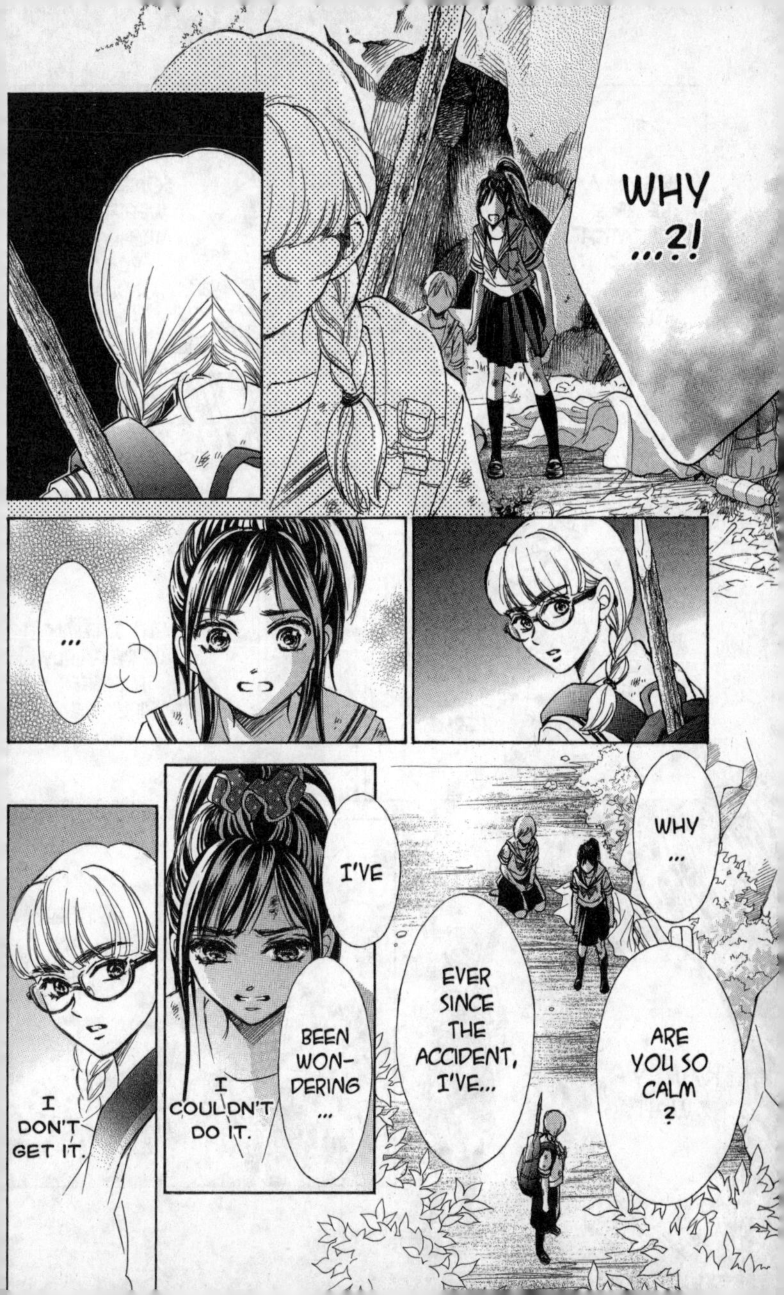
WHY ...?!
...
WHY ...
ARE YOU SO CALM?
EVER SINCE THE ACCIDENT, I'VE...
I'VE
BEEN WONDERING ...
I COULDN'T DO IT.
I DON'T GET IT.

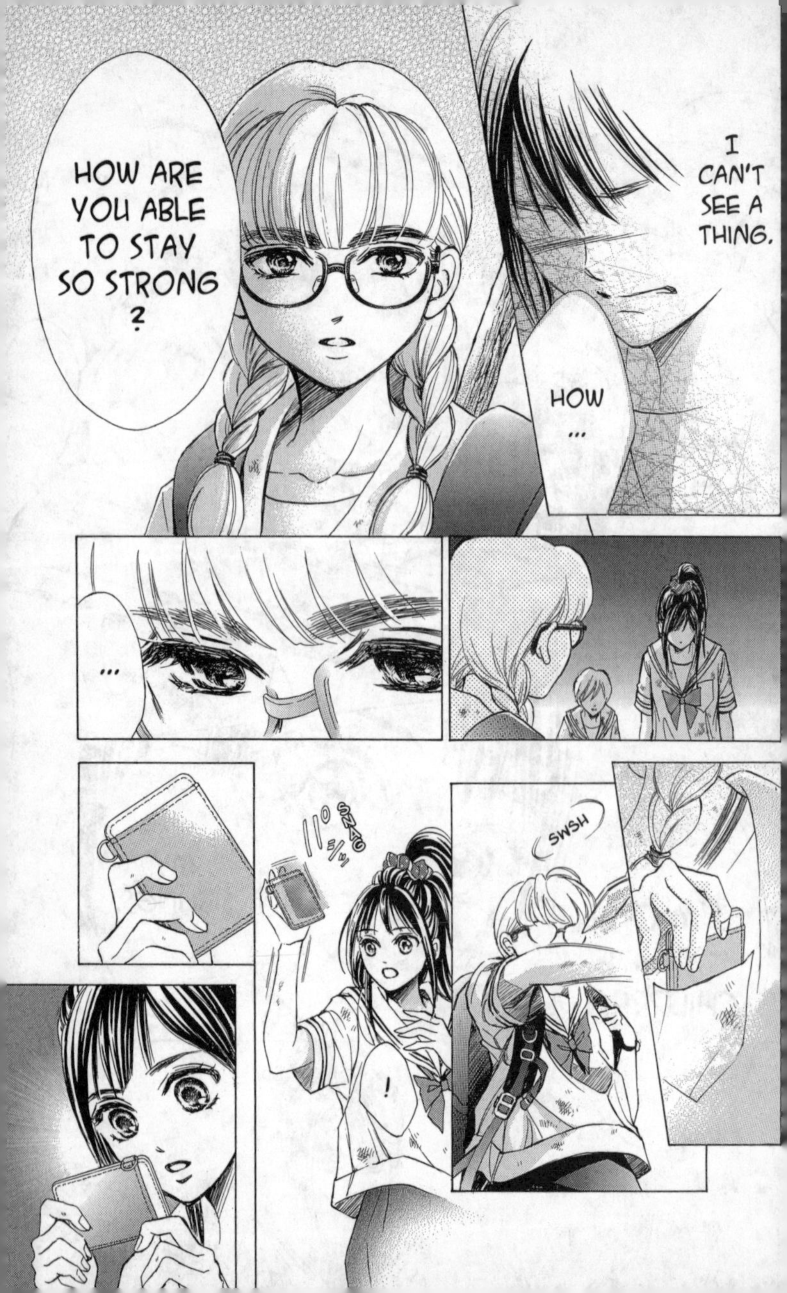
I CAN'T SEE A THING.
HOW ...
HOW ARE YOU ABLE TO STAY SO STRONG?
...
SWSH
SNAG
!

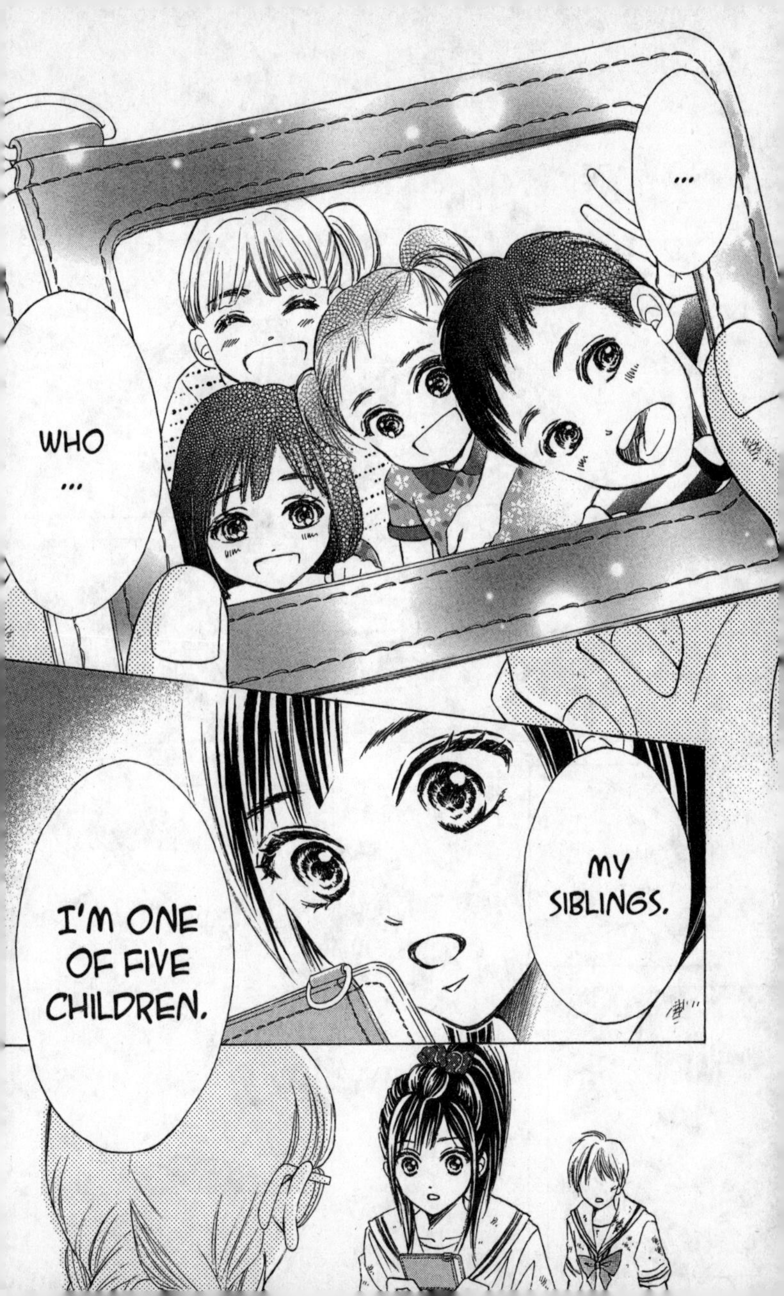
...
WHO ...
MY SIBLINGS.
I'M ONE OF FIVE CHILDREN.

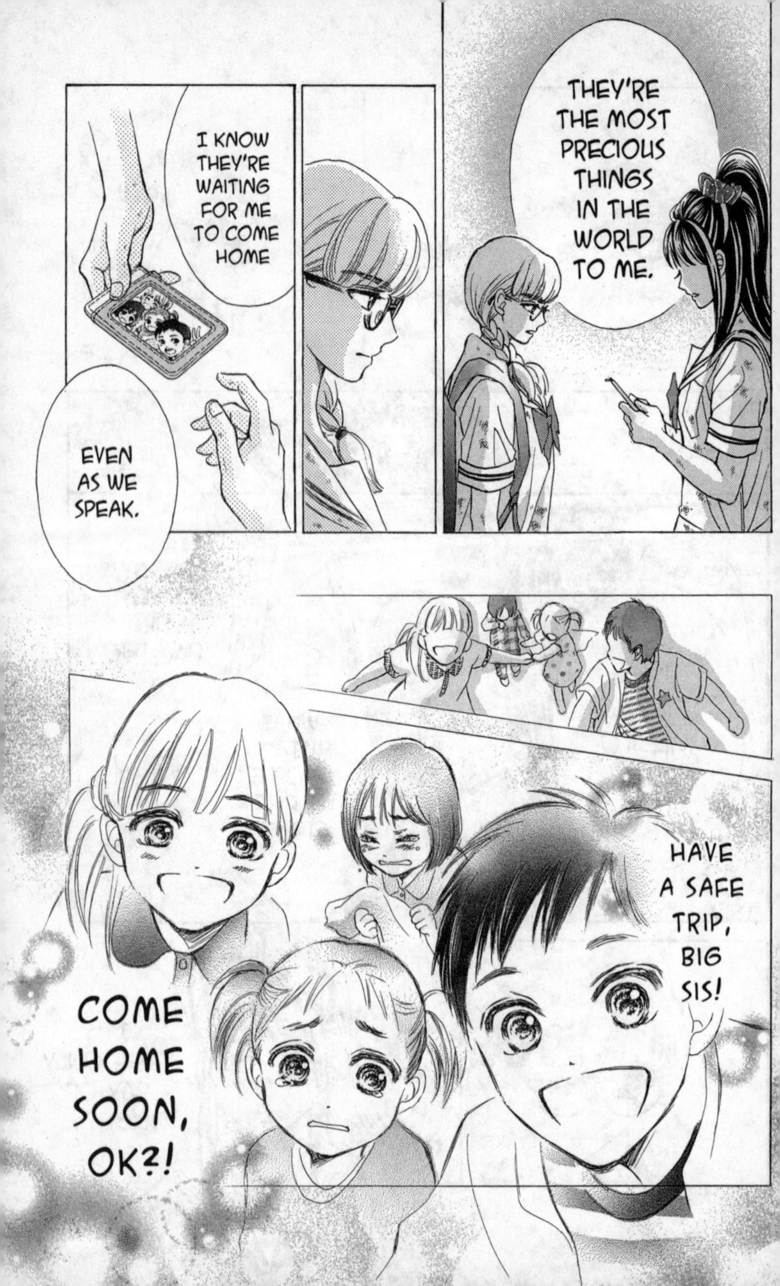
THEY'RE THE MOST PRECIOUS THINGS IN THE WORLD TO ME.
I KNOW THEY'RE WAITING FOR ME TO COME HOME
EVEN AS WE SPEAK.
HAVE A SAFE TRIP, BIG SIS!
COME HOME SOON, OK?!

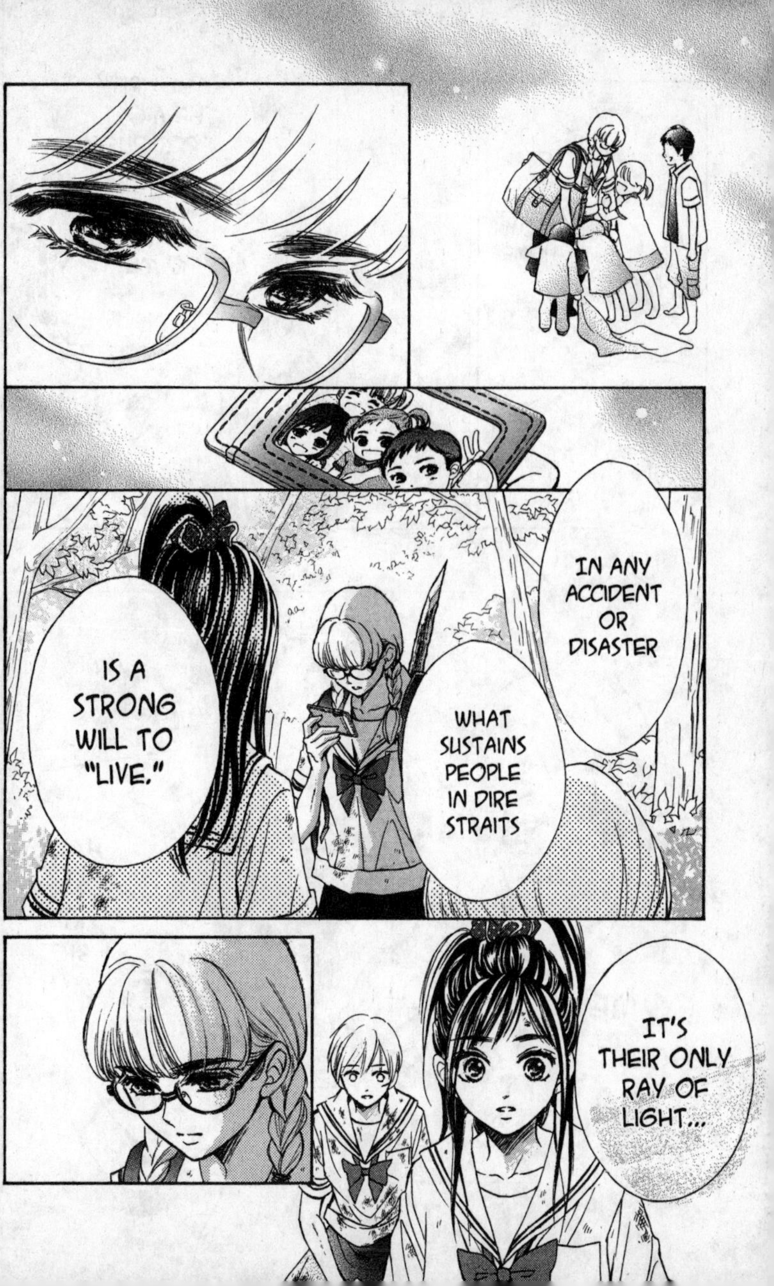
IN ANY ACCIDENT OR DISASTER
WHAT SUSTAINS PEOPLE IN DIRE STRAITS
IS A STRONG WILL TO "LIVE."
IT'S THEIR ONLY RAY OF LIGHT...

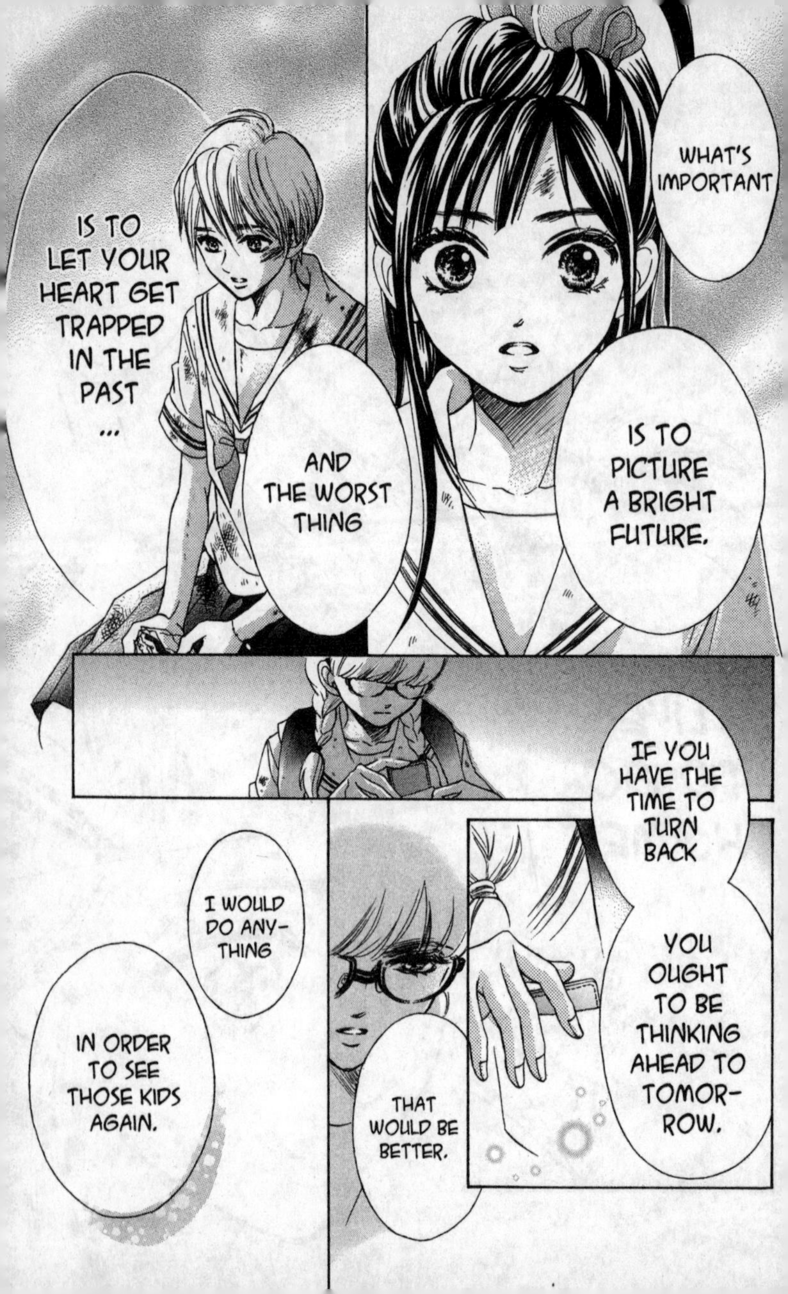
WHAT'S IMPORTANT
IS TO PICTURE A BRIGHT FUTURE.
AND THE WORST THING
IS TO LET YOUR HEART GET TRAPPED IN THE PAST ...
IF YOU HAVE THE TIME TO TURN BACK
YOU OUGHT TO BE THINKING AHEAD TO TOMOR-ROW.
THAT WOULD BE BETTER.
I WOULD DO ANY-THING
IN ORDER TO SEE THOSE KIDS AGAIN.

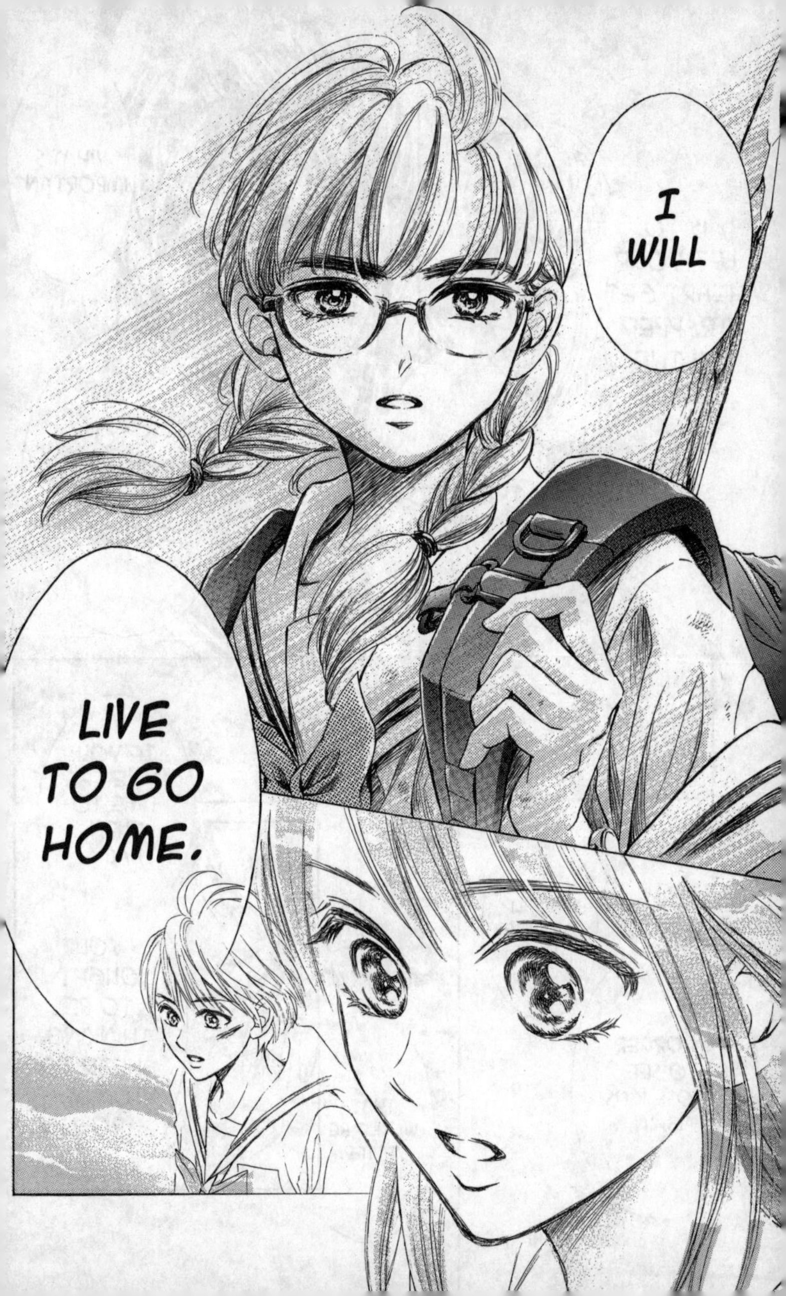
I WILL
LIVE TO GO HOME.

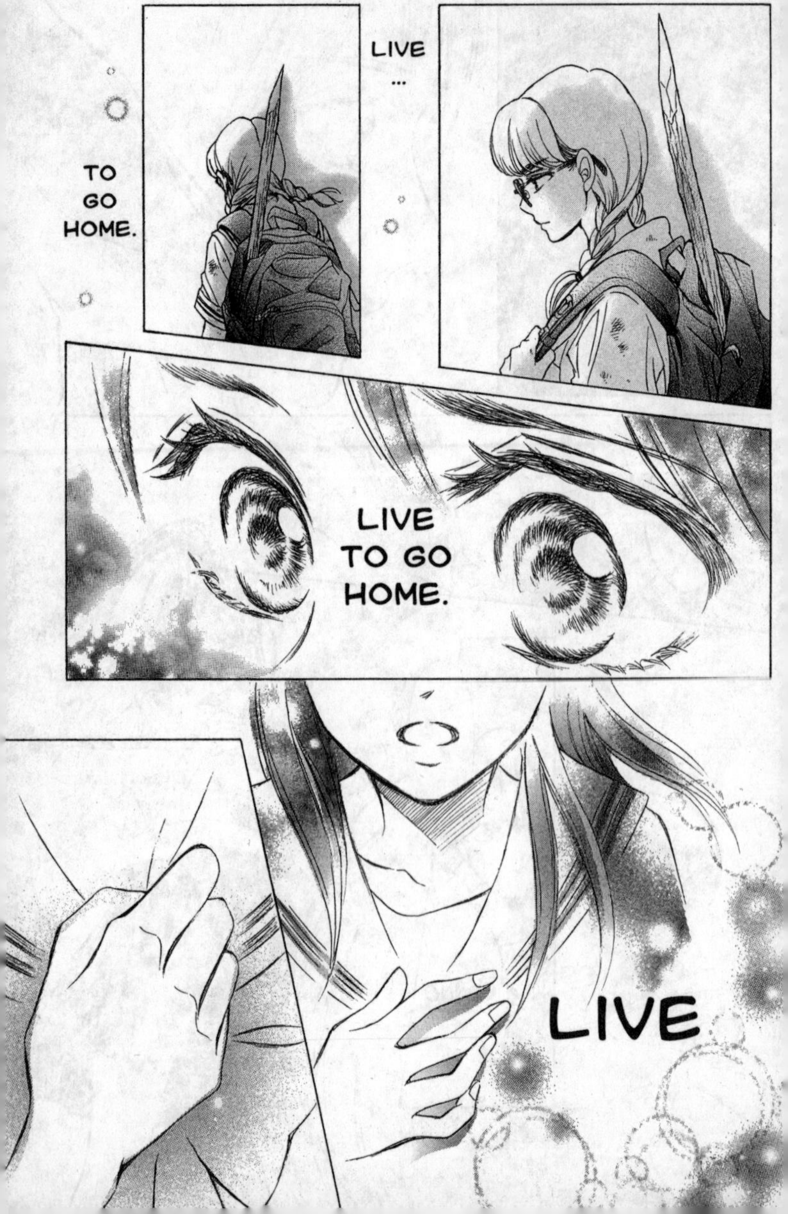
LIVE ...
TO GO HOME.
LIVE TO GO HOME.
LIVE

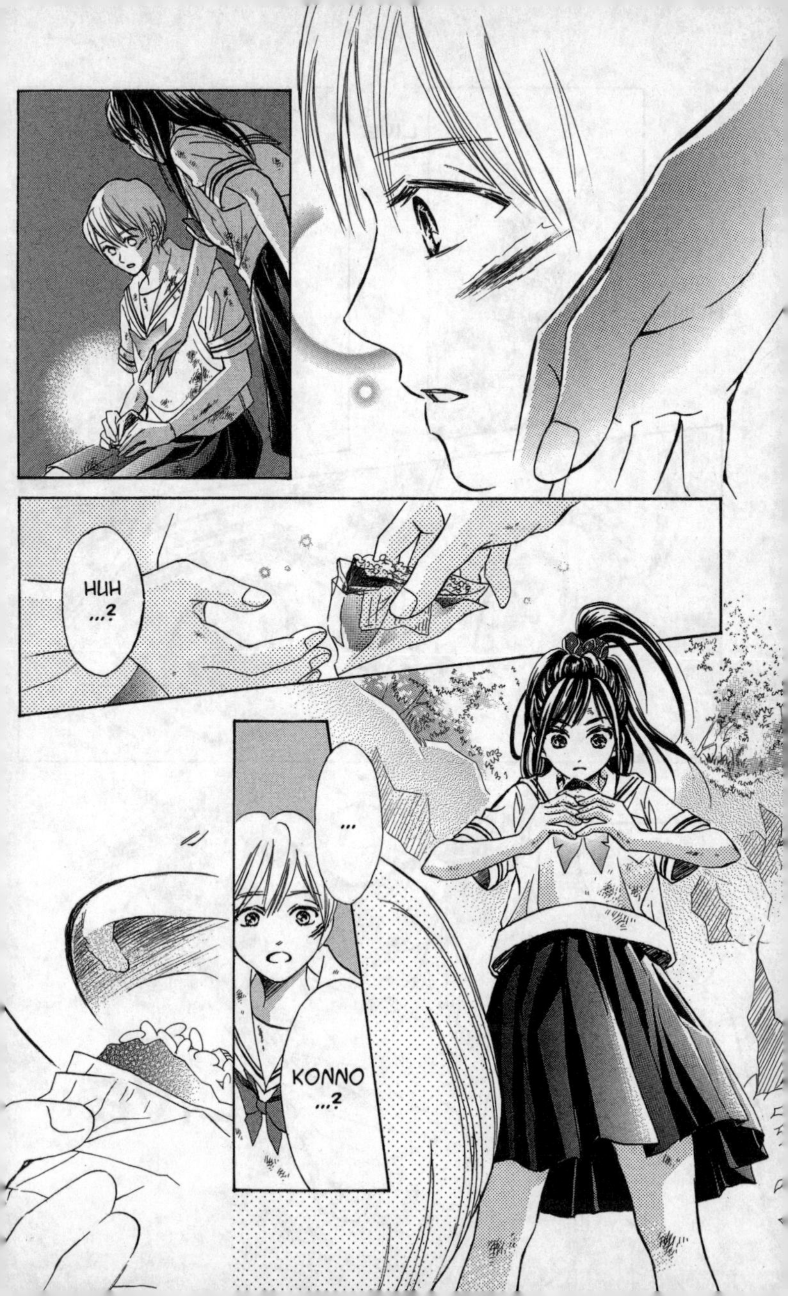
HUH
...?
...
KONNO
...?

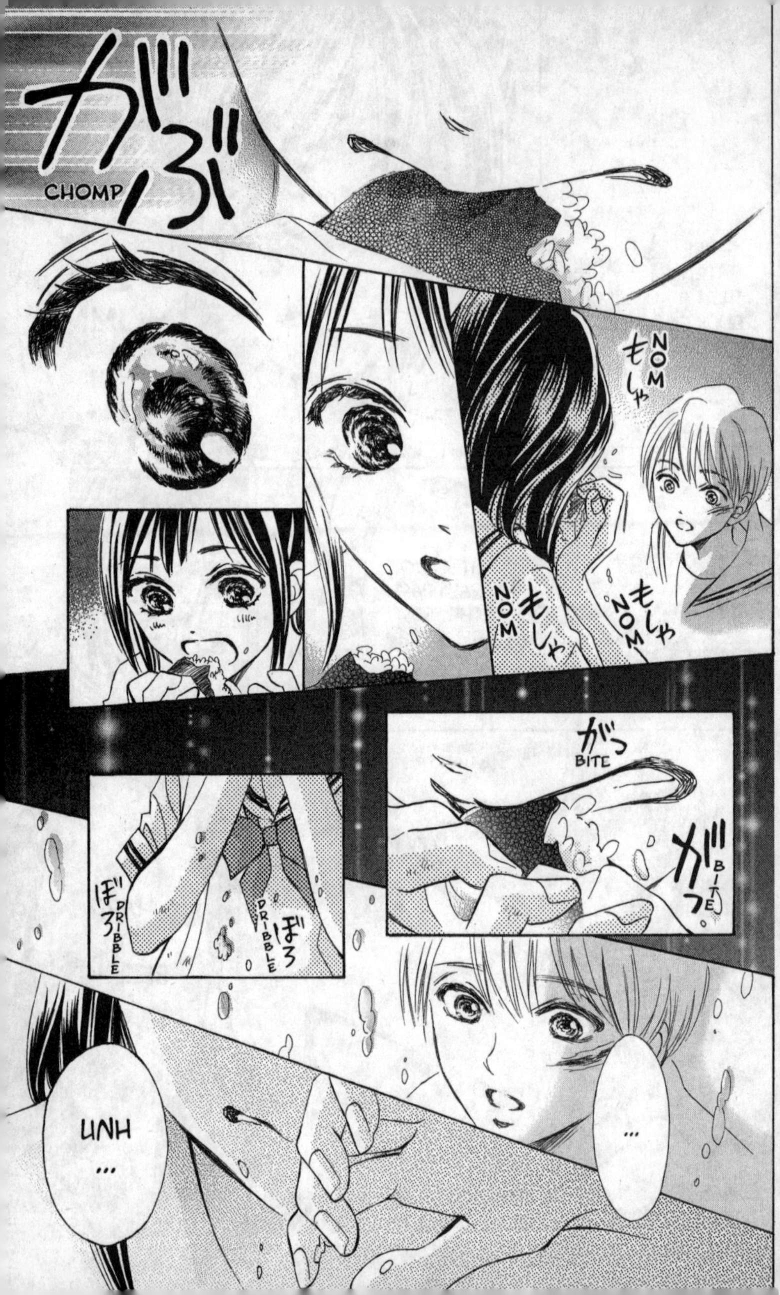
がぶ
CHOMP
もしゃ
NOM
もしゃ
NOM
もしゃ
NOM
がつ
BITE
がつ
BITE
ぼろ
DRIBBLE
ぼろ
DRIBBLE
...
UNH ...

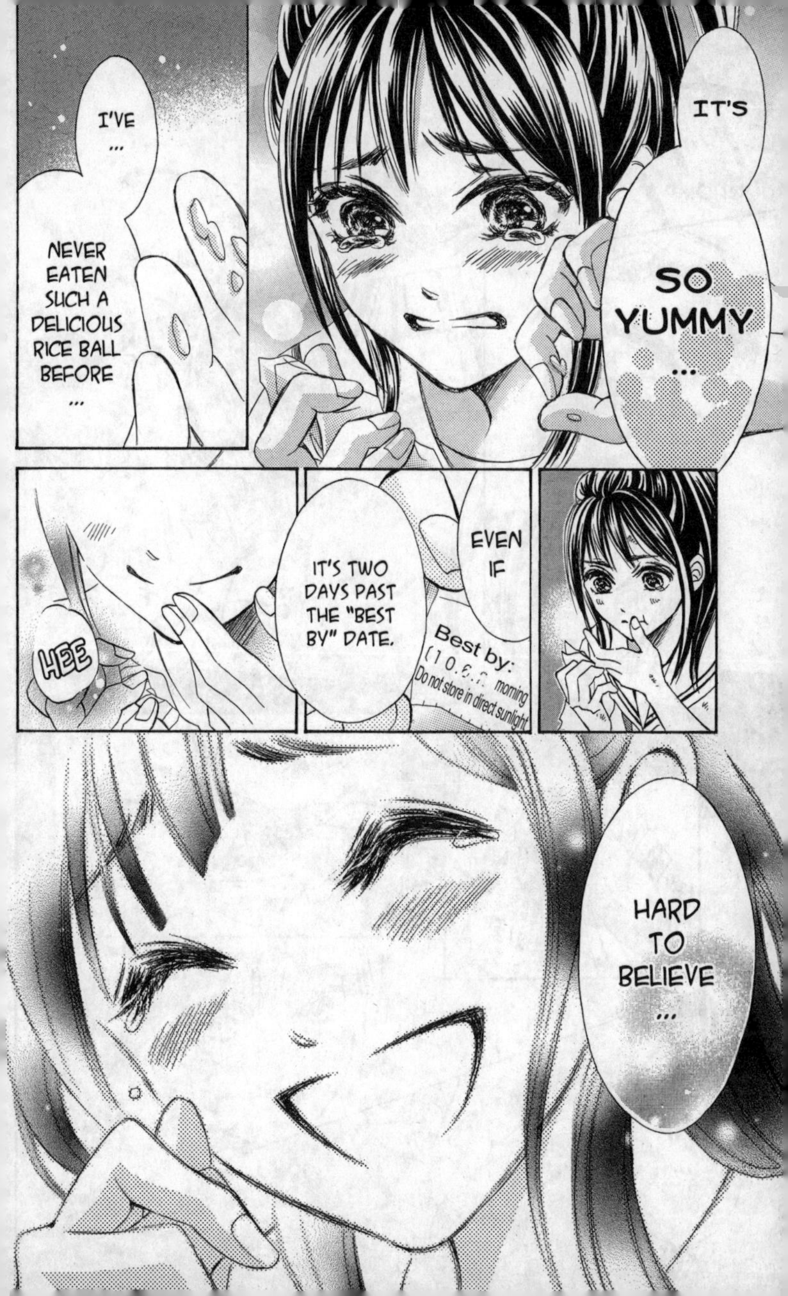
IT'S
SO YUMMY ...
I'VE ...
NEVER EATEN SUCH A DELICIOUS RICE BALL BEFORE ...
EVEN IF
IT'S TWO DAYS PAST THE "BEST BY" DATE.
Best by:
morning
Do not store in direct sunlight
HEE
HARD TO BELIEVE ...

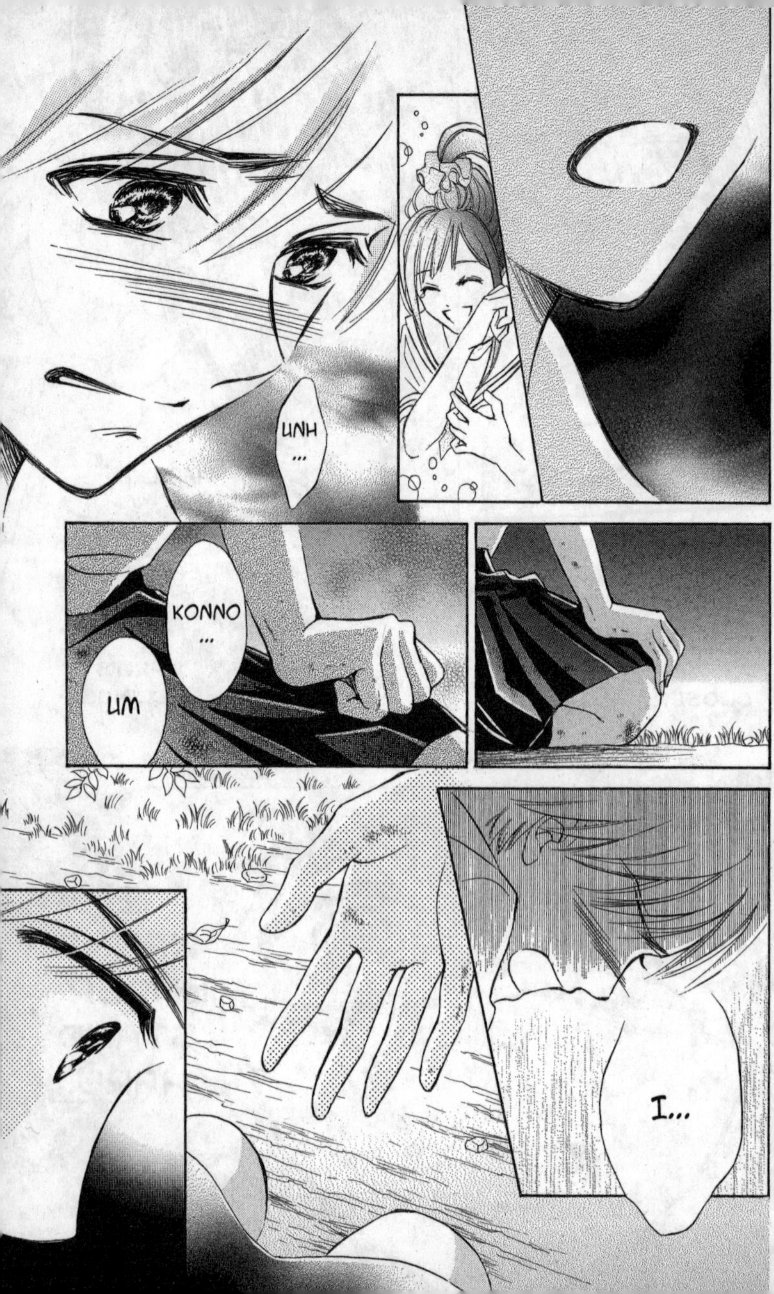
UNH ...
KONNO ...
UM
I...

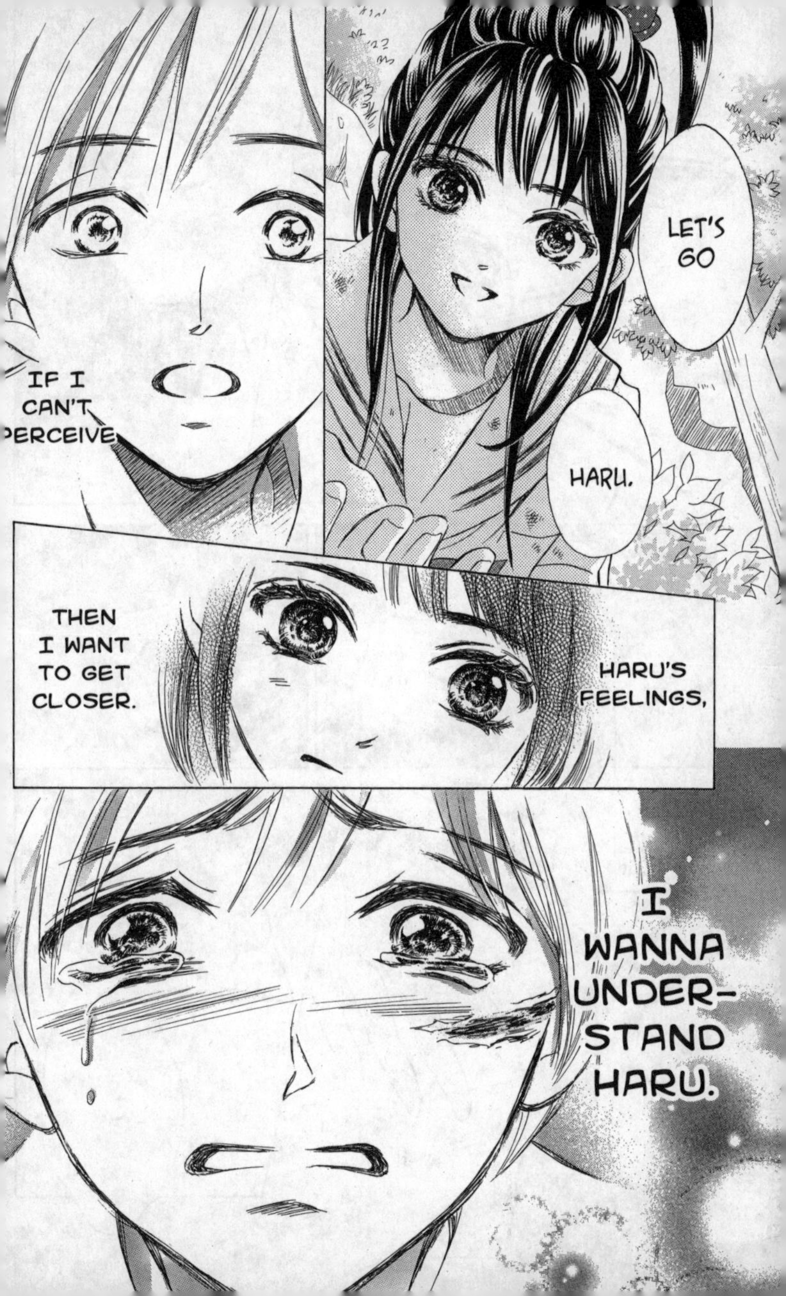
LET'S GO
HARU.
IF I CAN'T PERCEIVE
HARU'S FEELINGS,
THEN I WANT TO GET CLOSER.
I WANNA UNDER-STAND HARU.

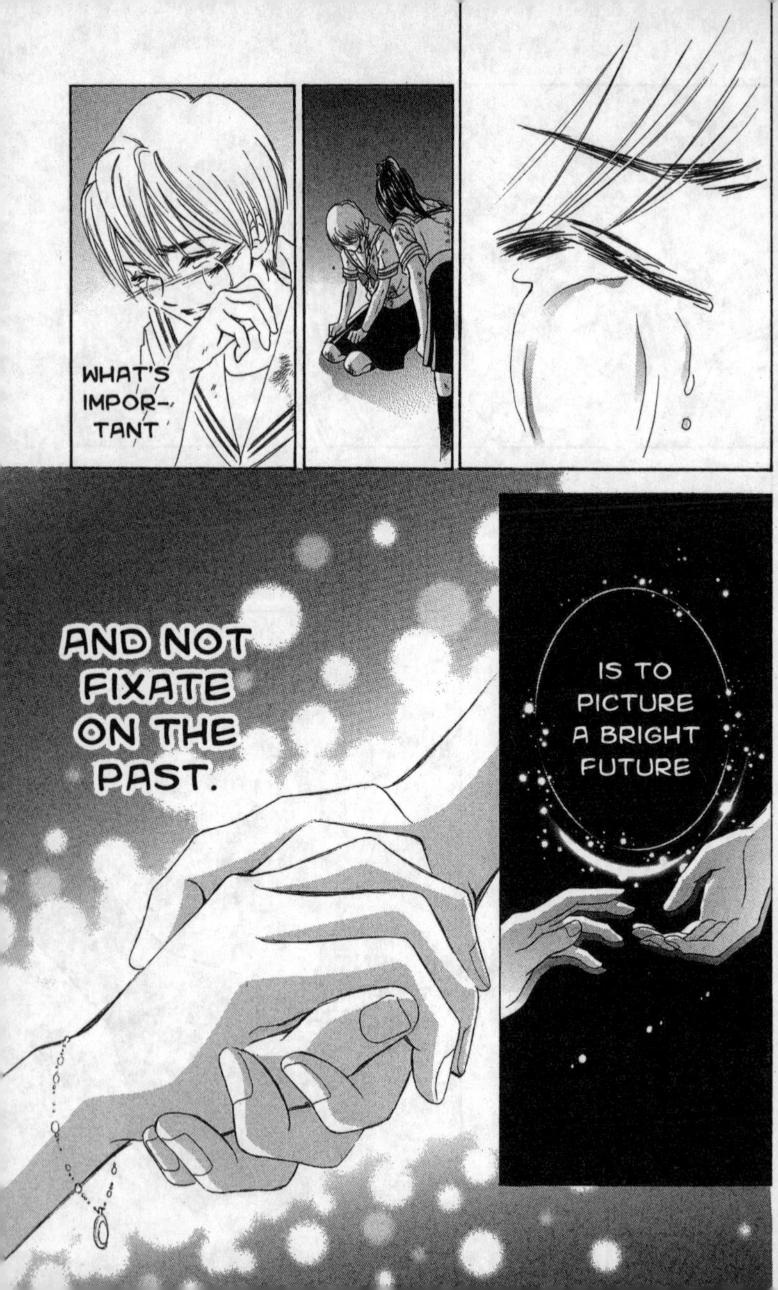
WHAT'S IMPORTANT
IS TO PICTURE A BRIGHT FUTURE
AND NOT FIXATE ON THE PAST.

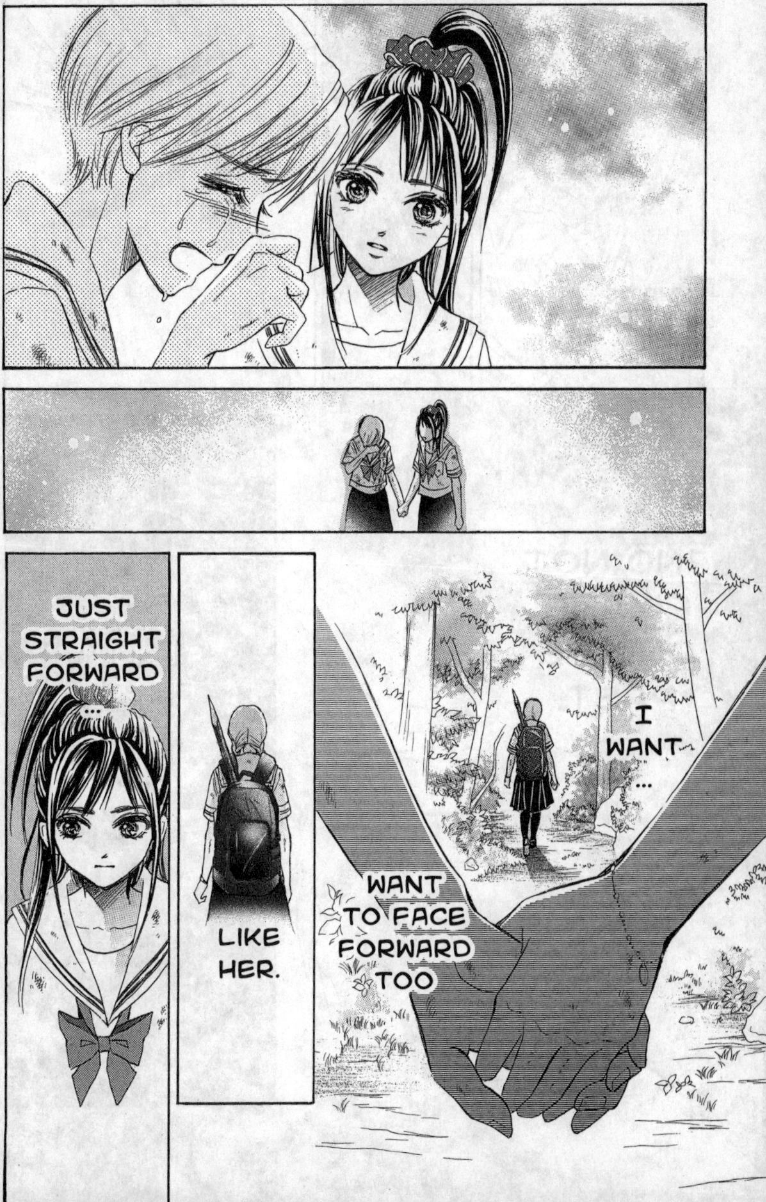
I WANT ...
WANT TO FACE FORWARD TOO
LIKE HER.
JUST STRAIGHT FORWARD ...

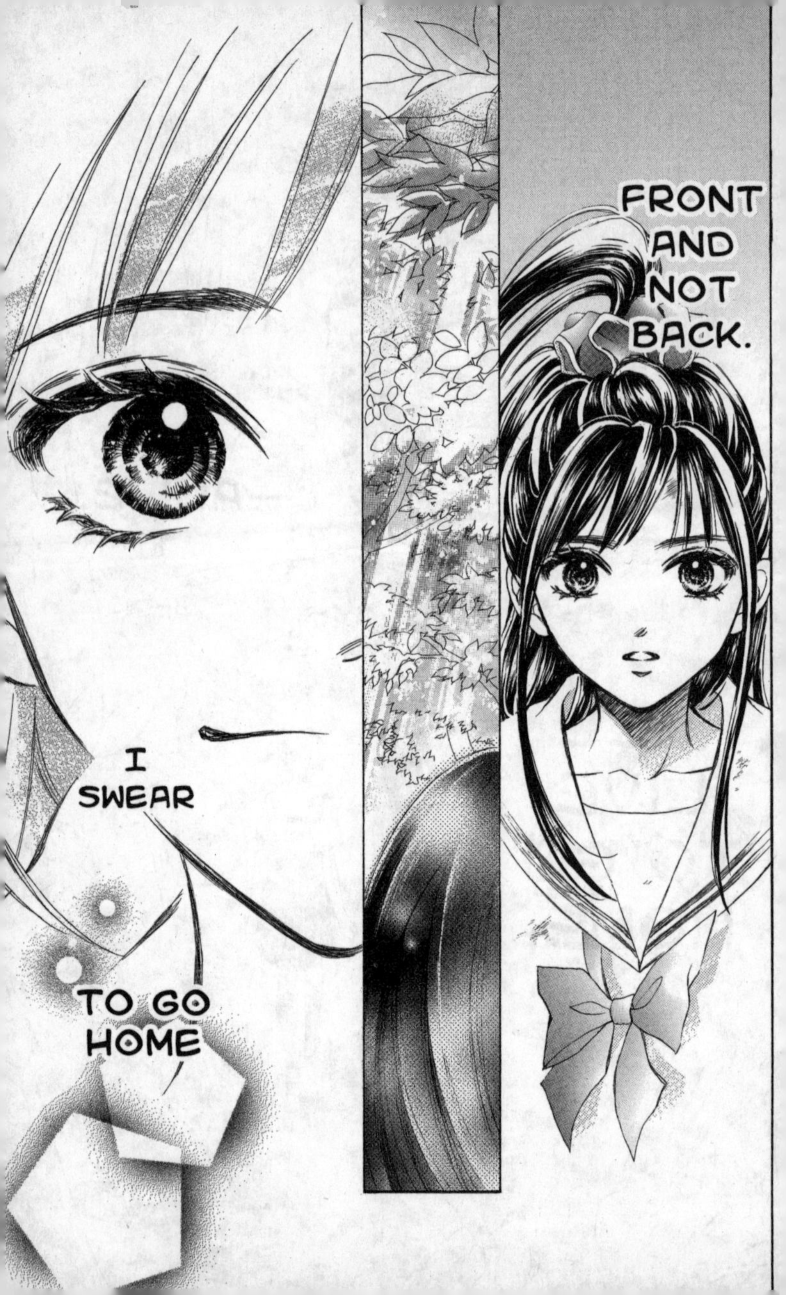
FRONT AND NOT BACK.
I SWEAR
TO GO HOME

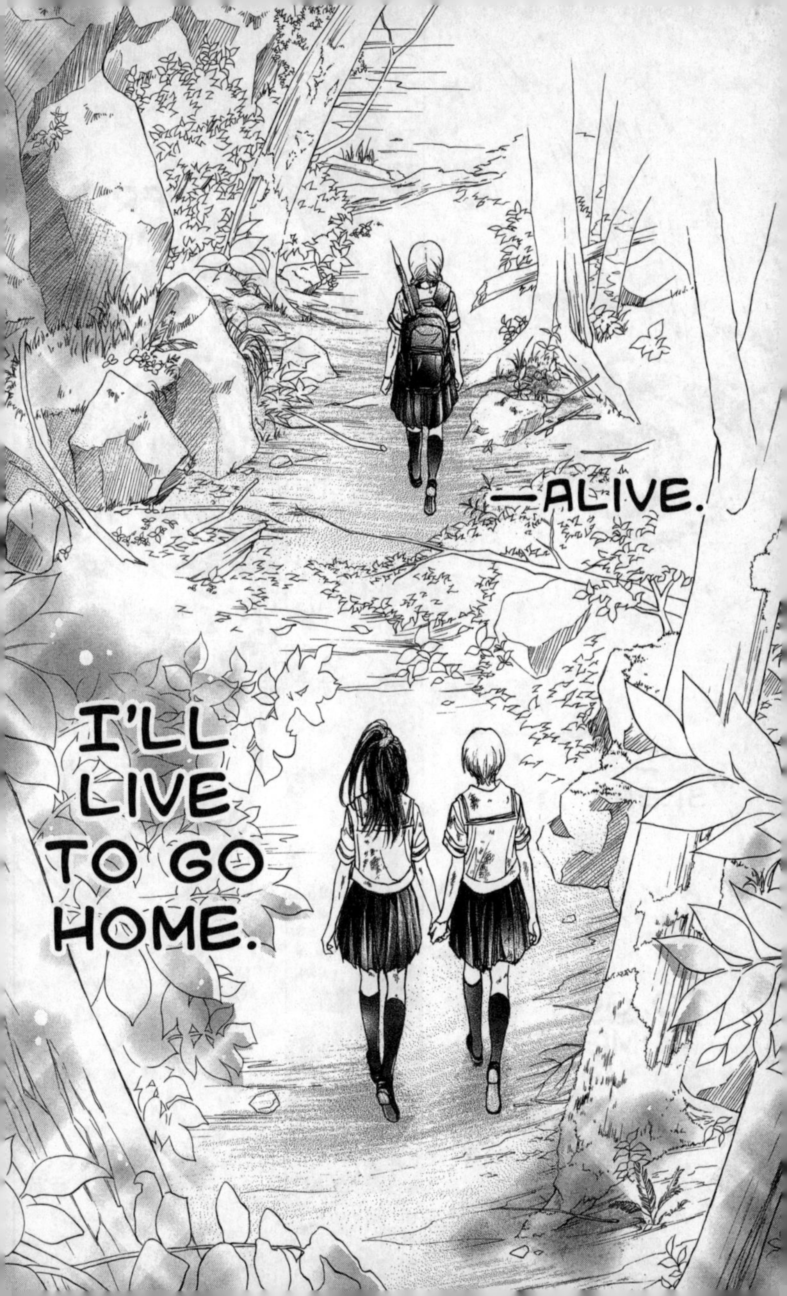
—ALIVE.
I'LL LIVE TO GO HOME.

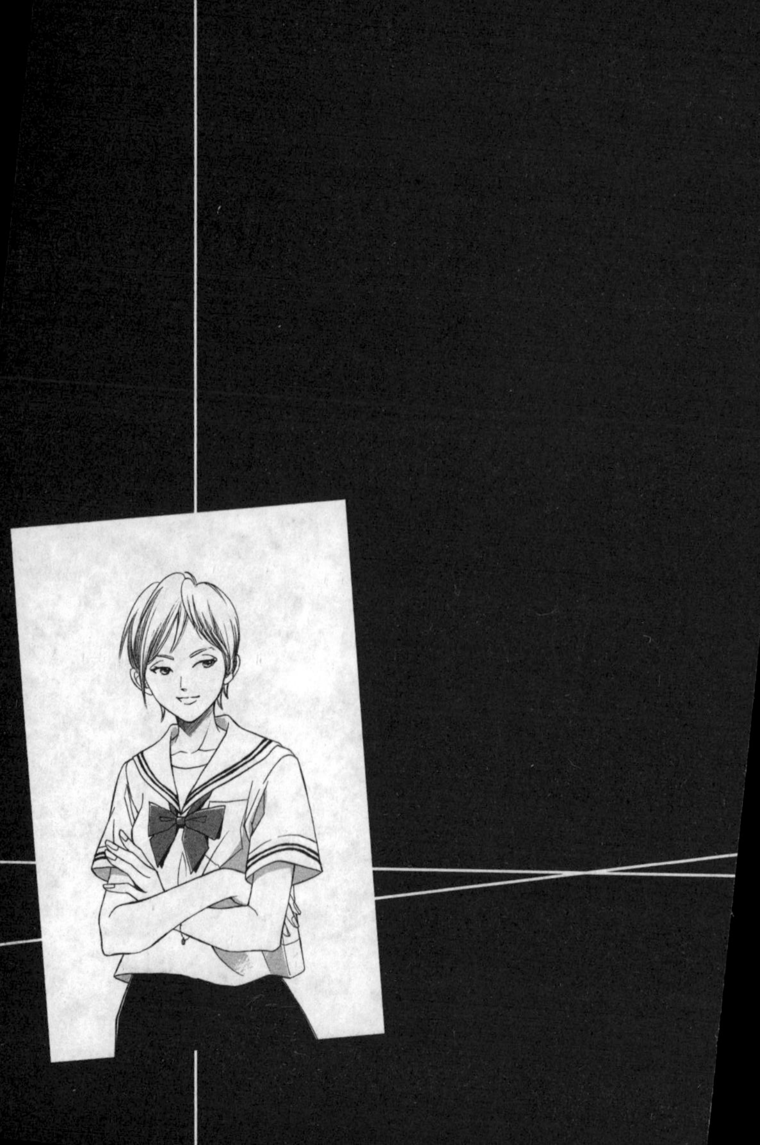

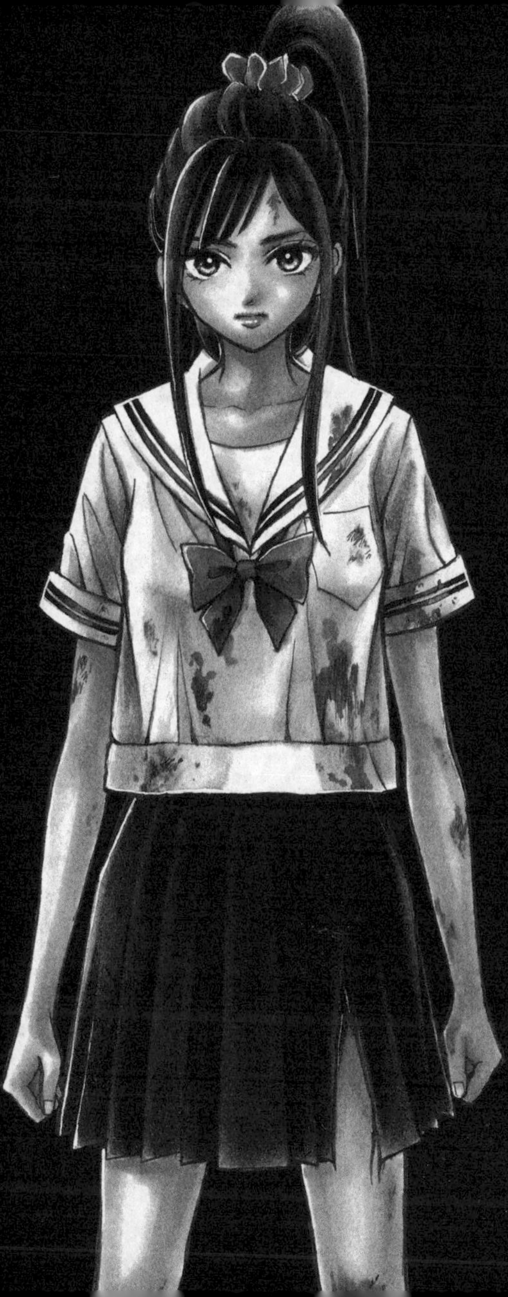

Scene.5
Take It Into Your Own Hands

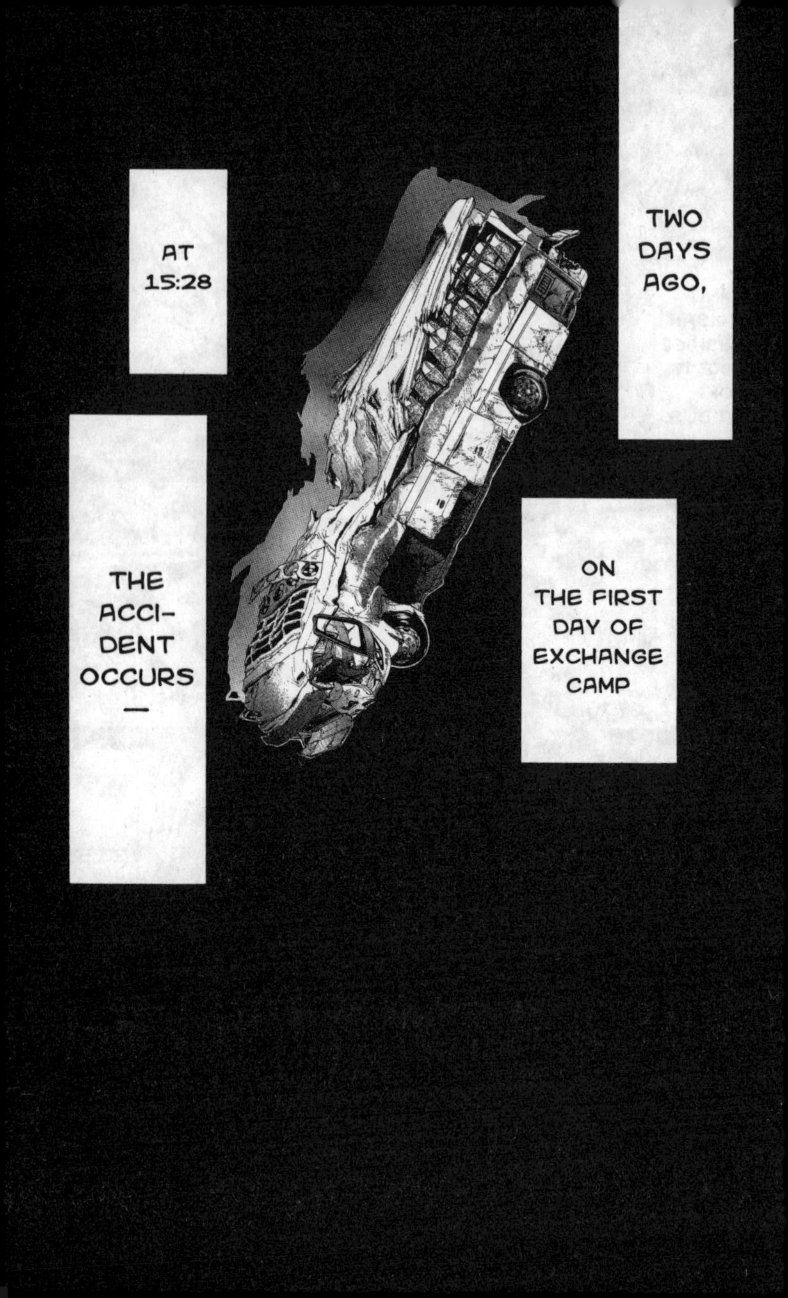
TWO DAYS AGO,
ON THE FIRST DAY OF EXCHANGE CAMP
AT 15:28
THE ACCI- DENT OCCURS —

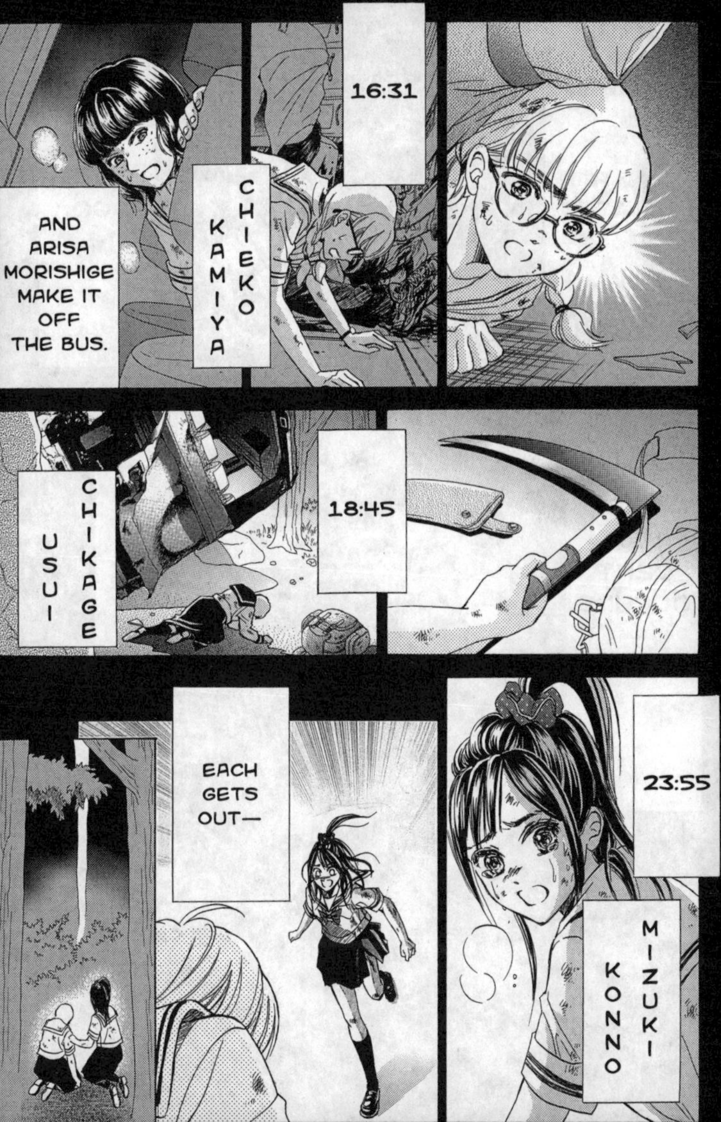
16:31
CHIEKO KAMIYA
AND ARISA MORISHIGE MAKE IT OFF THE BUS.
18:45
CHIKAGE USUI
23:55
MIZUKI KONNO
EACH GETS OUT—

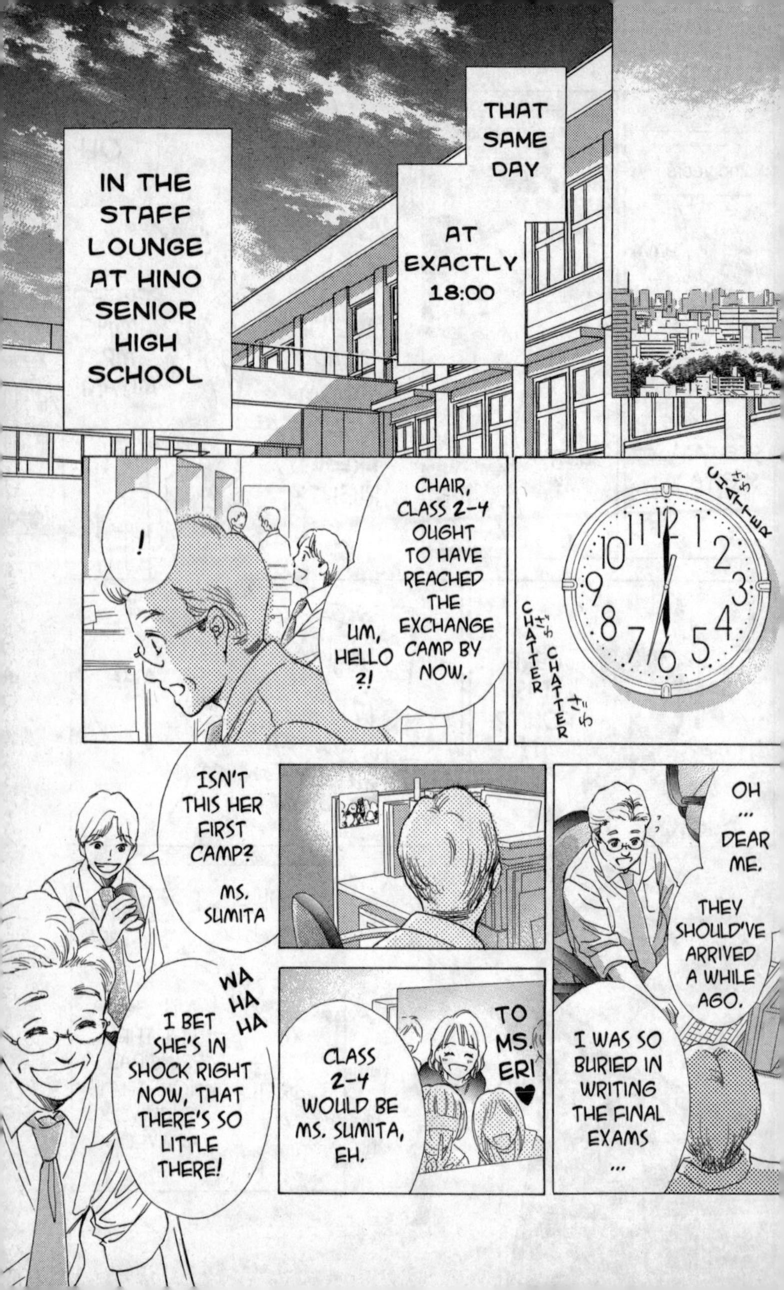
THAT SAME DAY
AT EXACTLY 18:00
IN THE STAFF LOUNGE AT HINO SENIOR HIGH SCHOOL
CHATTER
CHATTER
CHATTER
CHAIR, CLASS 2-4 OUGHT TO HAVE REACHED THE EXCHANGE CAMP BY NOW.
UM, HELLO ?!
!
OH ... DEAR ME.
THEY SHOULD'VE ARRIVED A WHILE AGO.
I WAS SO BURIED IN WRITING THE FINAL EXAMS ...
TO MS. ERI ♥
CLASS 2-4 WOULD BE MS. SUMITA, EH.
ISN'T THIS HER FIRST CAMP?
MS. SUMITA
WA HA HA
I BET SHE'S IN SHOCK RIGHT NOW, THAT THERE'S SO LITTLE THERE!

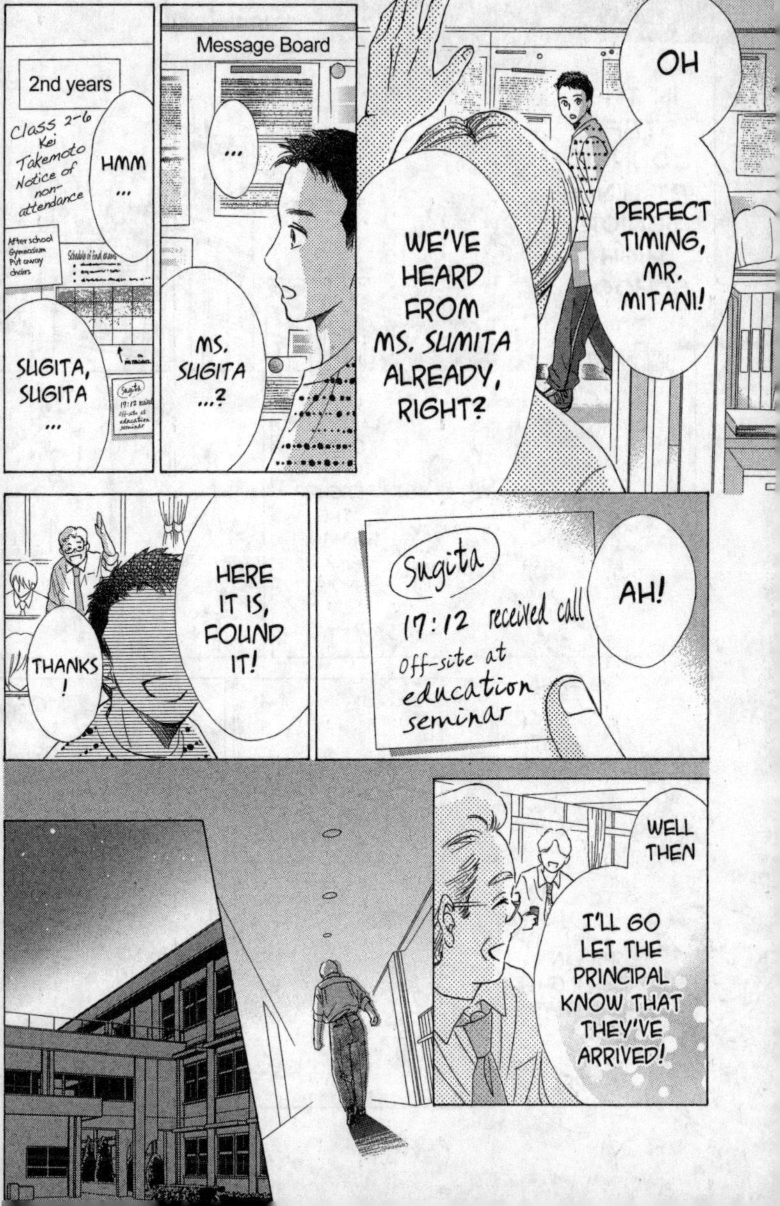
OH
PERFECT TIMING, MR. MITANI!
WE'VE HEARD FROM MS. SUMITA ALREADY, RIGHT?
Message Board
...
MS. SUGITA ...?
2nd years
Class 2-6 Kei Takemoto Notice of non-attendance
HMM ...
After school Gymnasium Put away chairs
Schedule of final exams
SUGITA, SUGITA ...
Sugita 17:12 received off-site at education seminar
Sugita
17:12 received call
Off-site at education seminar
AH!
HERE IT IS, FOUND IT!
THANKS!
WELL THEN
I'LL GO LET THE PRINCIPAL KNOW THAT THEY'VE ARRIVED!

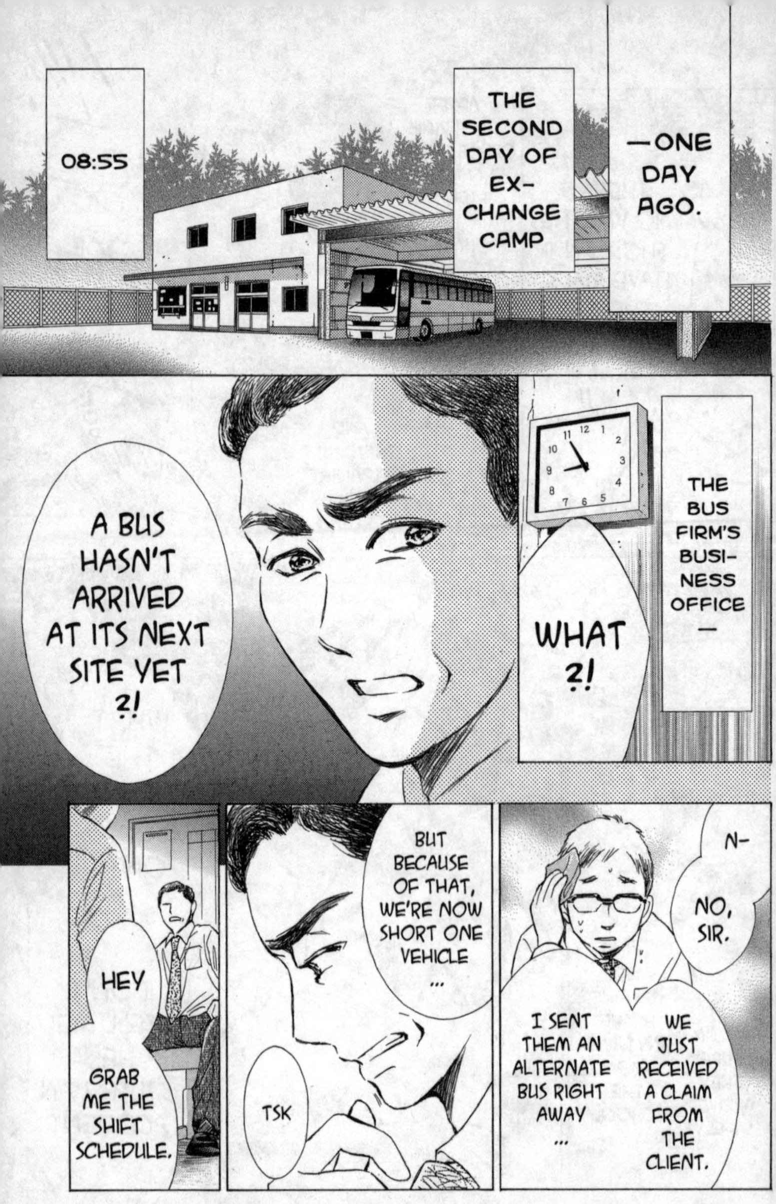
—ONE DAY AGO.
THE SECOND DAY OF EX-CHANGE CAMP
08:55
THE BUS FIRM'S BUSI-NESS OFFICE —
WHAT ?!
A BUS HASN'T ARRIVED AT ITS NEXT SITE YET ?!
N-NO, SIR.
WE JUST RECEIVED A CLAIM FROM THE CLIENT.
I SENT THEM AN ALTERNATE BUS RIGHT AWAY ...
BUT BECAUSE OF THAT, WE'RE NOW SHORT ONE VEHICLE ...
TSK
HEY
GRAB ME THE SHIFT SCHEDULE.

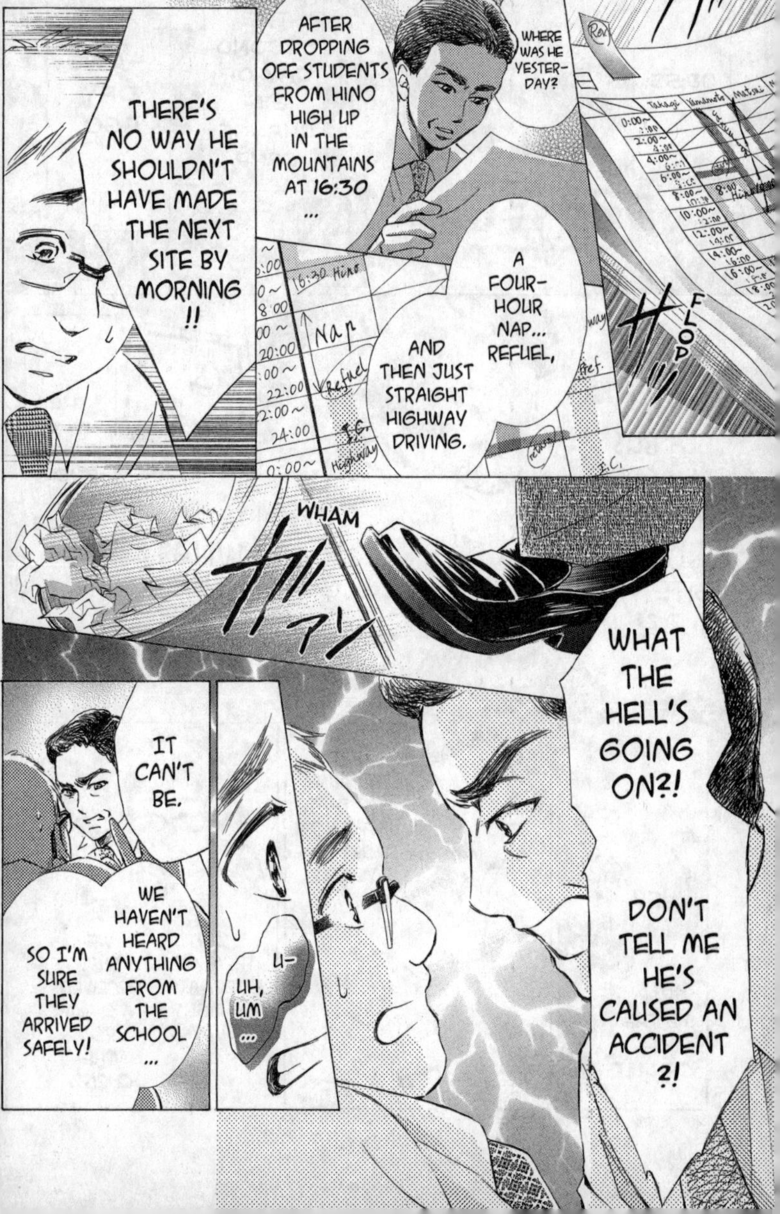
FLOP
WHERE WAS HE YESTERDAY?
AFTER DROPPING OFF STUDENTS FROM HINO HIGH UP IN THE MOUNTAINS AT 16:30 ...
A FOUR-HOUR NAP... REFUEL,
AND THEN JUST STRAIGHT HIGHWAY DRIVING.
THERE'S NO WAY HE SHOULDN'T HAVE MADE THE NEXT SITE BY MORNING !!
WHAM
WHAT THE HELL'S GOING ON?!
DON'T TELL ME HE'S CAUSED AN ACCIDENT ?!
U-UH, UM ...
IT CAN'T BE.
WE HAVEN'T HEARD ANYTHING FROM THE SCHOOL ...
SO I'M SURE THEY ARRIVED SAFELY!

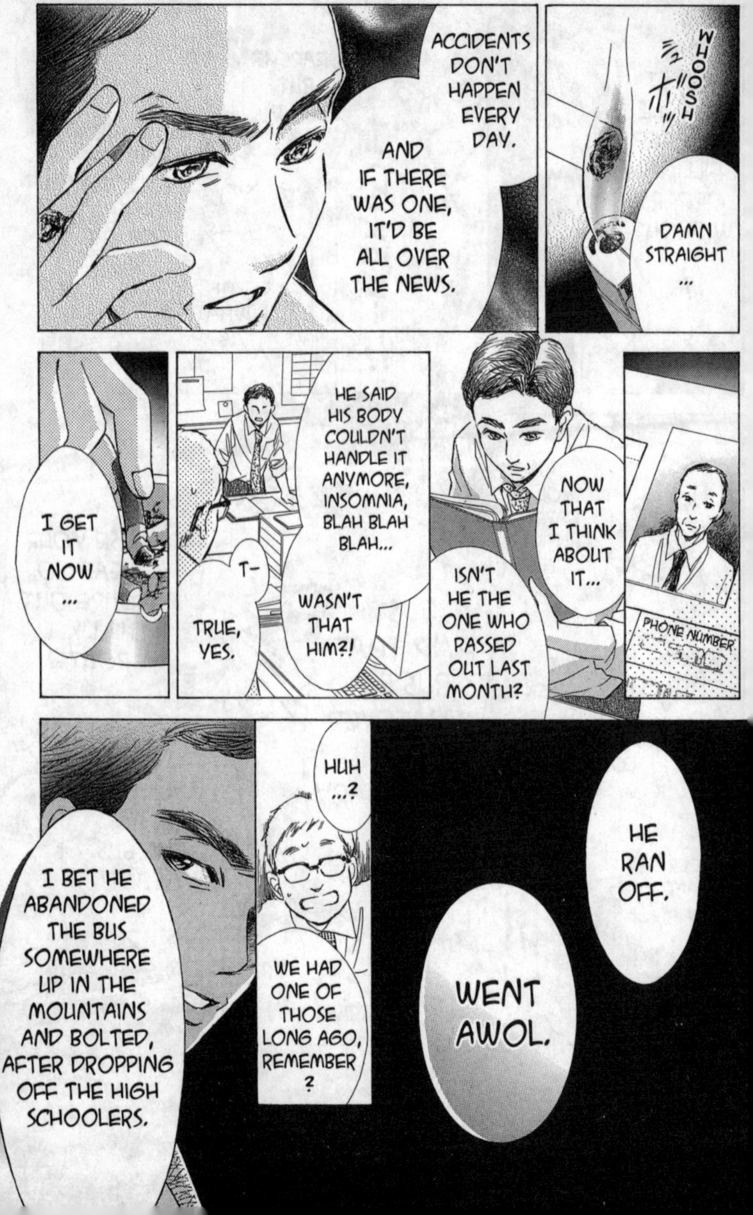
WHOOSH
DAMN STRAIGHT...
ACCIDENTS DON'T HAPPEN EVERY DAY.
AND IF THERE WAS ONE, IT'D BE ALL OVER THE NEWS.
PHONE NUMBER
NOW THAT I THINK ABOUT IT...
ISN'T HE THE ONE WHO PASSED OUT LAST MONTH?
HE SAID HIS BODY COULDN'T HANDLE IT ANYMORE, INSOMNIA, BLAH BLAH BLAH...
WASN'T THAT HIM?!
T-
TRUE, YES.
I GET IT NOW...
HE RAN OFF.
WENT AWOL.
HUH...?
WE HAD ONE OF THOSE LONG AGO, REMEMBER?
I BET HE ABANDONED THE BUS SOMEWHERE UP IN THE MOUNTAINS AND BOLTED, AFTER DROPPING OFF THE HIGH SCHOOLERS.

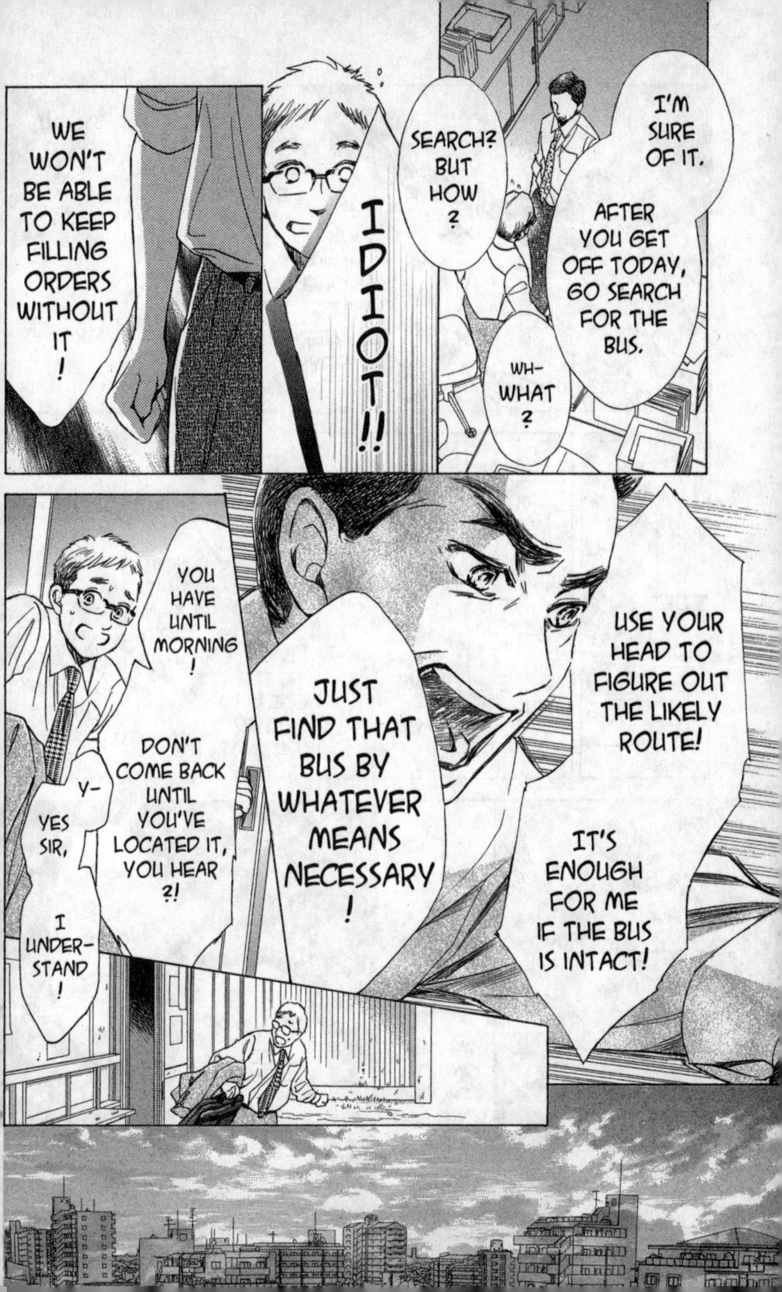
I'M SURE OF IT.
AFTER YOU GET OFF TODAY, GO SEARCH FOR THE BUS.
WH- WHAT?
SEARCH? BUT HOW?
IDIOT!!
WE WON'T BE ABLE TO KEEP FILLING ORDERS WITHOUT IT!
USE YOUR HEAD TO FIGURE OUT THE LIKELY ROUTE!
IT'S ENOUGH FOR ME IF THE BUS IS INTACT!
JUST FIND THAT BUS BY WHATEVER MEANS NECESSARY!
YOU HAVE UNTIL MORNING!
DON'T COME BACK UNTIL YOU'VE LOCATED IT, YOU HEAR?!
Y- YES SIR,
I UNDERSTAND!

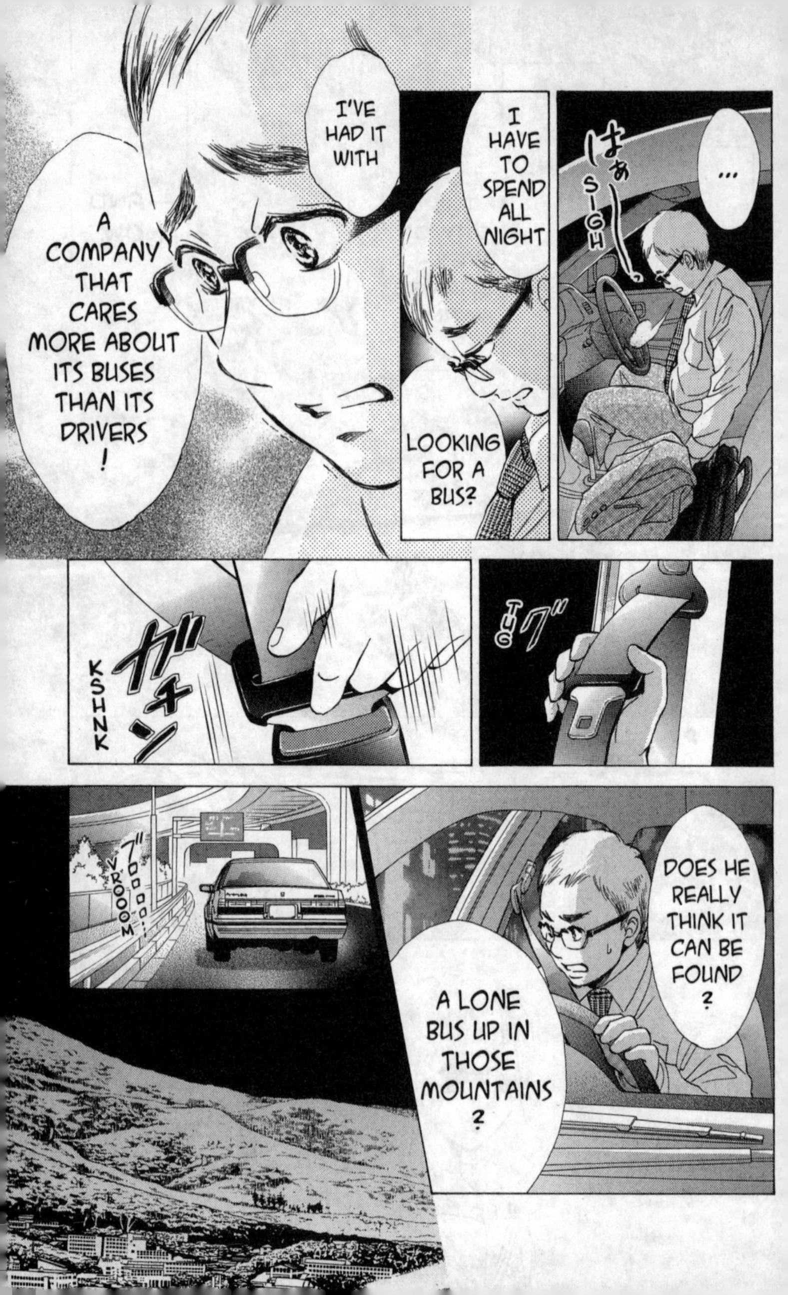
...
はぁ
SIGH
I HAVE TO SPEND ALL NIGHT
LOOKING FOR A BUS?
I'VE HAD IT WITH
A COMPANY THAT CARES MORE ABOUT ITS BUSES THAN ITS DRIVERS!
グ
TUG
ガチン
KSHNK
DOES HE REALLY THINK IT CAN BE FOUND?
A LONE BUS UP IN THOSE MOUNTAINS?
ブロロロ…
VROOOOM

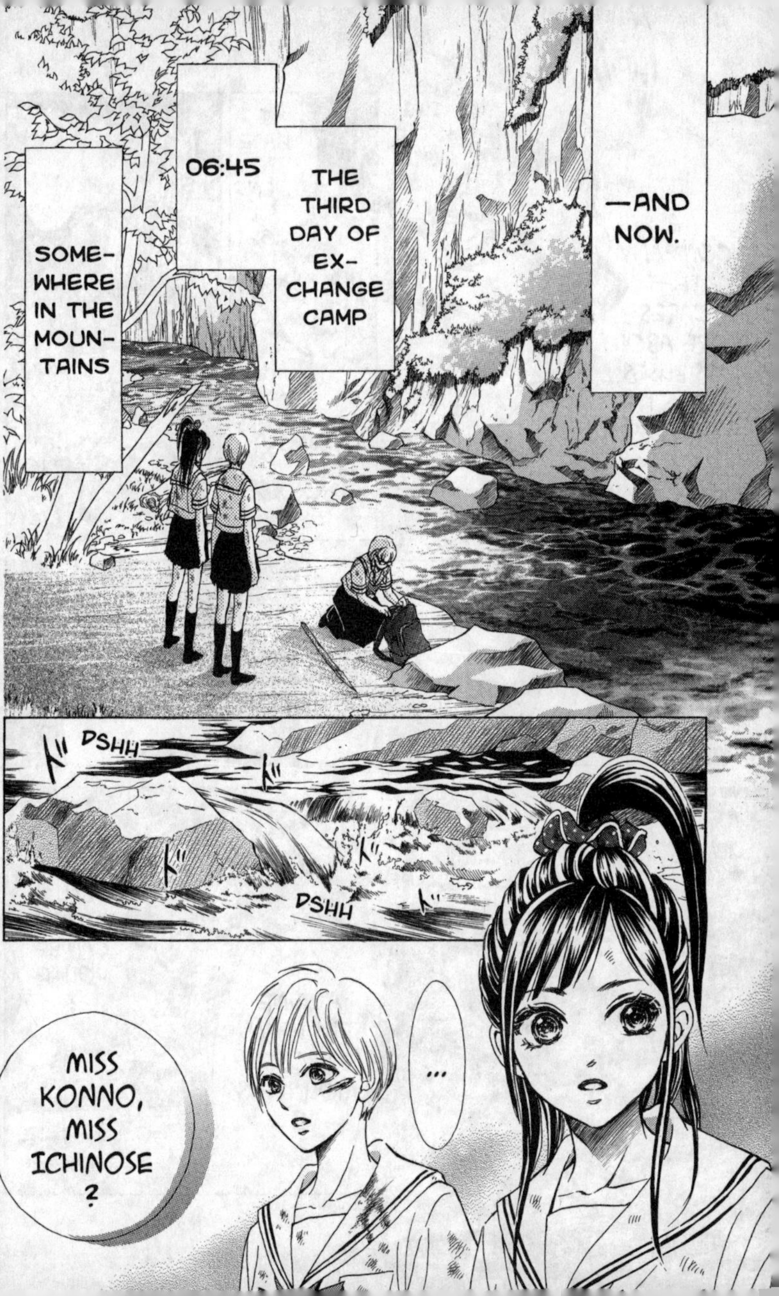
—AND NOW.
THE THIRD DAY OF EX-CHANGE CAMP
06:45
SOMEWHERE IN THE MOUN-TAINS
ド
DSHH
ド
ド
ド
DSHH
ド
...
MISS KONNO, MISS ICHINOSE?

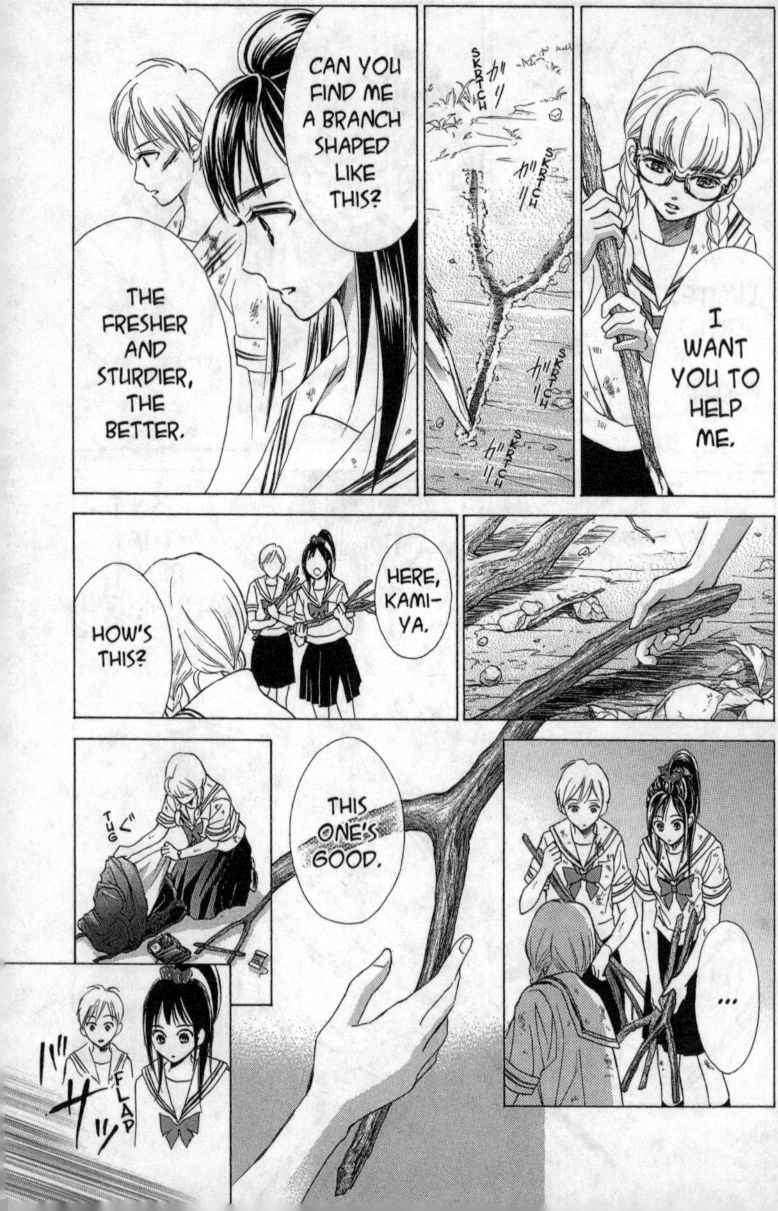
I WANT YOU TO HELP ME.
SKRTCH
SKRTCH
SKRTCH
SKRTCH
CAN YOU FIND ME A BRANCH SHAPED LIKE THIS?
THE FRESHER AND STURDIER, THE BETTER.
HERE, KAMI-YA.
HOW'S THIS?
...
THIS ONE'S GOOD.
TUG
FLAP

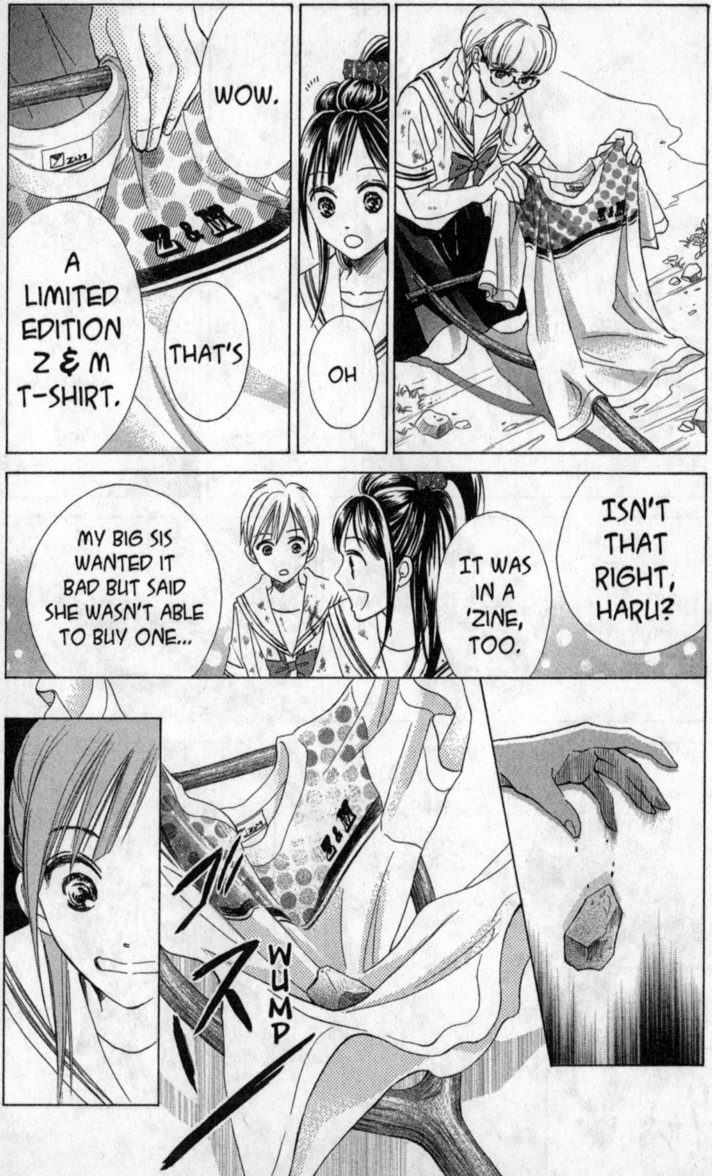
OH
WOW.
THAT'S
A LIMITED EDITION Z & M T-SHIRT.
ISN'T THAT RIGHT, HARU?
IT WAS IN A 'ZINE, TOO.
MY BIG SIS WANTED IT BAD BUT SAID SHE WASN'T ABLE TO BUY ONE...
WUMP

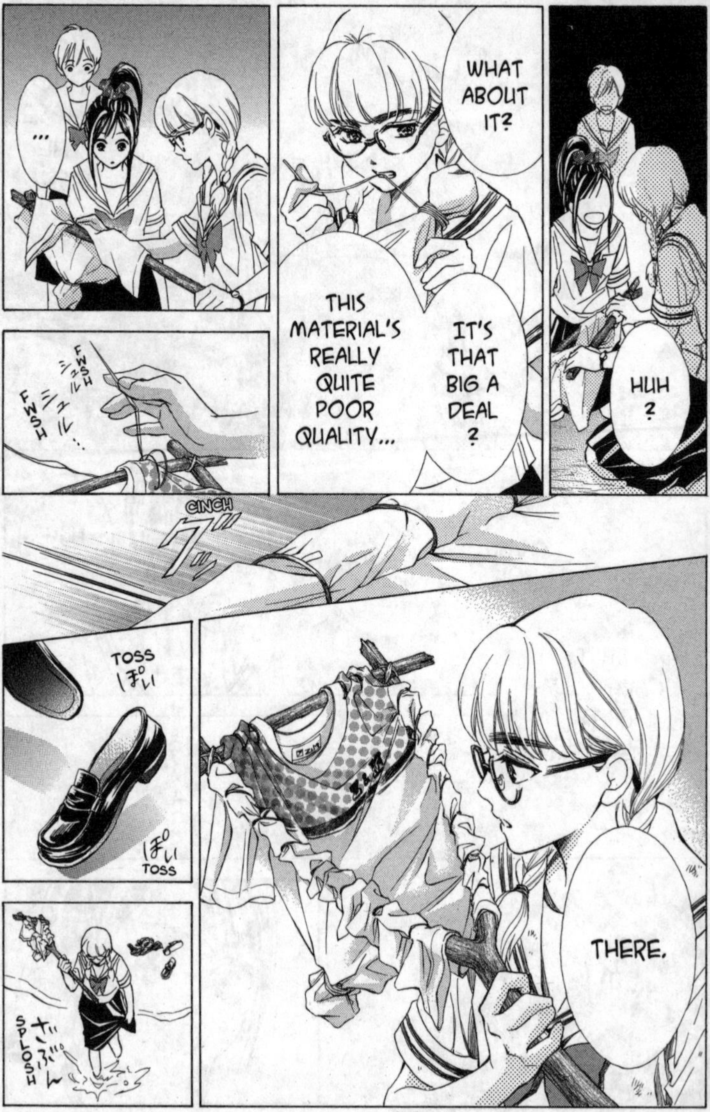
HUH ?
WHAT ABOUT IT?
IT'S THAT BIG A DEAL ?
THIS MATERIAL'S REALLY QUITE POOR QUALITY...
...
FWSH
シュル
FWSH
シュル...
CINCH
THERE.
TOSS
ぽい
ぽい
TOSS
SPLOSH

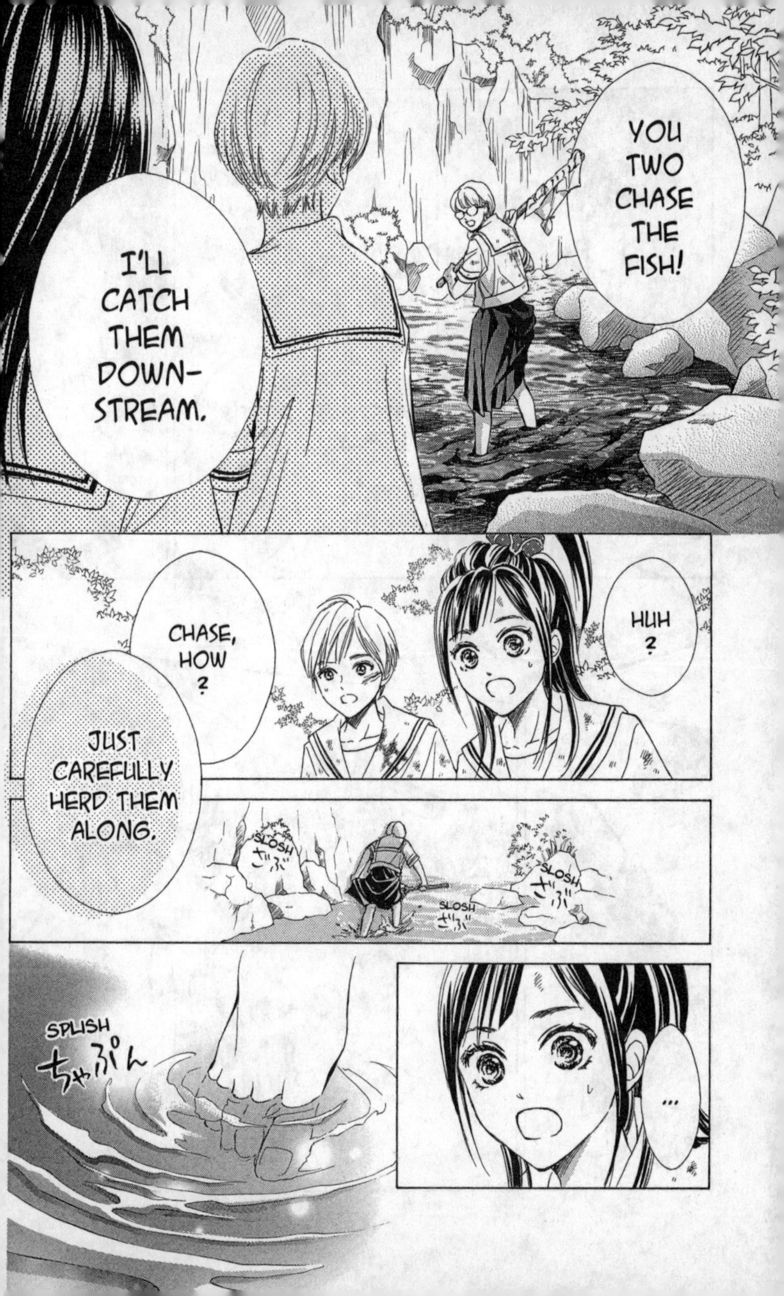
YOU TWO CHASE THE FISH!
I'LL CATCH THEM DOWN-STREAM.
HUH?
CHASE, HOW?
JUST CAREFULLY HERD THEM ALONG.
SLOSH ざぶ
SLOSH ざぶ
SLOSH ざぶ
...
SPLISH ちゃぷん

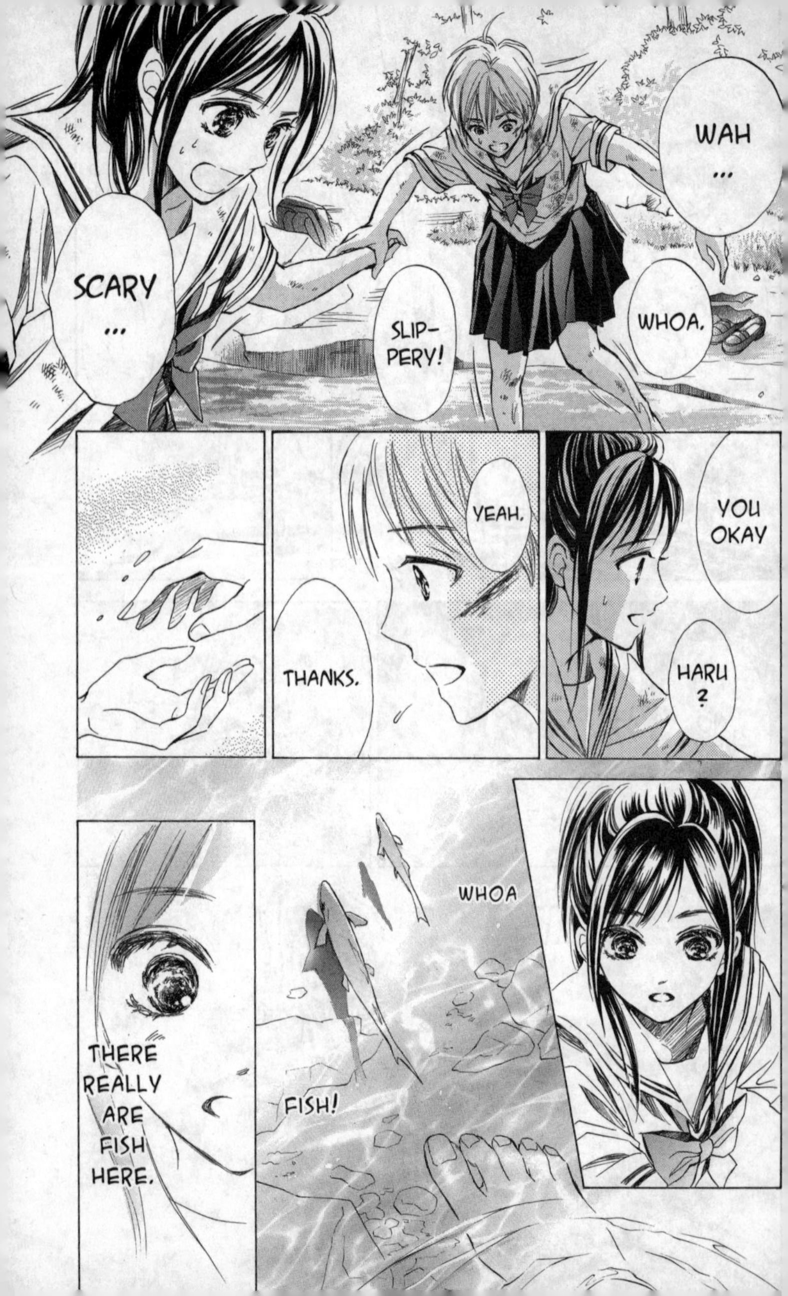
WAH ...
WHOA.
SLIP-PERY!
SCARY ...
YOU OKAY HARU?
YEAH.
THANKS.
WHOA
FISH!
THERE REALLY ARE FISH HERE.

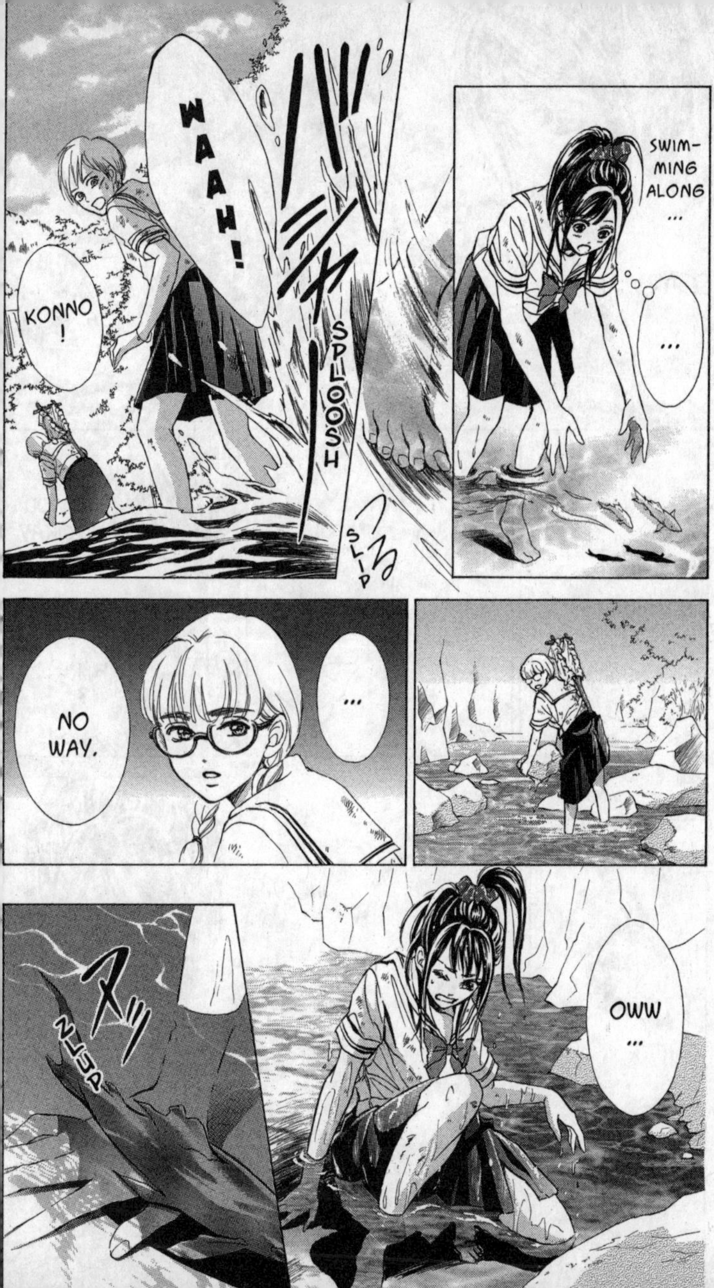
SWIM-MING ALONG ...
...
WAAH!
SPLOOSH
SLIP
KONNO!
...
NO WAY.
OWW ...
ZLUP

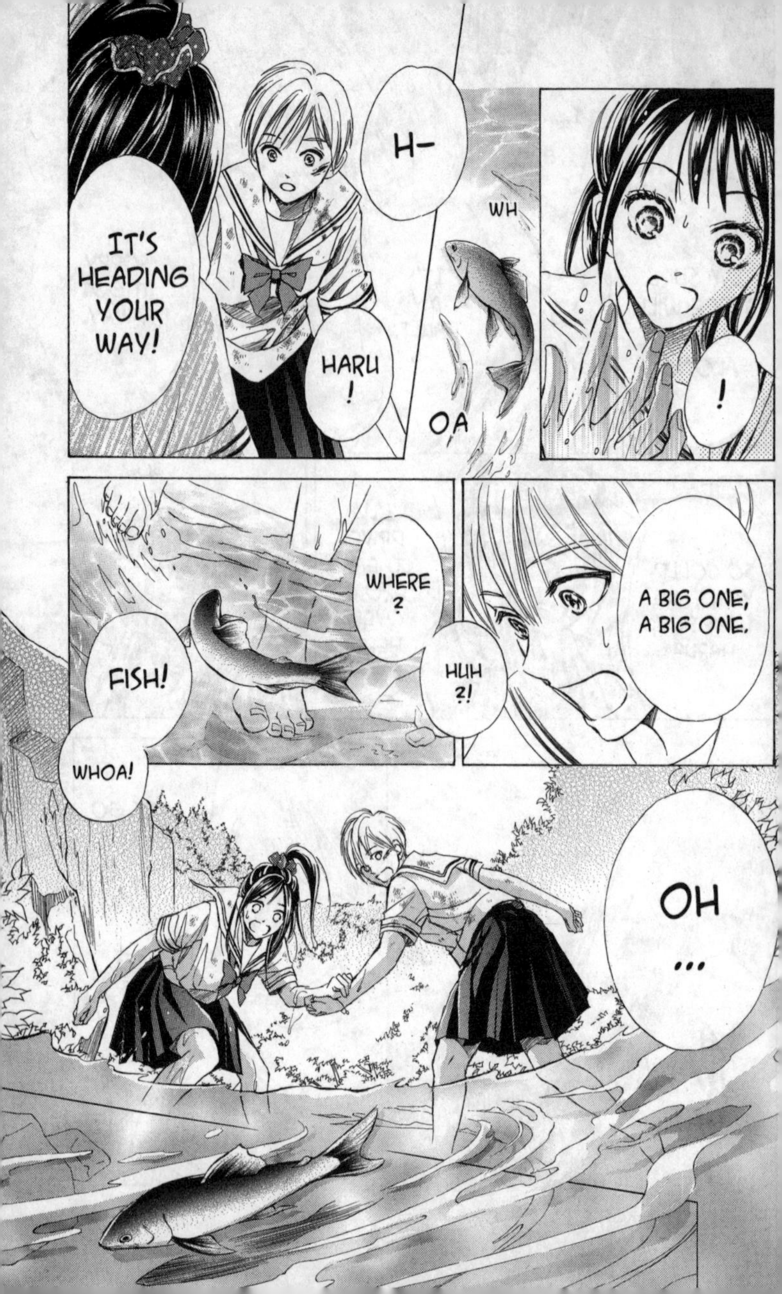
!
WH
OA
H-
HARU!
IT'S HEADING YOUR WAY!
A BIG ONE, A BIG ONE.
HUH?!
WHERE?
FISH!
WHOA!
OH ...

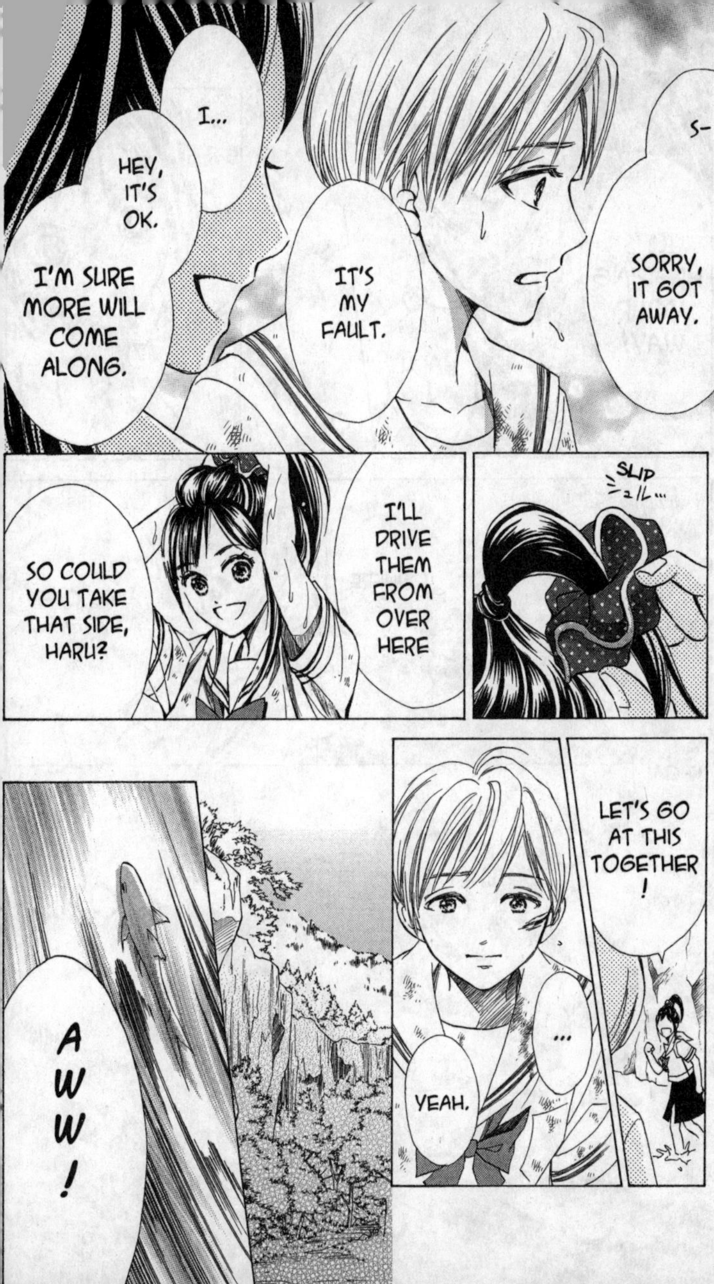
S-
SORRY, IT GOT AWAY.
IT'S MY FAULT.
I...
HEY, IT'S OK.
I'M SURE MORE WILL COME ALONG.
SLIP
ュル...
I'LL DRIVE THEM FROM OVER HERE
SO COULD YOU TAKE THAT SIDE, HARU?
LET'S GO AT THIS TOGETHER!
...
YEAH.
AWW!

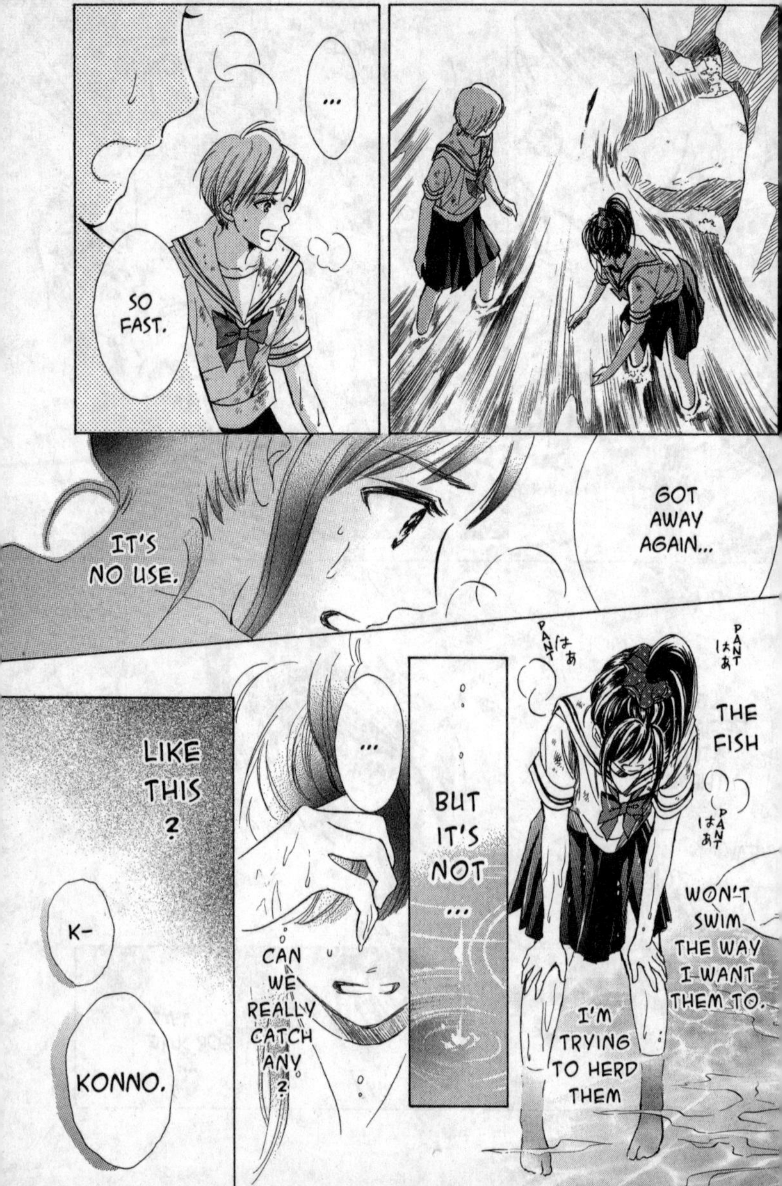
...
SO FAST.
GOT AWAY AGAIN...
IT'S NO USE.
PANT はあ
PANT はあ
THE FISH
PANT はあ
WON'T SWIM THE WAY I WANT THEM TO.
I'M TRYING TO HERD THEM
BUT IT'S NOT ...
...
CAN WE REALLY CATCH ANY ?
LIKE THIS ?
K-
KONNO.

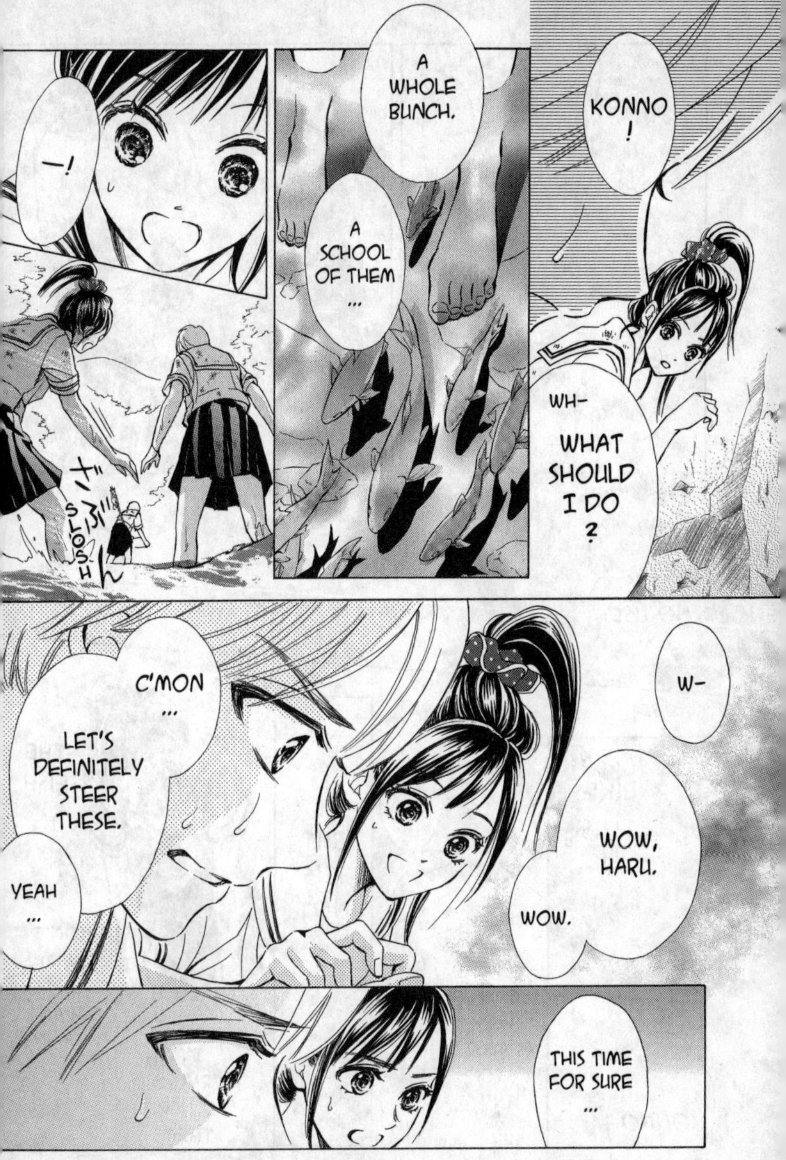
KONNO!
WH- WHAT SHOULD I DO?
A WHOLE BUNCH.
A SCHOOL OF THEM...
—!
SLOSH
W-
WOW, HARU.
WOW.
C'MON...
LET'S DEFINITELY STEER THESE.
YEAH...
THIS TIME FOR SURE...

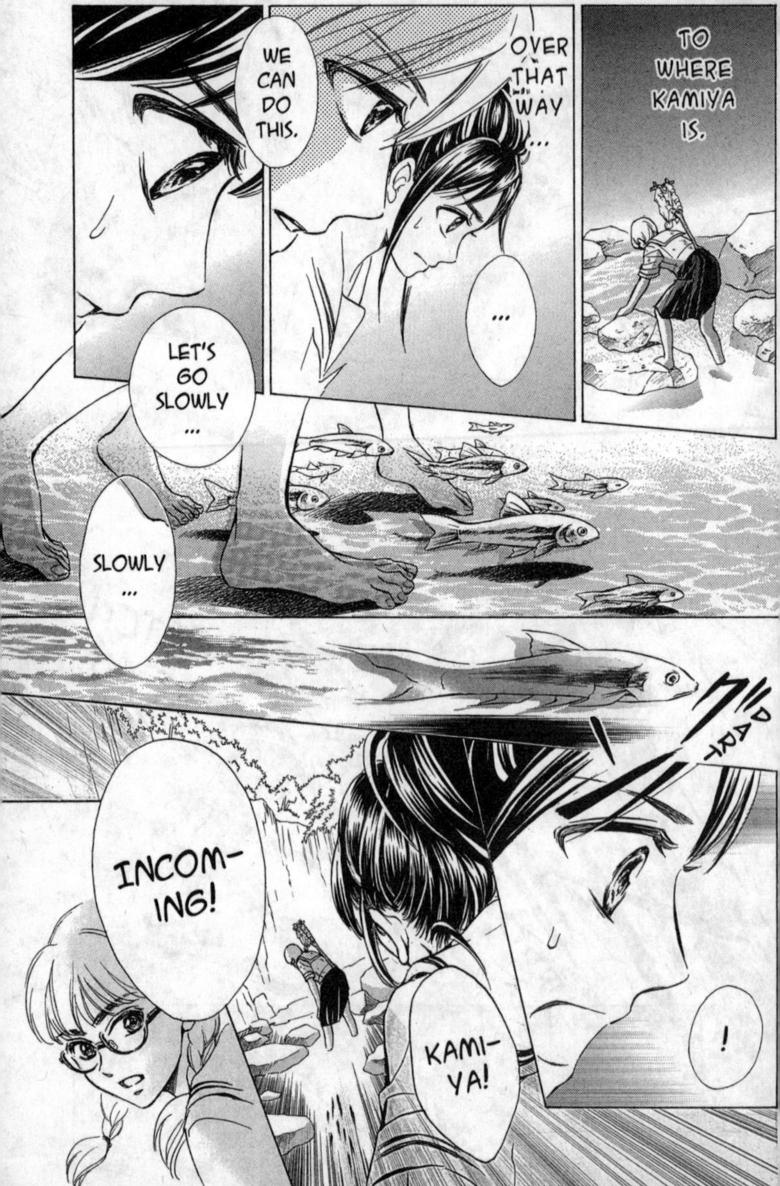
TO WHERE KAMIYA IS.
OVER THAT WAY...
WE CAN DO THIS.
...
LET'S GO SLOWLY...
SLOWLY...
DART
!
KAMI-YA!
INCOM-ING!

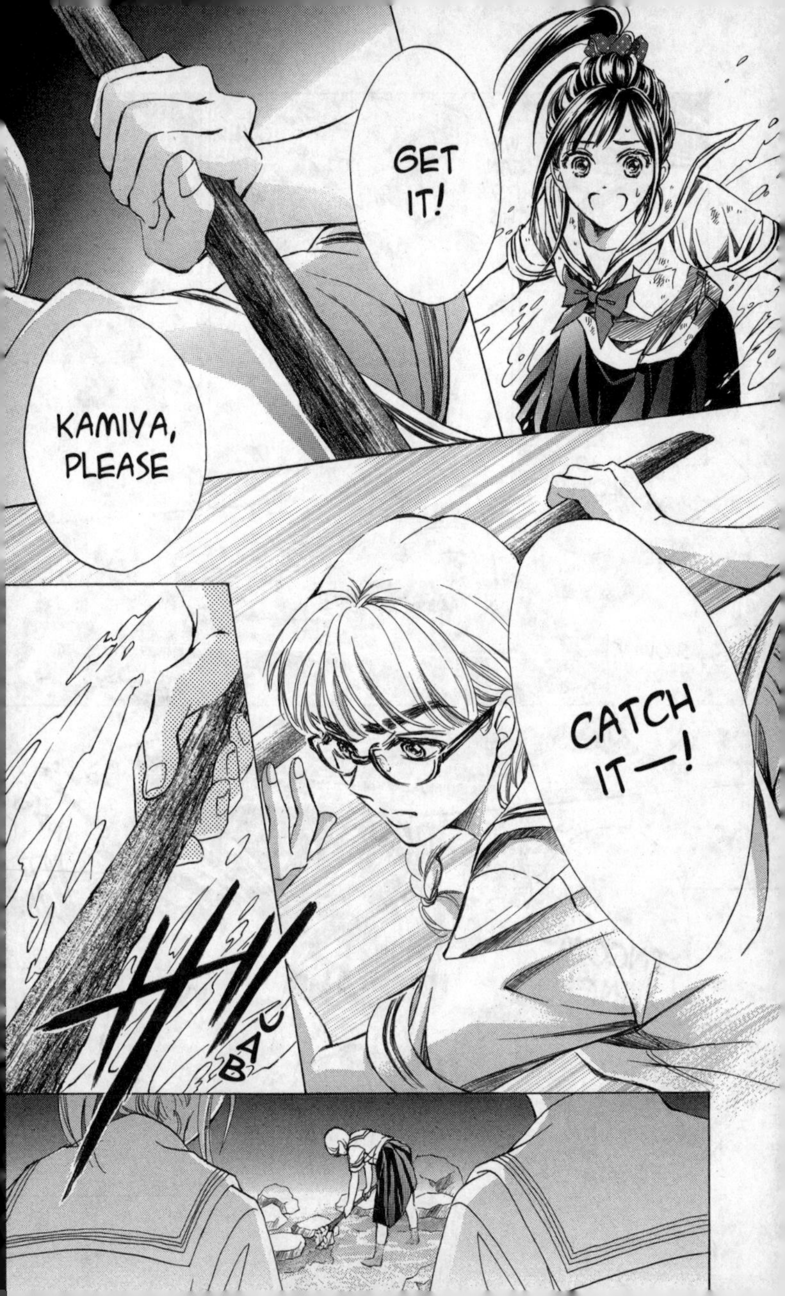
GET IT!
KAMIYA, PLEASE
CATCH IT—!
BAU

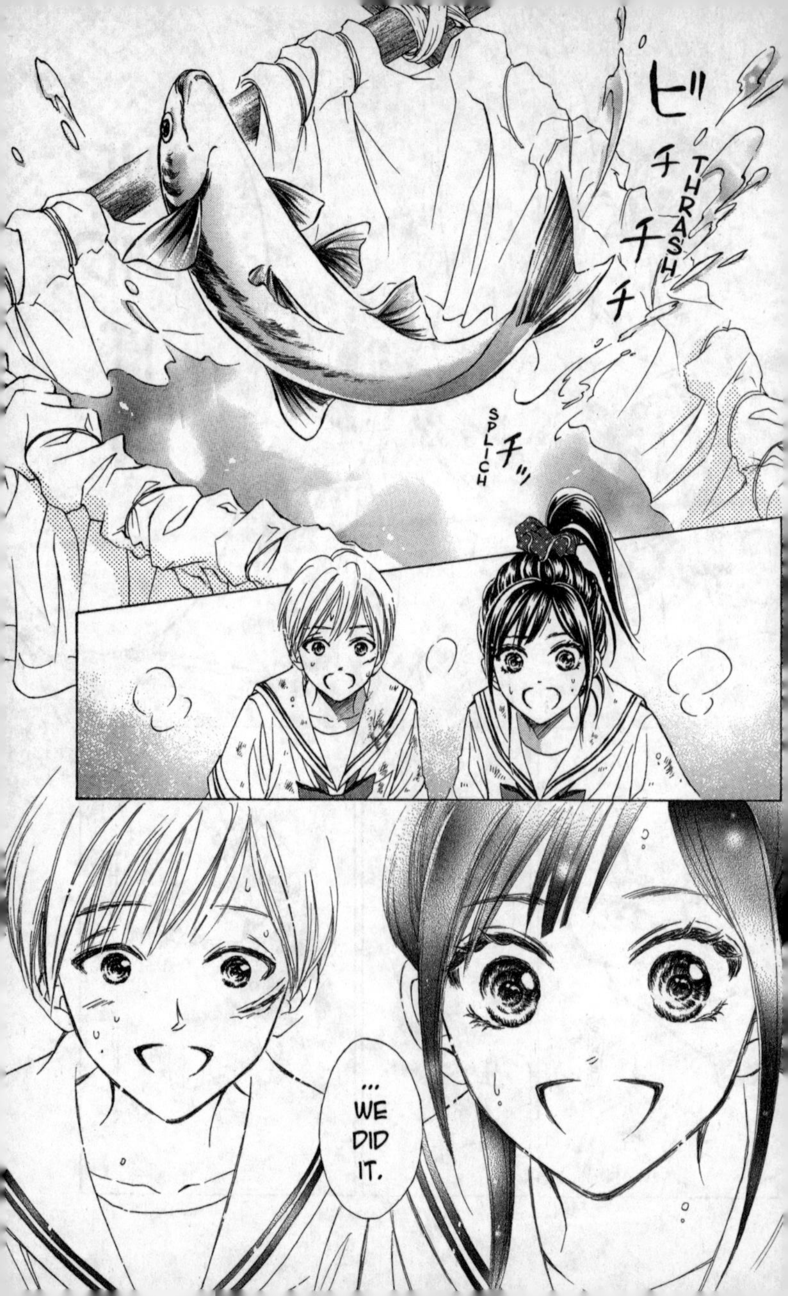
ビチチチ
THRASH
チッ
SPLICH
...WE DID IT.

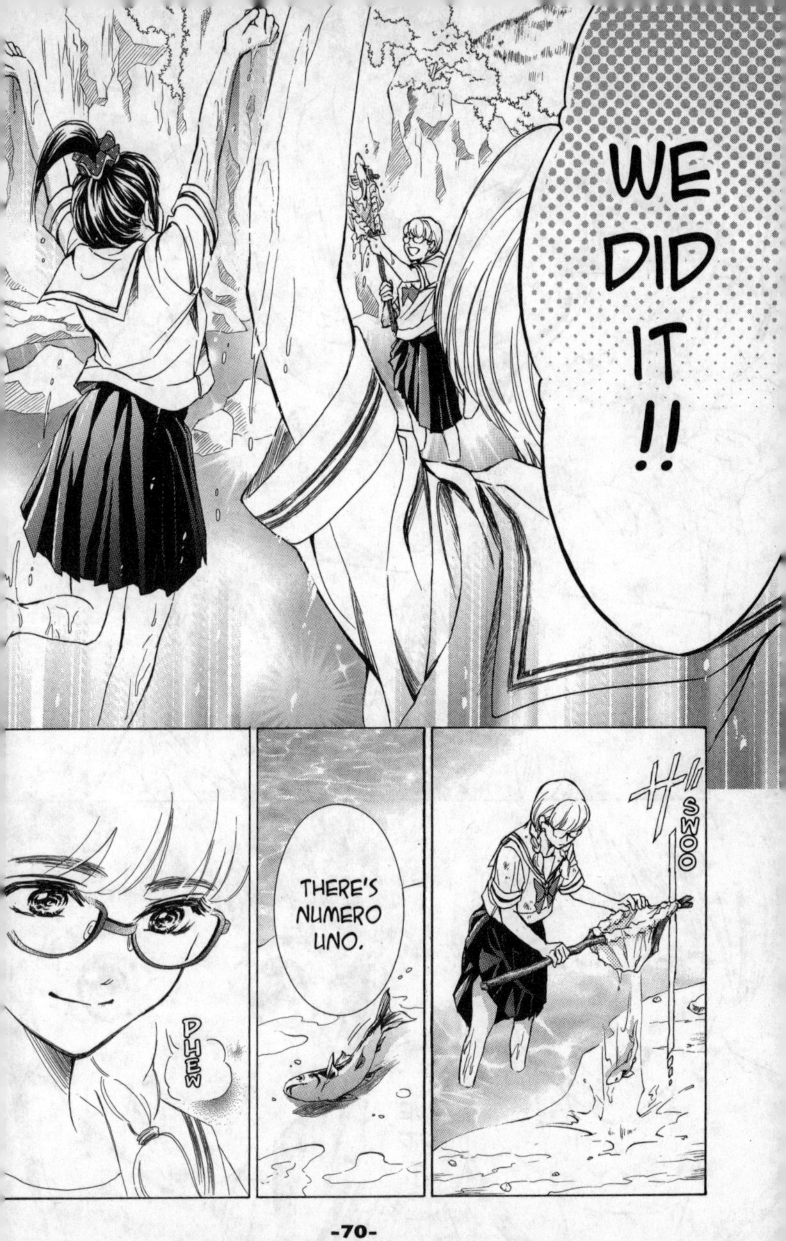
WE DID IT!!
SWOO
THERE'S NUMERO UNO.
PHEW

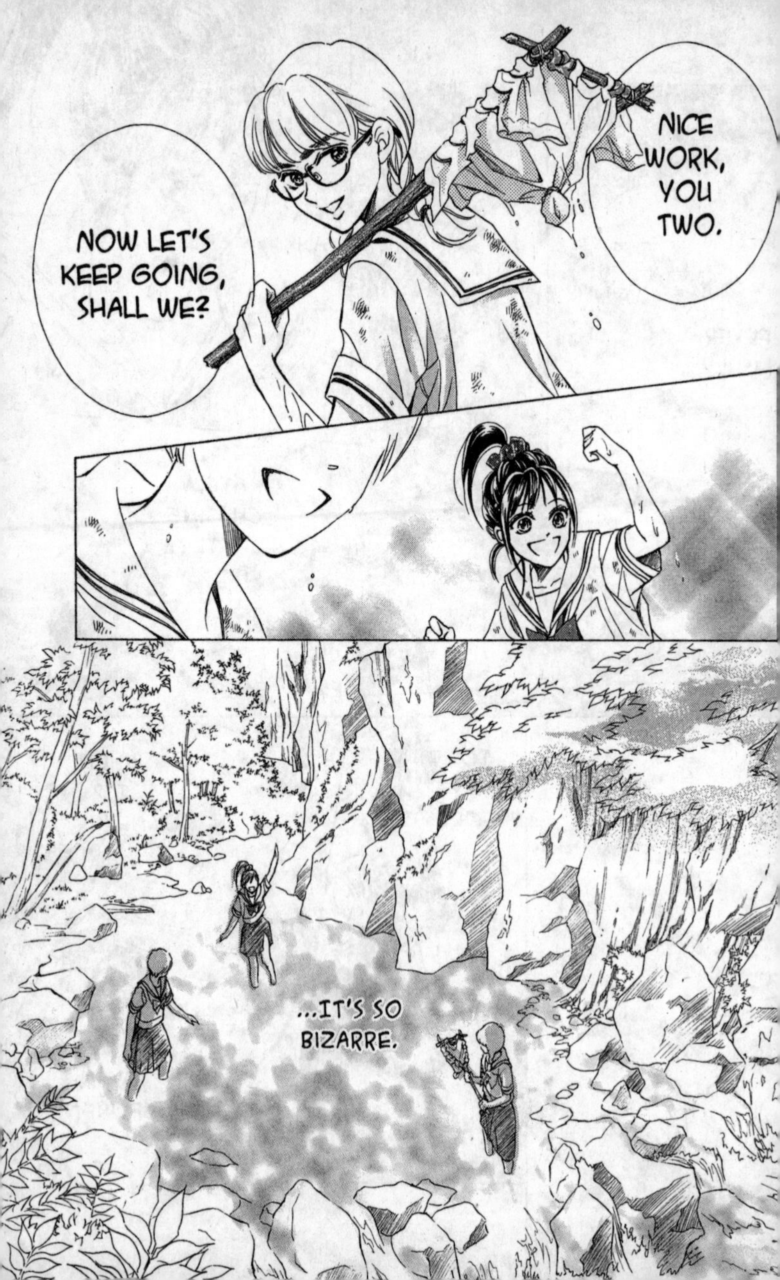
NICE WORK, YOU TWO.
NOW LET'S KEEP GOING, SHALL WE?
...IT'S SO BIZARRE.

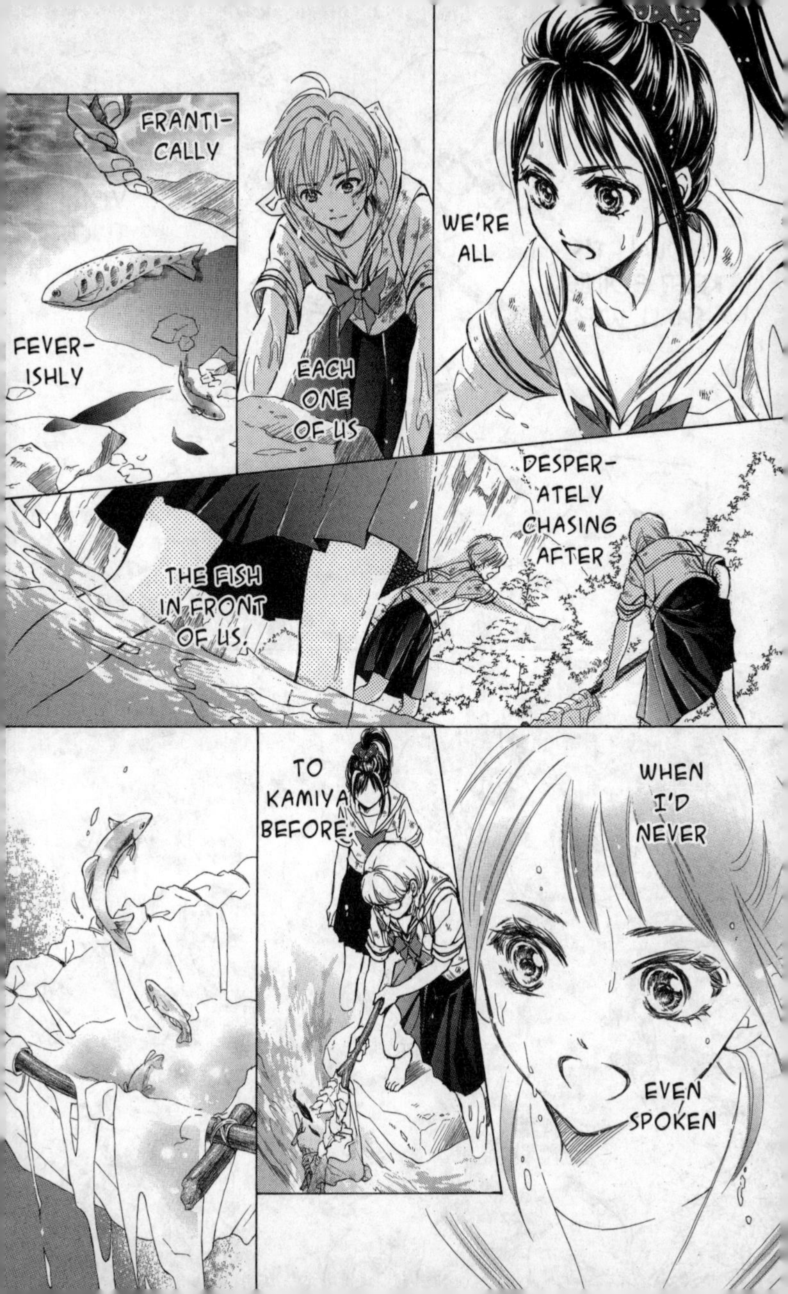
WE'RE ALL
EACH ONE OF US
FRANTI-CALLY
FEVER-ISHLY
DESPER-ATELY CHASING AFTER
THE FISH IN FRONT OF US.
WHEN I'D NEVER
EVEN SPOKEN
TO KAMIYA BEFORE.

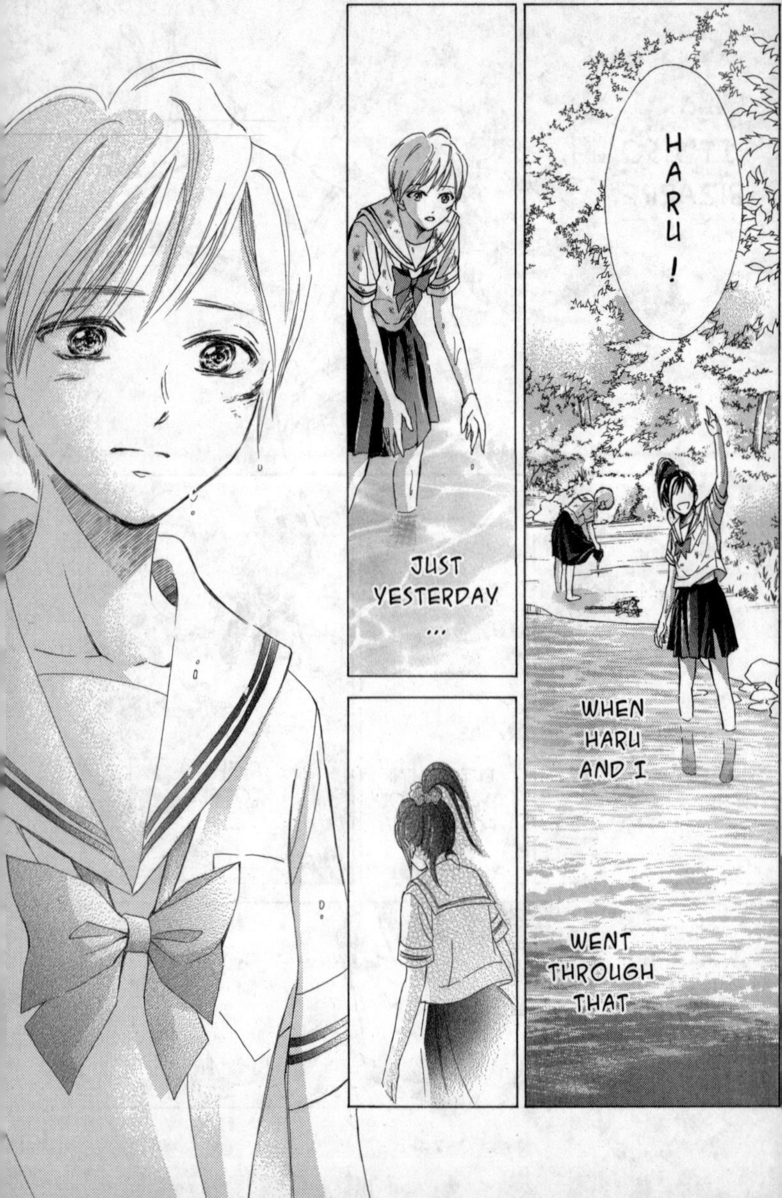
HARU!
WHEN HARU AND I
WENT THROUGH THAT
JUST YESTERDAY ...

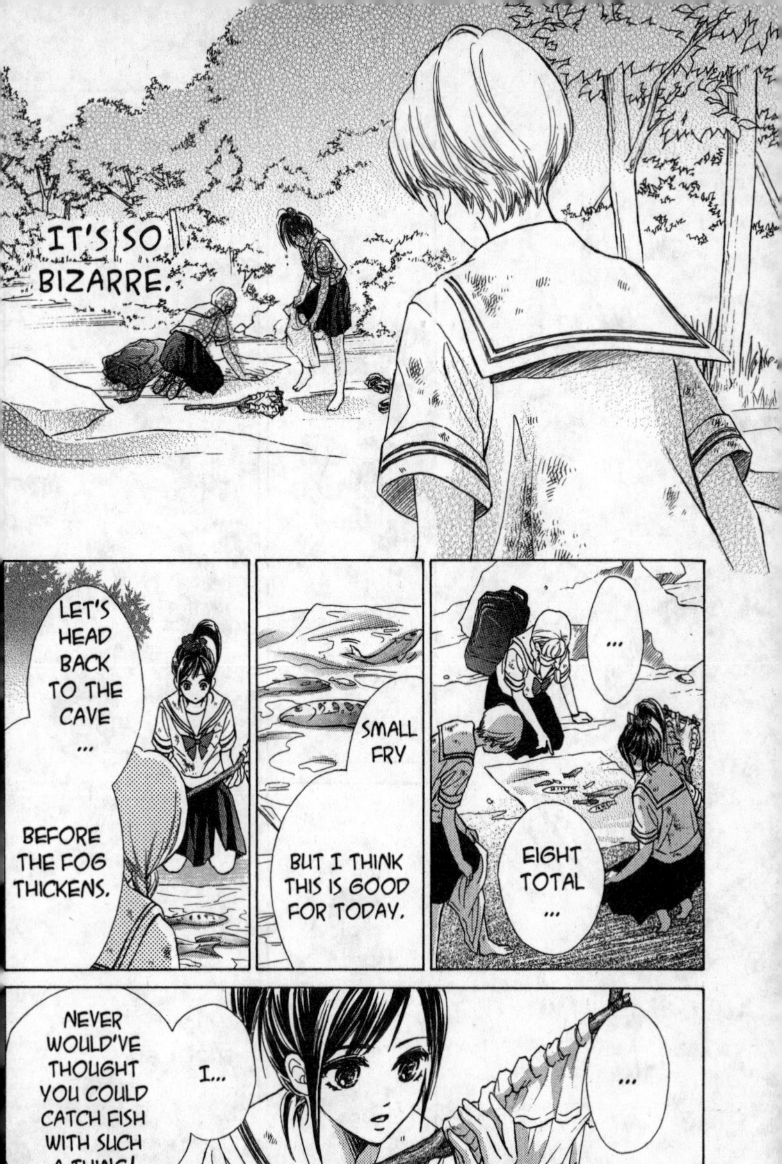
IT'S SO BIZARRE.
...
EIGHT TOTAL ...
SMALL FRY
BUT I THINK THIS IS GOOD FOR TODAY.
LET'S HEAD BACK TO THE CAVE ...
BEFORE THE FOG THICKENS.
...
I...
NEVER WOULD'VE THOUGHT YOU COULD CATCH FISH WITH SUCH A THING!

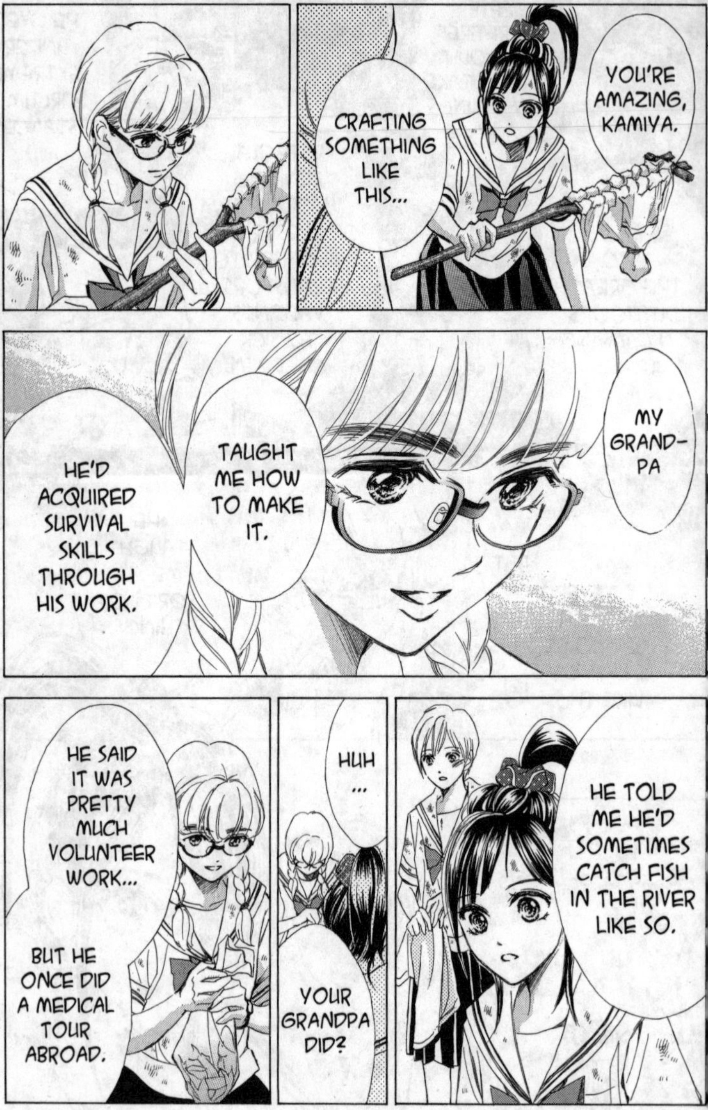
YOU'RE AMAZING, KAMIYA.
CRAFTING SOMETHING LIKE THIS...
MY GRAND-PA
TAUGHT ME HOW TO MAKE IT.
HE'D ACQUIRED SURVIVAL SKILLS THROUGH HIS WORK.
HE TOLD ME HE'D SOMETIMES CATCH FISH IN THE RIVER LIKE SO.
HUH ...
YOUR GRANDPA DID?
HE SAID IT WAS PRETTY MUCH VOLUNTEER WORK...
BUT HE ONCE DID A MEDICAL TOUR ABROAD.

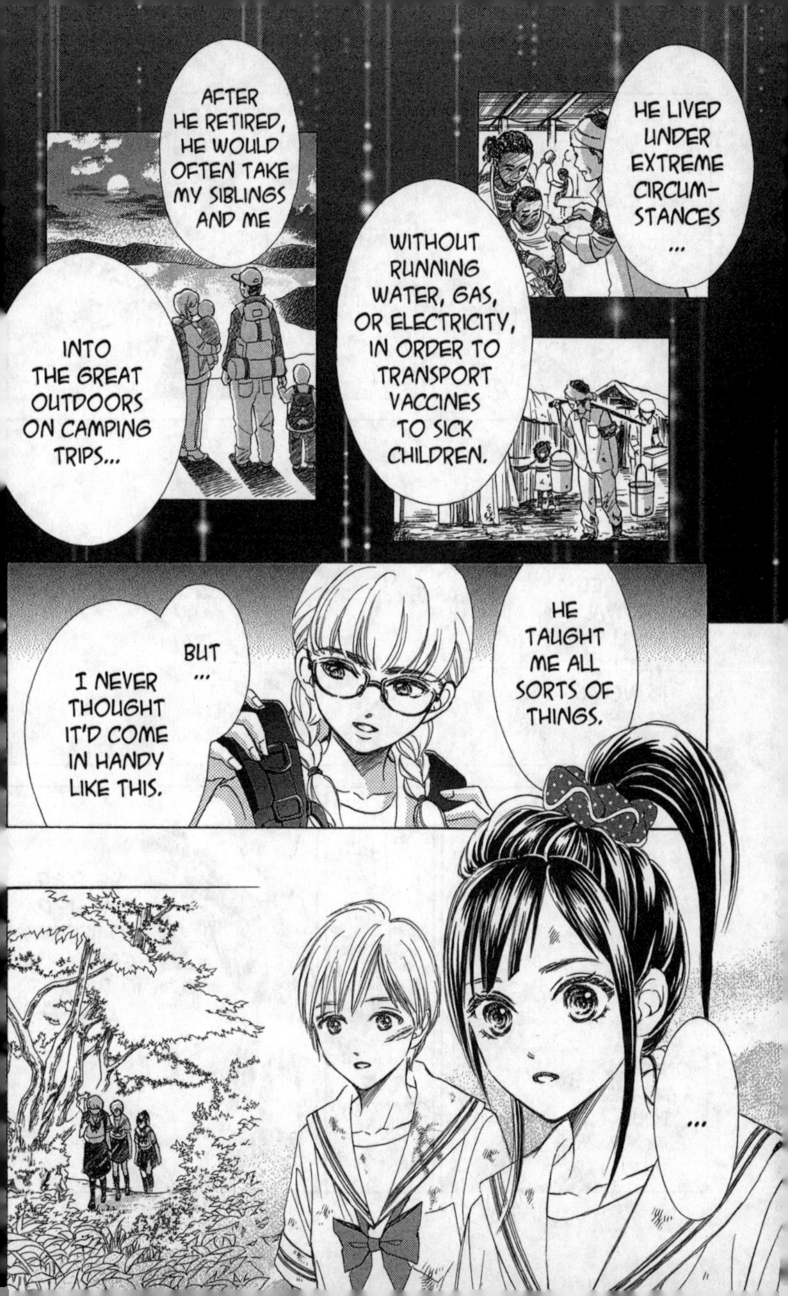
HE LIVED UNDER EXTREME CIRCUM-STANCES ...
WITHOUT RUNNING WATER, GAS, OR ELECTRICITY, IN ORDER TO TRANSPORT VACCINES TO SICK CHILDREN.
AFTER HE RETIRED, HE WOULD OFTEN TAKE MY SIBLINGS AND ME
INTO THE GREAT OUTDOORS ON CAMPING TRIPS...
HE TAUGHT ME ALL SORTS OF THINGS.
BUT ...
I NEVER THOUGHT IT'D COME IN HANDY LIKE THIS.
...

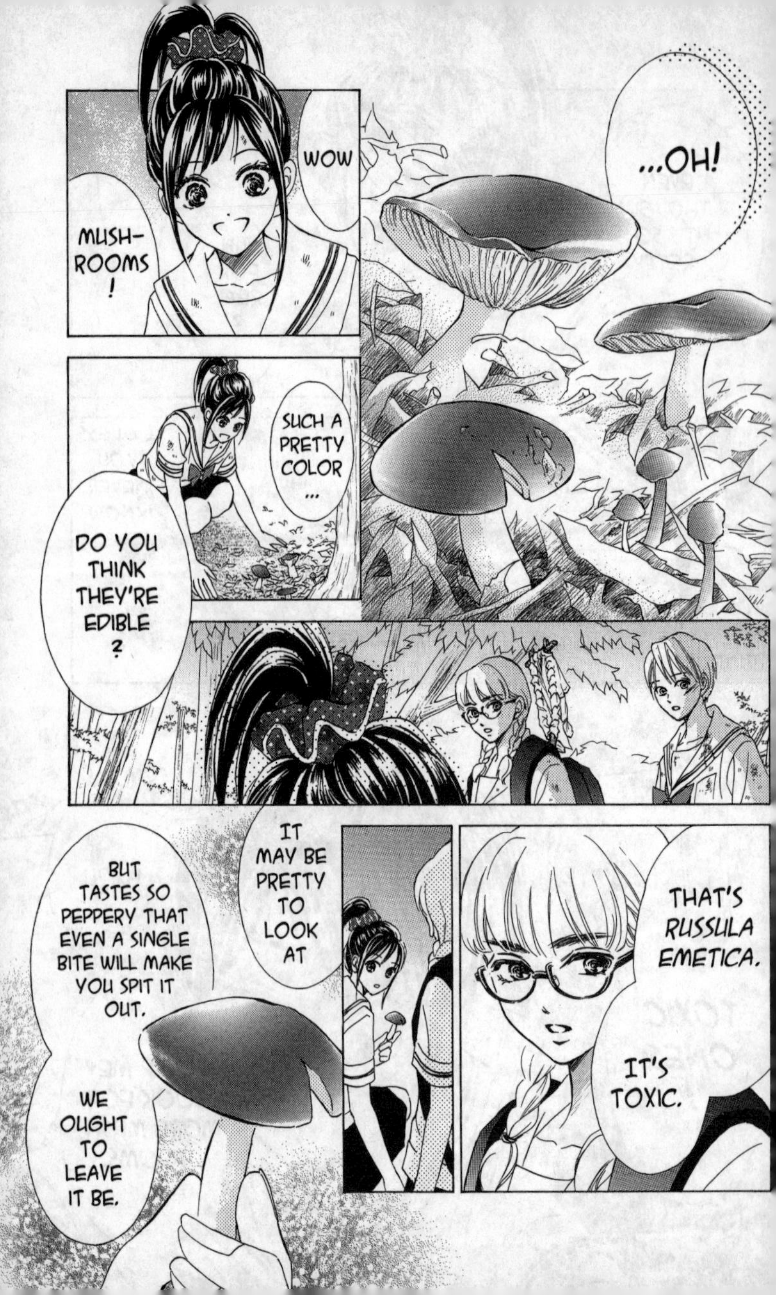
...OH!
WOW
MUSH-ROOMS!
SUCH A PRETTY COLOR...
DO YOU THINK THEY'RE EDIBLE?
THAT'S RUSSULA EMETICA.
IT'S TOXIC.
IT MAY BE PRETTY TO LOOK AT
BUT TASTES SO PEPPERY THAT EVEN A SINGLE BITE WILL MAKE YOU SPIT IT OUT.
WE OUGHT TO LEAVE IT BE.

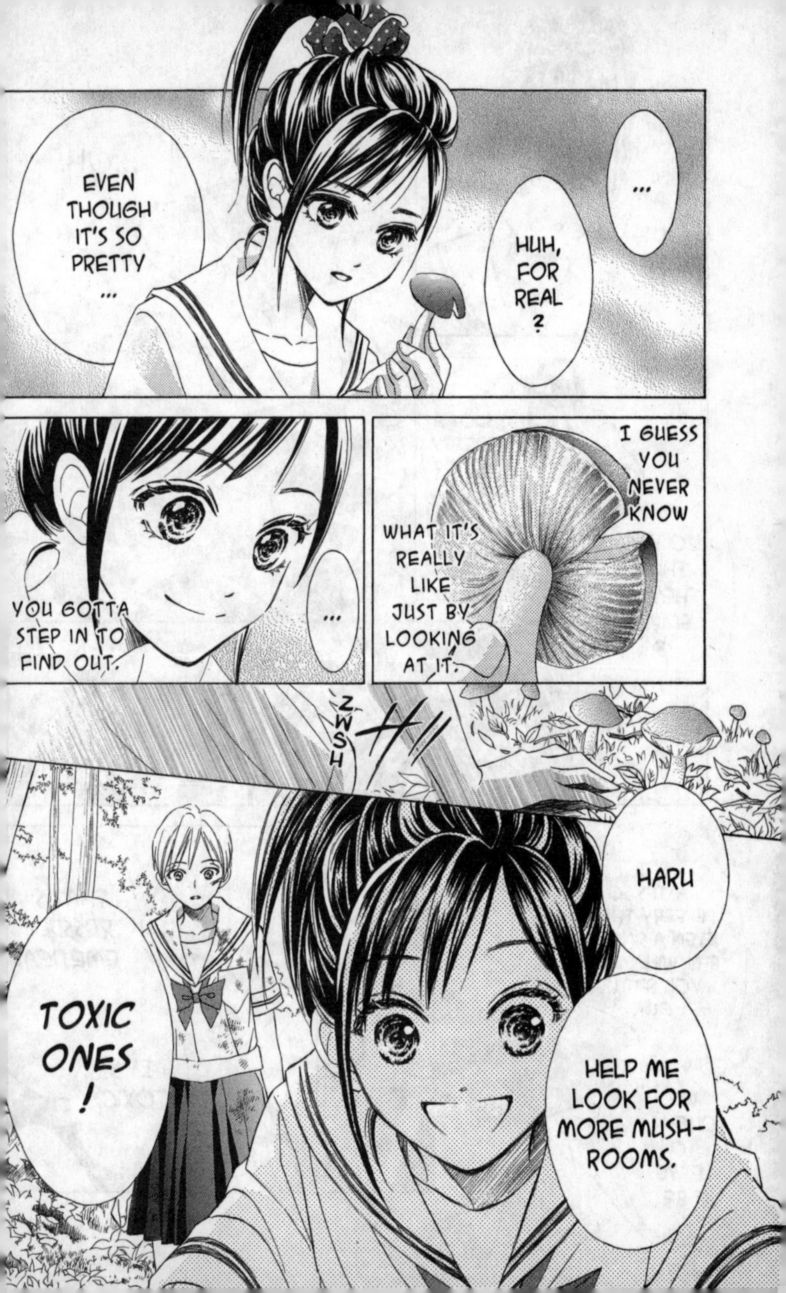
...
HUH, FOR REAL?
EVEN THOUGH IT'S SO PRETTY ...
I GUESS YOU NEVER KNOW
WHAT IT'S REALLY LIKE JUST BY LOOKING AT IT.
...
YOU GOTTA STEP IN TO FIND OUT.
ZWSH
HARU
HELP ME LOOK FOR MORE MUSH-ROOMS.
TOXIC ONES!

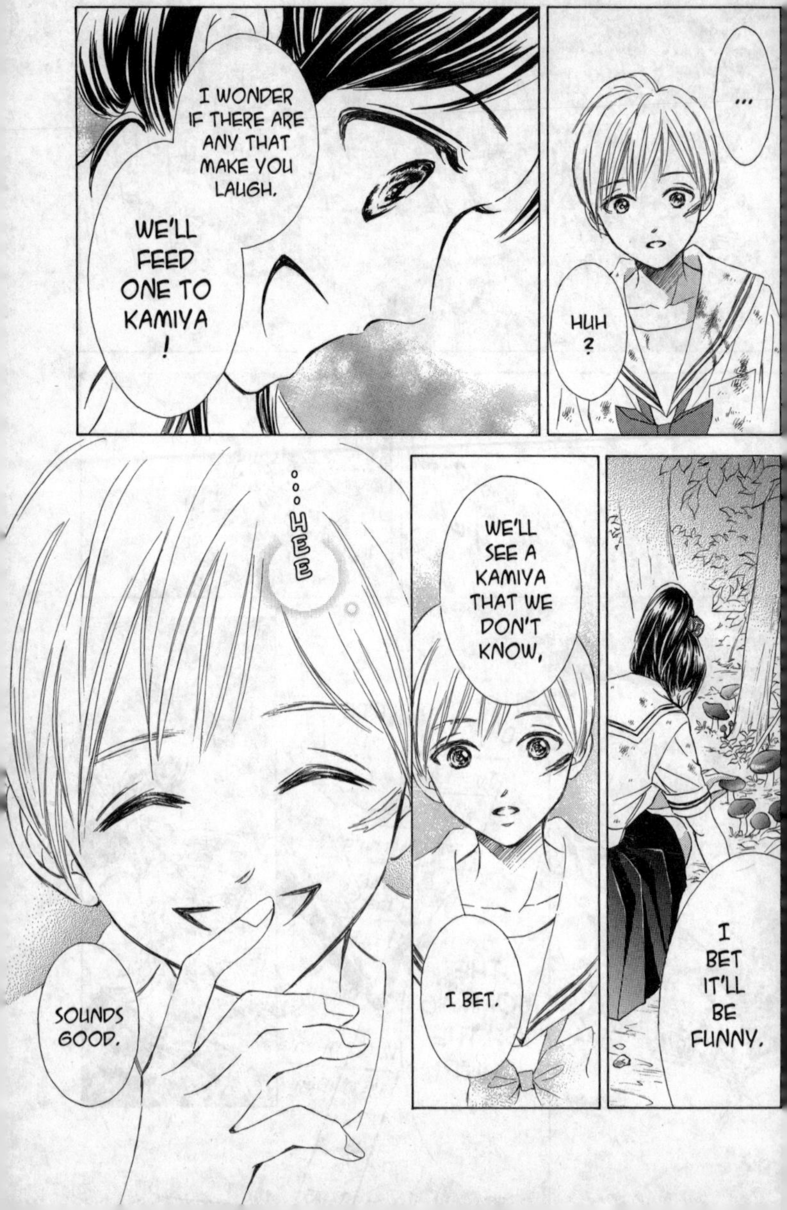
...
HUH?
I WONDER IF THERE ARE ANY THAT MAKE YOU LAUGH.
WE'LL FEED ONE TO KAMIYA!
I BET IT'LL BE FUNNY.
WE'LL SEE A KAMIYA THAT WE DON'T KNOW,
I BET.
...HEE
SOUNDS GOOD.

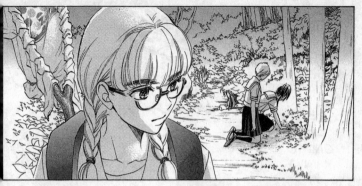

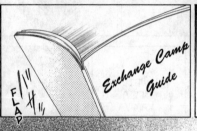

Exchange Camp Guide

...

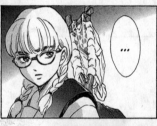

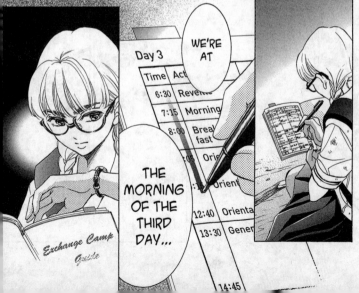

WE'RE AT

Day 3

Time	Act
6:30	Reveil...
7:15	Morning
8:00	Break fast
:05	Ori...
	Orient...
12:40	Orienta...
13:30	Gener...
14:45	

THE MORNING OF THE THIRD DAY...

Exchange Camp Guide

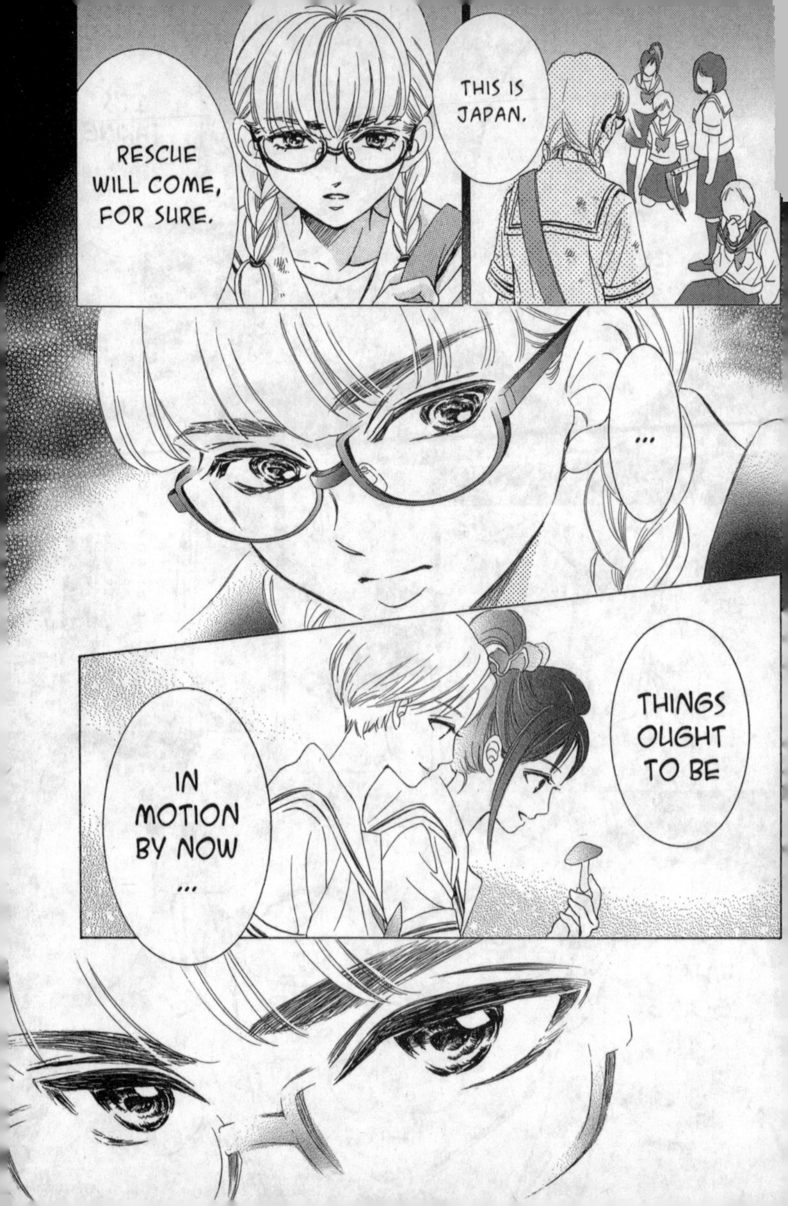
THIS IS JAPAN.
RESCUE WILL COME, FOR SURE.
...
THINGS OUGHT TO BE
IN MOTION BY NOW ...

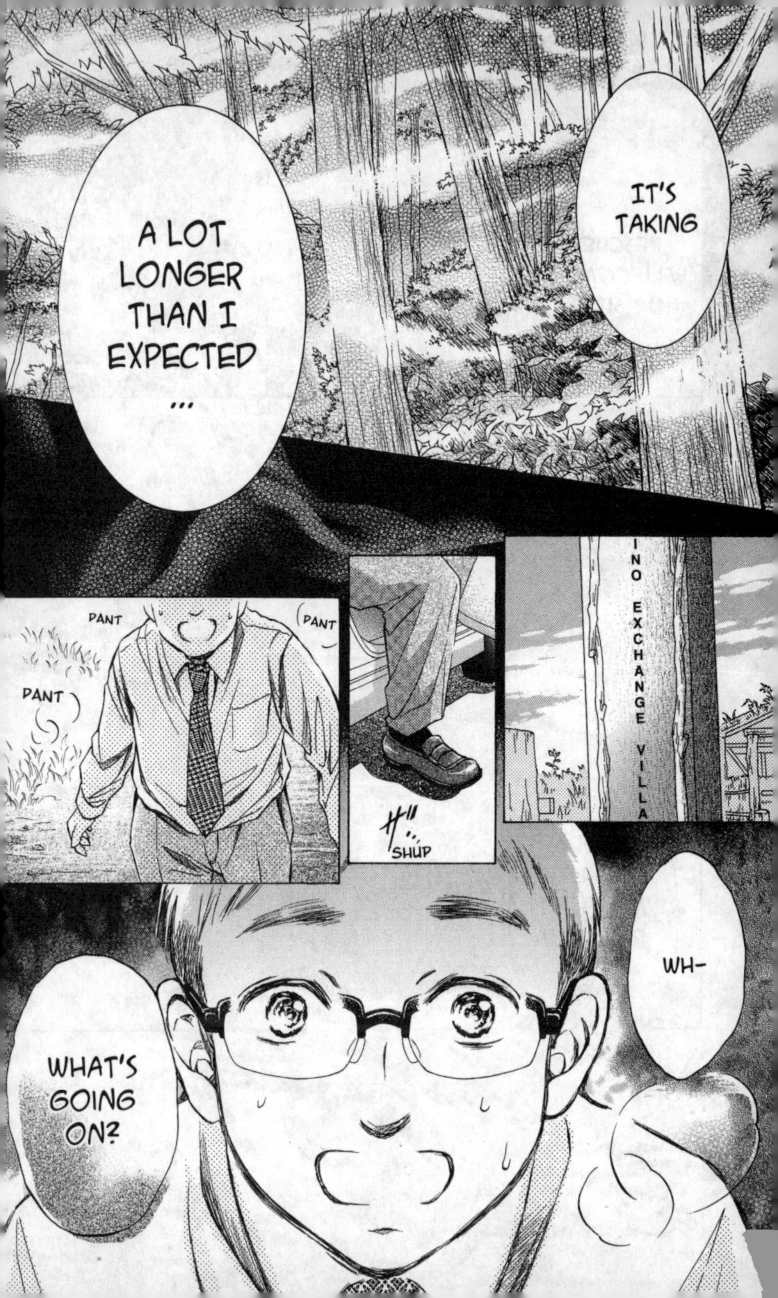
IT'S TAKING
A LOT LONGER THAN I EXPECTED ...
INO EXCHANGE VILLA
SHUP
PANT
PANT
PANT
WH-
WHAT'S GOING ON?

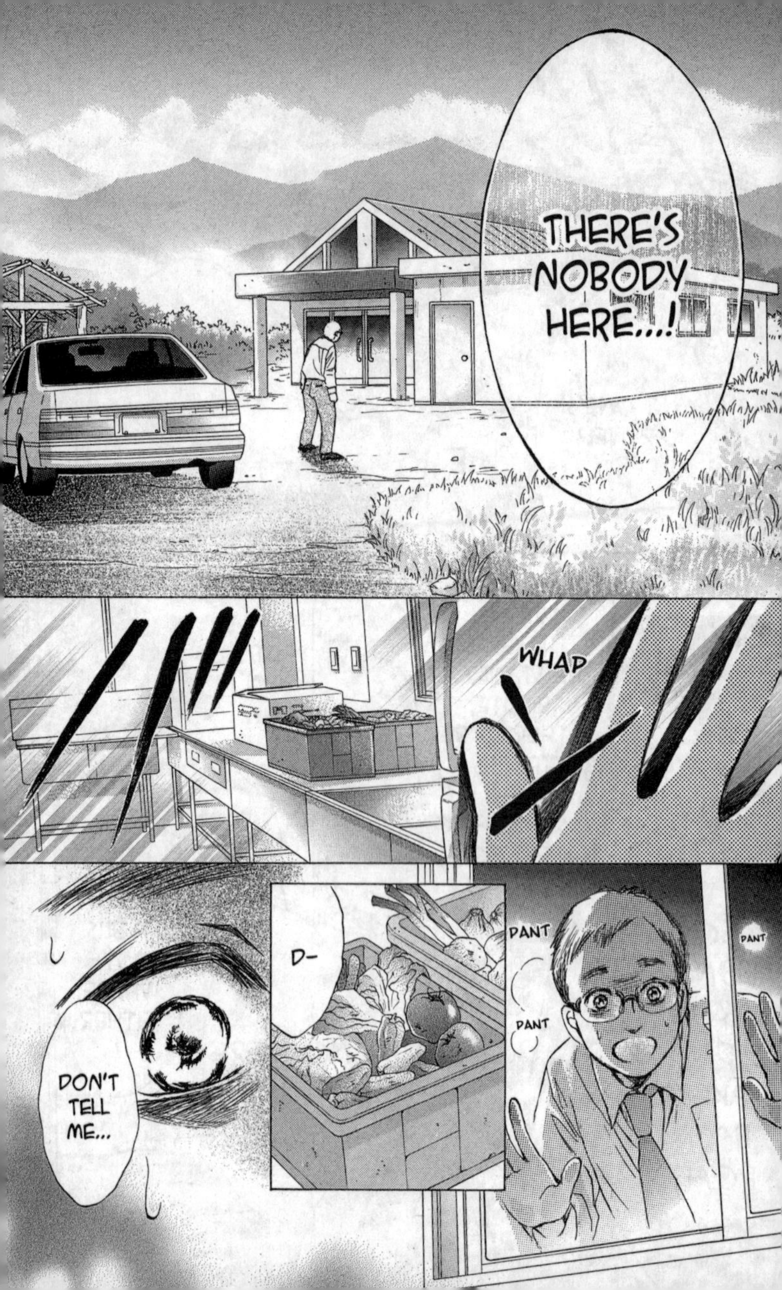
THERE'S NOBODY HERE...!
WHAP
PANT
PANT
PANT
D-
DON'T TELL ME...

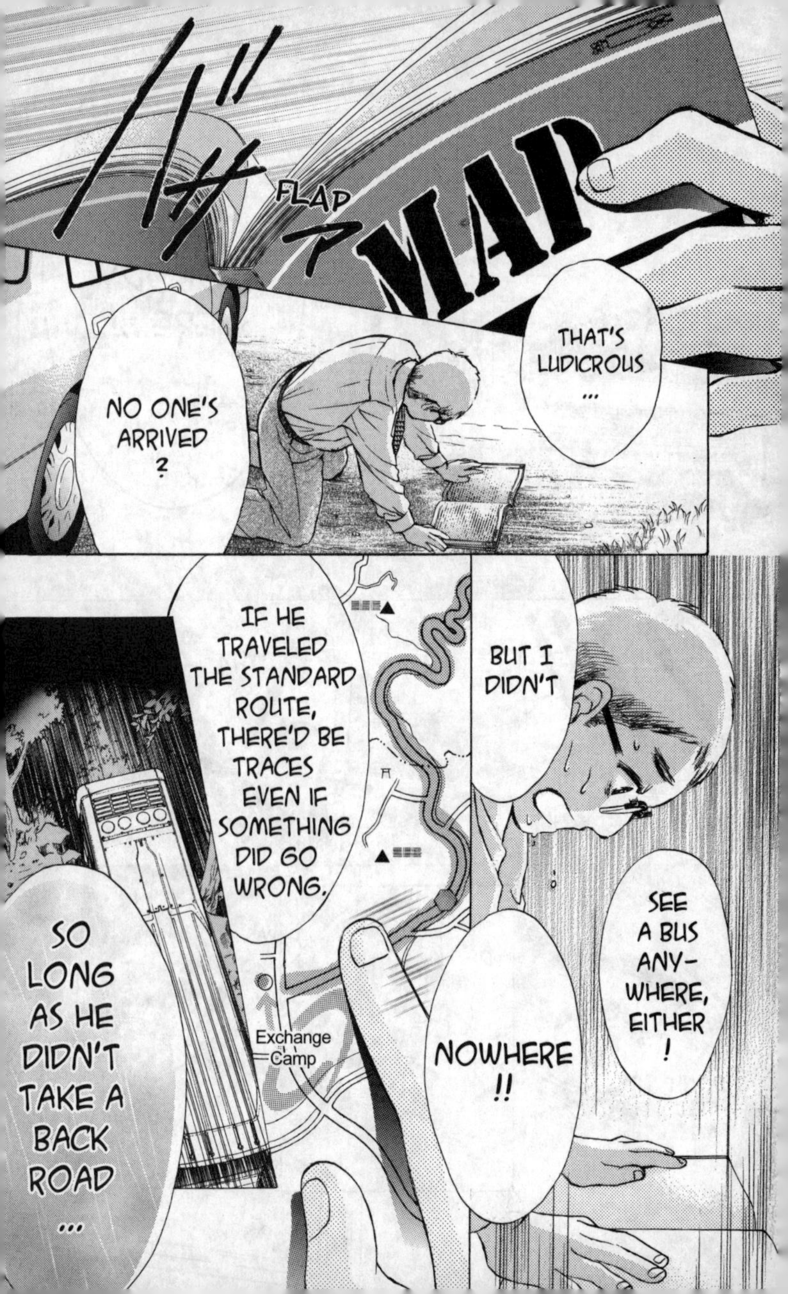
バサァ
FLAP
MAP
THAT'S LUDICROUS ...
NO ONE'S ARRIVED?
BUT I DIDN'T
SEE A BUS ANY-WHERE, EITHER!
NOWHERE!!
IF HE TRAVELED THE STANDARD ROUTE, THERE'D BE TRACES EVEN IF SOMETHING DID GO WRONG.
Exchange Camp
SO LONG AS HE DIDN'T TAKE A BACK ROAD ...

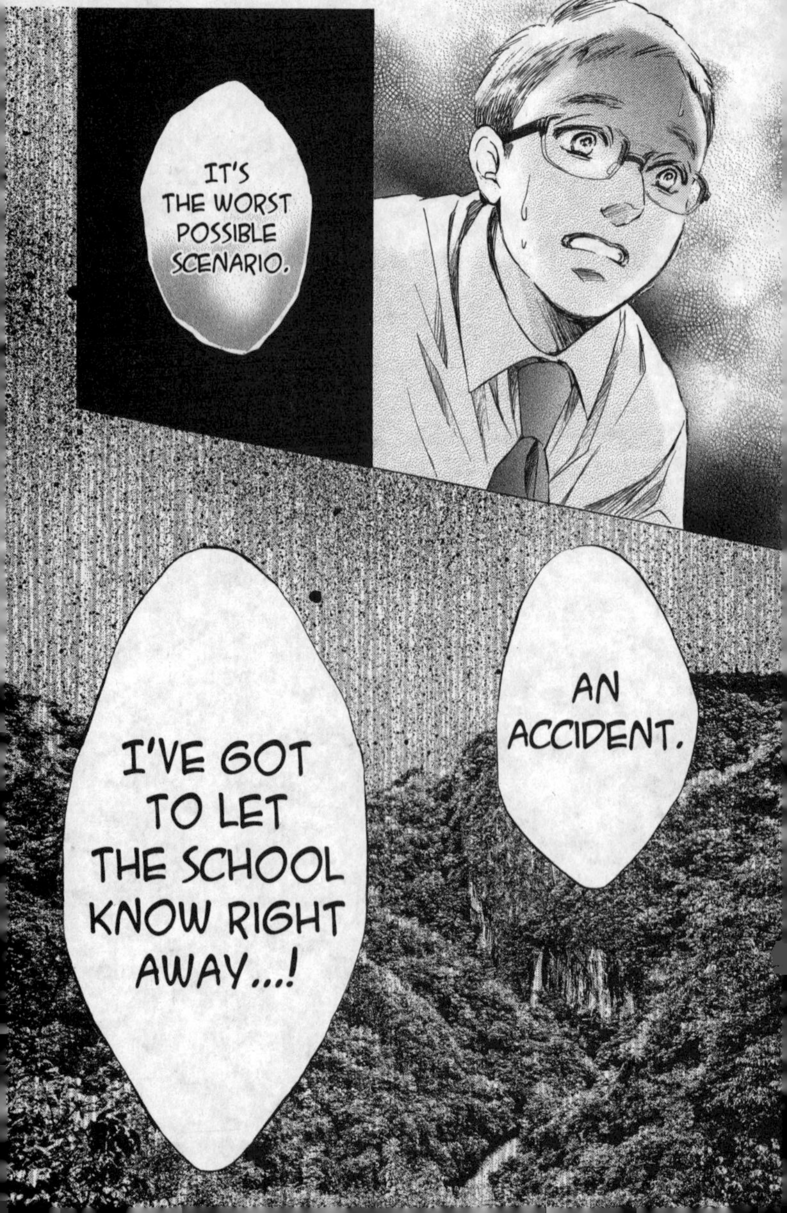
IT'S THE WORST POSSIBLE SCENARIO.
AN ACCIDENT.
I'VE GOT TO LET THE SCHOOL KNOW RIGHT AWAY...!

Scene.6 The Black Shadow

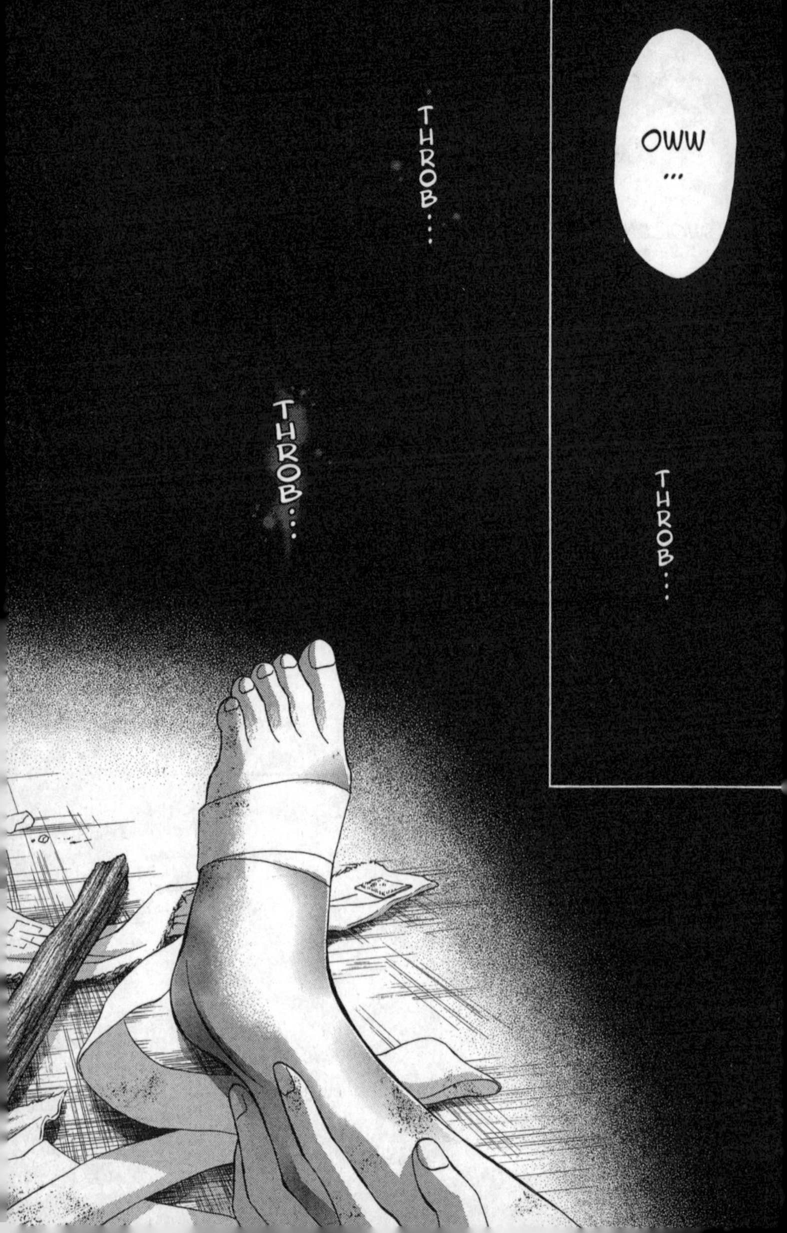
OWW ...
THROB...
THROB...
THROB...

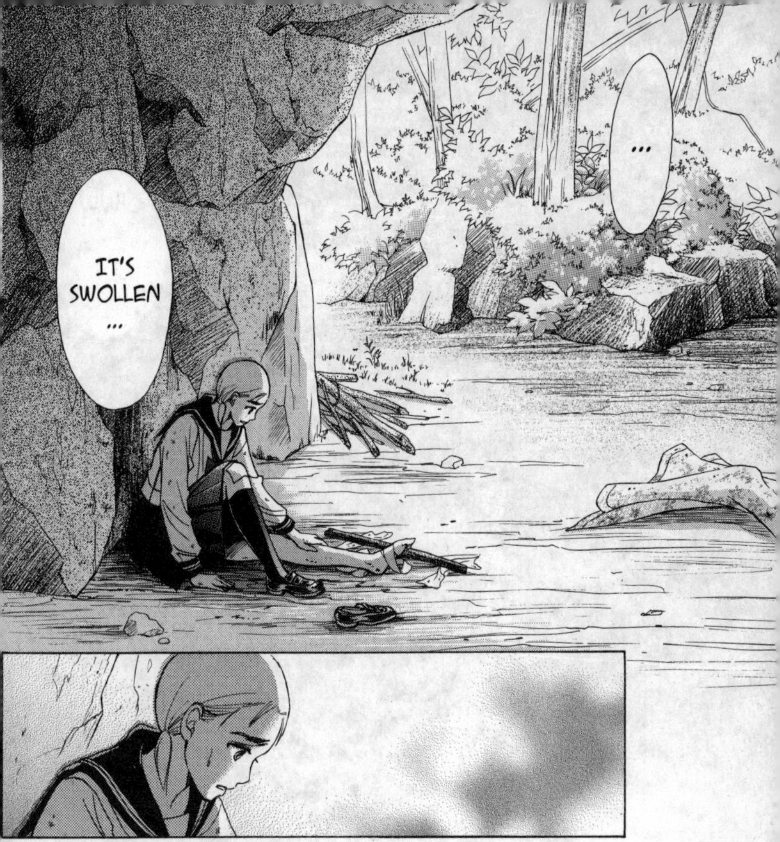
...
IT'S SWOLLEN ...

LIMIT

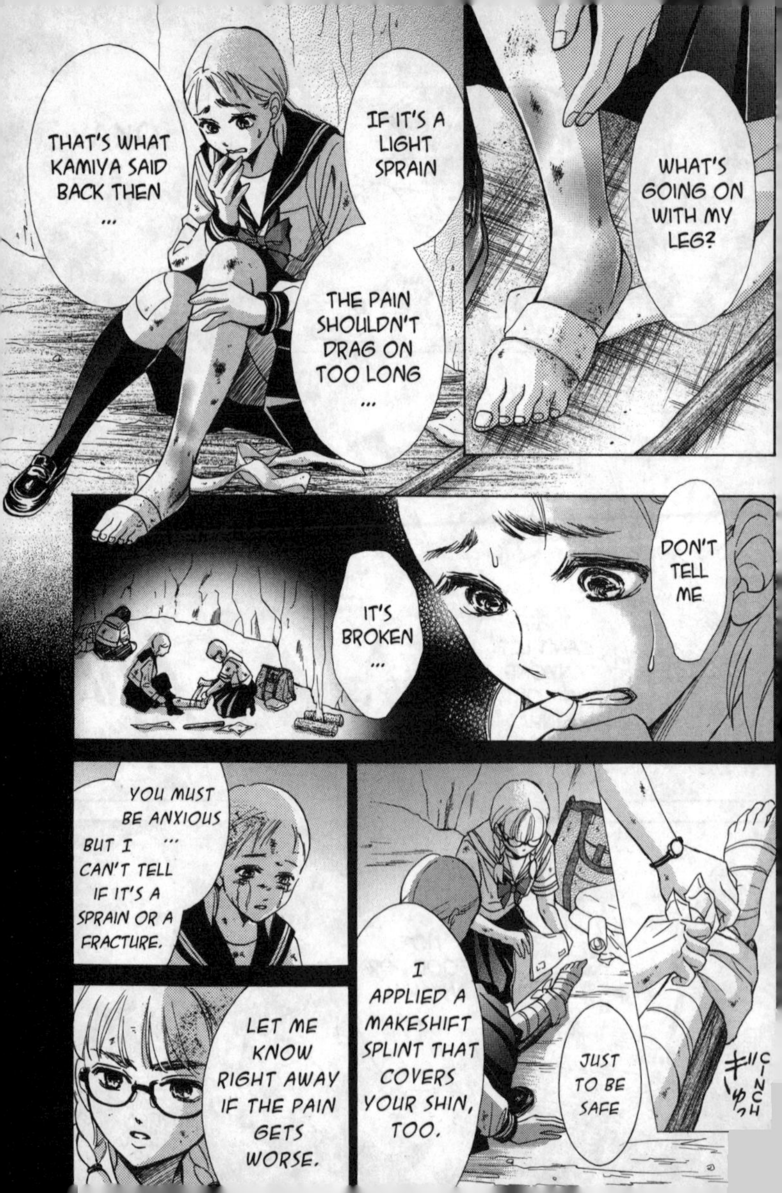
WHAT'S GOING ON WITH MY LEG?
IF IT'S A LIGHT SPRAIN
THAT'S WHAT KAMIYA SAID BACK THEN ...
THE PAIN SHOULDN'T DRAG ON TOO LONG ...
DON'T TELL ME
IT'S BROKEN ...
CINCH
JUST TO BE SAFE
I APPLIED A MAKESHIFT SPLINT THAT COVERS YOUR SHIN, TOO.
YOU MUST BE ANXIOUS ... BUT I CAN'T TELL IF IT'S A SPRAIN OR A FRACTURE.
LET ME KNOW RIGHT AWAY IF THE PAIN GETS WORSE.

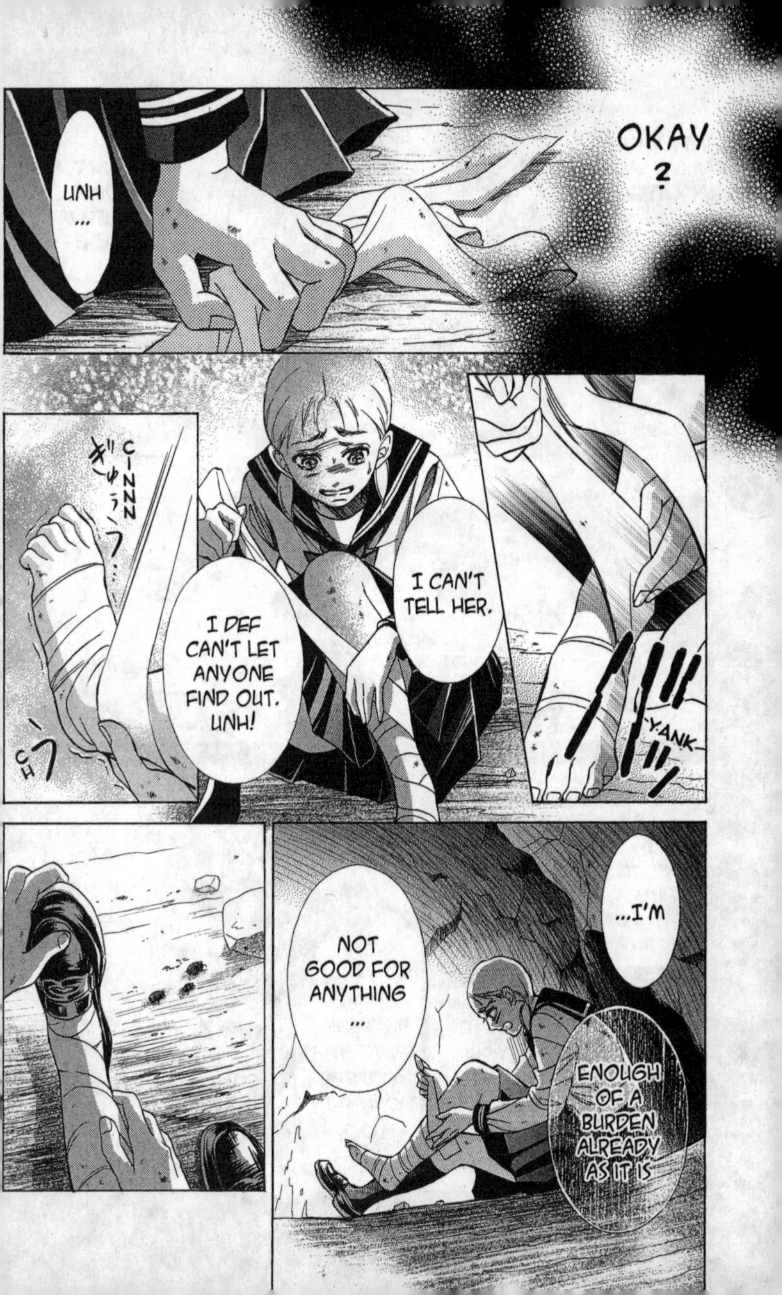
OKAY ?
UNH ...
YANK
I CAN'T TELL HER.
I DEF CAN'T LET ANYONE FIND OUT. UNH!
CINNN
CH
...I'M
NOT GOOD FOR ANYTHING ...
ENOUGH OF A BURDEN ALREADY AS IT IS

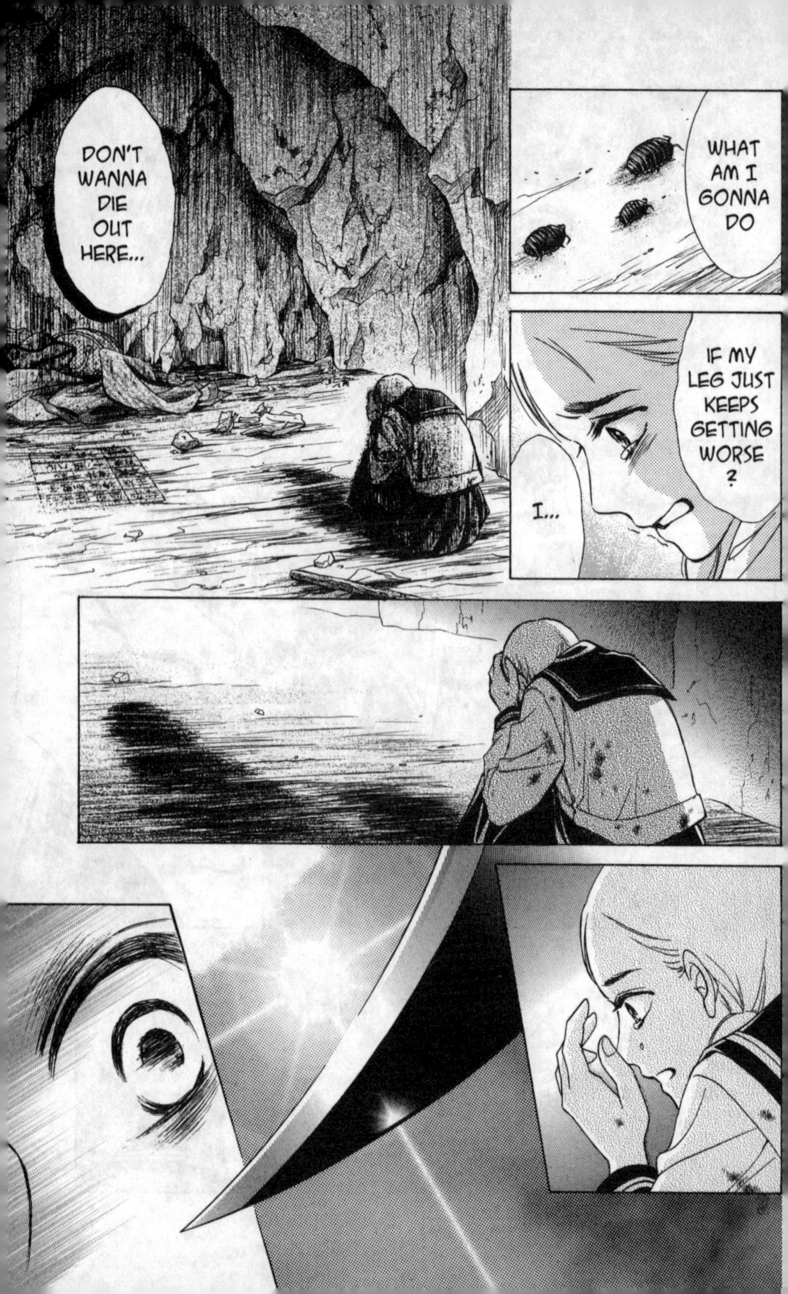
WHAT AM I GONNA DO
IF MY LEG JUST KEEPS GETTING WORSE ?
I...
DON'T WANNA DIE OUT HERE...

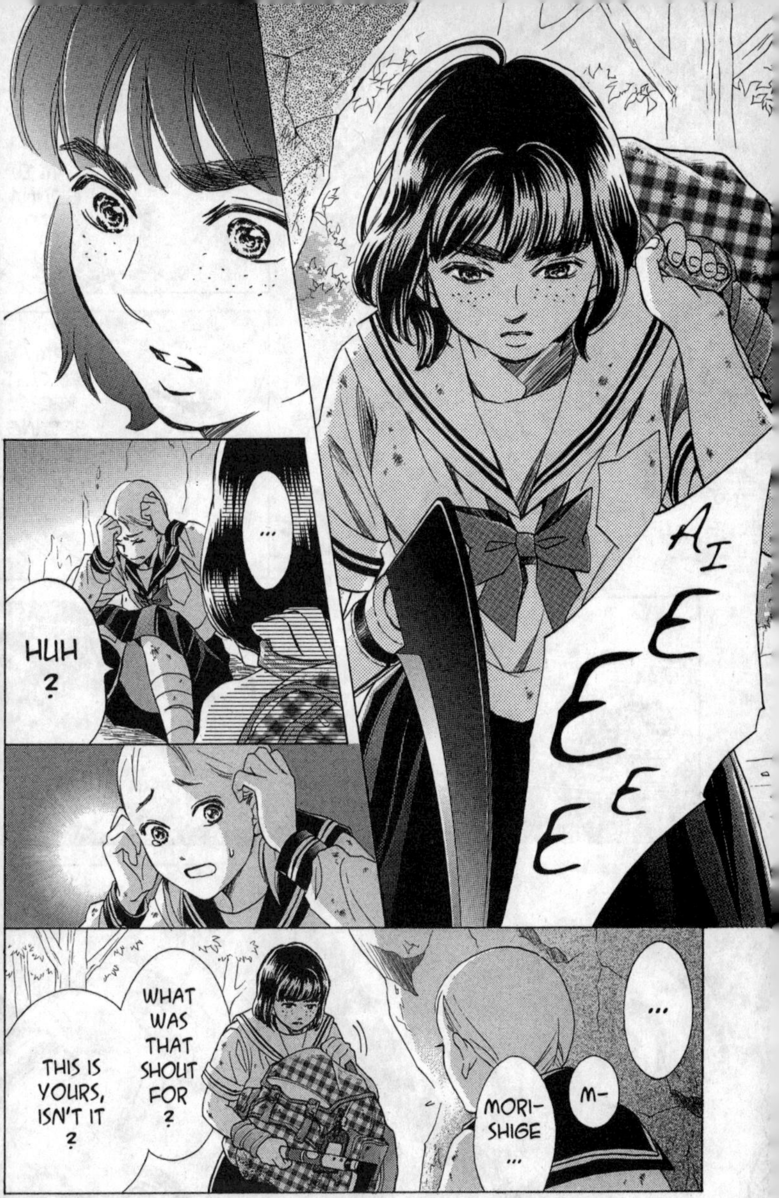
AIEEEEE
...
HUH ?
...
M-
MORI-SHIGE ...
WHAT WAS THAT SHOUT FOR ?
THIS IS YOURS, ISN'T IT ?

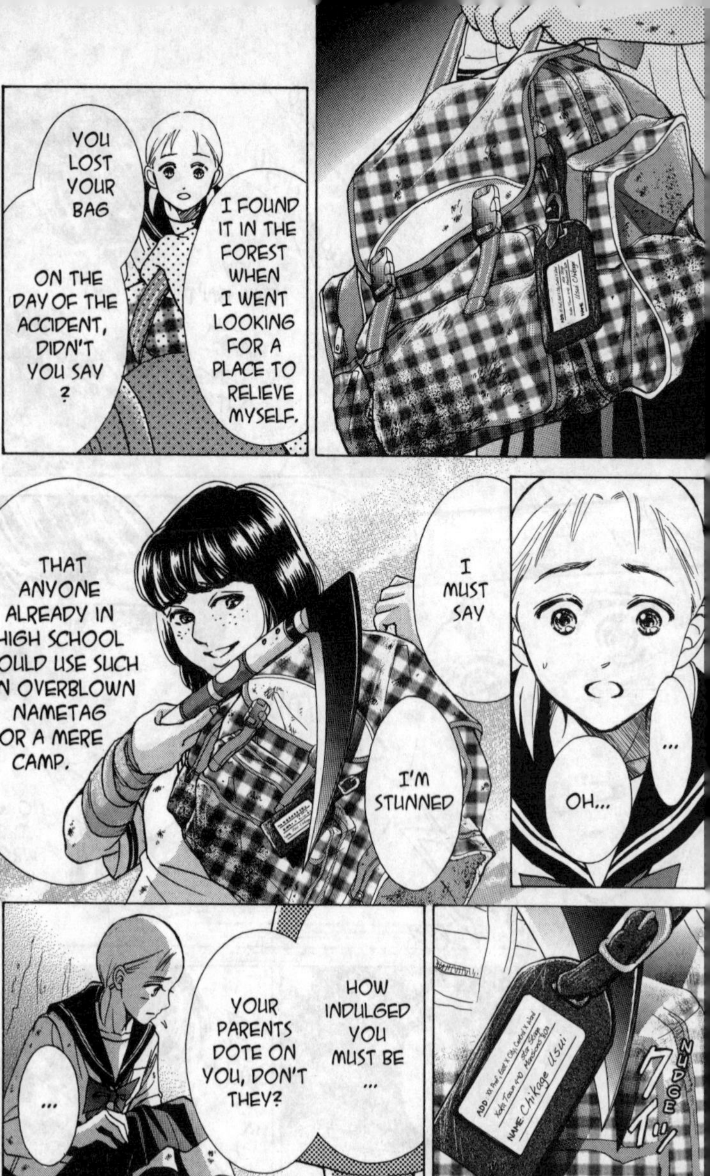
I FOUND IT IN THE FOREST WHEN I WENT LOOKING FOR A PLACE TO RELIEVE MYSELF.
YOU LOST YOUR BAG
ON THE DAY OF THE ACCIDENT, DIDN'T YOU SAY ?
I MUST SAY
...
OH...
I'M STUNNED
THAT ANYONE ALREADY IN HIGH SCHOOL WOULD USE SUCH AN OVERBLOWN NAMETAG FOR A MERE CAMP.
NUDGE
ADD XX Pref., East X City, Central X Ward
Xoko Town 440 Star Stage Mansions 303
NAME Chikage Usui
HOW INDULGED YOU MUST BE ...
YOUR PARENTS DOTE ON YOU, DON'T THEY?
...

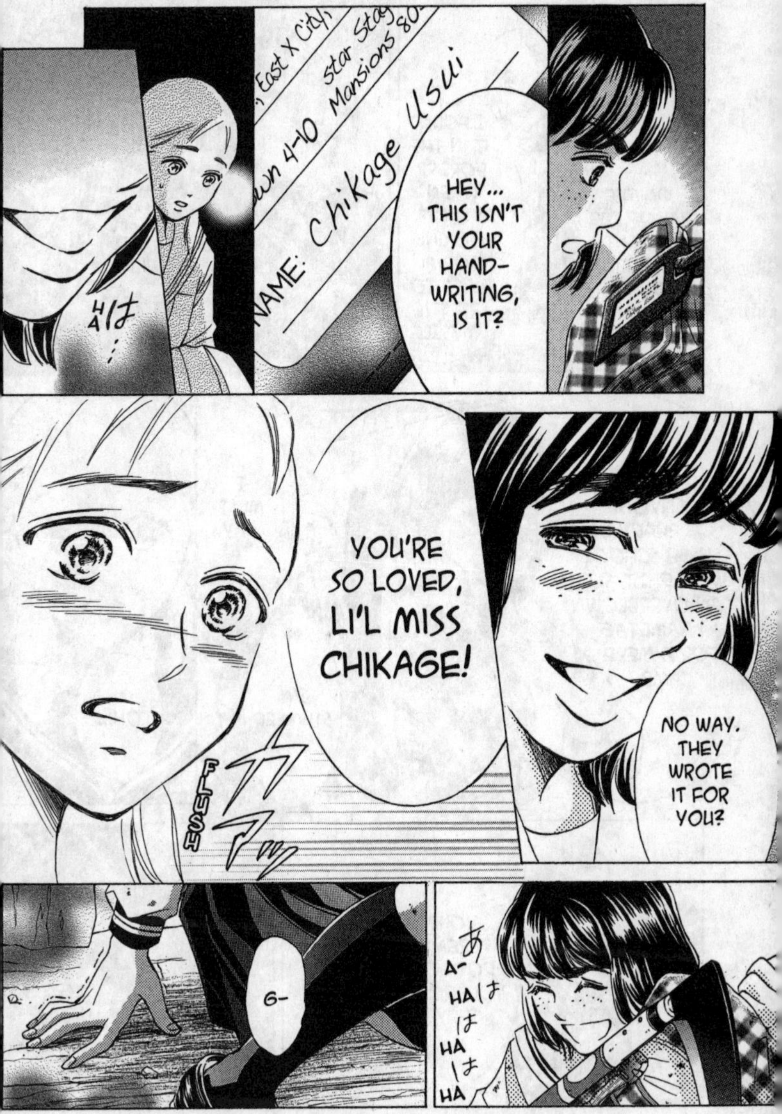
HEY... THIS ISN'T YOUR HAND-WRITING, IS IT?
, East X City,
wn 4-10 star Stag
Mansions 80-
NAME: Chikage Usui
HA は
NO WAY. THEY WROTE IT FOR YOU?
YOU'RE SO LOVED, LI'L MISS CHIKAGE!
FLUSH
A- あ HA は は HA は HA
G-

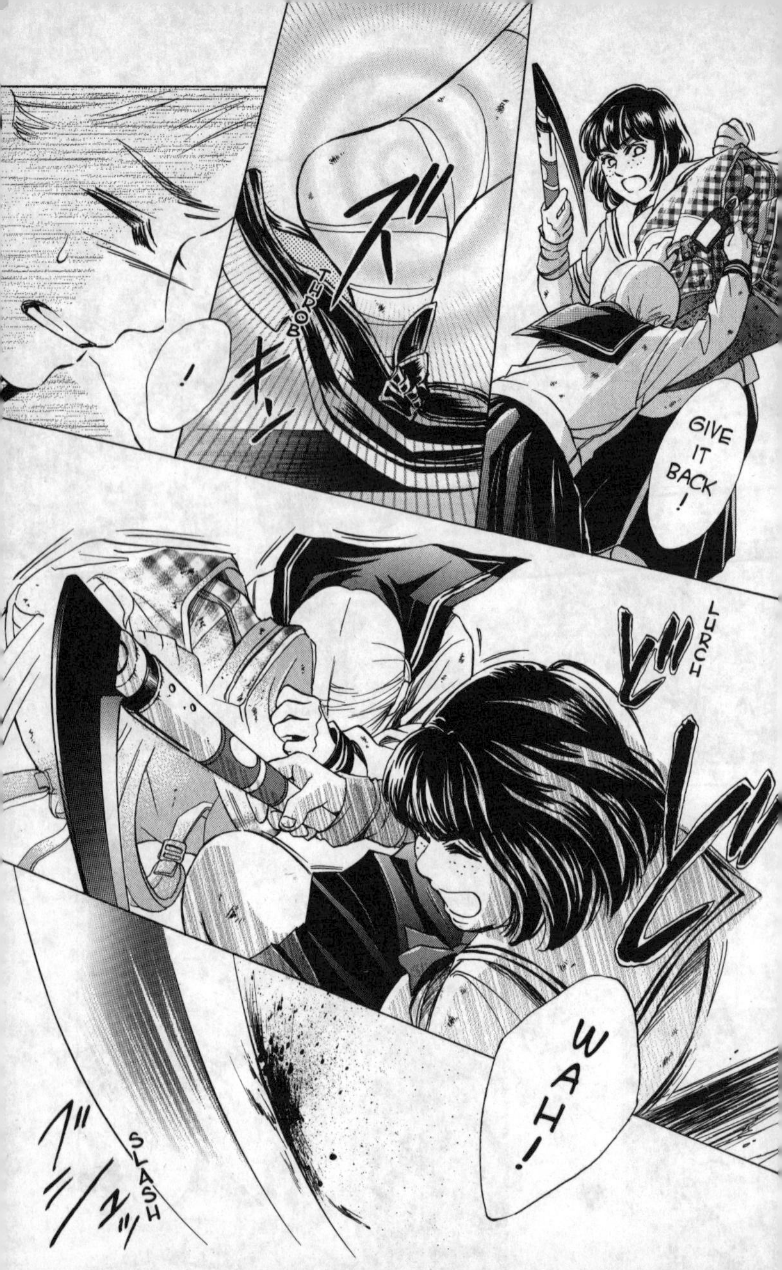
GIVE IT BACK!
THROB
!
LURCH
WAH!
SLASH

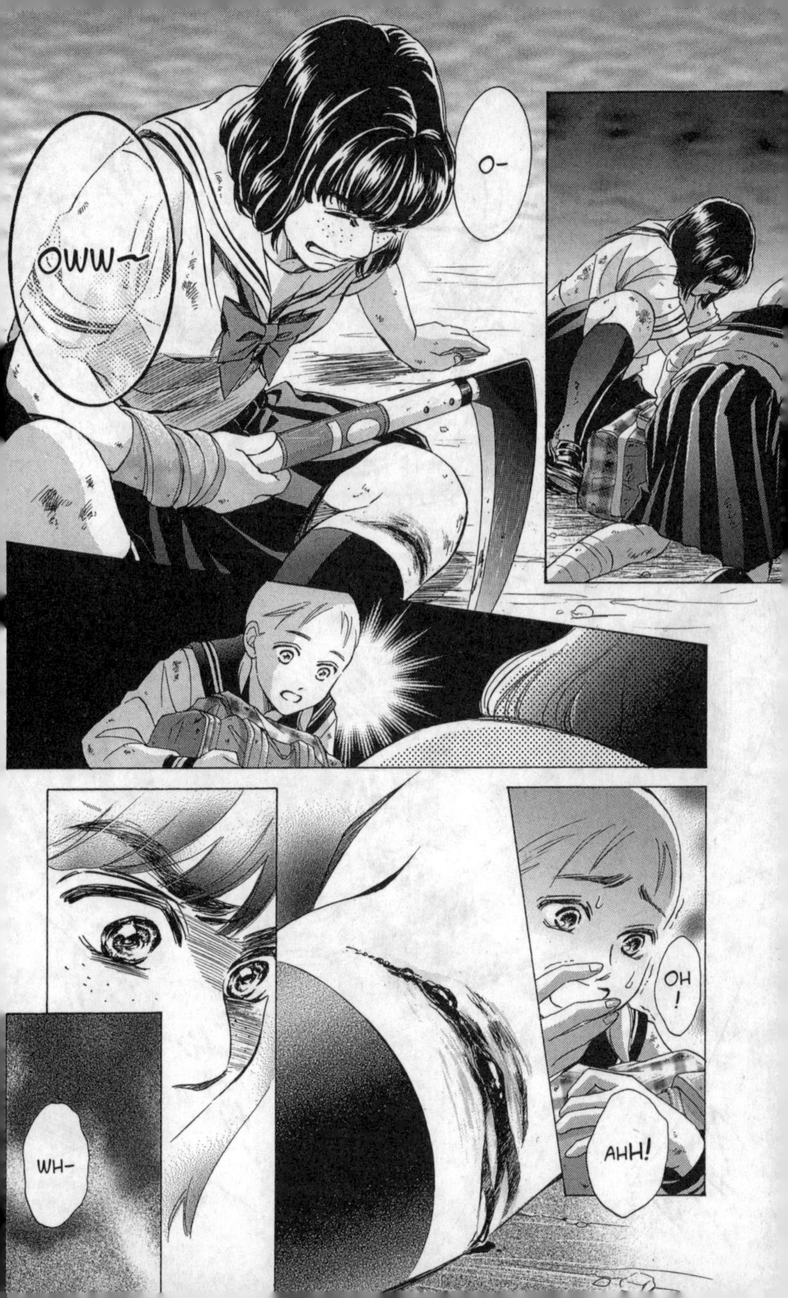
O-
OWW~
OH!
AHH!
WH-

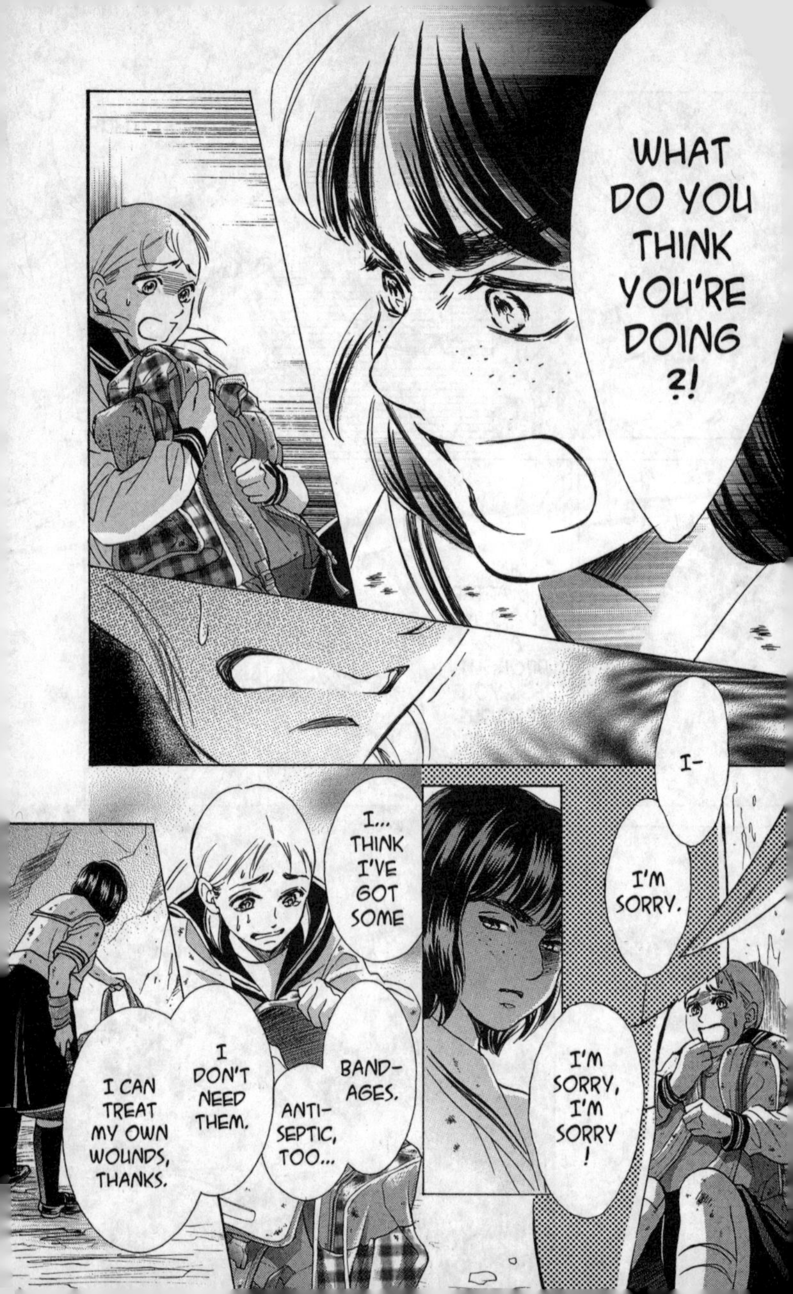
WHAT DO YOU THINK YOU'RE DOING?!
I-
I'M SORRY.
I'M SORRY, I'M SORRY!
I... THINK I'VE GOT SOME
BAND-AGES.
ANTI-SEPTIC, TOO...
I DON'T NEED THEM.
I CAN TREAT MY OWN WOUNDS, THANKS.

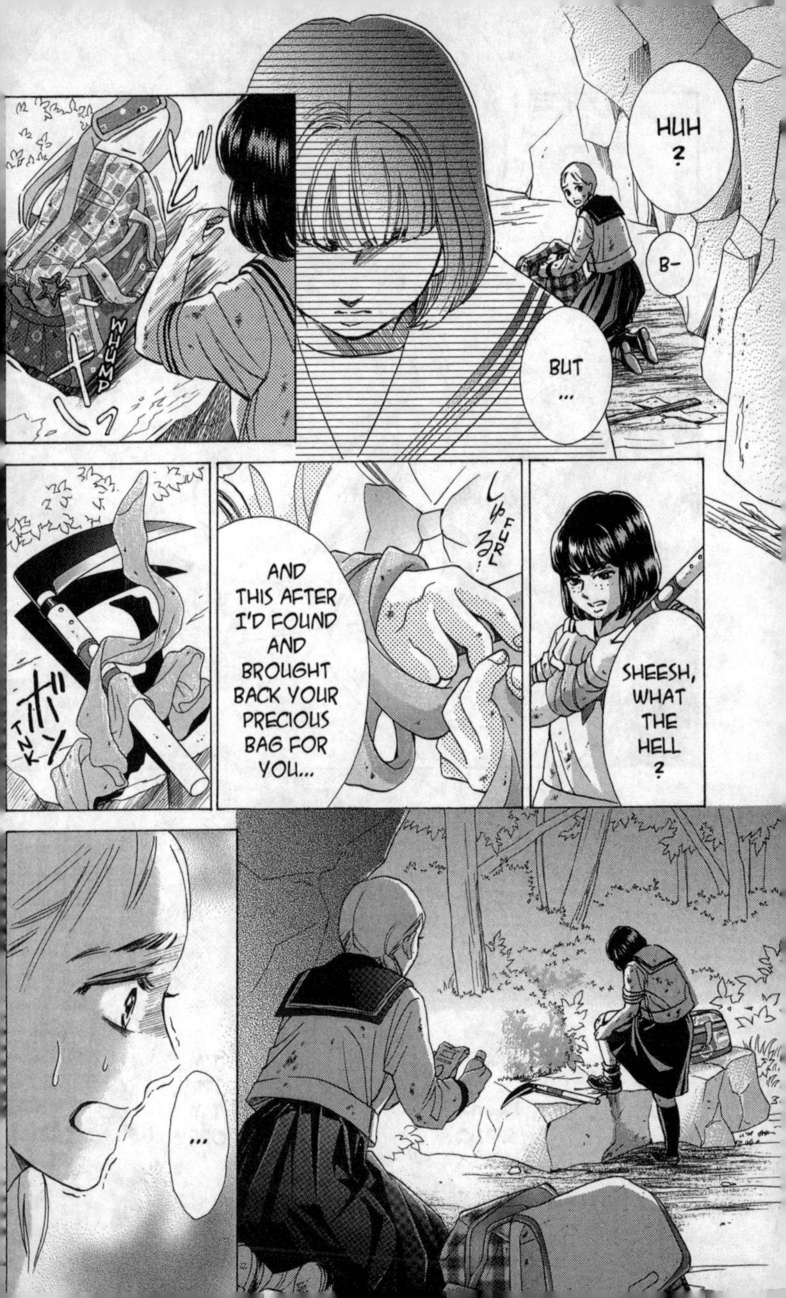
HUH ?
B-
BUT ...
WHUMP
SHEESH, WHAT THE HELL ?
しゅる
FURL
AND THIS AFTER I'D FOUND AND BROUGHT BACK YOUR PRECIOUS BAG FOR YOU...
ボン
TNK
...

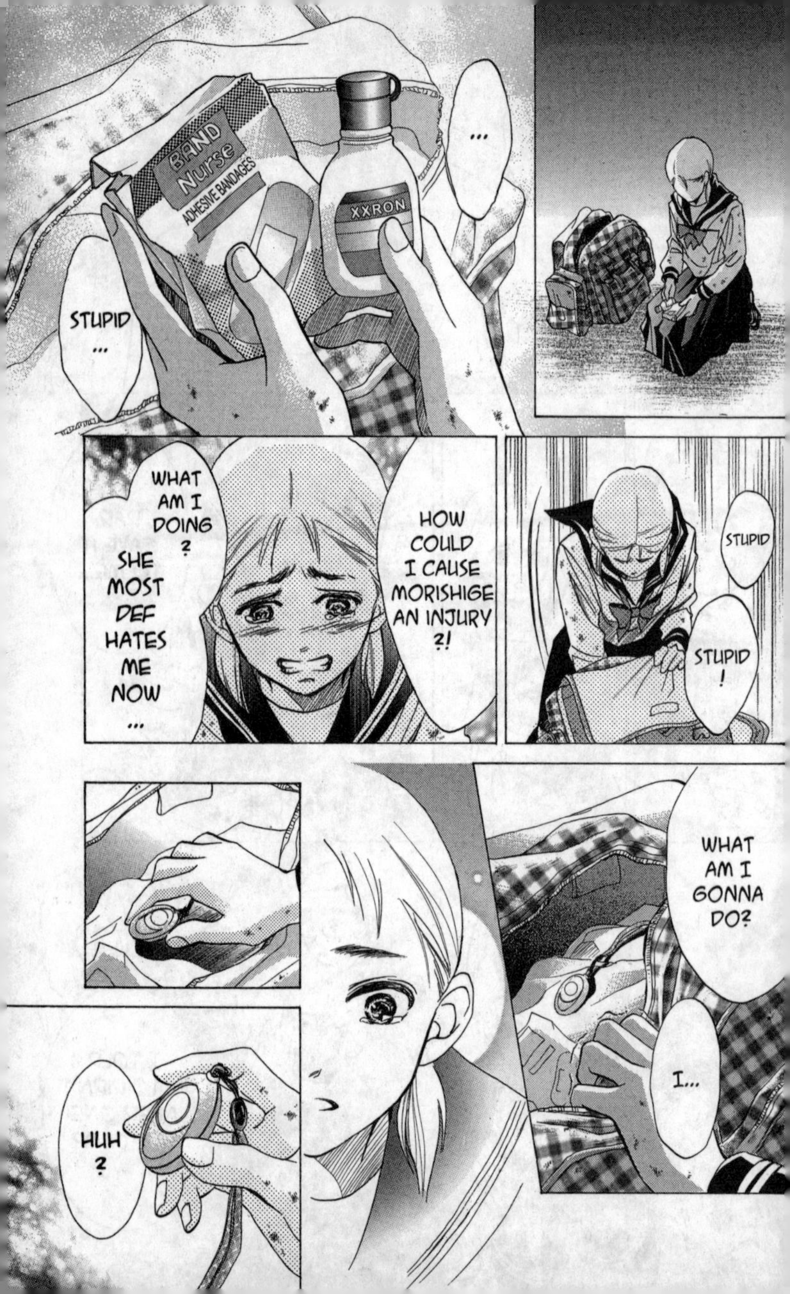
...
BAND Nurse ADHESIVE BANDAGES
XXRON
STUPID ...
STUPID
STUPID!
HOW COULD I CAUSE MORISHIGE AN INJURY?!
WHAT AM I DOING?
SHE MOST DEF HATES ME NOW ...
WHAT AM I GONNA DO?
I...
HUH?

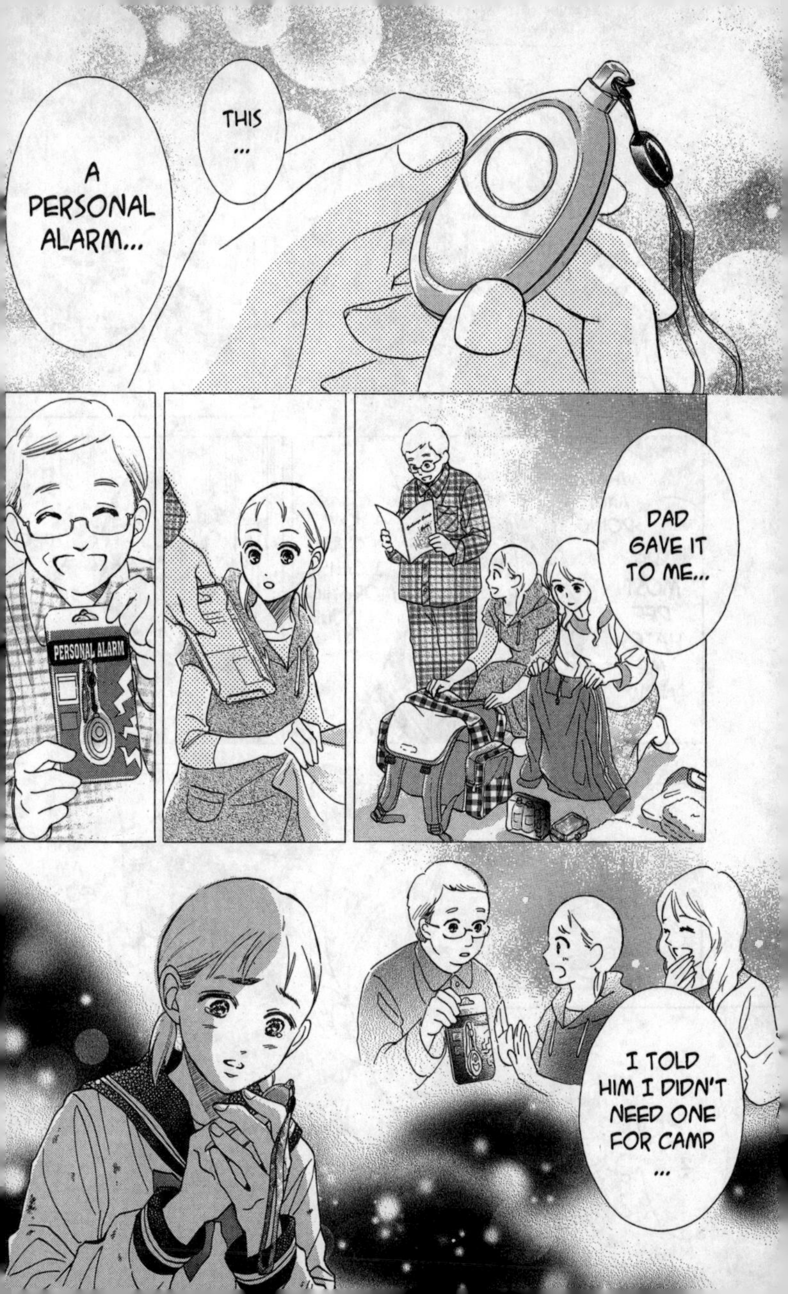
THIS ...
A PERSONAL ALARM...
DAD GAVE IT TO ME...
PERSONAL ALARM
I TOLD HIM I DIDN'T NEED ONE FOR CAMP ...

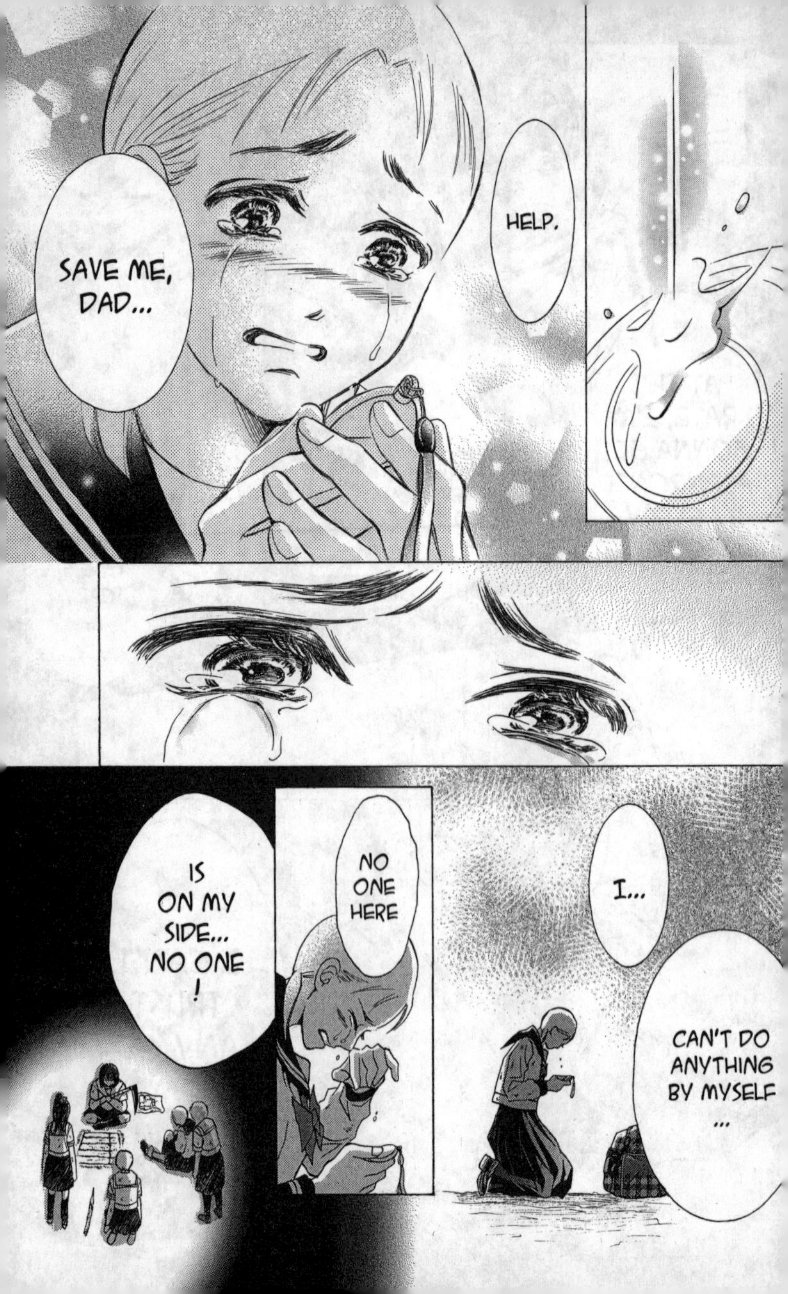
HELP.
SAVE ME, DAD...
I...
CAN'T DO ANYTHING BY MYSELF ...
NO ONE HERE
IS ON MY SIDE... NO ONE !

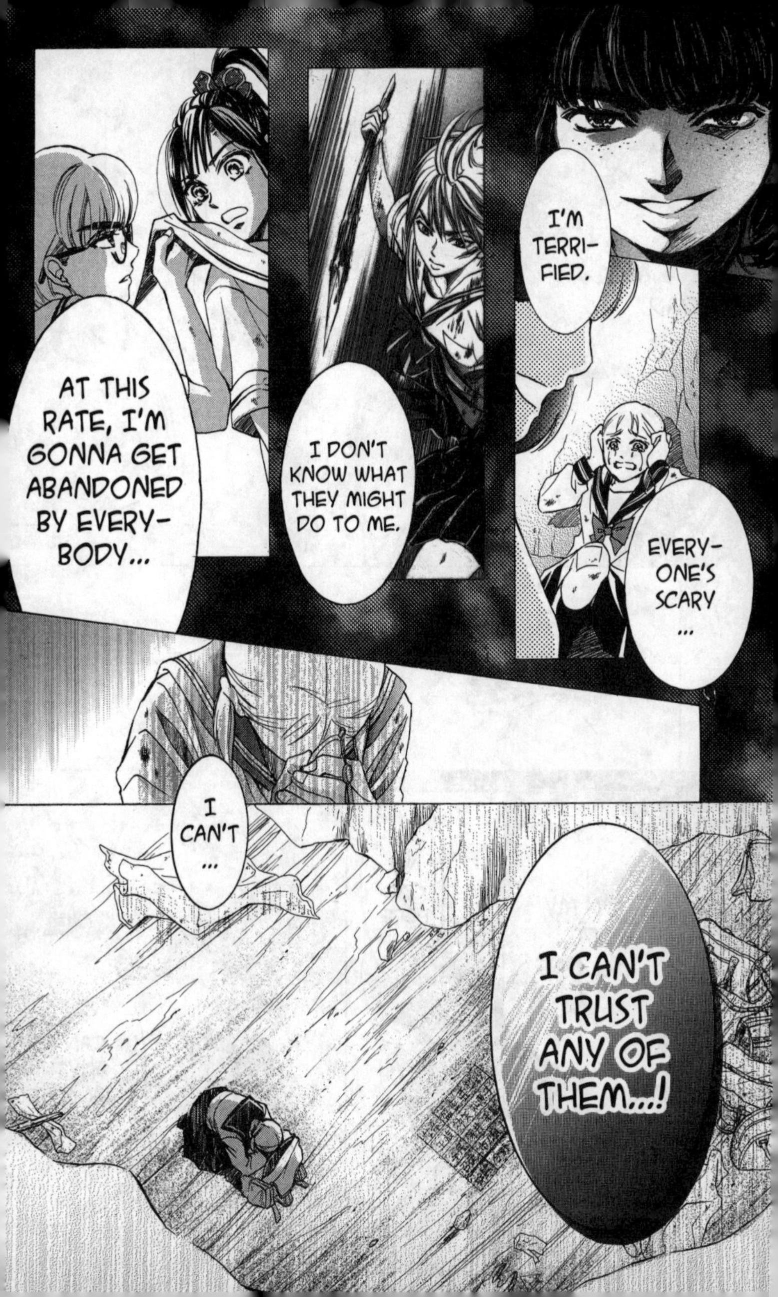
I'M TERRI-FIED.
EVERY-ONE'S SCARY ...
I DON'T KNOW WHAT THEY MIGHT DO TO ME.
AT THIS RATE, I'M GONNA GET ABANDONED BY EVERY-BODY...
I CAN'T ...
I CAN'T TRUST ANY OF THEM...!

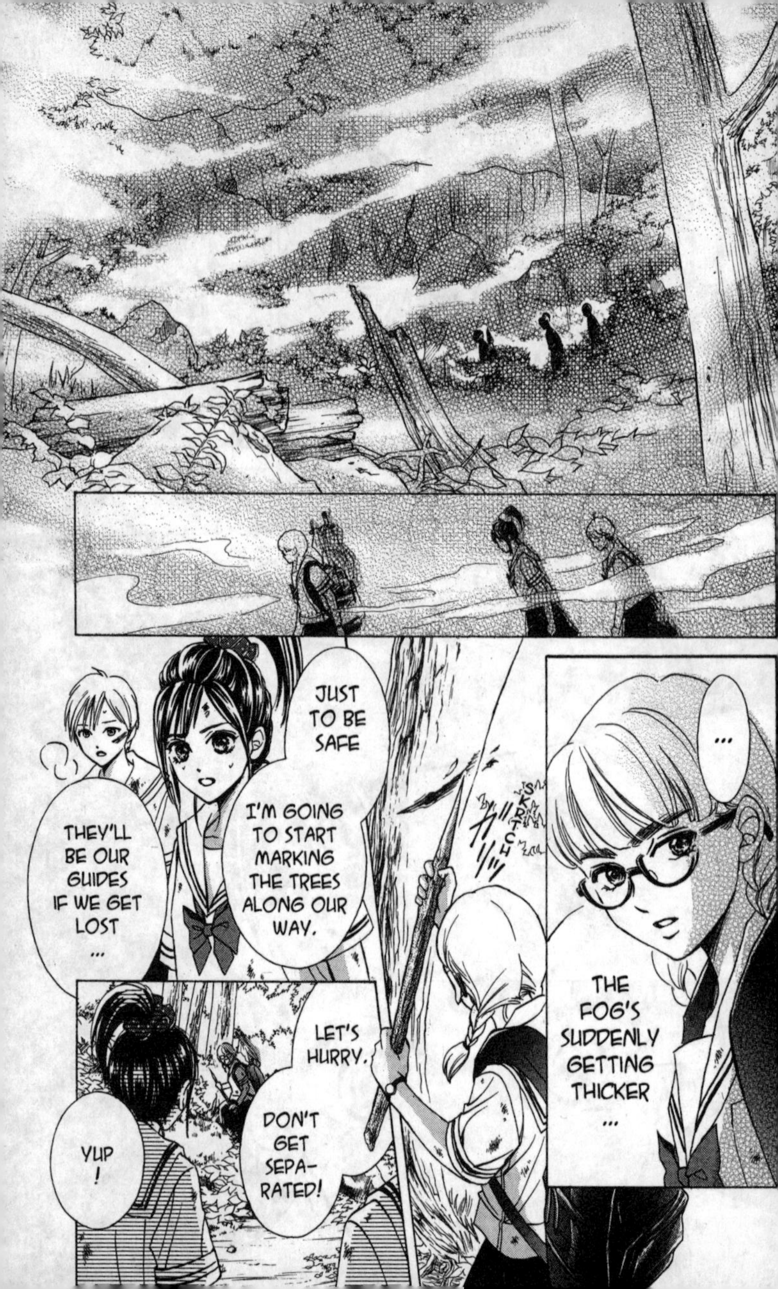
...
THE FOG'S SUDDENLY GETTING THICKER ...
JUST TO BE SAFE
I'M GOING TO START MARKING THE TREES ALONG OUR WAY.
SKRTCH
THEY'LL BE OUR GUIDES IF WE GET LOST ...
LET'S HURRY.
DON'T GET SEPA-RATED!
YUP!

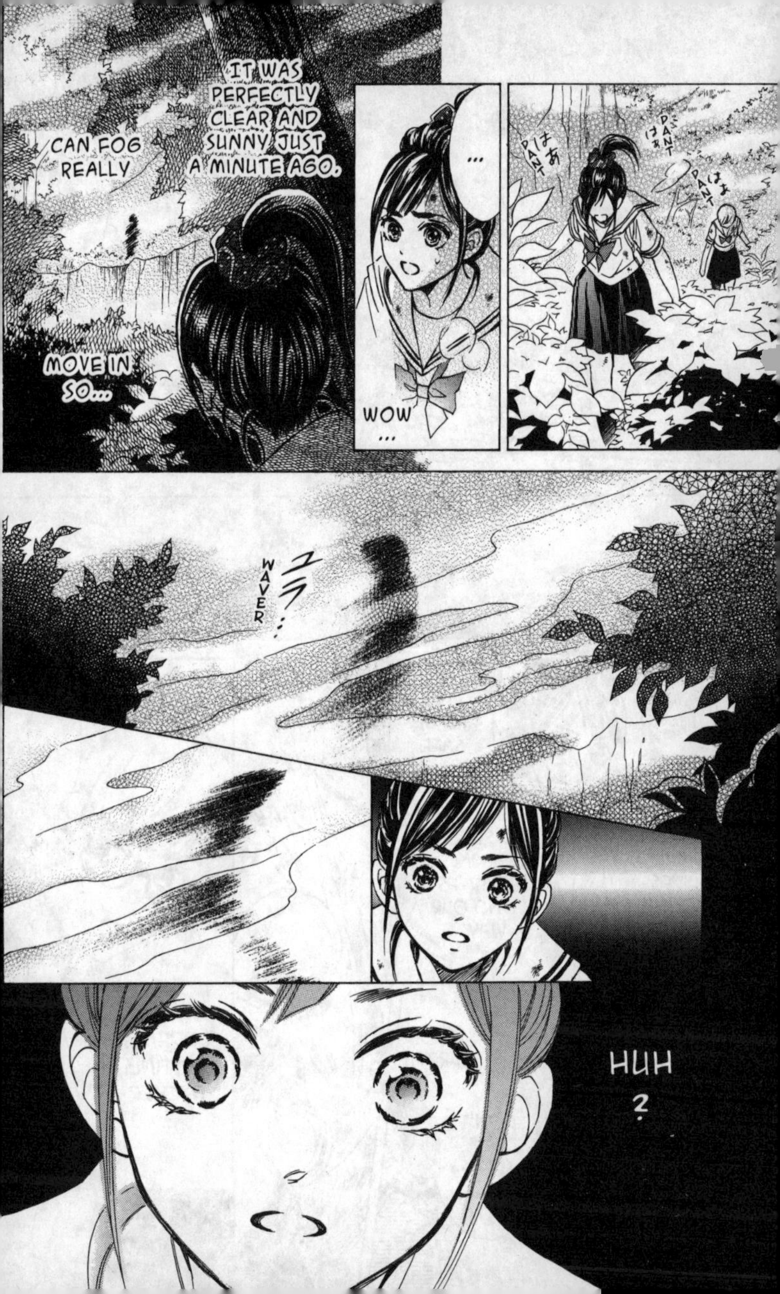

はあ PANT
はあ PANT
はぁ PANT
...
WOW ...
IT WAS PERFECTLY CLEAR AND SUNNY JUST A MINUTE AGO.
CAN FOG REALLY
MOVE IN SO...
ユラ... WAVER
HUH ?

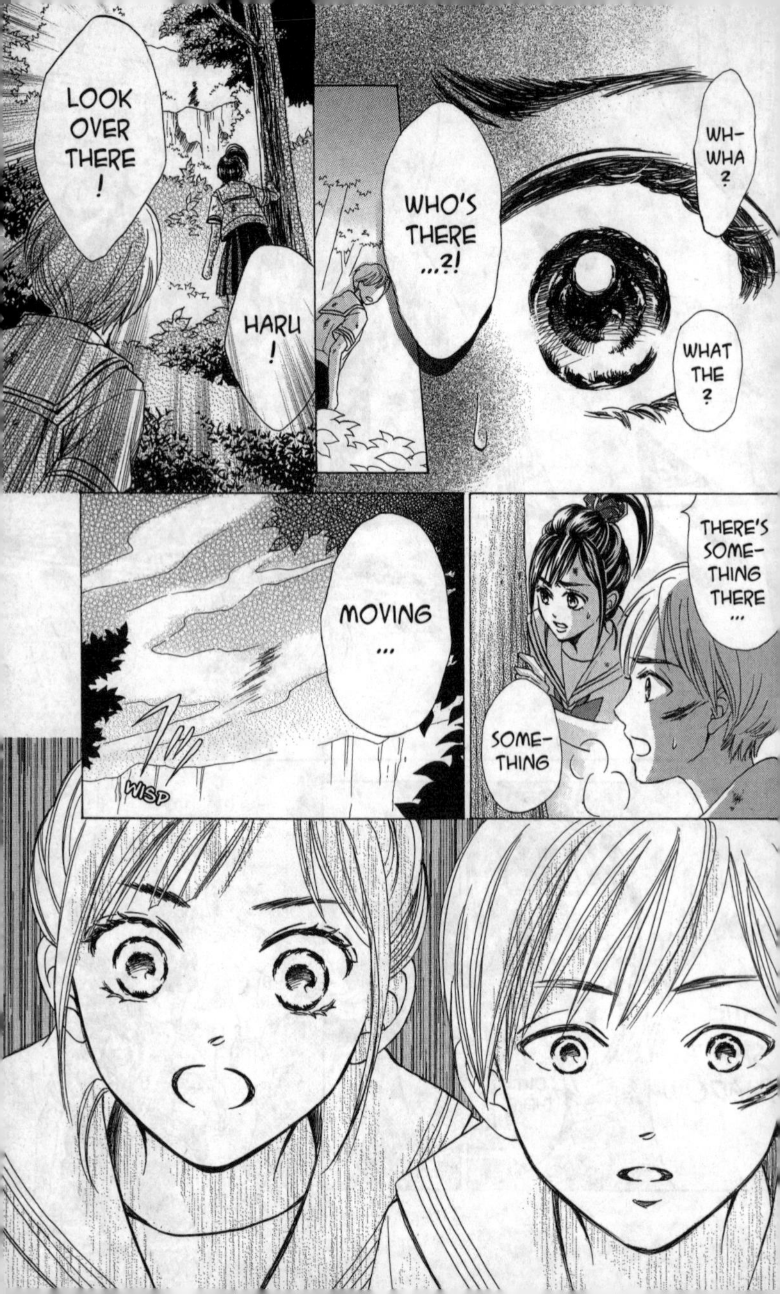
WH- WHA?
WHAT THE?
WHO'S THERE ...?!
LOOK OVER THERE!
HARU!
THERE'S SOME-THING THERE ...
SOME-THING
MOVING ...
WISP

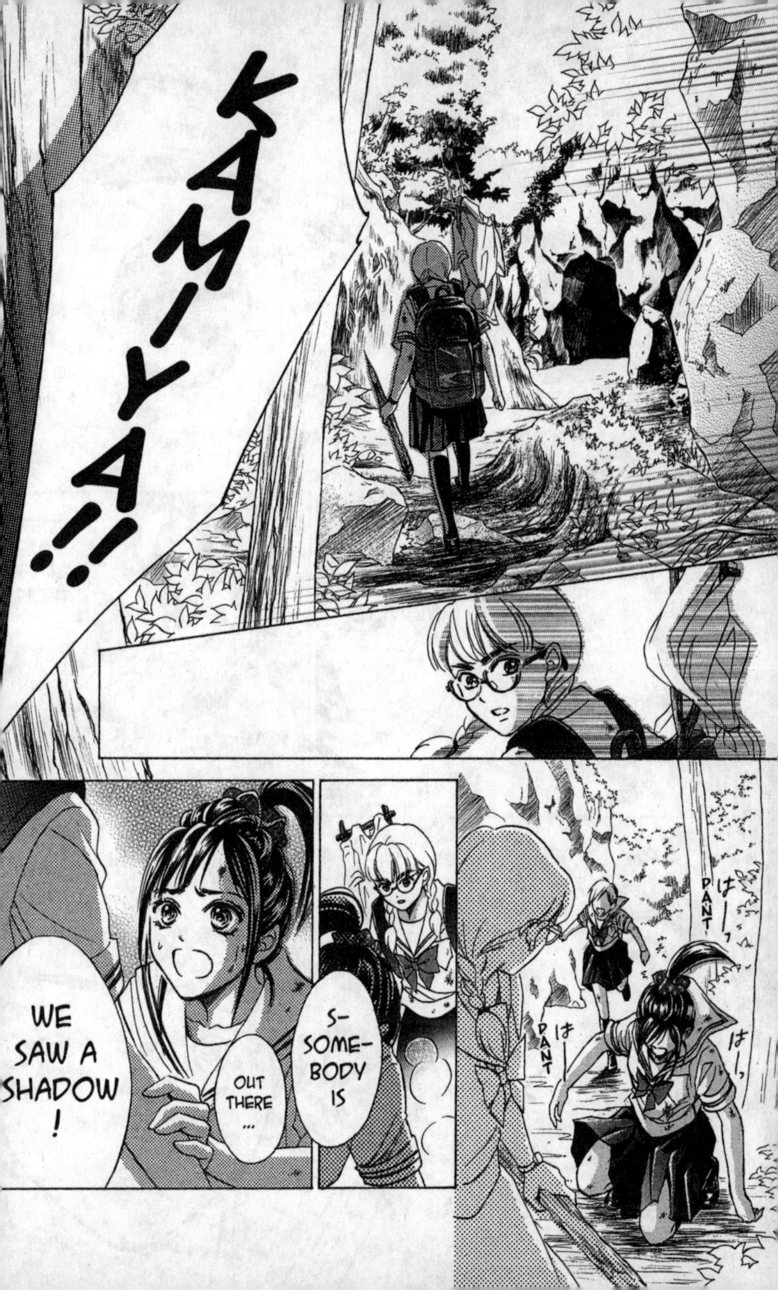
KAMIYAA!!
PANT
はーっ
PANT
はー,
は
S-SOMEBODY IS
OUT THERE...
WE SAW A SHADOW!

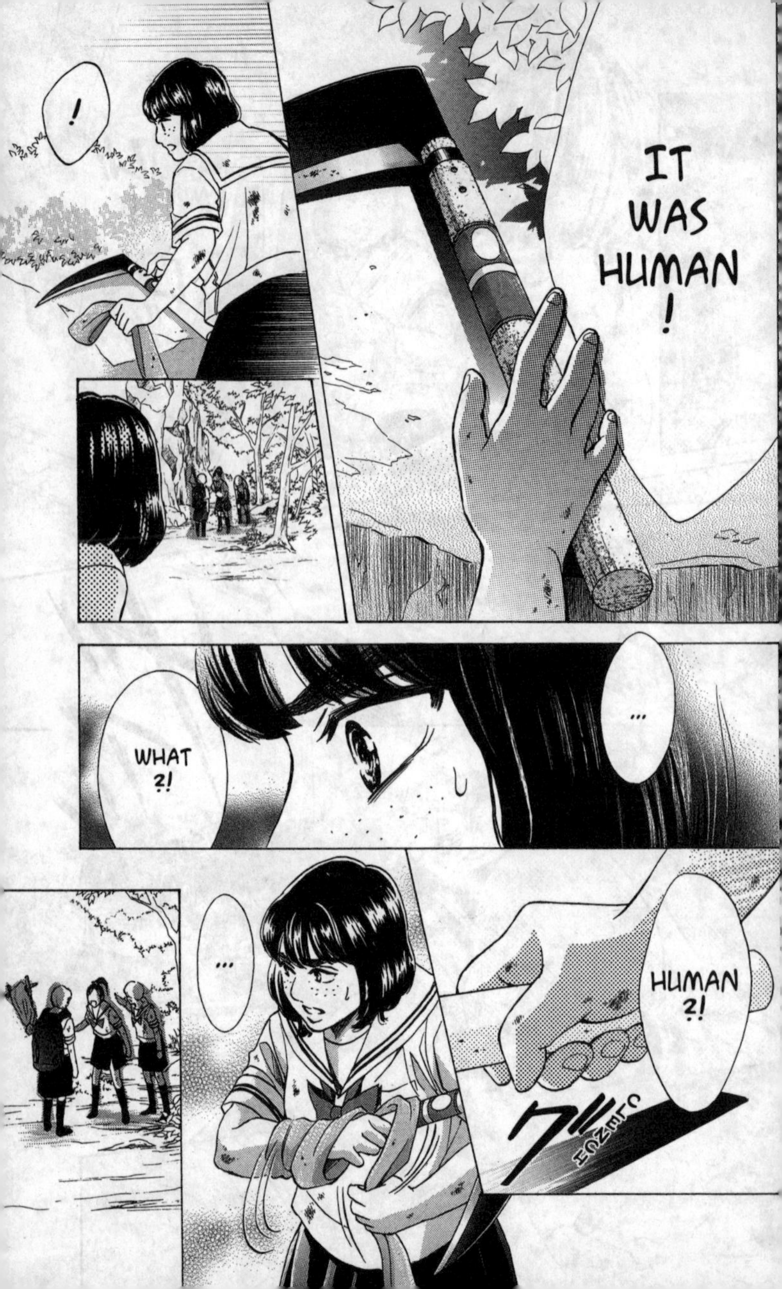
IT WAS HUMAN!
!
...
WHAT?!
HUMAN?!
ク''
CLENCH
...

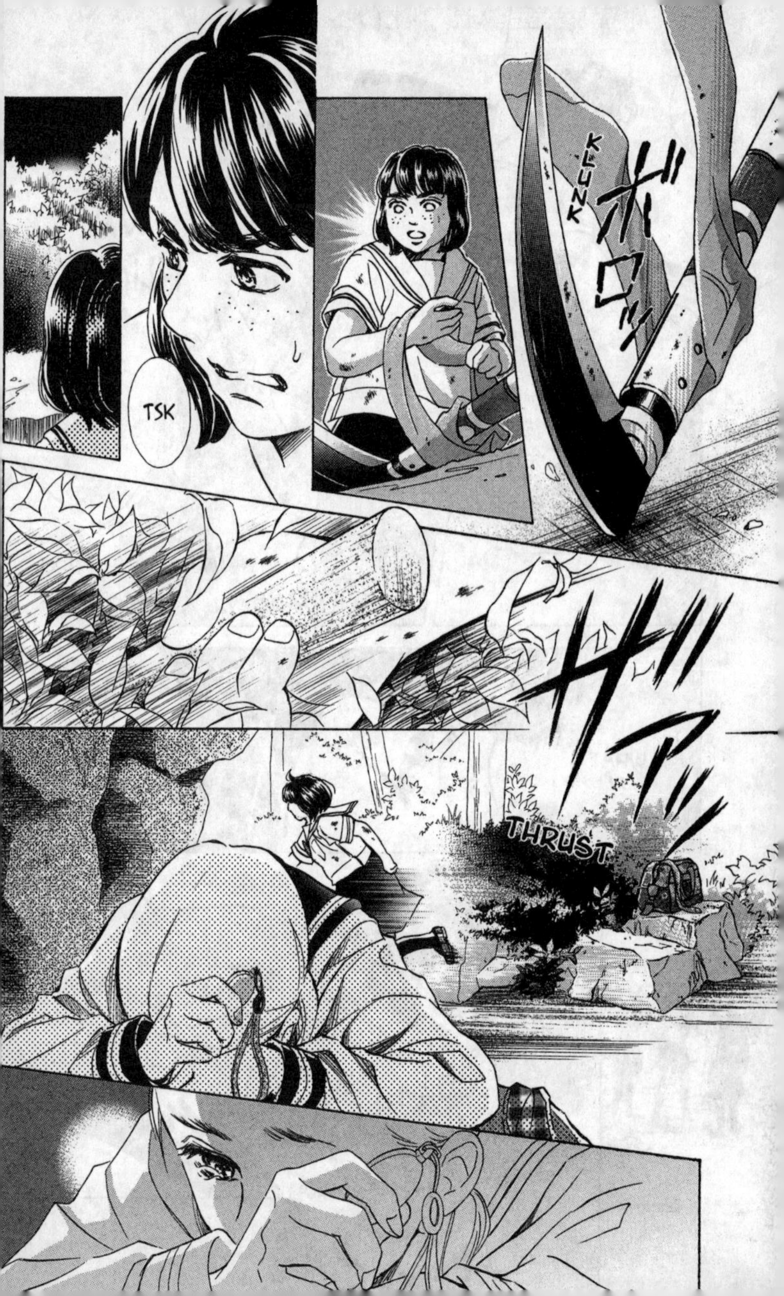
KLUNK
TSK
THRUST

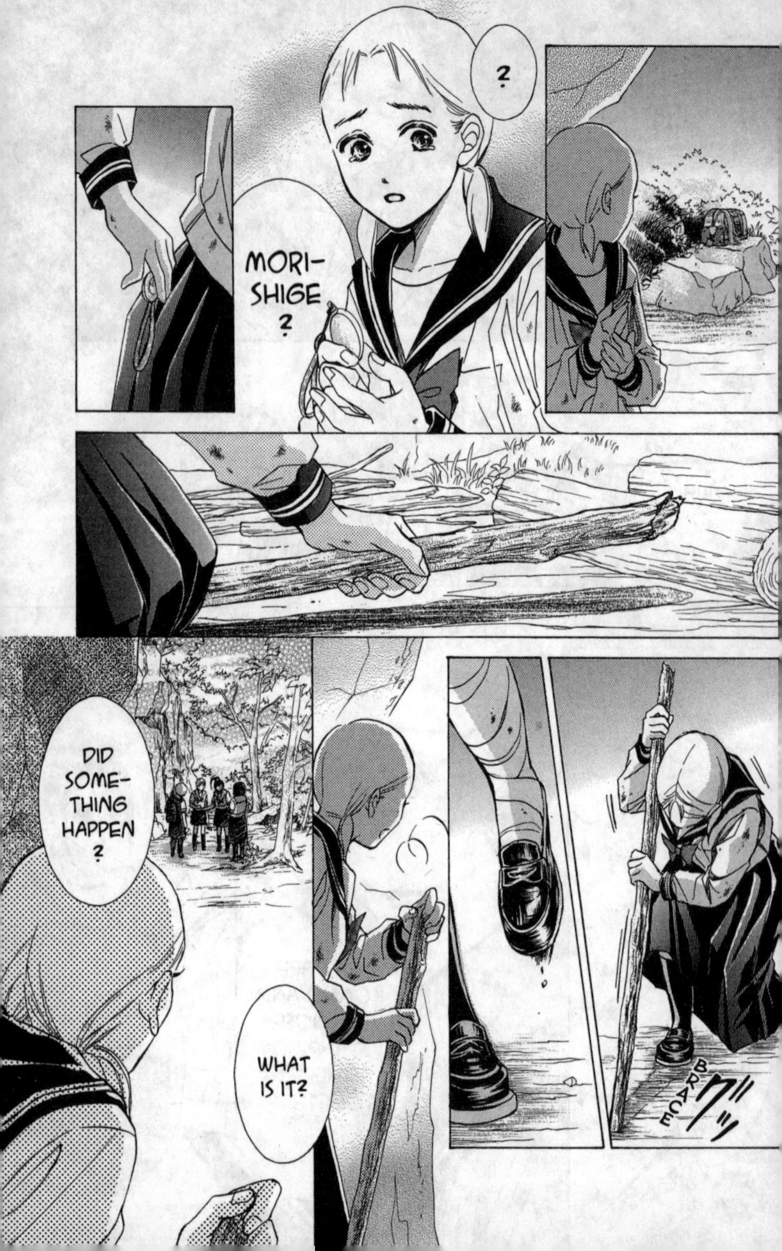
?
MORI-SHIGE?
BRACE
WHAT IS IT?
DID SOME-THING HAPPEN?

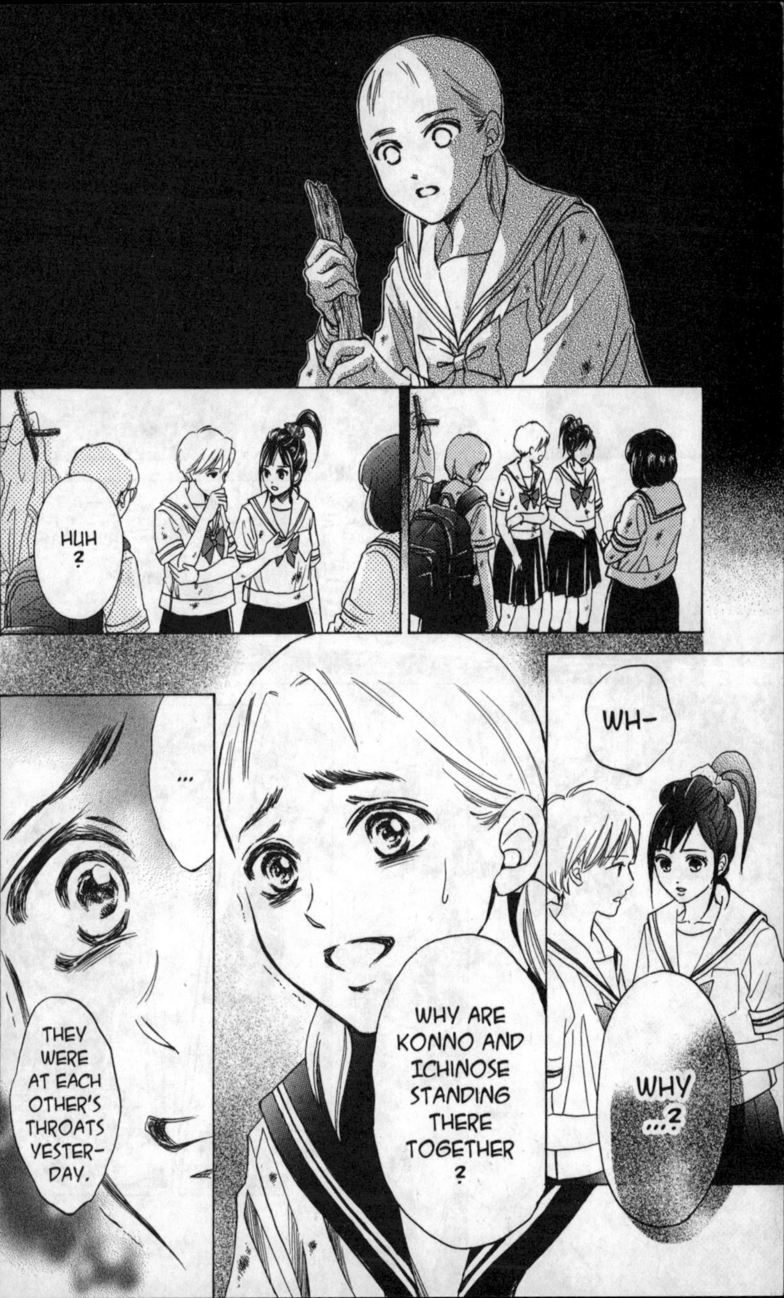
HUH?
WH-
WHY...?
WHY ARE KONNO AND ICHINOSE STANDING THERE TOGETHER?
...
THEY WERE AT EACH OTHER'S THROATS YESTER-DAY.

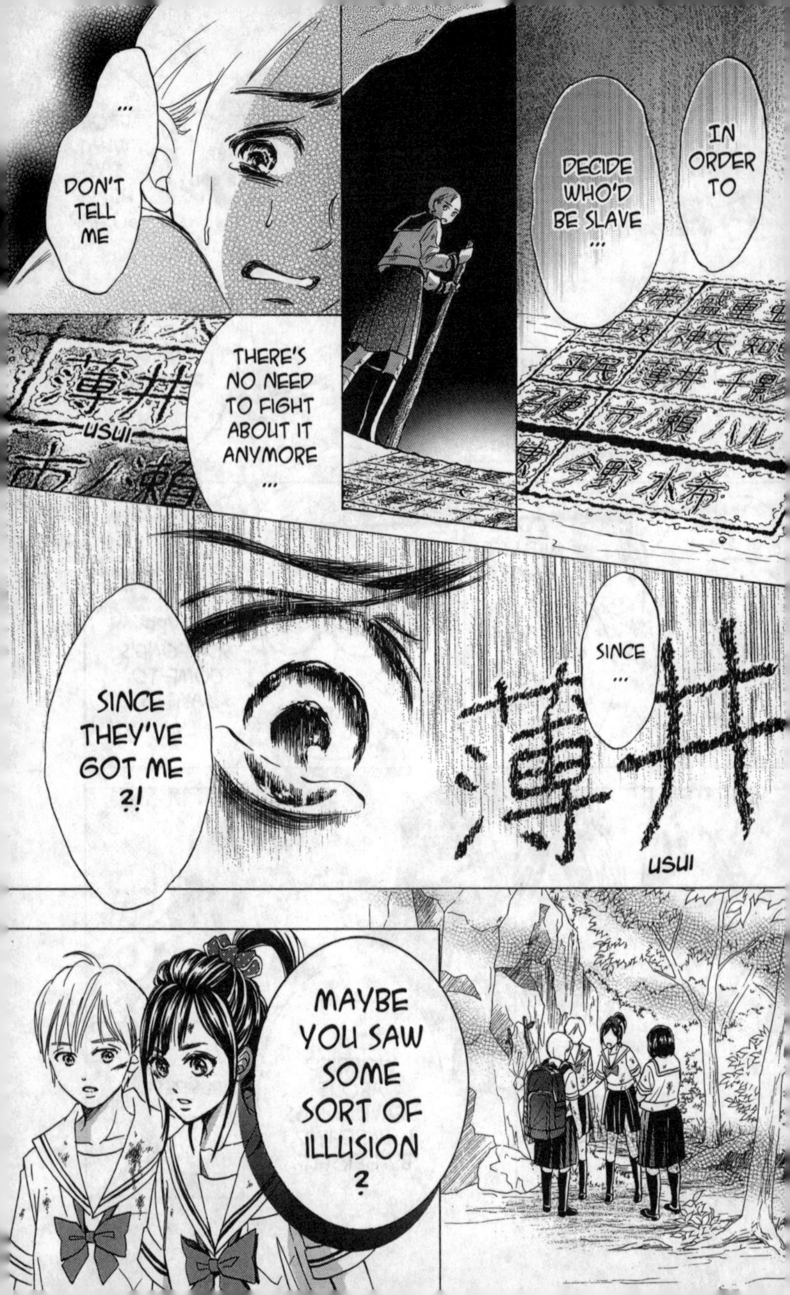

IN ORDER TO
DECIDE WHO'D BE SLAVE ...
... DON'T TELL ME
THERE'S NO NEED TO FIGHT ABOUT IT ANYMORE ...
USUI
SINCE ...
USUI
SINCE THEY'VE GOT ME ?!
MAYBE YOU SAW SOME SORT OF ILLUSION ?

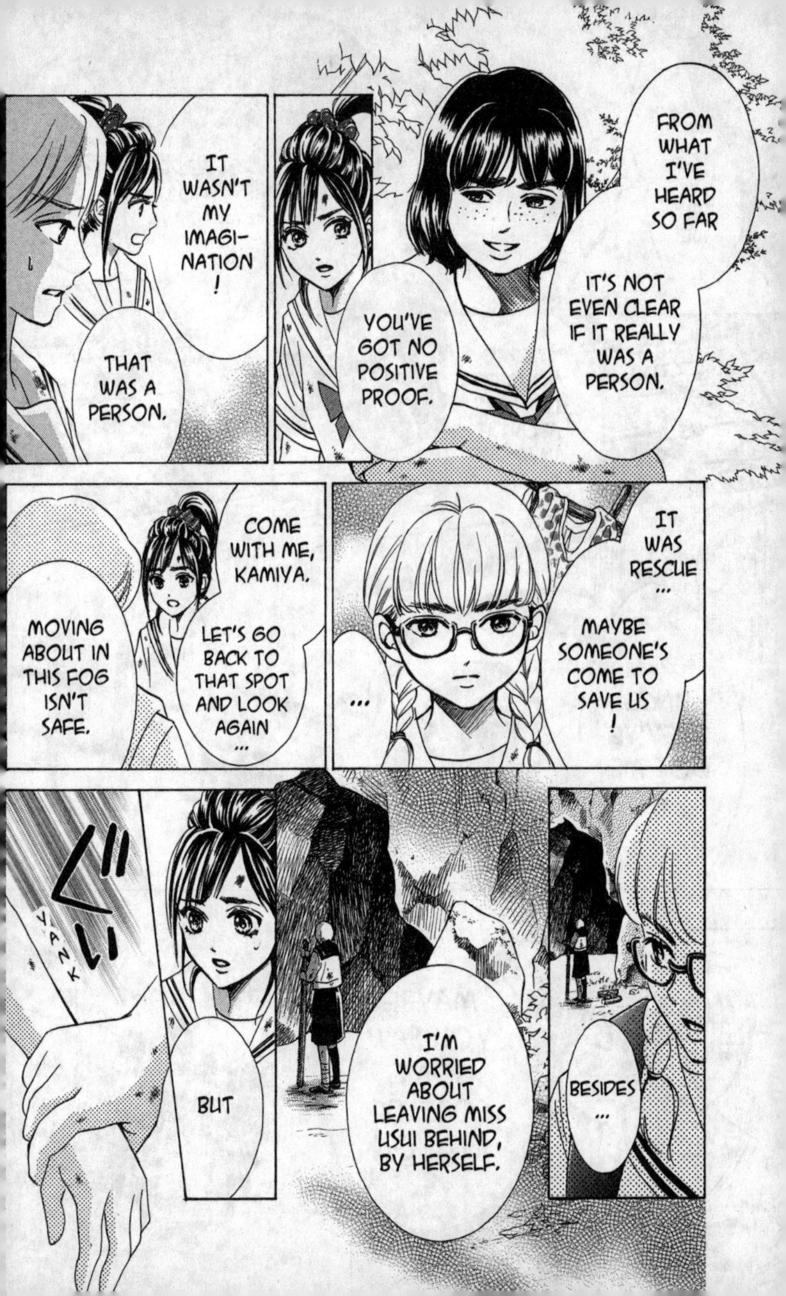
FROM WHAT I'VE HEARD SO FAR
IT'S NOT EVEN CLEAR IF IT REALLY WAS A PERSON.
YOU'VE GOT NO POSITIVE PROOF.
IT WASN'T MY IMAGINATION!
THAT WAS A PERSON.
IT WAS RESCUE...
MAYBE SOMEONE'S COME TO SAVE US!
...
COME WITH ME, KAMIYA.
LET'S GO BACK TO THAT SPOT AND LOOK AGAIN...
MOVING ABOUT IN THIS FOG ISN'T SAFE.
BESIDES...
I'M WORRIED ABOUT LEAVING MISS USUI BEHIND, BY HERSELF.
BUT
ぐい
YANK

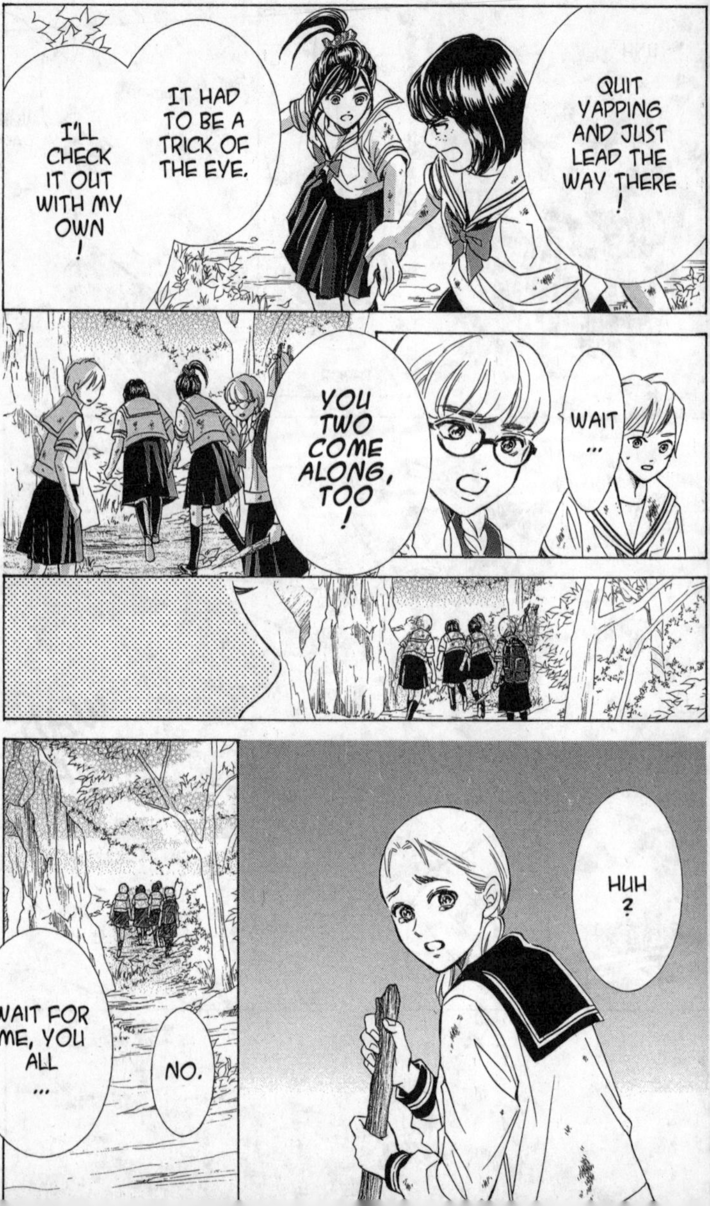
QUIT YAPPING AND JUST LEAD THE WAY THERE!
IT HAD TO BE A TRICK OF THE EYE.
I'LL CHECK IT OUT WITH MY OWN!
WAIT...
YOU TWO COME ALONG, TOO!
HUH?
NO.
WAIT FOR ME, YOU ALL...

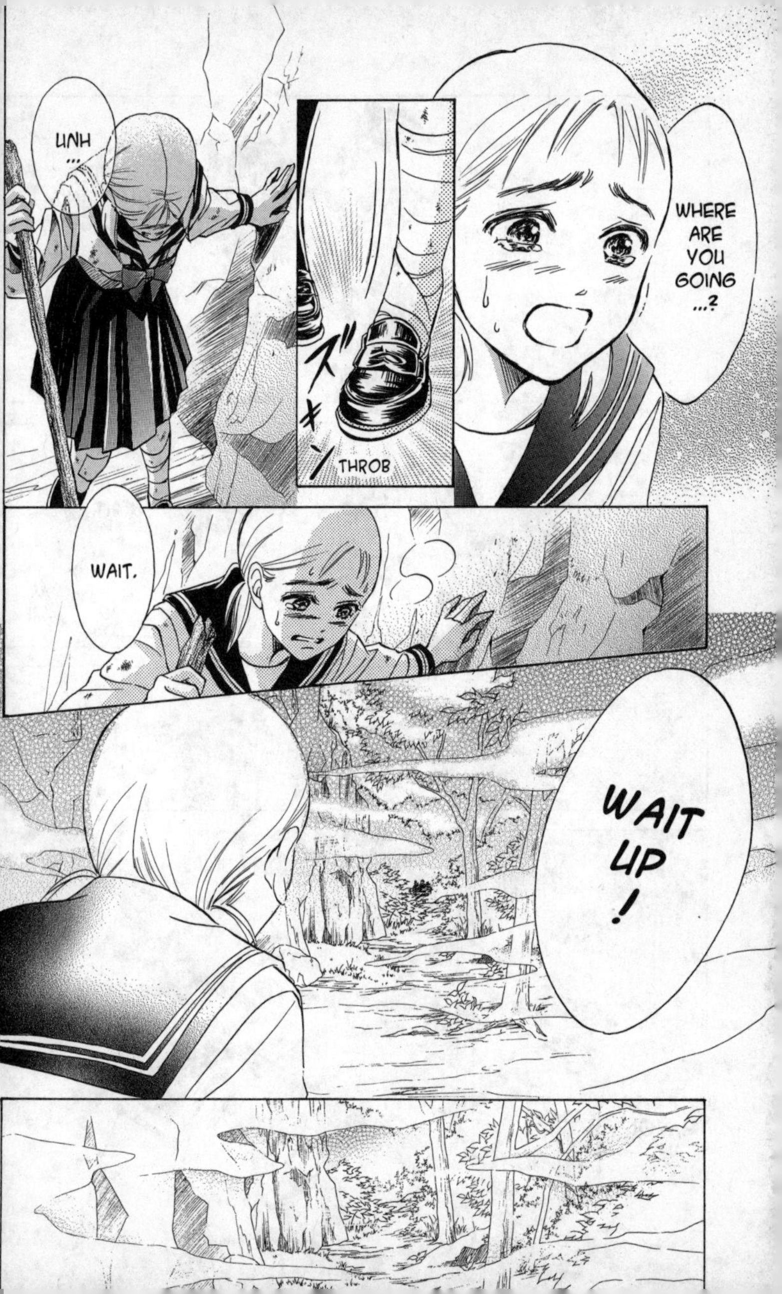
WHERE ARE YOU GOING ...?
ズキン
THROB
UNH ...
WAIT.
WAIT UP!

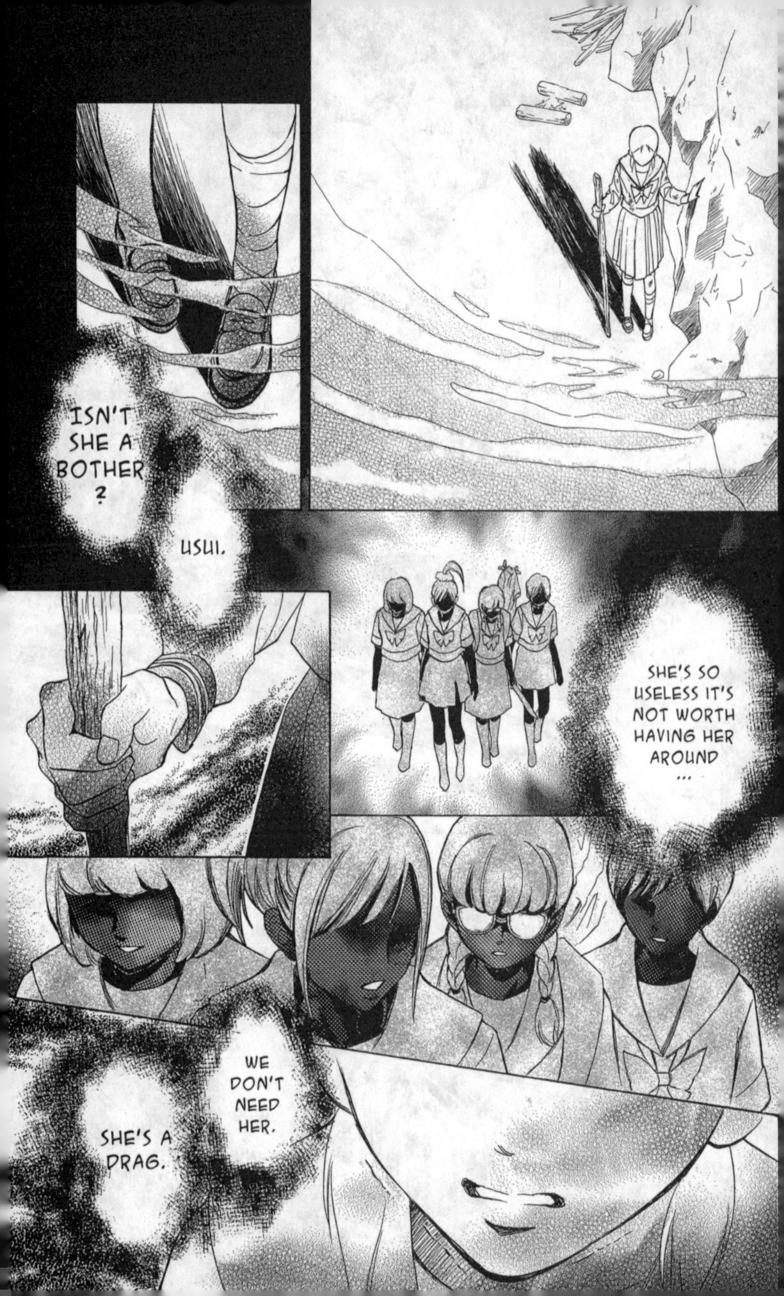
ISN'T SHE A BOTHER?
USUI.
SHE'S SO USELESS IT'S NOT WORTH HAVING HER AROUND...
WE DON'T NEED HER.
SHE'S A DRAG.

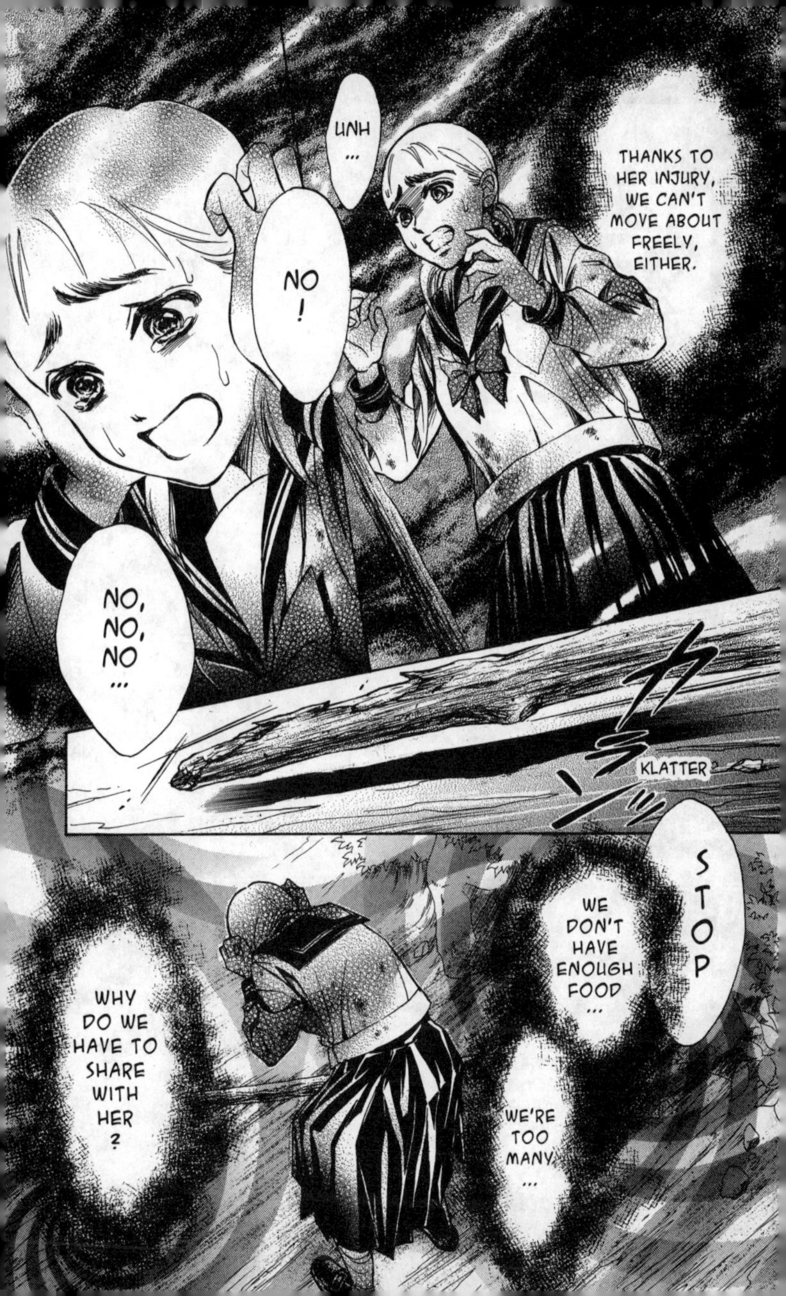
THANKS TO HER INJURY, WE CAN'T MOVE ABOUT FREELY, EITHER.
UNH ...
NO !
NO, NO, NO ...
KLATTER
STOP
WE DON'T HAVE ENOUGH FOOD ...
WE'RE TOO MANY ...
WHY DO WE HAVE TO SHARE WITH HER ?

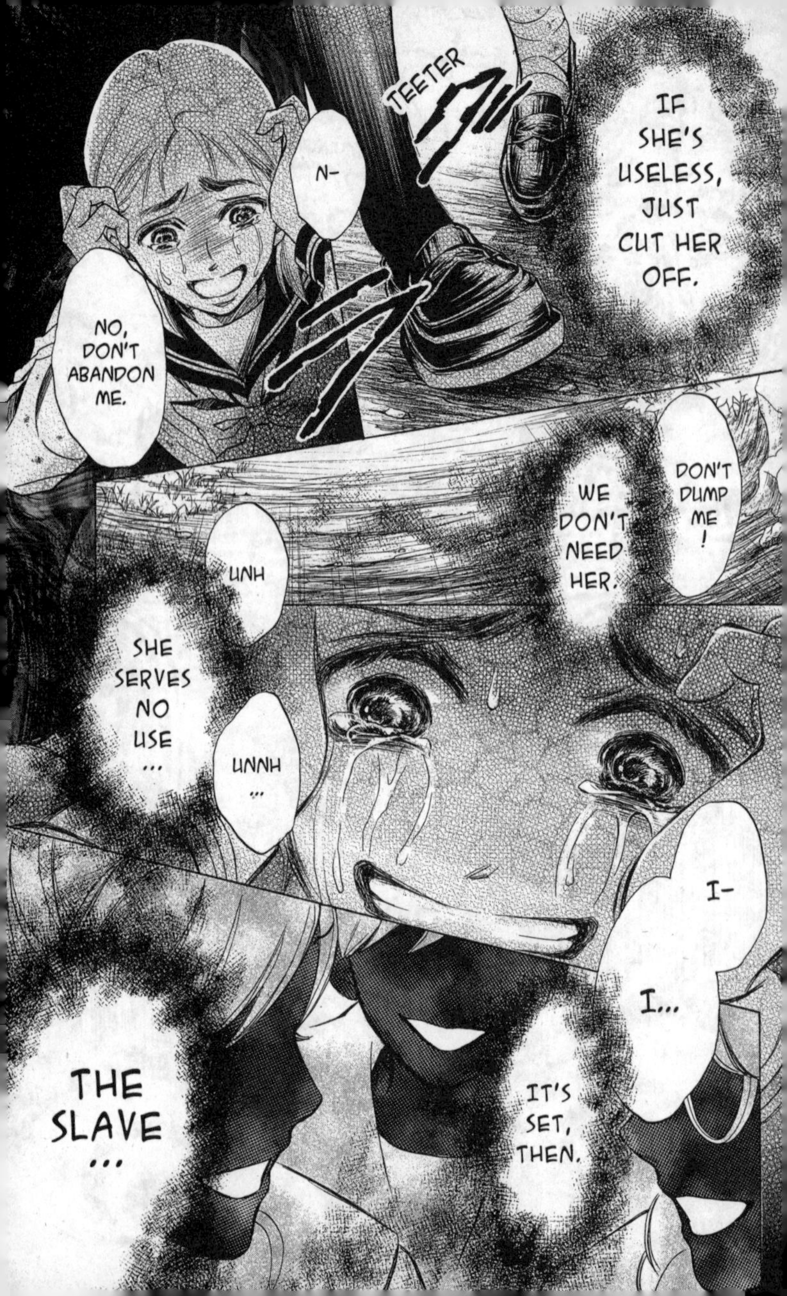
IF SHE'S USELESS, JUST CUT HER OFF.
TEETER
N-
NO, DON'T ABANDON ME.
DON'T DUMP ME!
WE DON'T NEED HER.
UNH
SHE SERVES NO USE...
UNNH...
I-
I...
IT'S SET, THEN.
THE SLAVE...

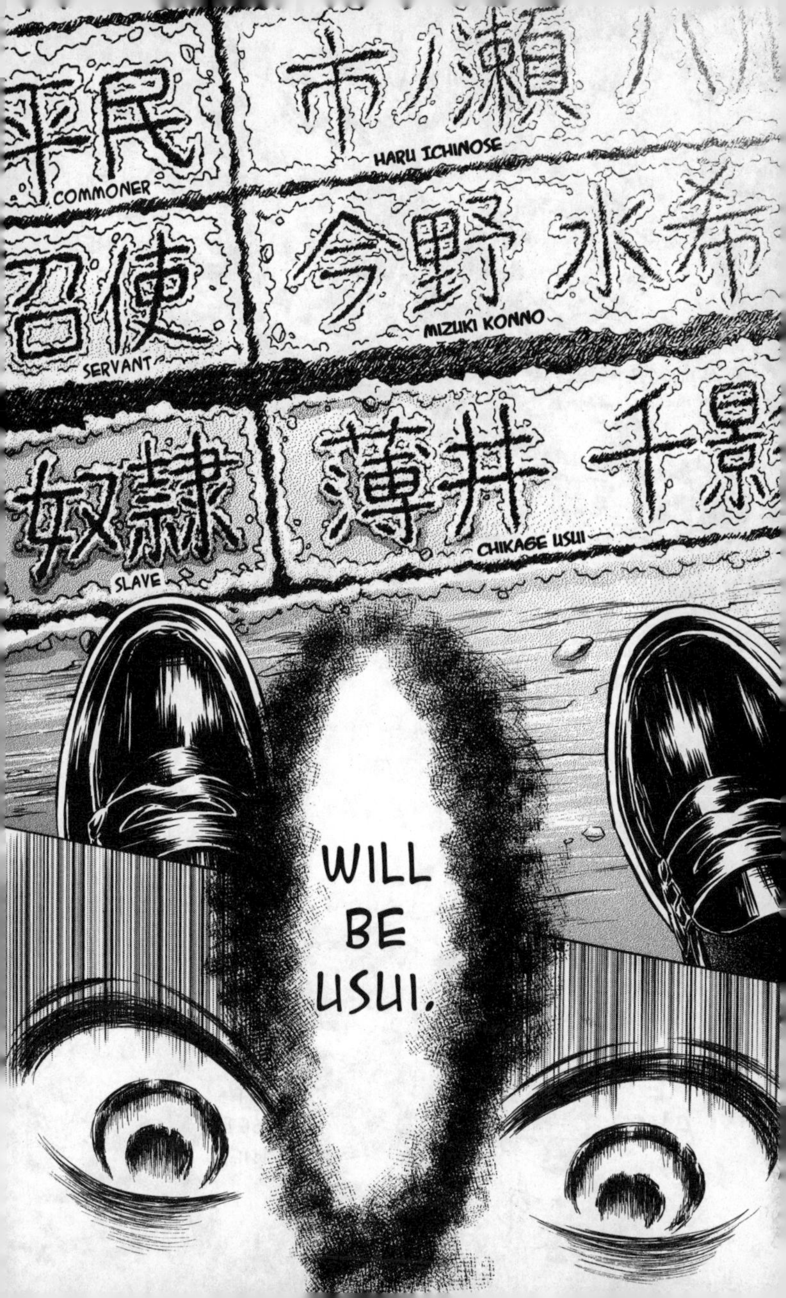
HARU ICHINOSE
COMMONER
MIZUKI KONNO
SERVANT
CHIKAGE USUI
SLAVE
WILL BE USUI.

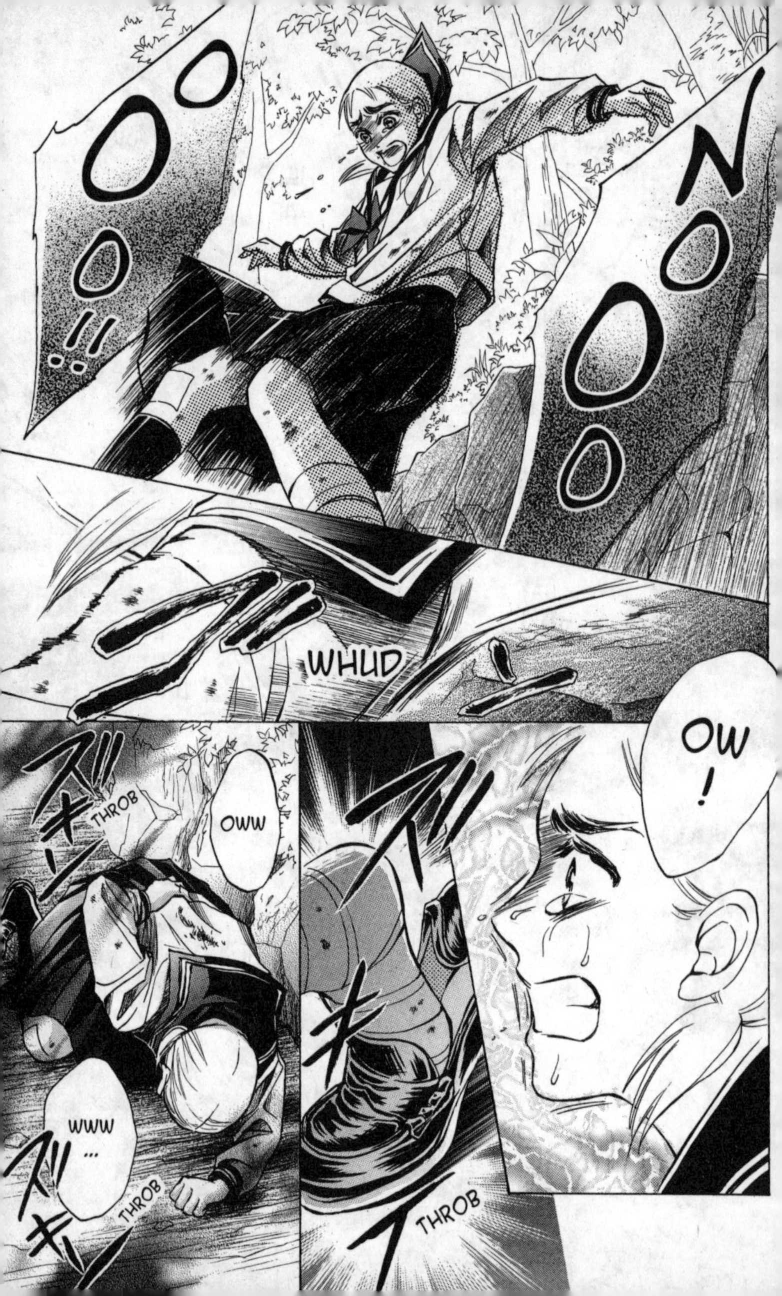
NOOOO
OOO!!
WHUD
OW!
THROB
OWW
THROB
WWW...
THROB

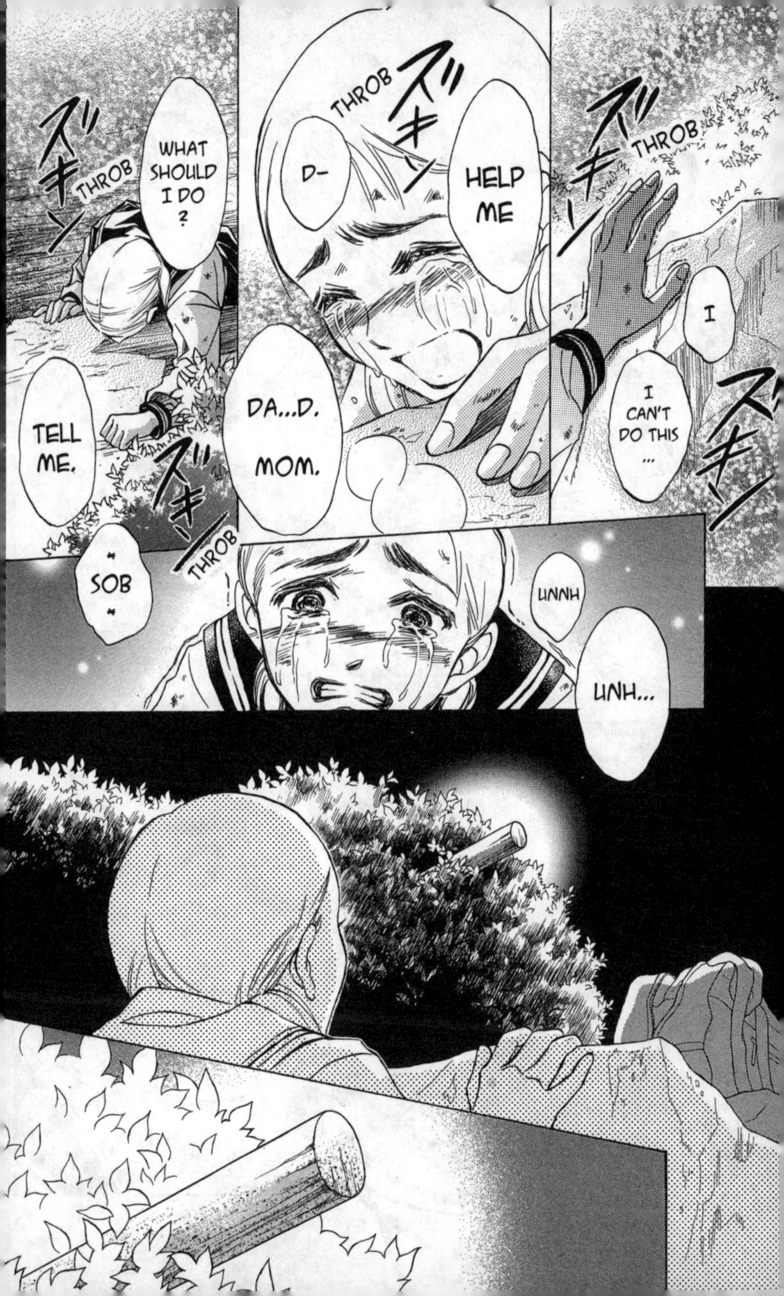
ズキン
THROB
I
I CAN'T DO THIS ...
ズキン
ズキン
THROB
HELP ME
D-
DA...D.
MOM.
ズキン
THROB
WHAT SHOULD I DO ?
TELL ME.
ズキン
THROB
UNNH
UNH...
* SOB *

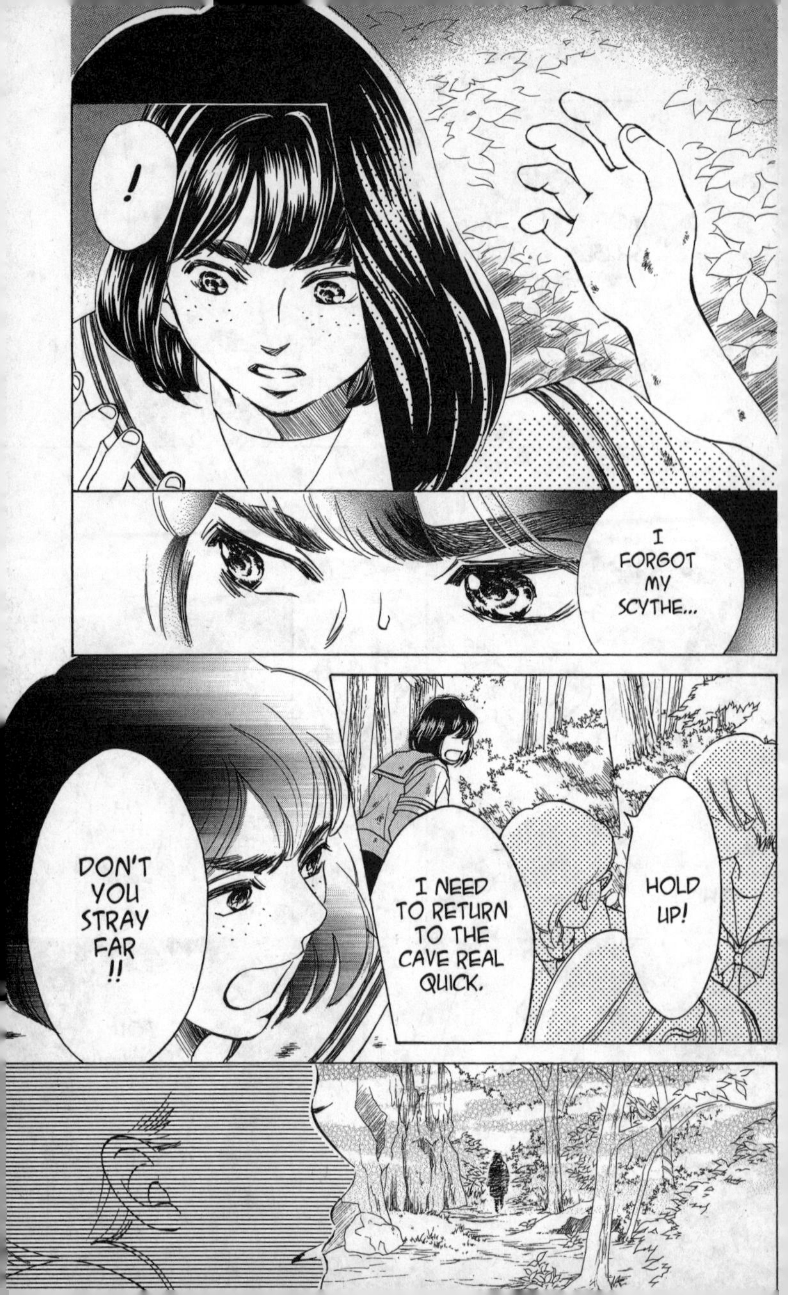
!
I FORGOT MY SCYTHE...
HOLD UP!
I NEED TO RETURN TO THE CAVE REAL QUICK.
DON'T YOU STRAY FAR !!

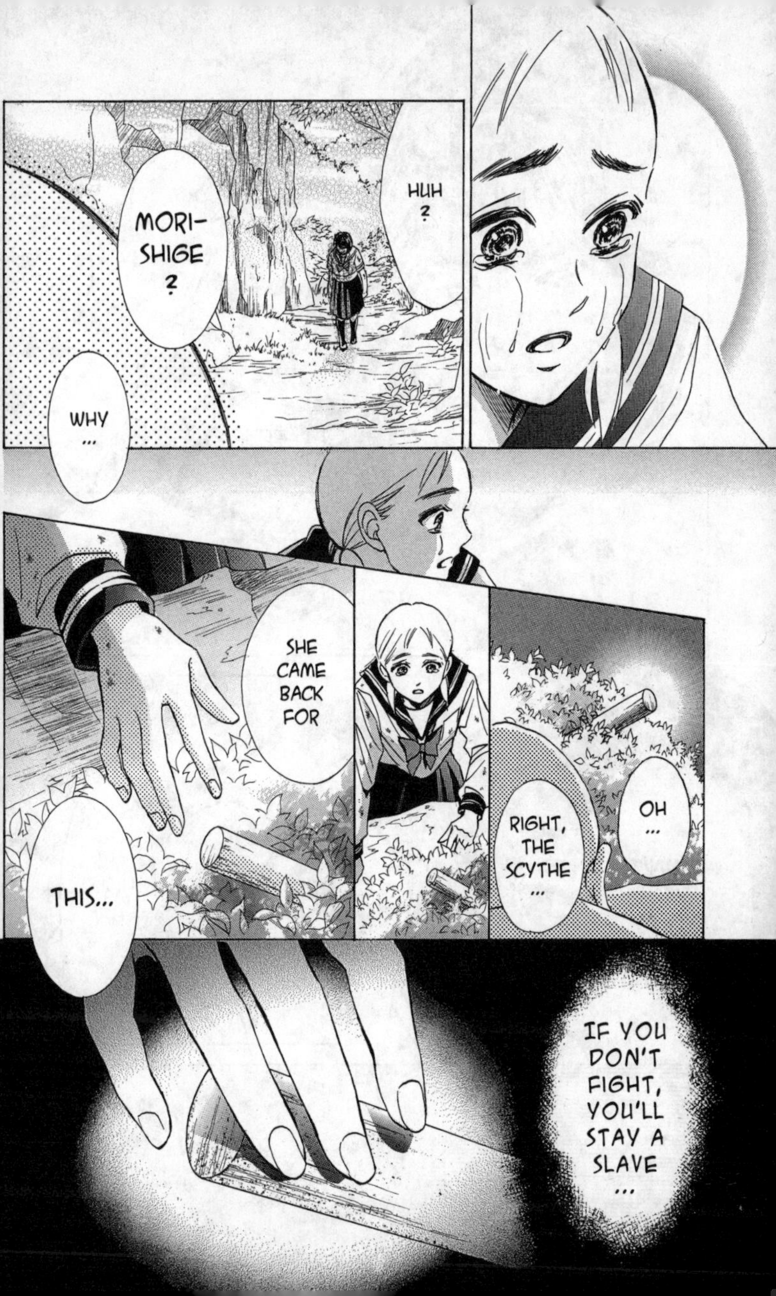
HUH ?
MORI-SHIGE ?
WHY ...
OH ...
RIGHT, THE SCYTHE ...
SHE CAME BACK FOR
THIS...
IF YOU DON'T FIGHT, YOU'LL STAY A SLAVE ...

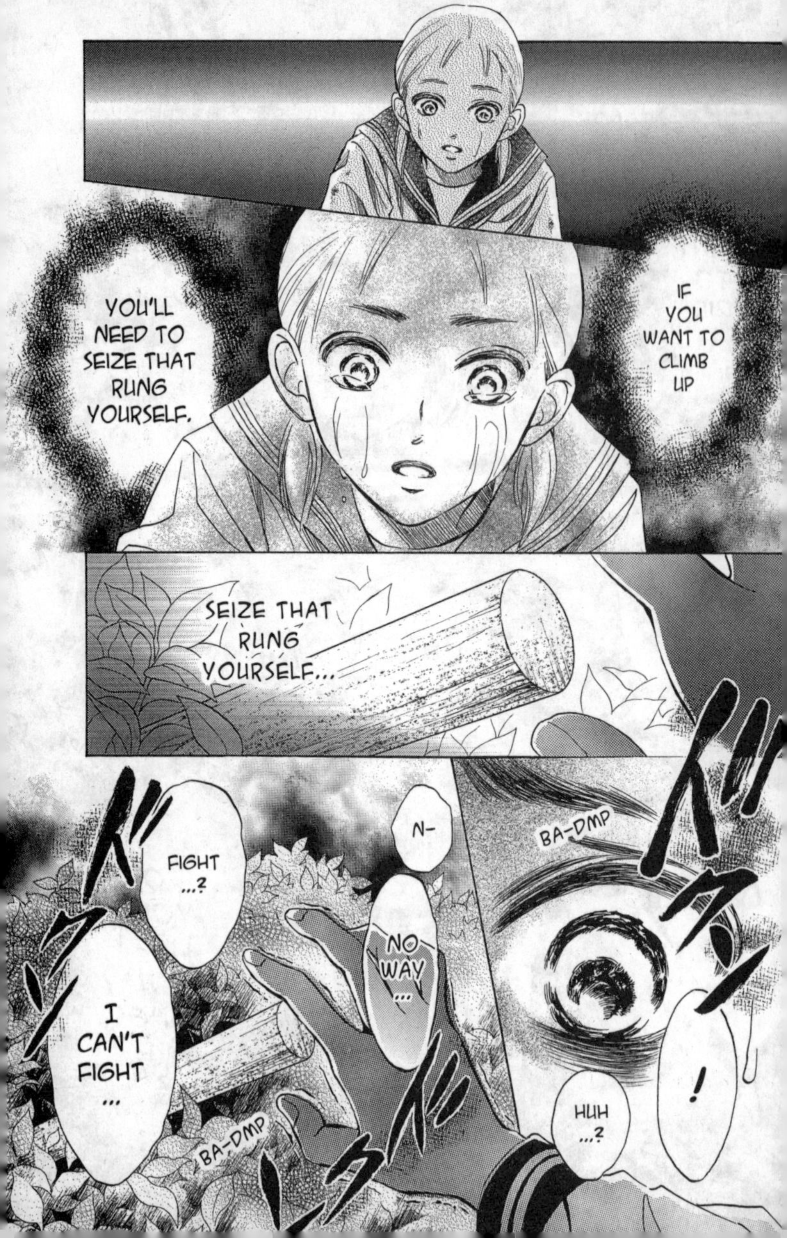
IF YOU WANT TO CLIMB UP
YOU'LL NEED TO SEIZE THAT RUNG YOURSELF.
SEIZE THAT RUNG YOURSELF...
BA-DMP
!
HUH ...?
N-
NO WAY ...
FIGHT ...?
I CAN'T FIGHT ...
BA-DMP

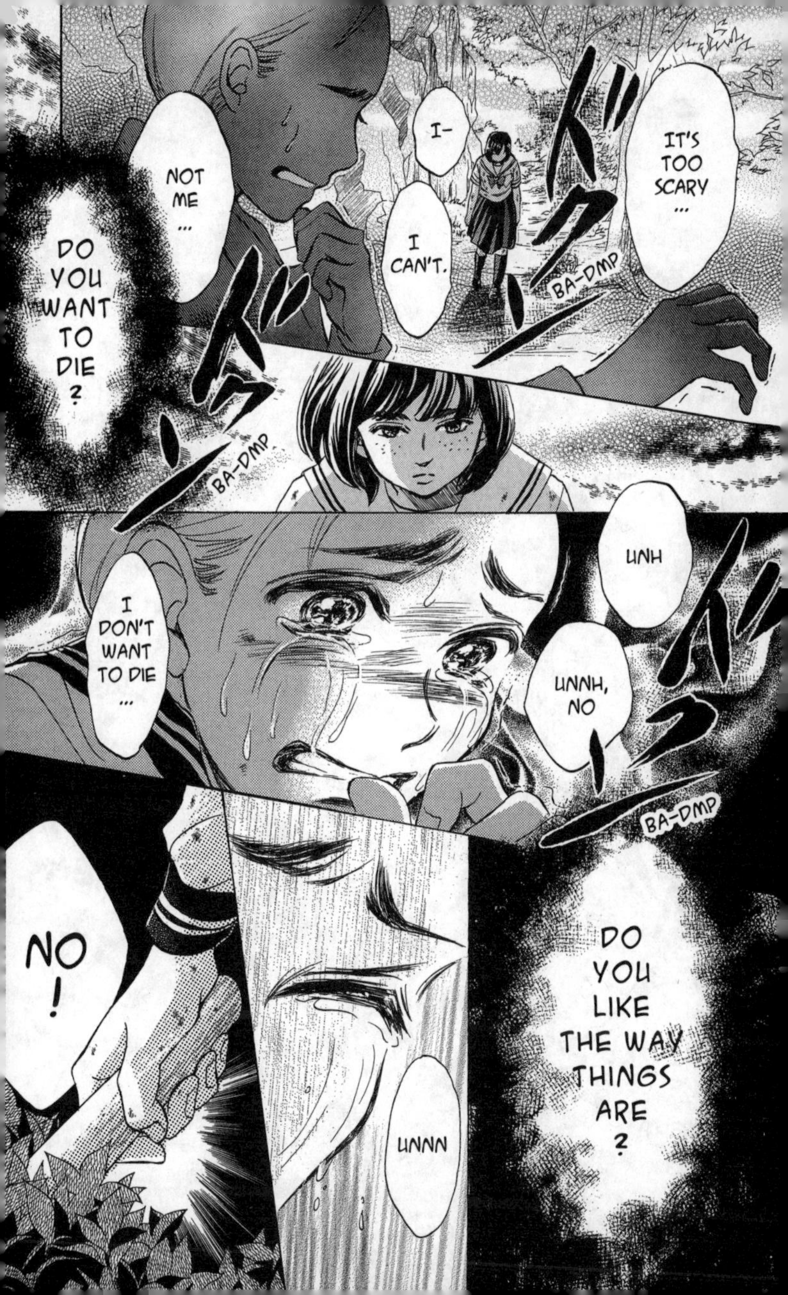
IT'S TOO SCARY ...
BA-DMP
I-
I CAN'T.
NOT ME ...
DO YOU WANT TO DIE?
BA-DMP
UNH
UNNH, NO
BA-DMP
I DON'T WANT TO DIE ...
DO YOU LIKE THE WAY THINGS ARE?
UNNN
NO!

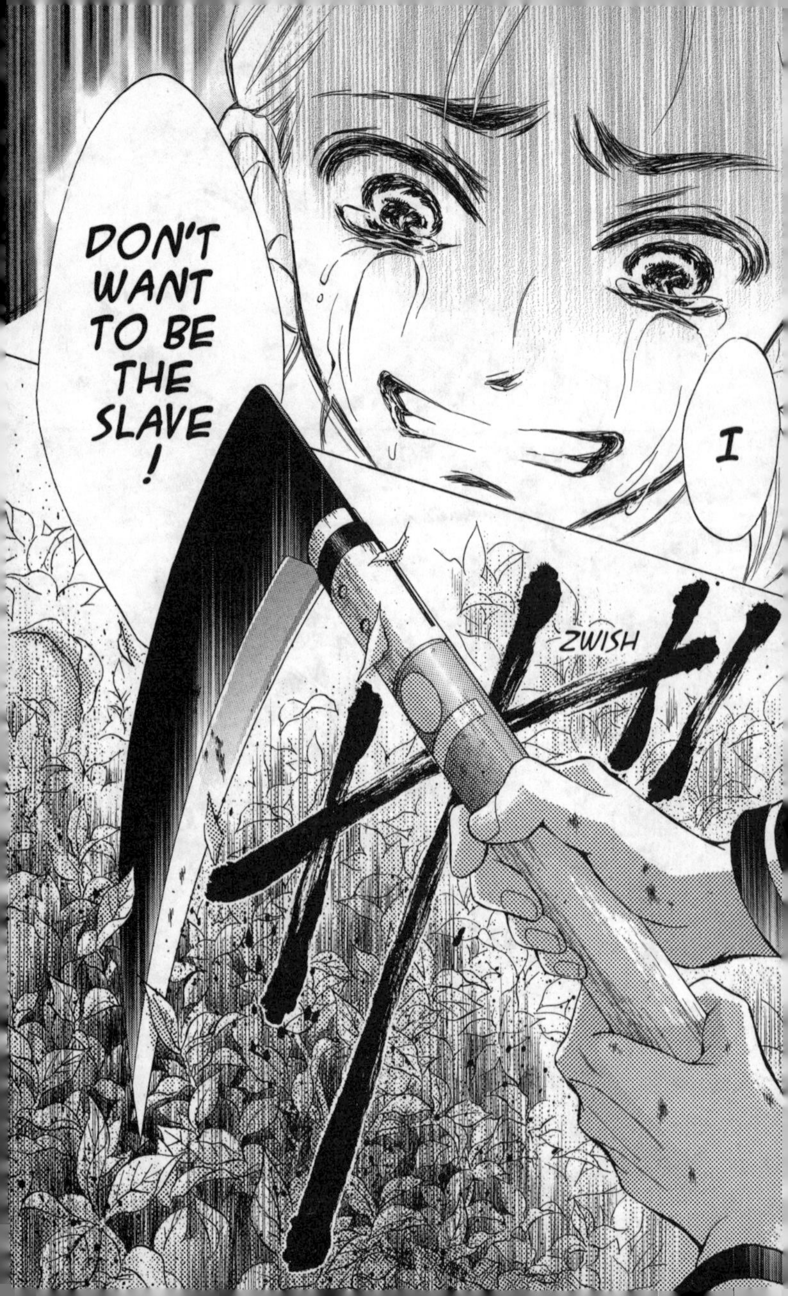
I
DON'T WANT TO BE THE SLAVE!
ZWISH

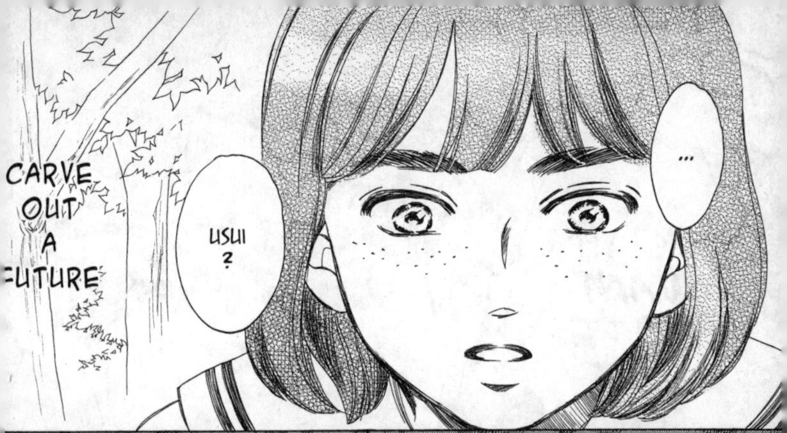
...
USUI ?
CARVE OUT A FUTURE
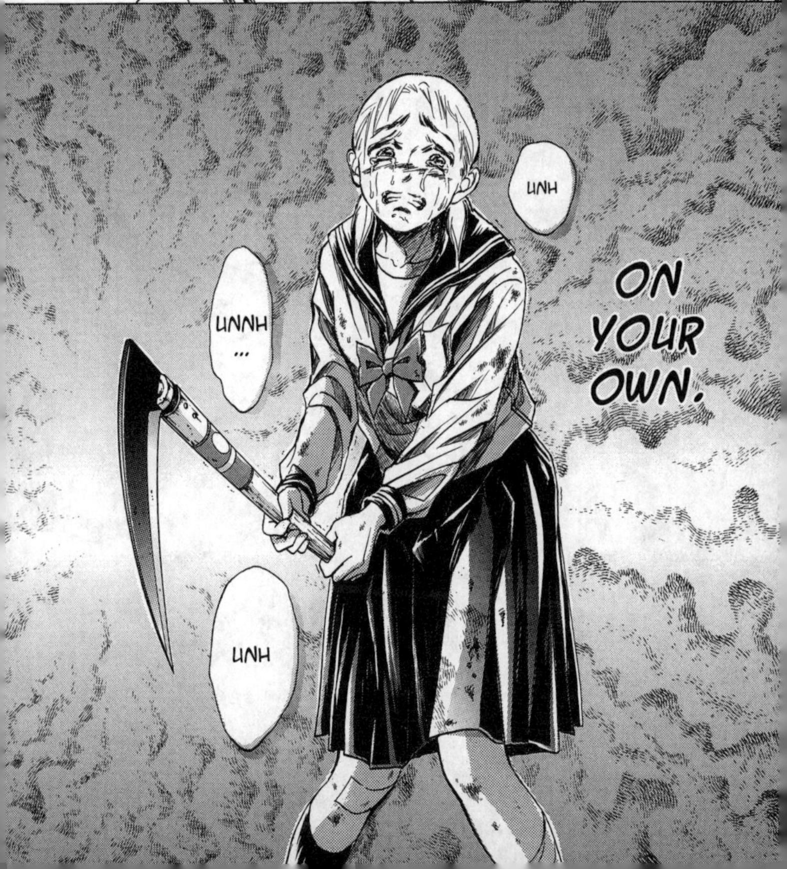
UNH
ON YOUR OWN.
UNNH ...
UNH

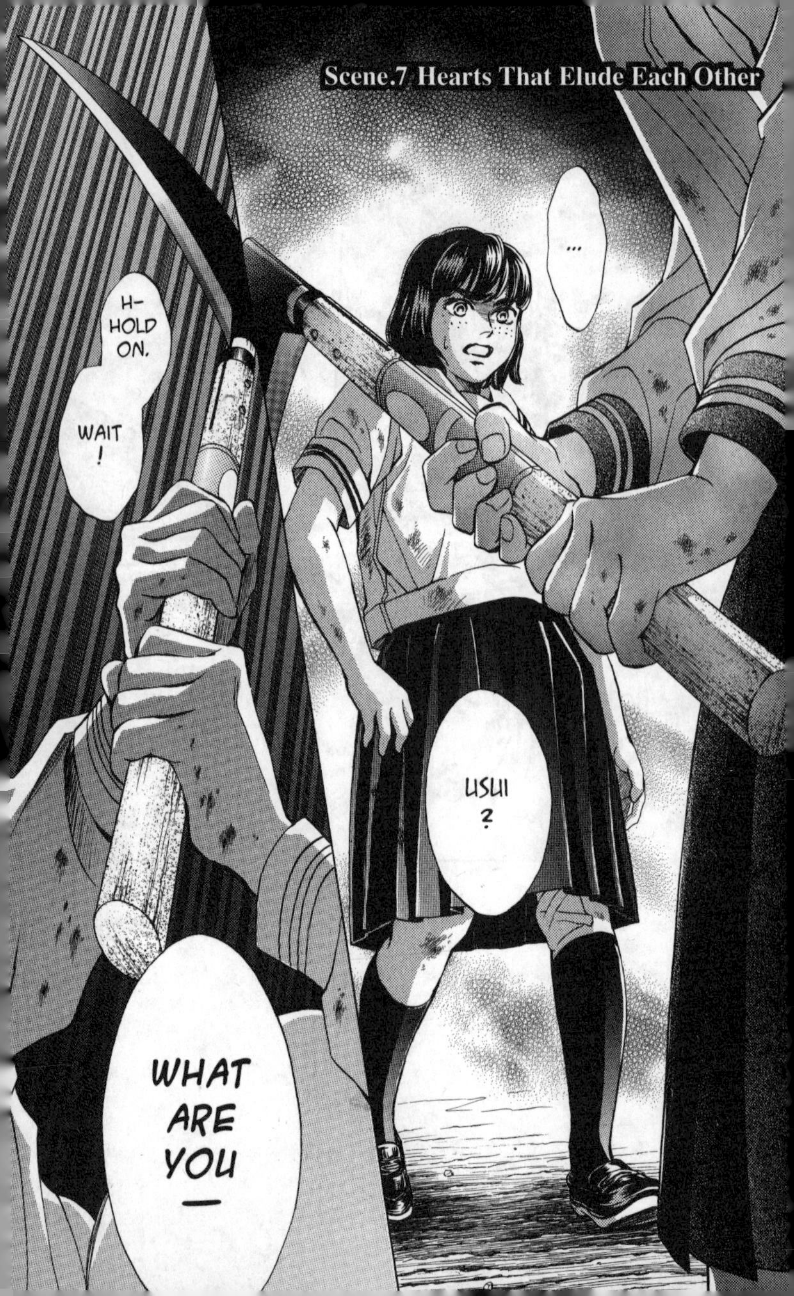
Scene.7 Hearts That Elude Each Other
...
H-HOLD ON.
WAIT!
USUI?
WHAT ARE YOU —

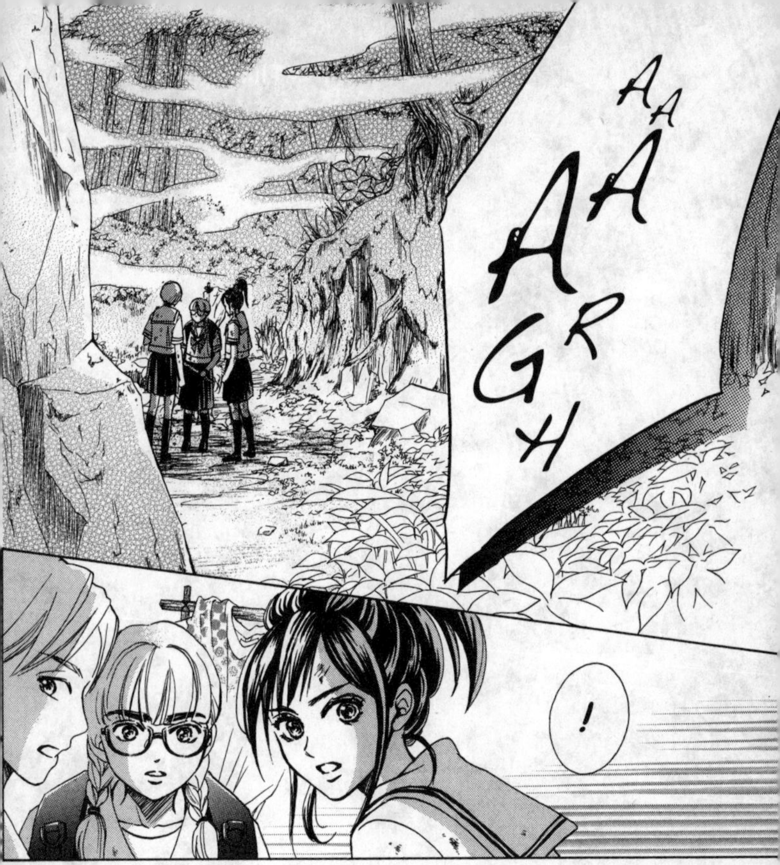
AAAARGH
!

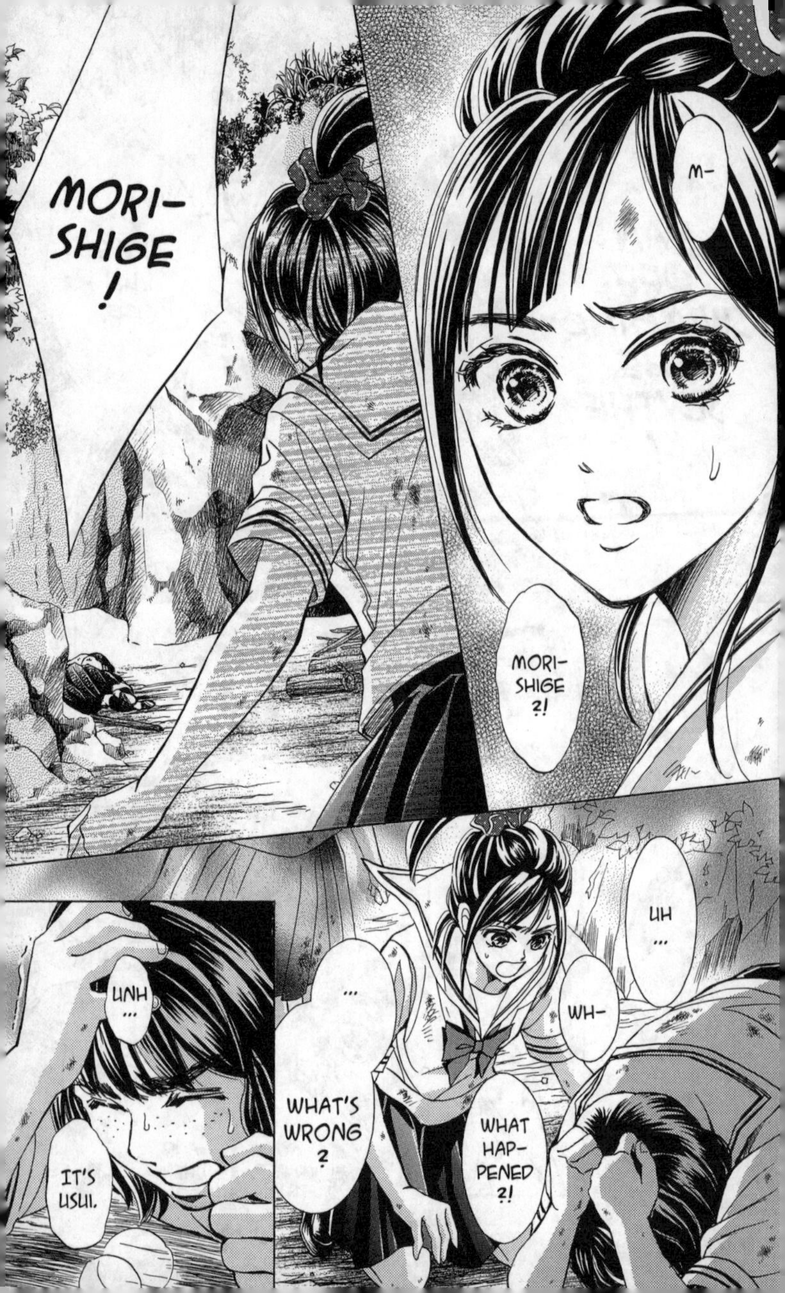
M-
MORI-SHIGE?!
MORI-SHIGE!
UH...
WH-
...
WHAT HAP-PENED?!
WHAT'S WRONG?
UNH...
IT'S USUI.

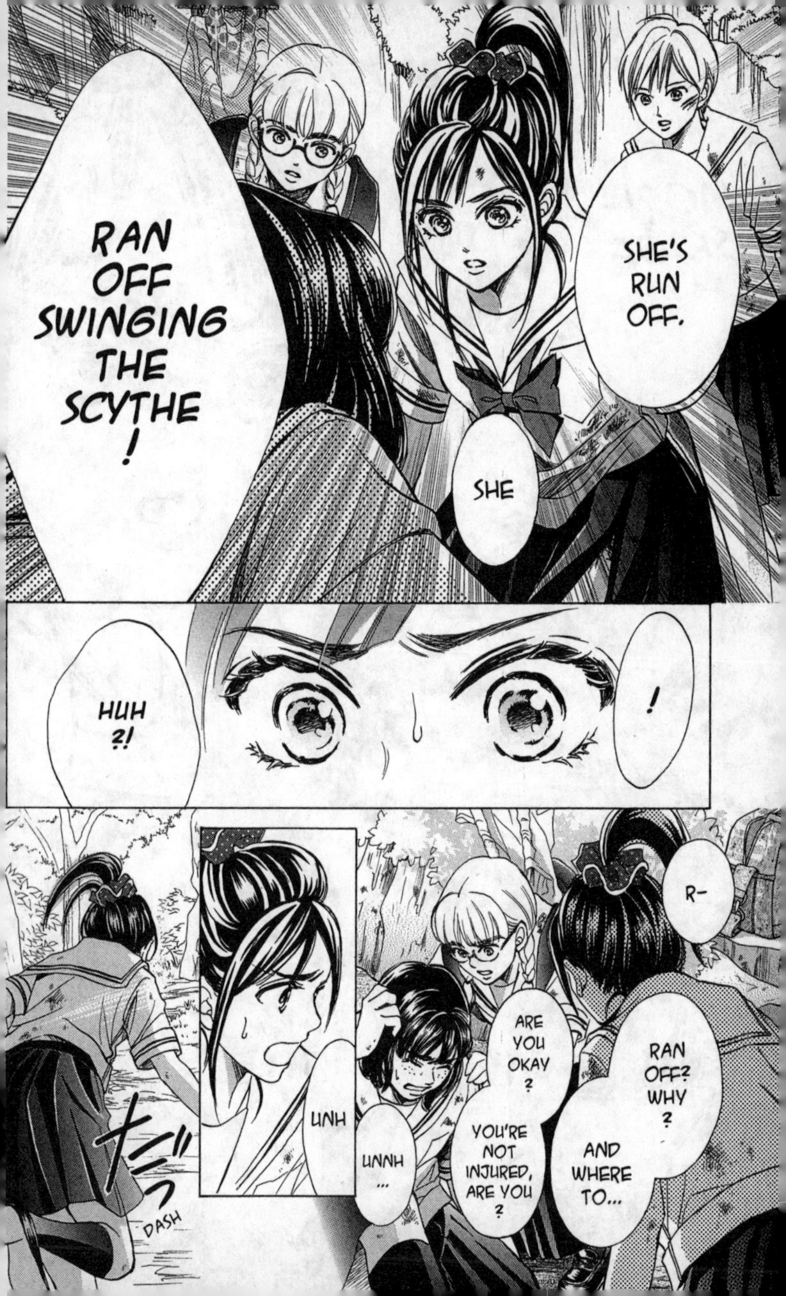
SHE'S RUN OFF.
SHE
RAN OFF SWINGING THE SCYTHE!
!
HUH?!
R-
RAN OFF? WHY?
AND WHERE TO...
ARE YOU OKAY?
YOU'RE NOT INJURED, ARE YOU?
UNNH...
UNH
DASH

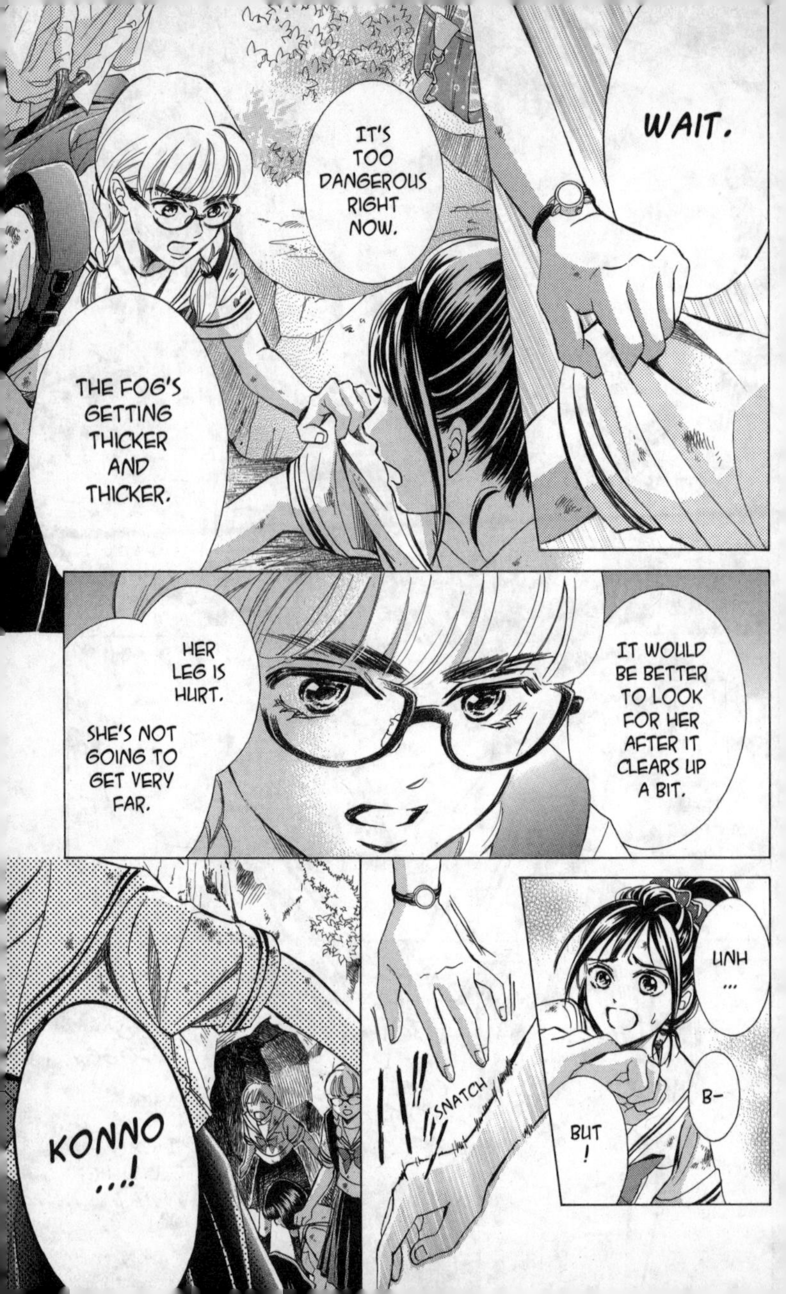
WAIT.
IT'S TOO DANGEROUS RIGHT NOW.
THE FOG'S GETTING THICKER AND THICKER.
IT WOULD BE BETTER TO LOOK FOR HER AFTER IT CLEARS UP A BIT.
HER LEG IS HURT.
SHE'S NOT GOING TO GET VERY FAR.
UNH ...
B-
BUT!
SNATCH
KONNO ...!

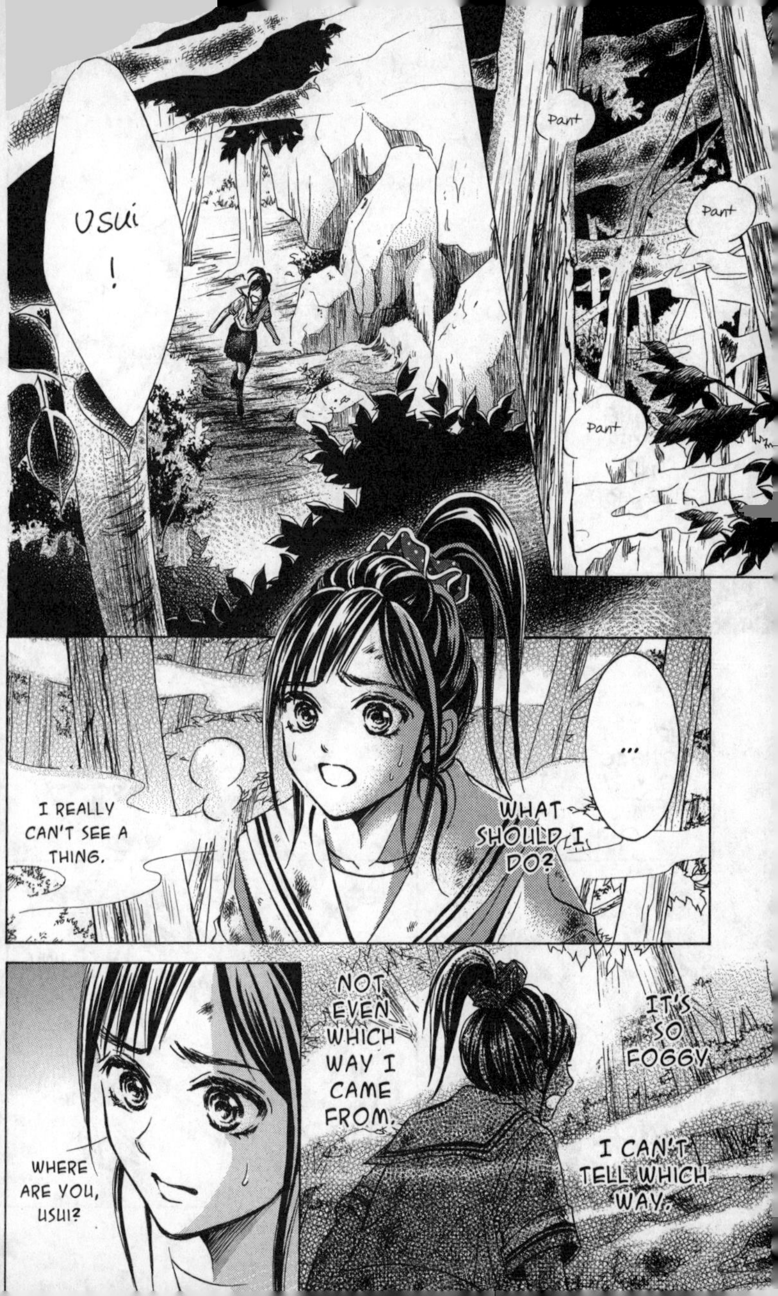
Pant
Pant
Pant
USUi !
...
WHAT SHOULD I DO?
I REALLY CAN'T SEE A THING.
IT'S SO FOGGY
I CAN'T TELL WHICH WAY.
NOT EVEN WHICH WAY I CAME FROM.
WHERE ARE YOU, USUI?

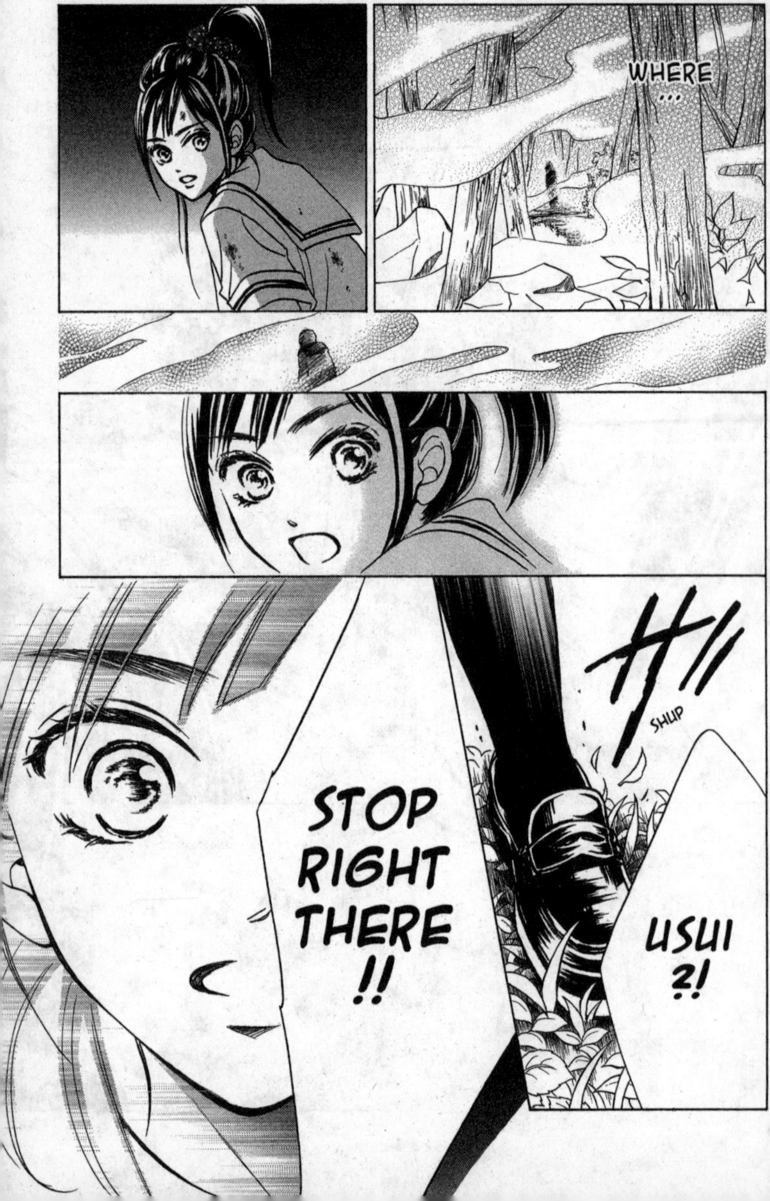
WHERE ...
SHUP
USUI ?!
STOP RIGHT THERE !!

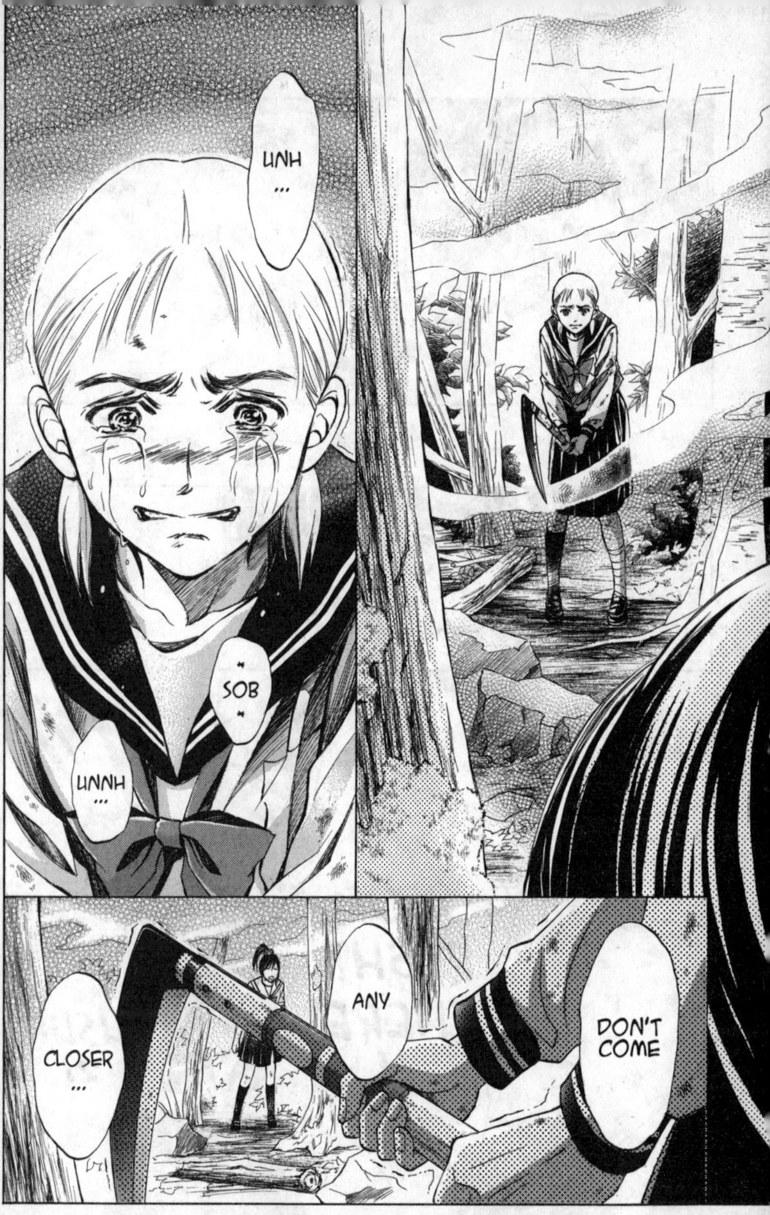
UNH …
* SOB *
UNNH …
DON'T COME
ANY
CLOSER …

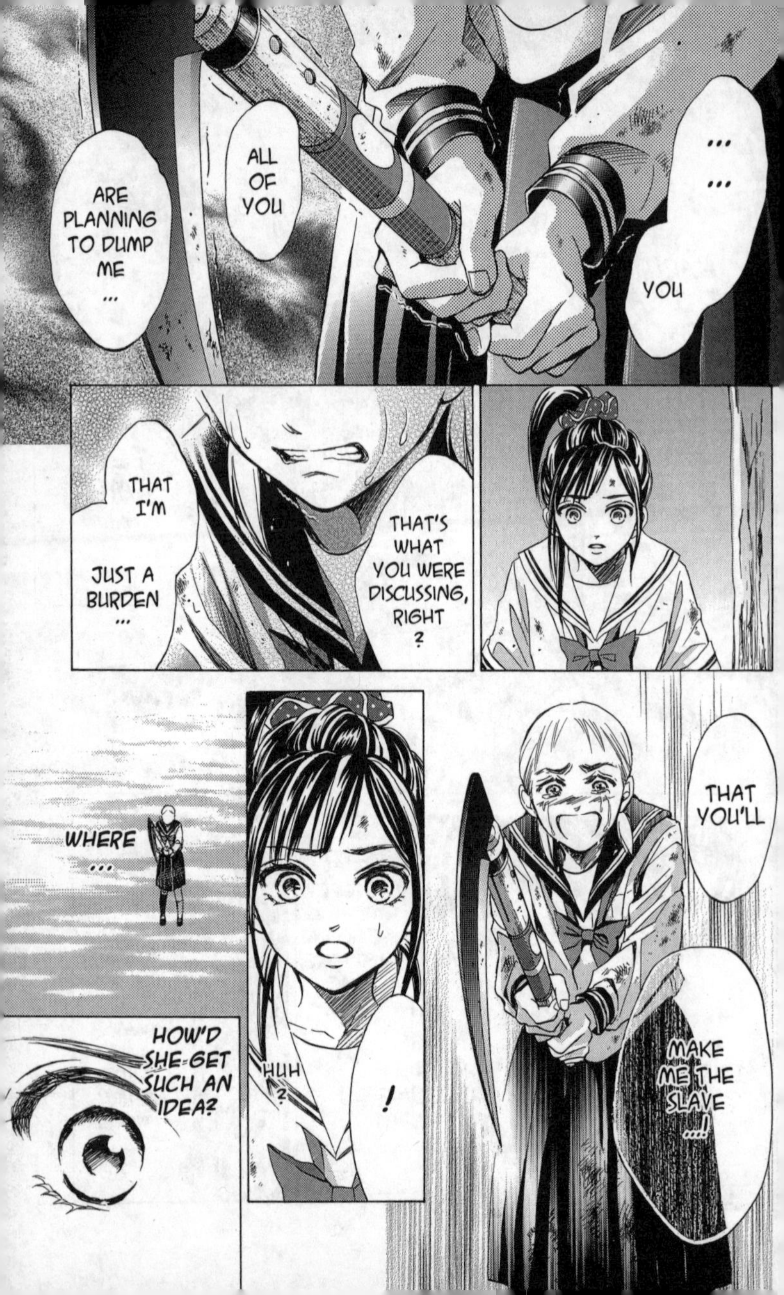
... ... YOU
ALL OF YOU
ARE PLANNING TO DUMP ME ...
THAT I'M
JUST A BURDEN ...
THAT'S WHAT YOU WERE DISCUSSING, RIGHT?
THAT YOU'LL
MAKE ME THE SLAVE ...!
!
HUH?
WHERE ...
HOW'D SHE GET SUCH AN IDEA?

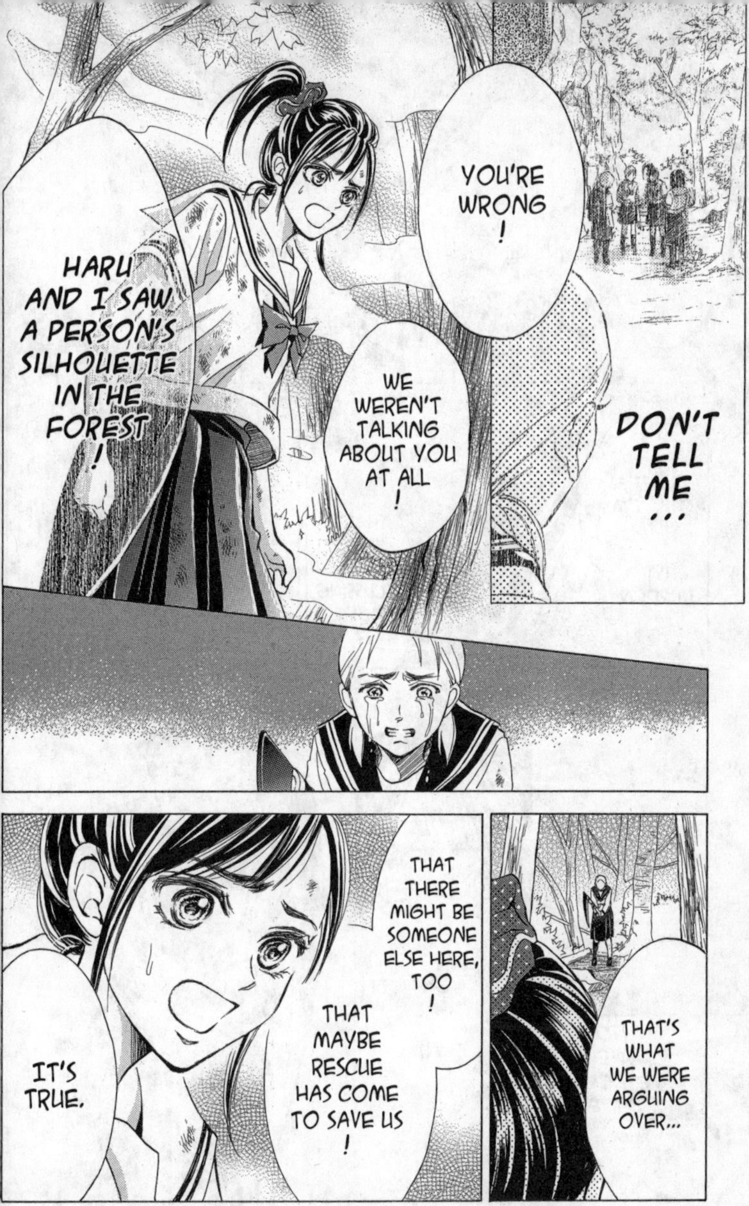
DON'T TELL ME...
YOU'RE WRONG!
WE WEREN'T TALKING ABOUT YOU AT ALL!
HARU AND I SAW A PERSON'S SILHOUETTE IN THE FOREST!
THAT'S WHAT WE WERE ARGUING OVER...
THAT THERE MIGHT BE SOMEONE ELSE HERE, TOO!
THAT MAYBE RESCUE HAS COME TO SAVE US!
IT'S TRUE.

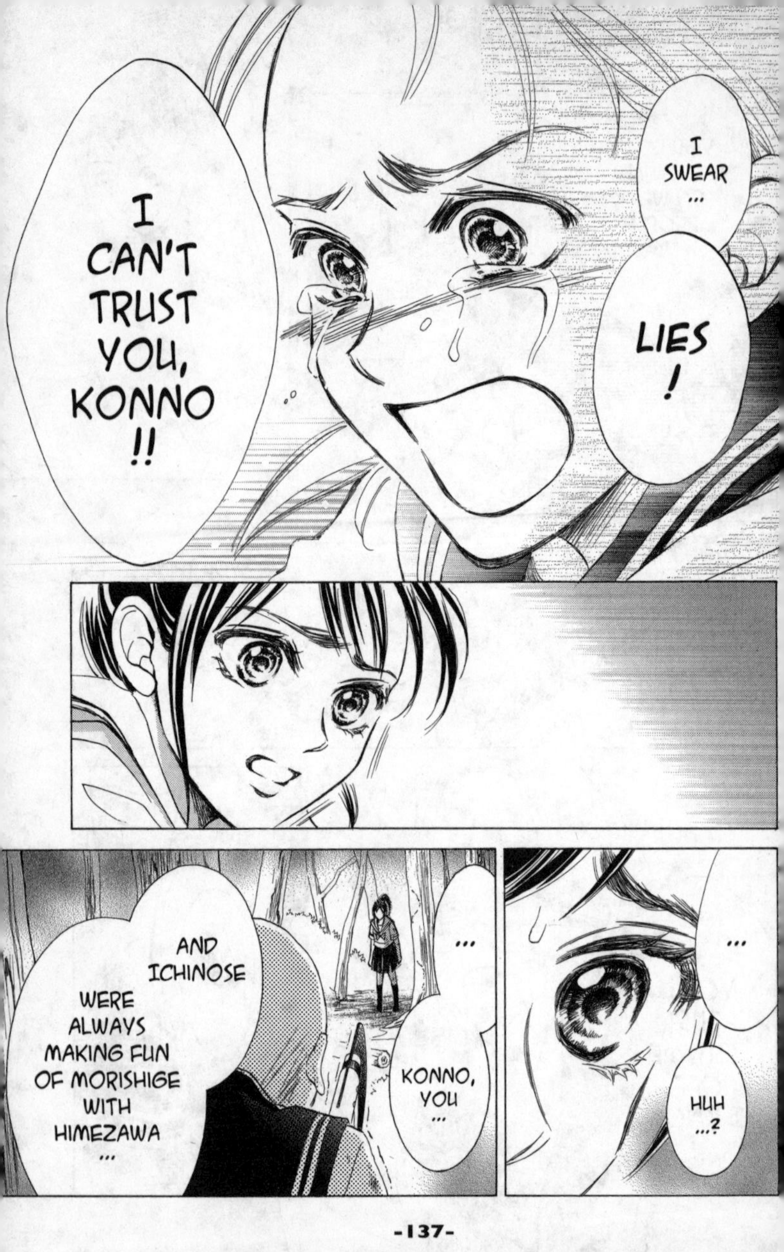
I SWEAR ...
LIES !
I CAN'T TRUST YOU, KONNO !!
...
HUH ...?
...
KONNO, YOU ...
AND ICHINOSE WERE ALWAYS MAKING FUN OF MORISHIGE WITH HIMEZAWA ...

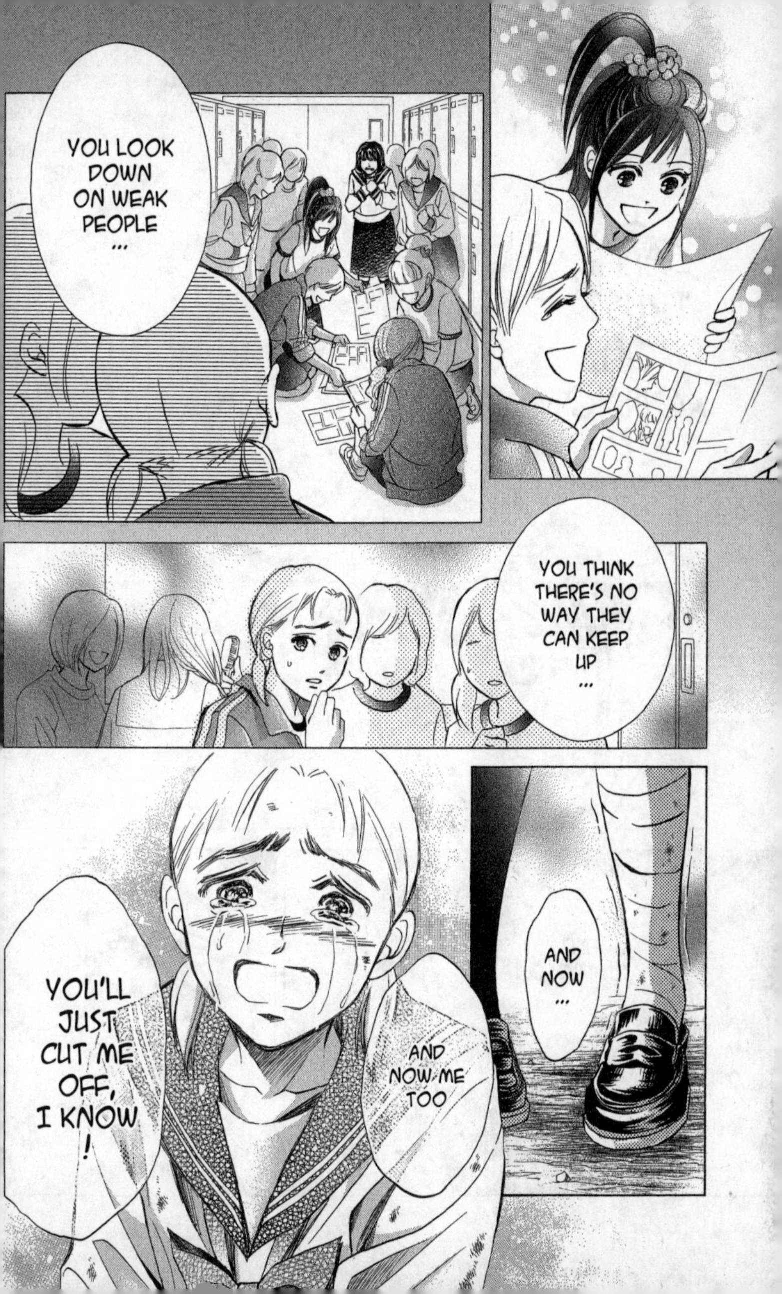
YOU LOOK DOWN ON WEAK PEOPLE ...
YOU THINK THERE'S NO WAY THEY CAN KEEP UP ...
AND NOW ...
AND NOW ME TOO
YOU'LL JUST CUT ME OFF, I KNOW !

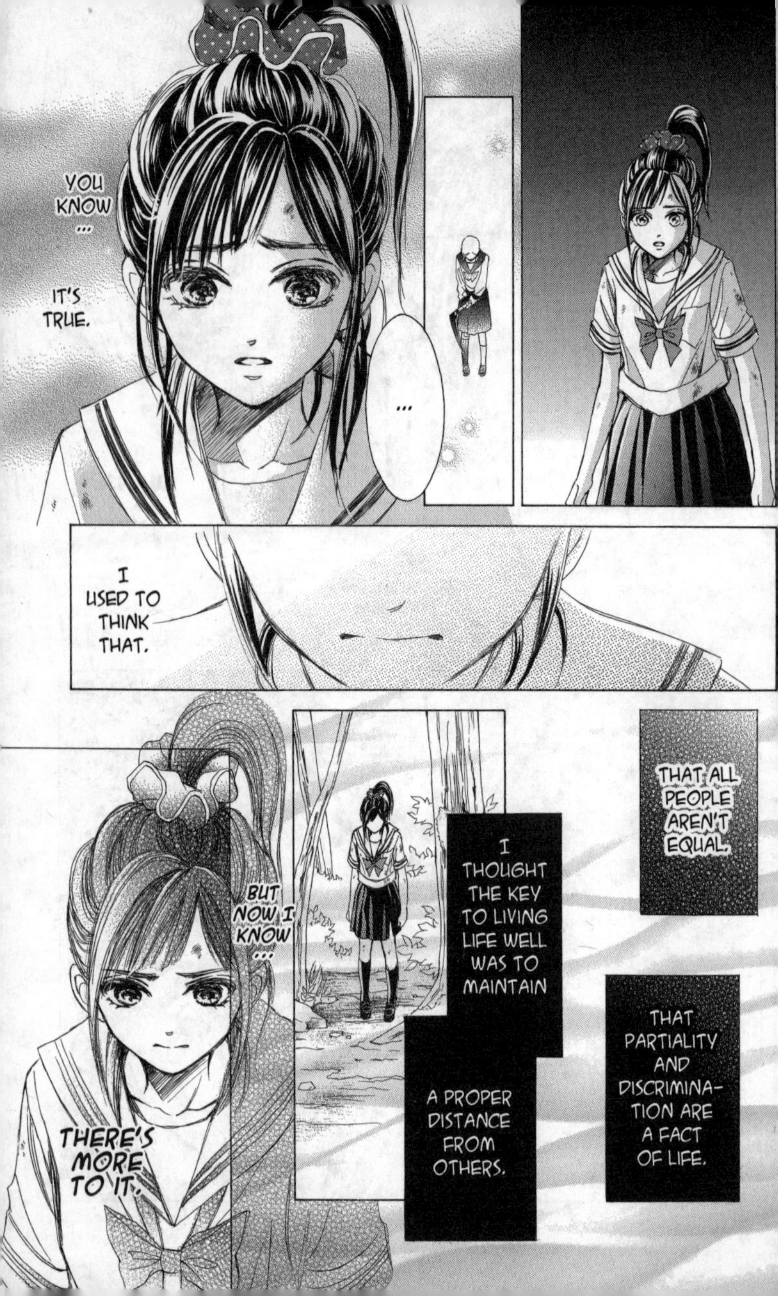
...
YOU KNOW ...
IT'S TRUE.
I USED TO THINK THAT.
THAT ALL PEOPLE AREN'T EQUAL.
THAT PARTIALITY AND DISCRIMINATION ARE A FACT OF LIFE.
I THOUGHT THE KEY TO LIVING LIFE WELL WAS TO MAINTAIN
A PROPER DISTANCE FROM OTHERS.
BUT NOW I KNOW ...
THERE'S MORE TO IT.

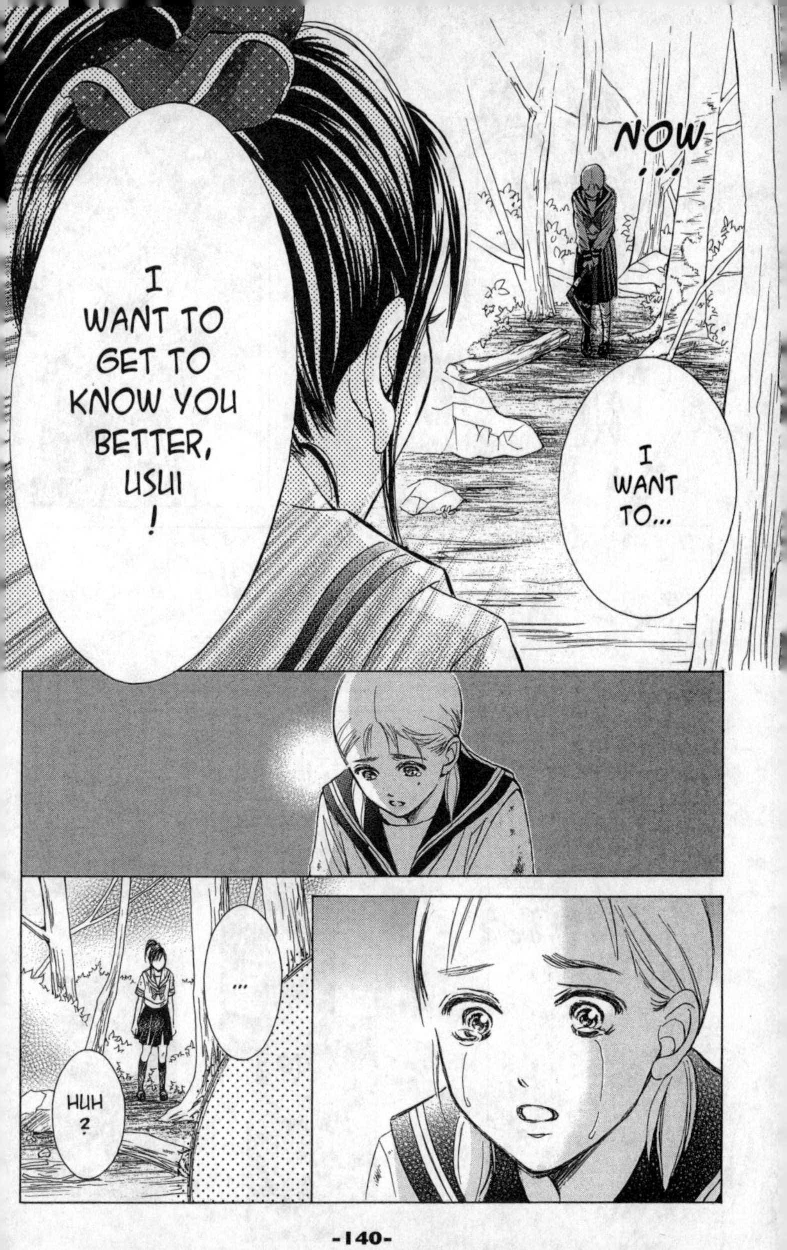
NOW...
I WANT TO...
I WANT TO GET TO KNOW YOU BETTER, USUI!
...
HUH?

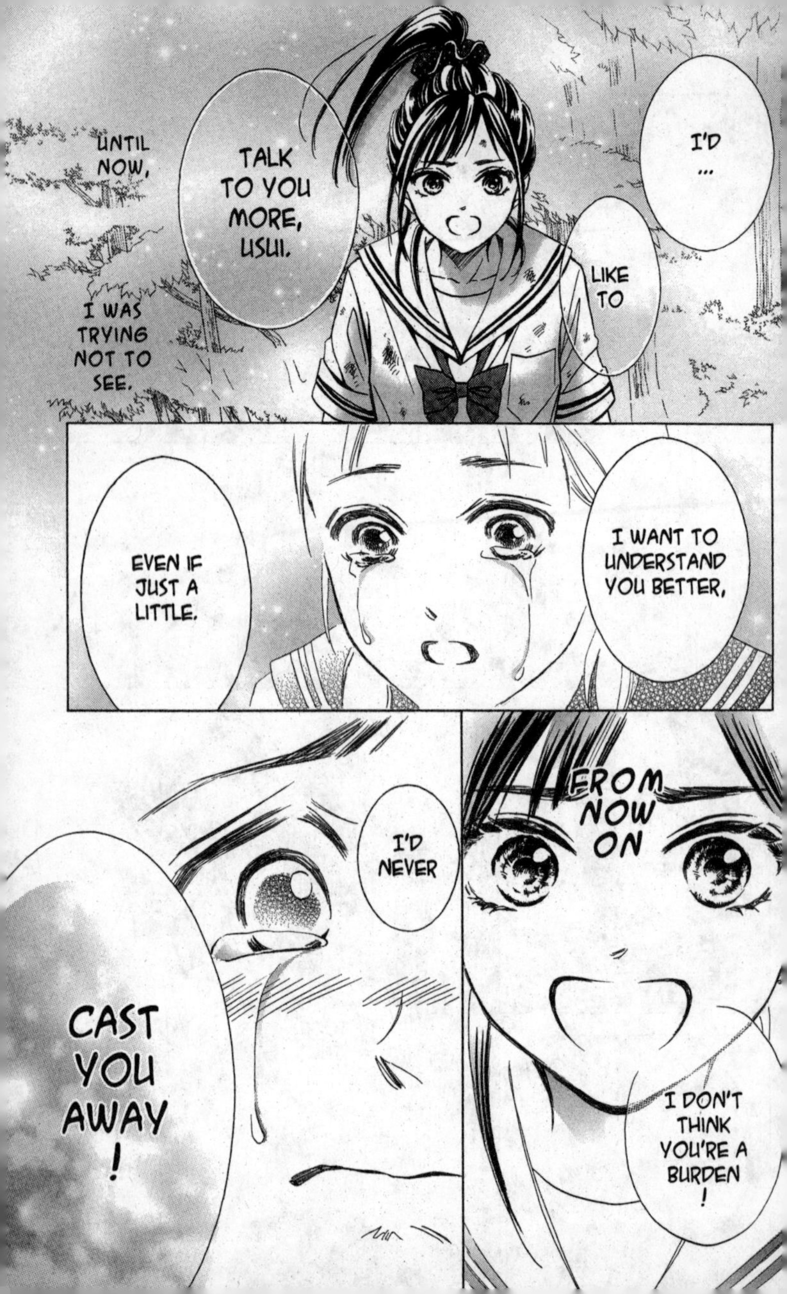
I'D ...
LIKE TO
TALK TO YOU MORE, USUI.
UNTIL NOW,
I WAS TRYING NOT TO SEE.
I WANT TO UNDERSTAND YOU BETTER,
EVEN IF JUST A LITTLE.
FROM NOW ON
I DON'T THINK YOU'RE A BURDEN!
I'D NEVER
CAST YOU AWAY!

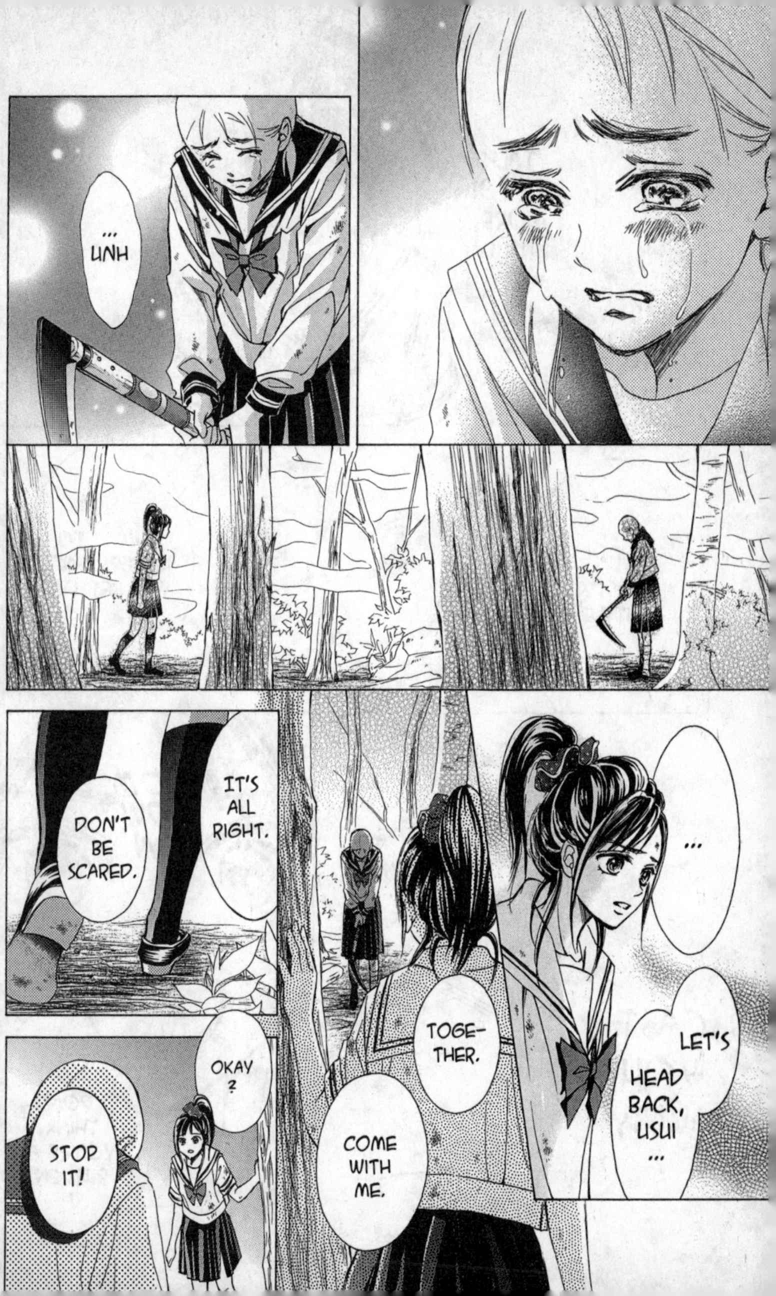
... UNH
...
LET'S HEAD BACK, USUI ...
TOGE-THER.
COME WITH ME.
IT'S ALL RIGHT.
DON'T BE SCARED.
OKAY?
STOP IT!

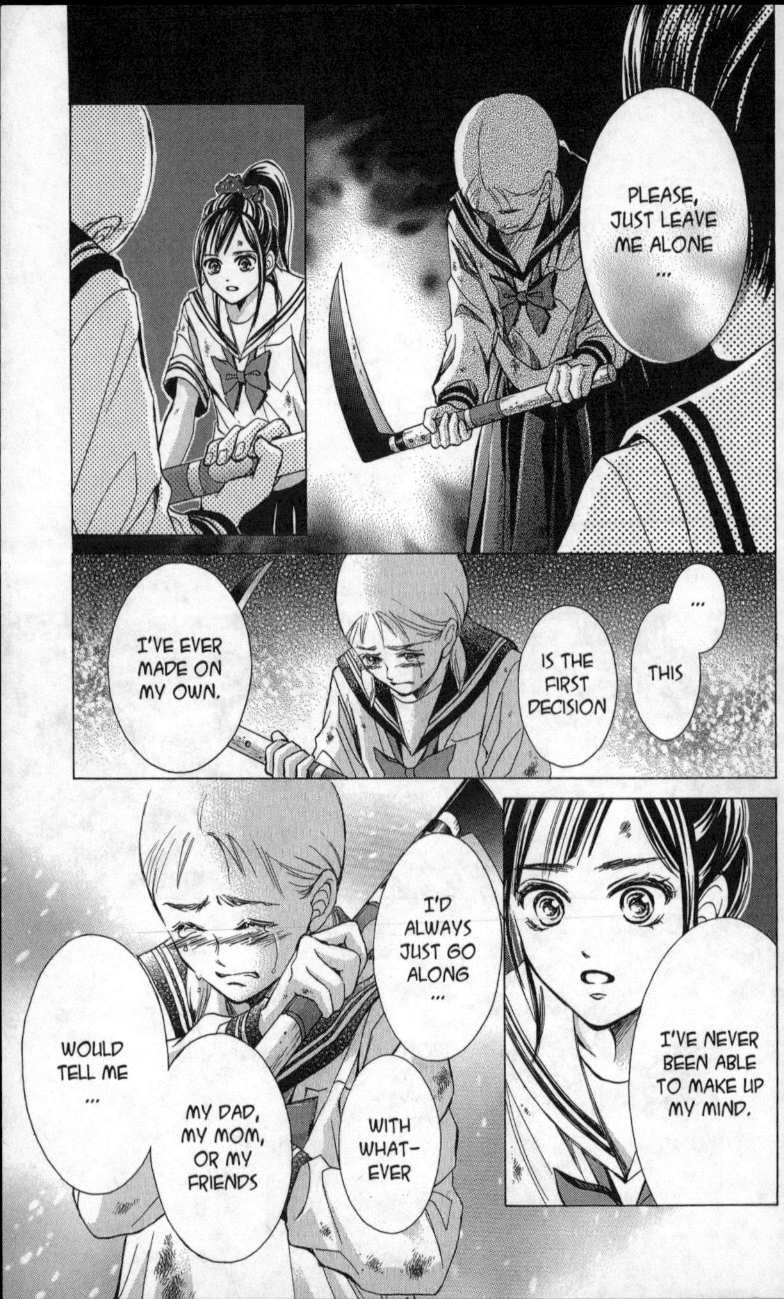
PLEASE, JUST LEAVE ME ALONE ...
...
THIS
IS THE FIRST DECISION
I'VE EVER MADE ON MY OWN.
I'VE NEVER BEEN ABLE TO MAKE UP MY MIND.
I'D ALWAYS JUST GO ALONG ...
WITH WHAT-EVER
MY DAD, MY MOM, OR MY FRIENDS
WOULD TELL ME ...

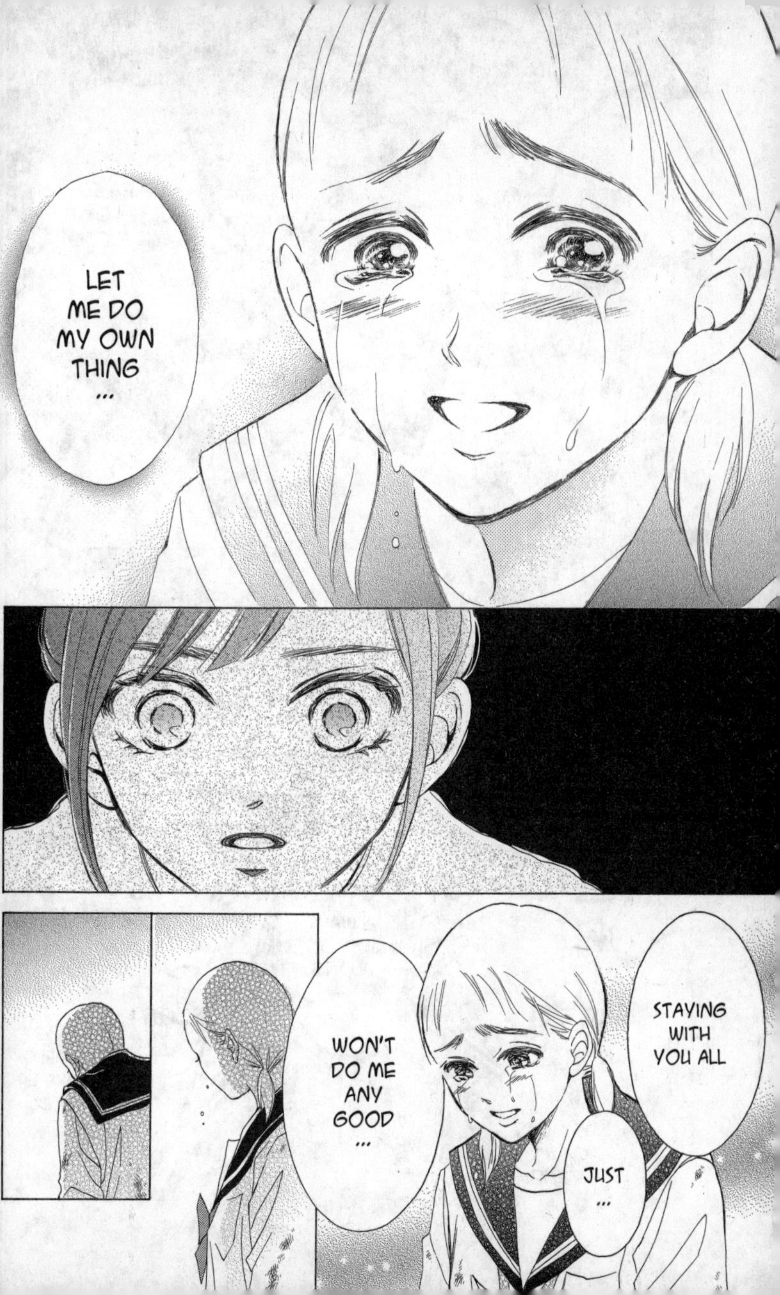
LET ME DO MY OWN THING ...
STAYING WITH YOU ALL
JUST ...
WON'T DO ME ANY GOOD ...

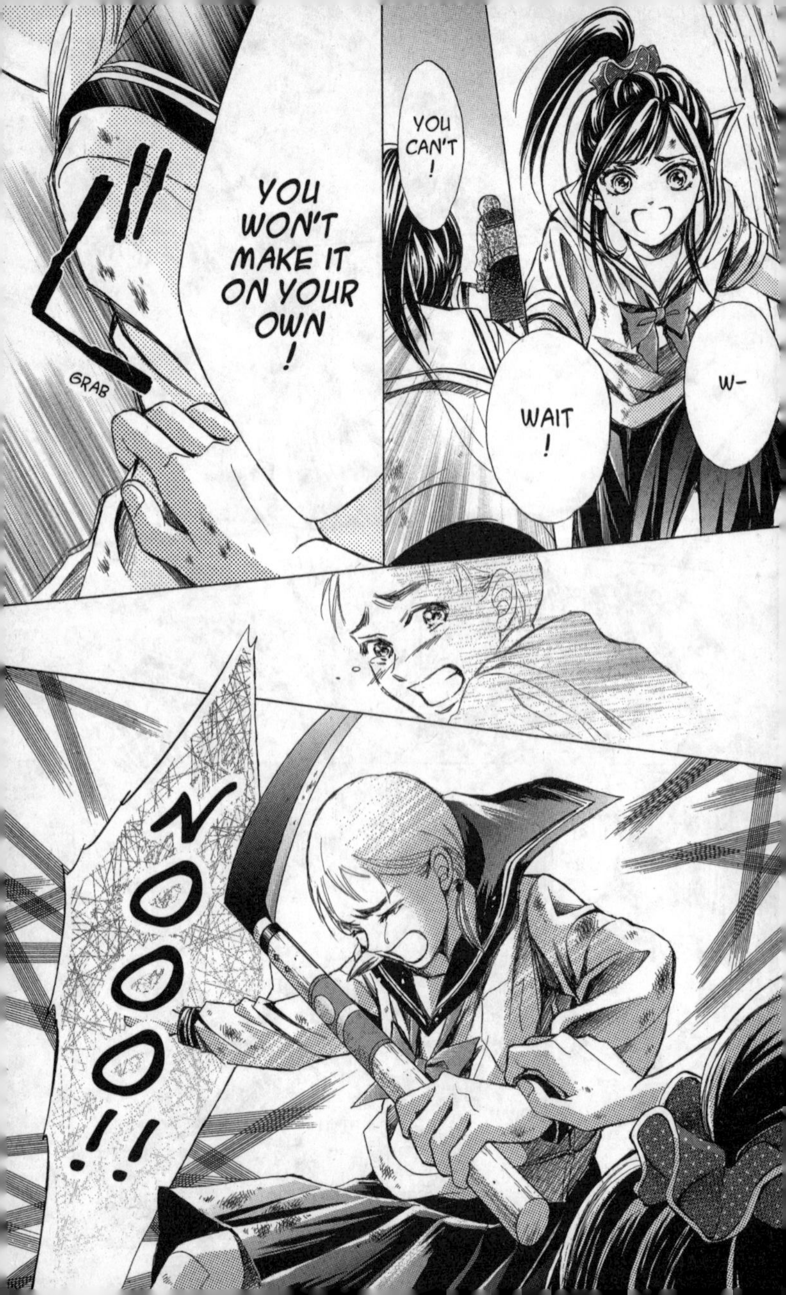
W-
WAIT!
YOU CAN'T!
YOU WON'T MAKE IT ON YOUR OWN!
GRAB
NOOOO!!

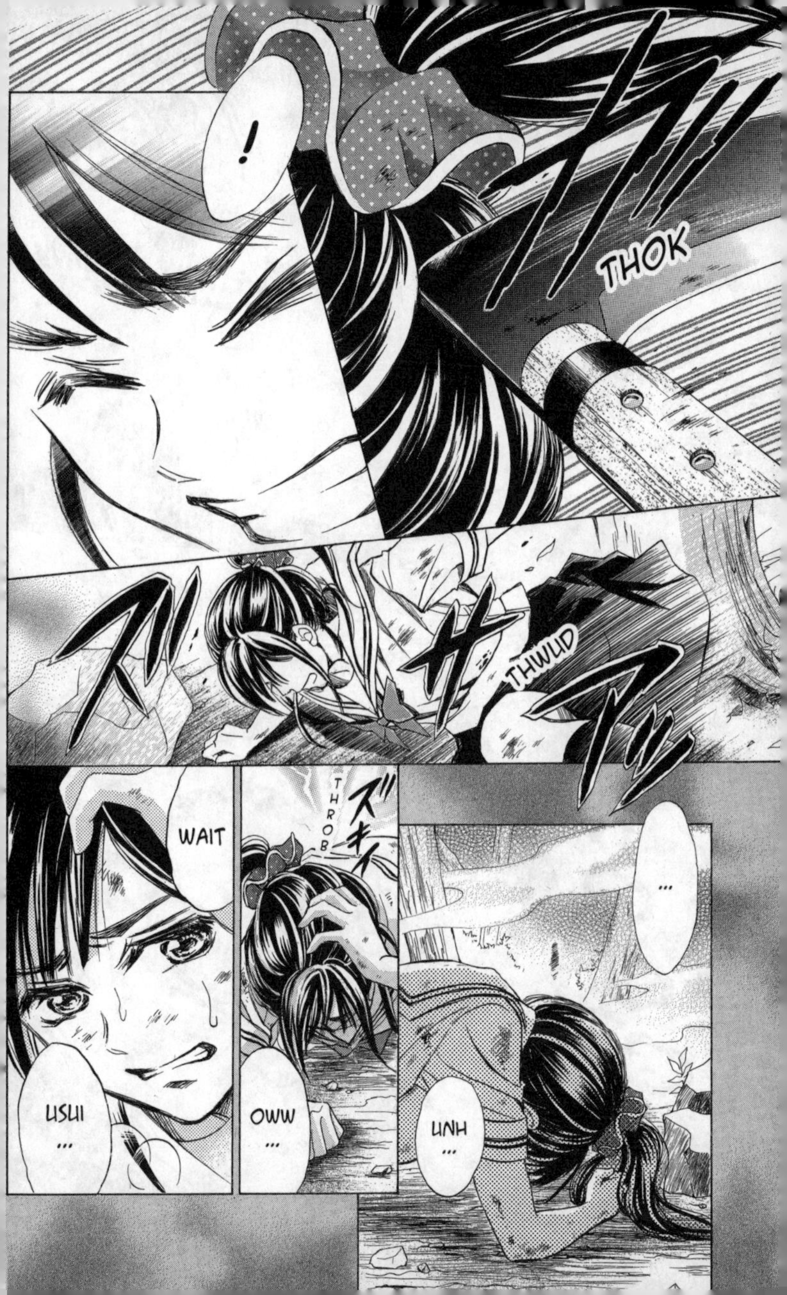
THOK
!
THWUD
...
UNH
...
THROB
OWW
...
WAIT
USUI
...

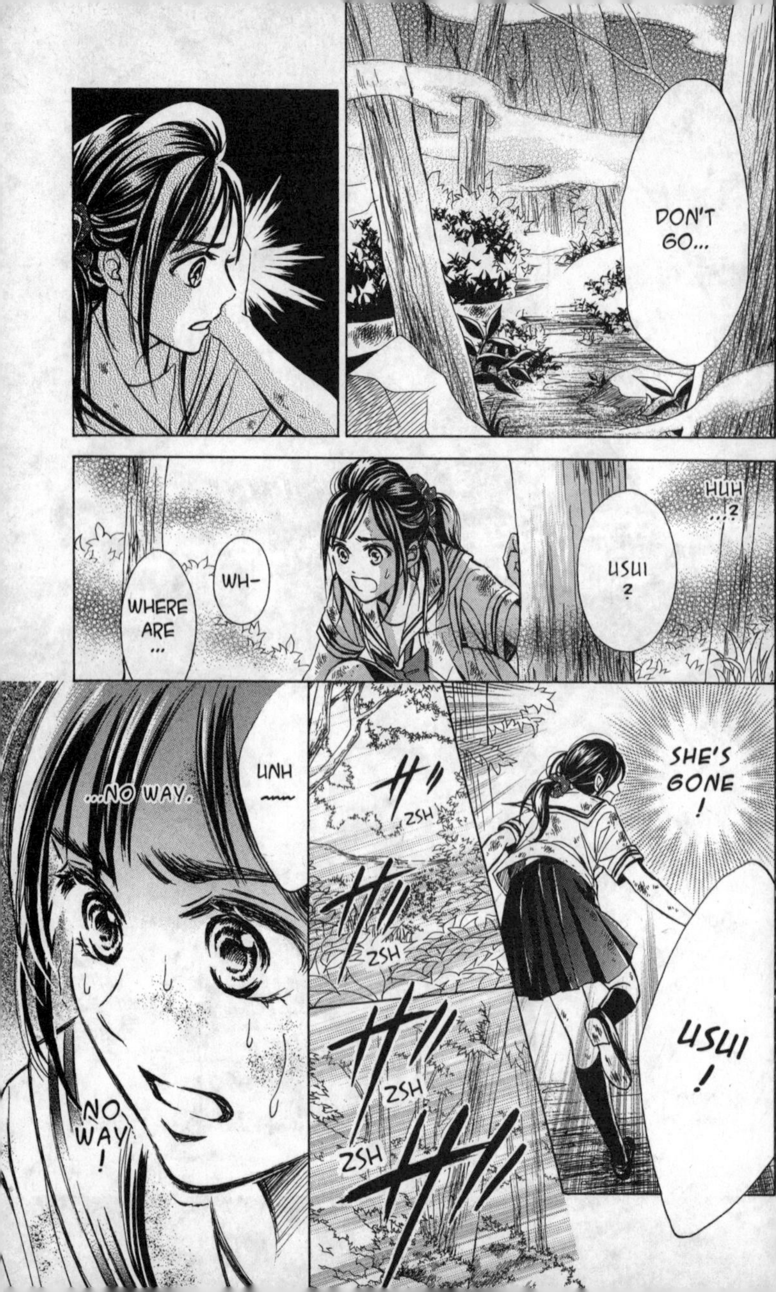
DON'T GO...
HUH...?
USUI?
WH-
WHERE ARE...
SHE'S GONE!
USUI!
ZSH
ZSH
ZSH
ZSH
UNH ~~
...NO WAY.
NO WAY!

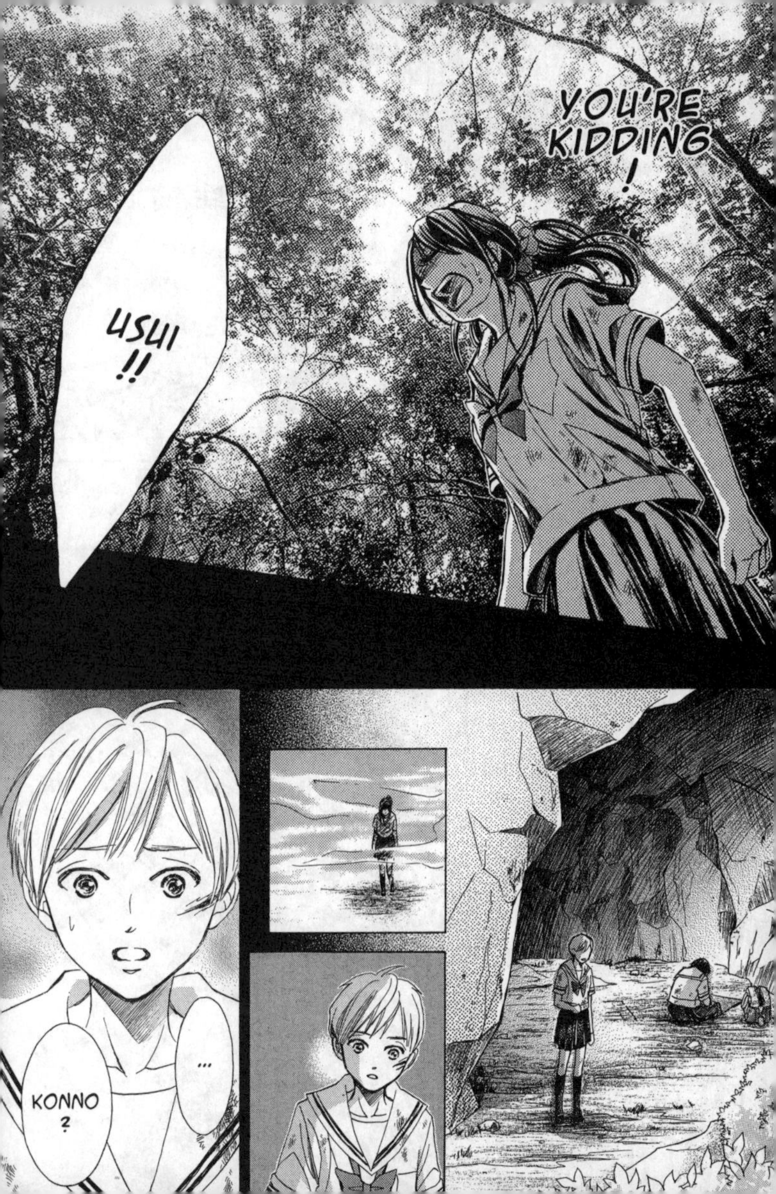
YOU'RE KIDDING!
USUI!!
...
KONNO?

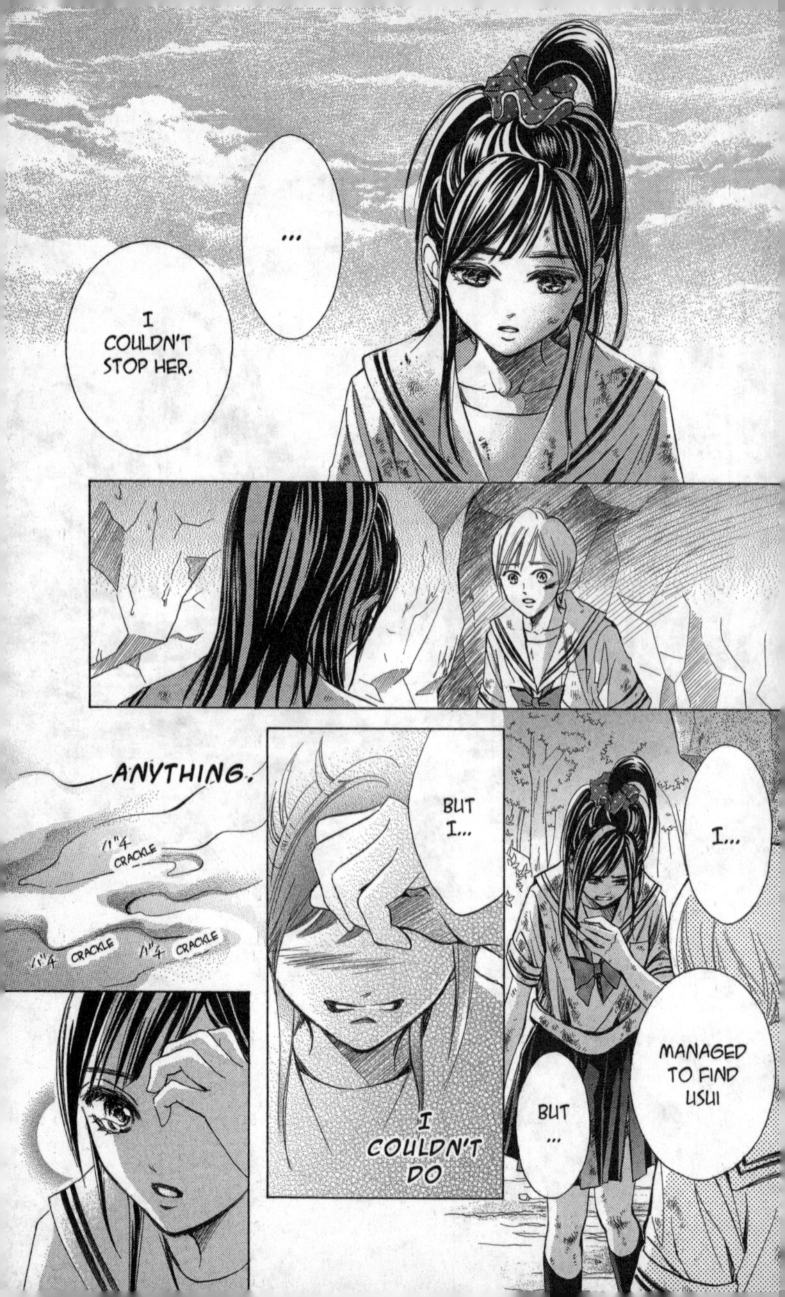
...
I COULDN'T STOP HER.
I...
MANAGED TO FIND USUI
BUT ...
BUT I...
I COULDN'T DO
ANYTHING.
CRACKLE
CRACKLE
CRACKLE

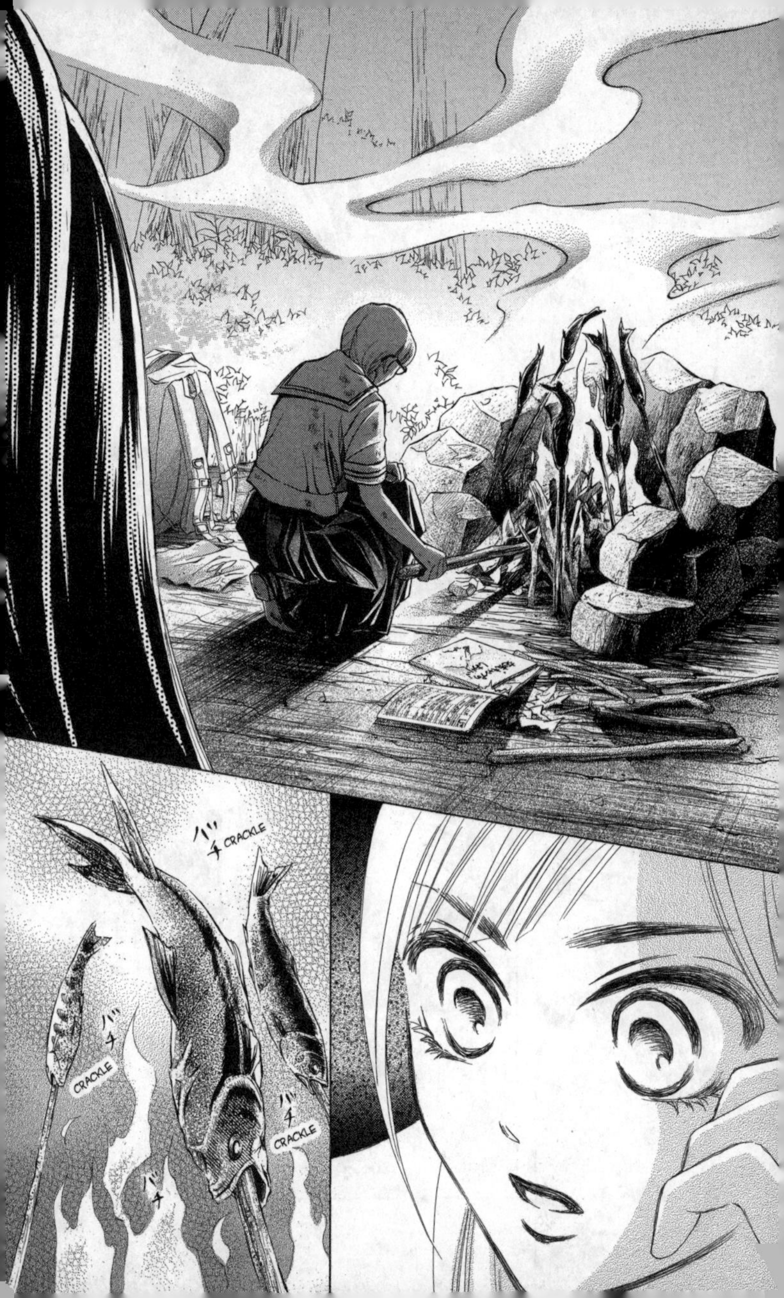
バチ CRACKLE
バチ CRACKLE
バチ CRACKLE
バチ

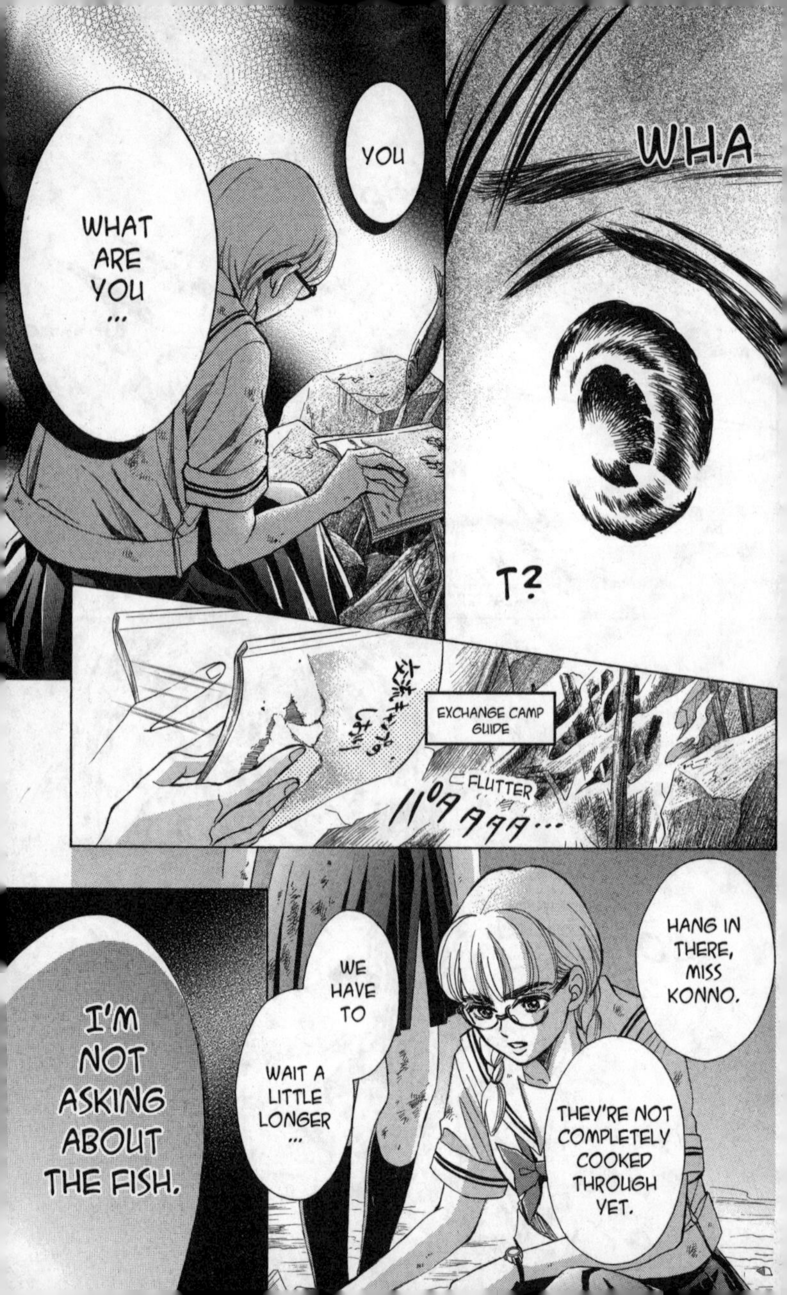

WHA
T?
YOU
WHAT ARE YOU ...
交流キャンプのしおり
EXCHANGE CAMP GUIDE
パタタタ…
FLUTTER
HANG IN THERE, MISS KONNO.
THEY'RE NOT COMPLETELY COOKED THROUGH YET.
WE HAVE TO
WAIT A LITTLE LONGER ...
I'M NOT ASKING ABOUT THE FISH.

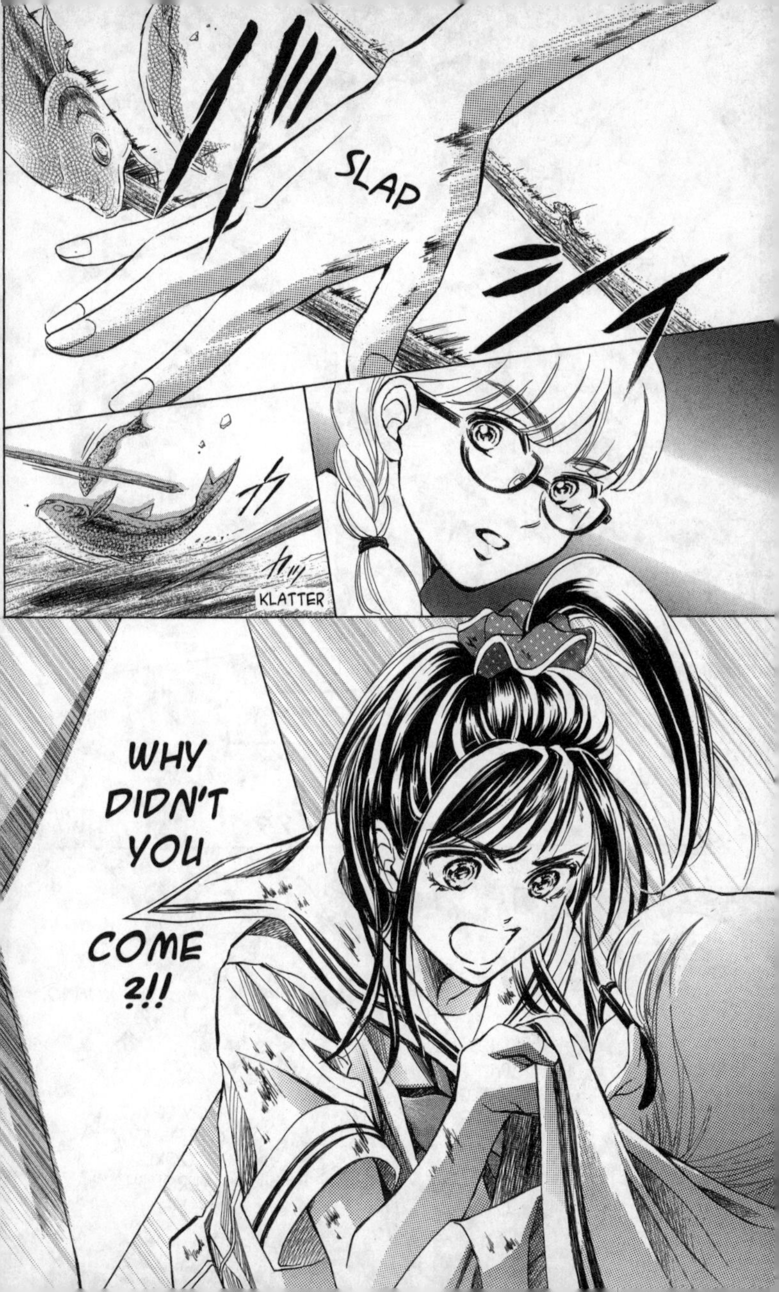
SLAP
KLATTER
WHY DIDN'T YOU COME ?!!

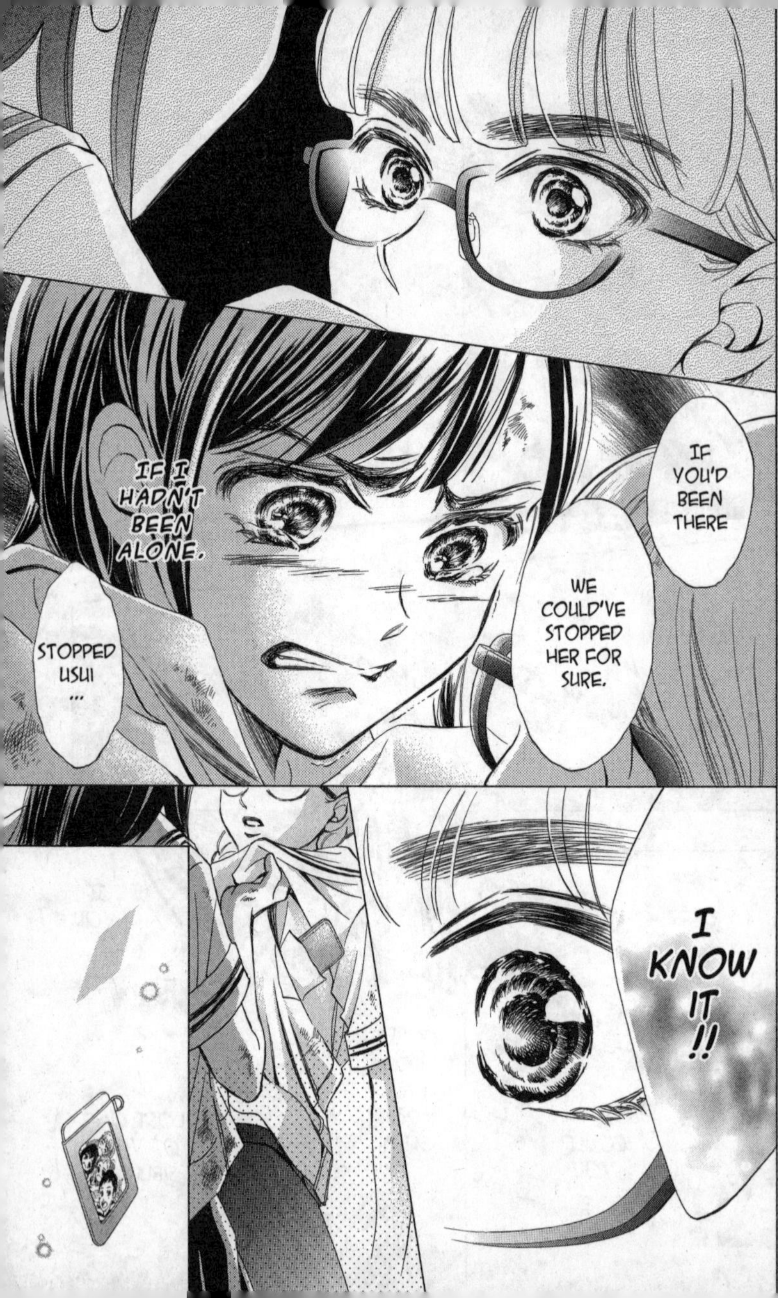
IF YOU'D BEEN THERE
WE COULD'VE STOPPED HER FOR SURE.
IF I HADN'T BEEN ALONE.
STOPPED USUI ...
I KNOW IT!!

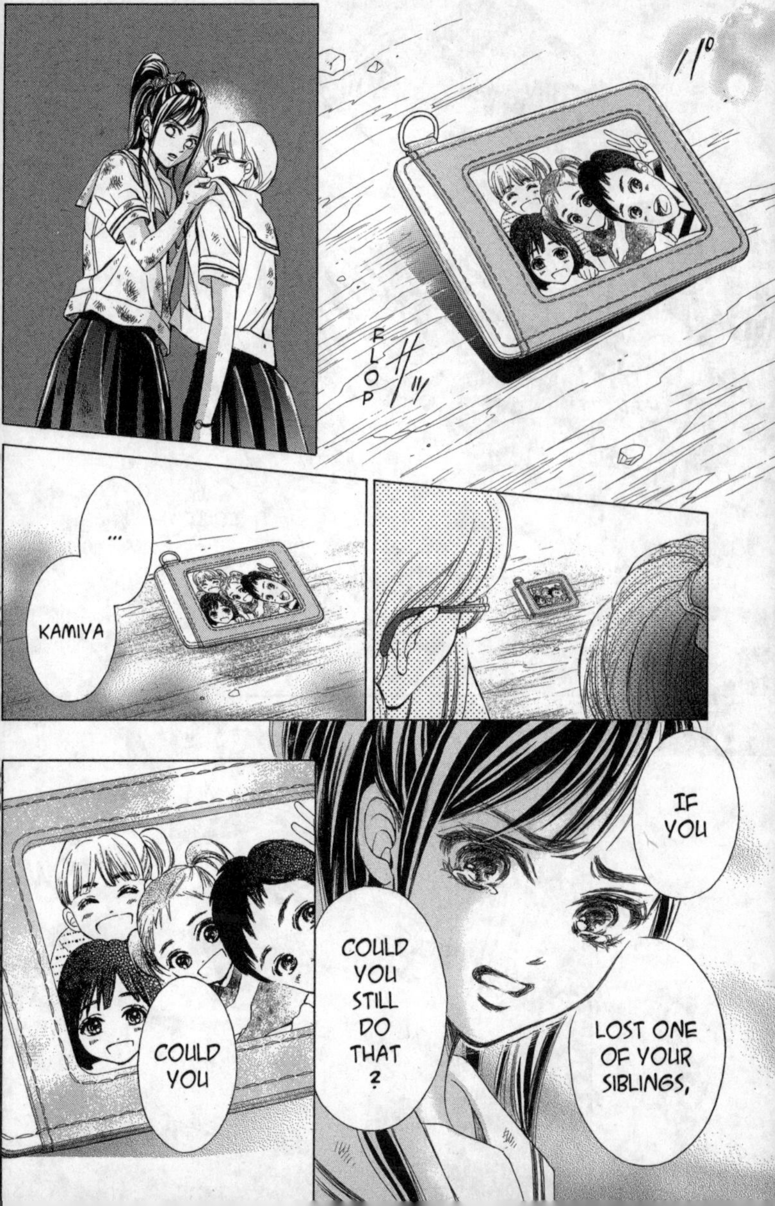
FLOP
...
KAMIYA
IF YOU
LOST ONE OF YOUR SIBLINGS,
COULD YOU STILL DO THAT?
COULD YOU

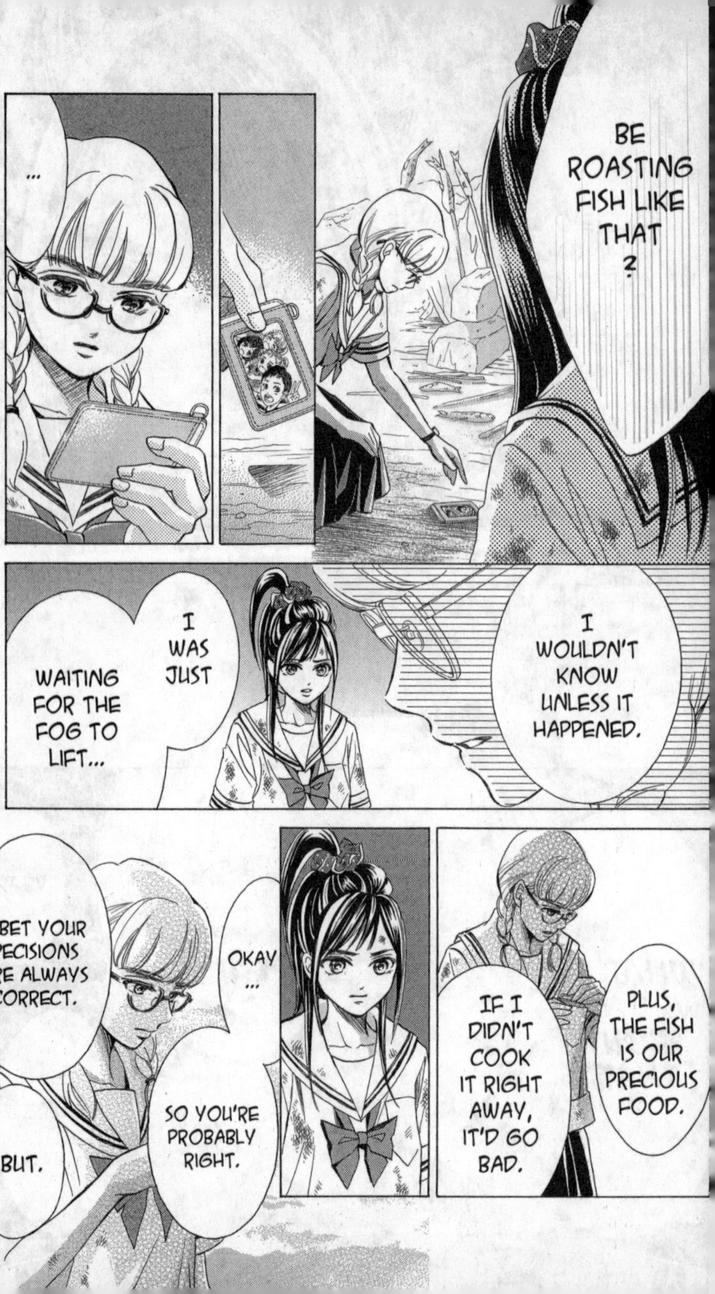
BE ROASTING FISH LIKE THAT?
...
I WOULDN'T KNOW UNLESS IT HAPPENED.
I WAS JUST
WAITING FOR THE FOG TO LIFT...
PLUS, THE FISH IS OUR PRECIOUS FOOD.
IF I DIDN'T COOK IT RIGHT AWAY, IT'D GO BAD.
OKAY...
I BET YOUR DECISIONS ARE ALWAYS CORRECT.
SO YOU'RE PROBABLY RIGHT.
BUT.

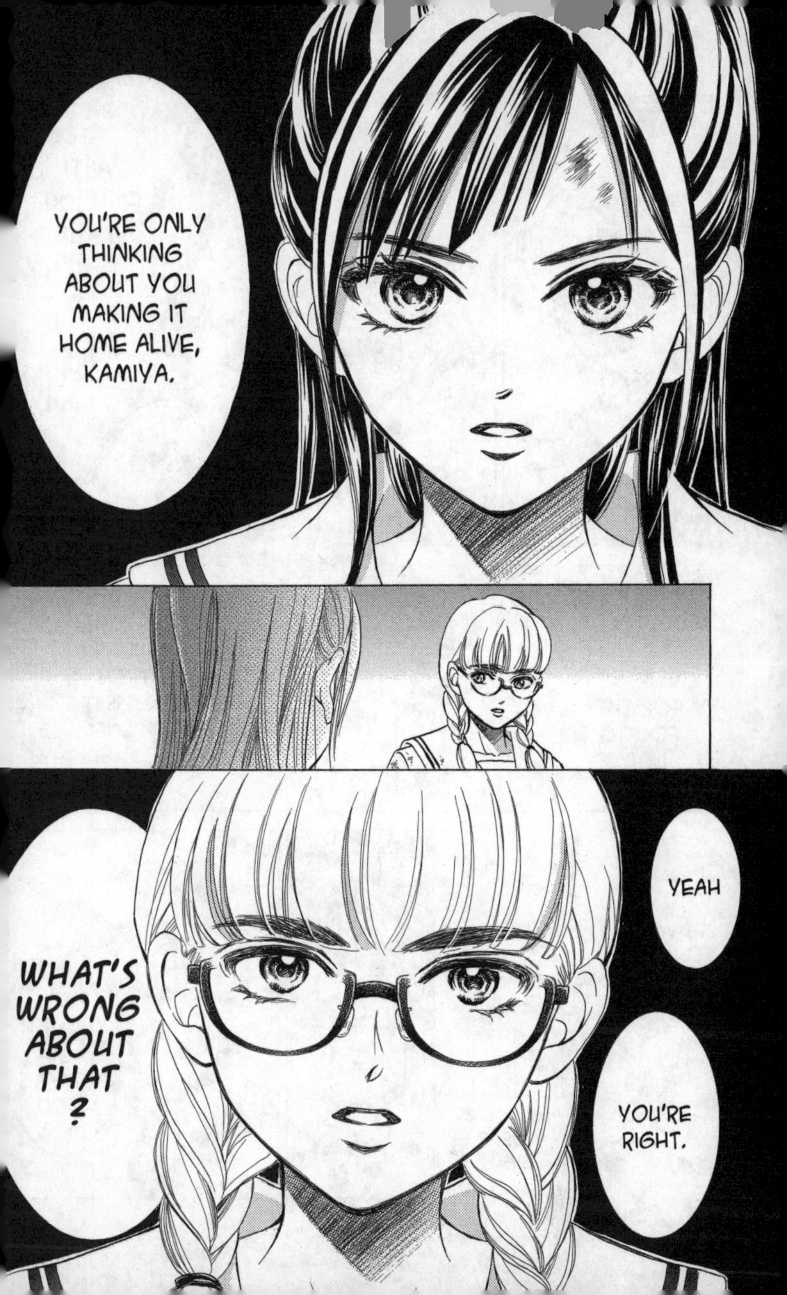
YOU'RE ONLY THINKING ABOUT YOU MAKING IT HOME ALIVE, KAMIYA.
YEAH
YOU'RE RIGHT.
WHAT'S WRONG ABOUT THAT?

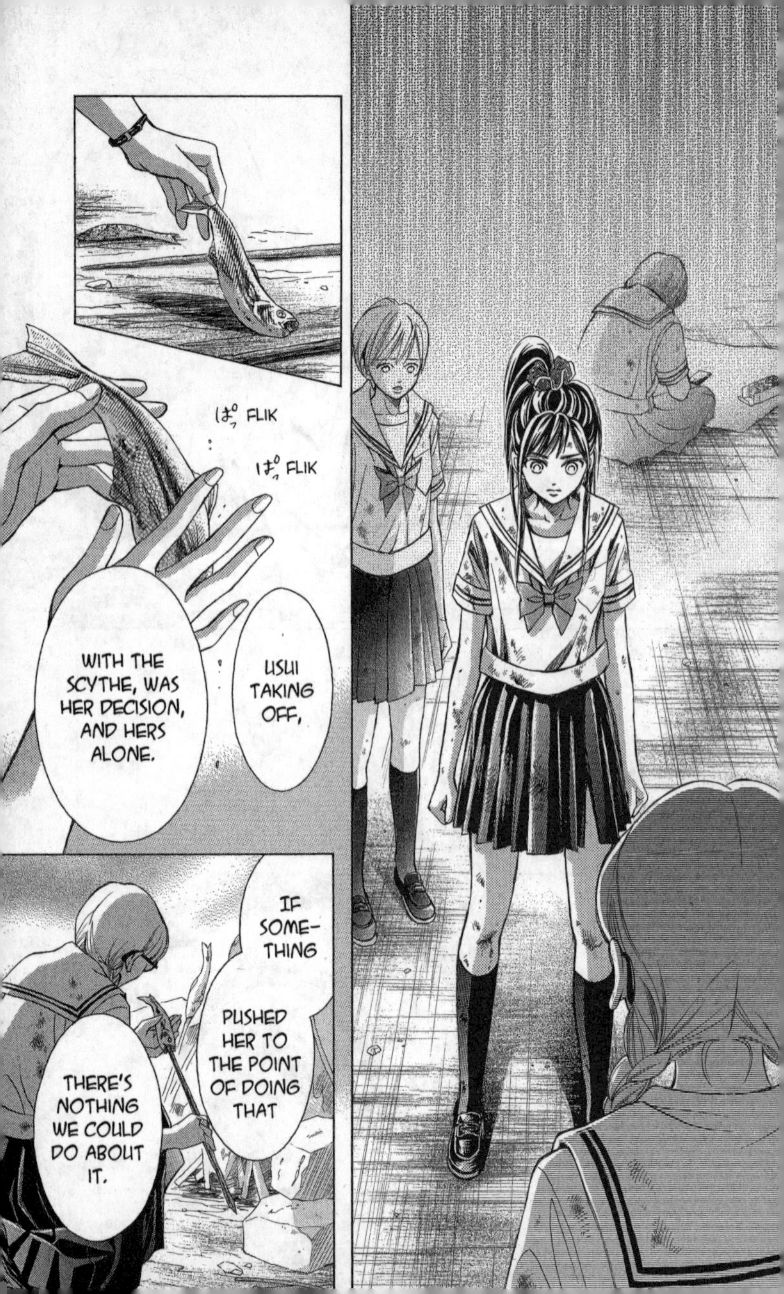
ぱっ FLIK
ぱっ FLIK
USUI TAKING OFF,
WITH THE SCYTHE, WAS HER DECISION, AND HERS ALONE.
IF SOME-THING
PUSHED HER TO THE POINT OF DOING THAT
THERE'S NOTHING WE COULD DO ABOUT IT.

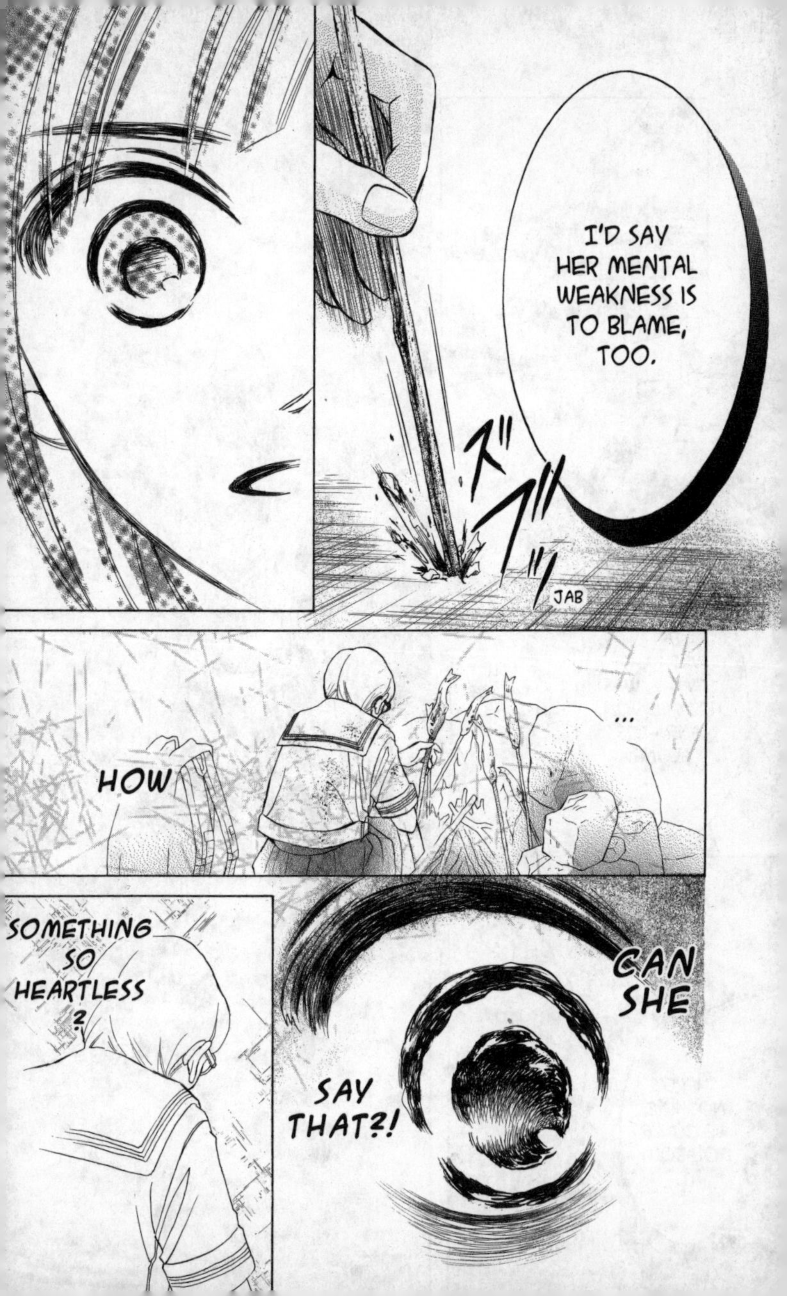
I'D SAY HER MENTAL WEAKNESS IS TO BLAME, TOO.
ズブッ
JAB
...
HOW
CAN SHE
SAY THAT?!
SOMETHING SO HEARTLESS ?

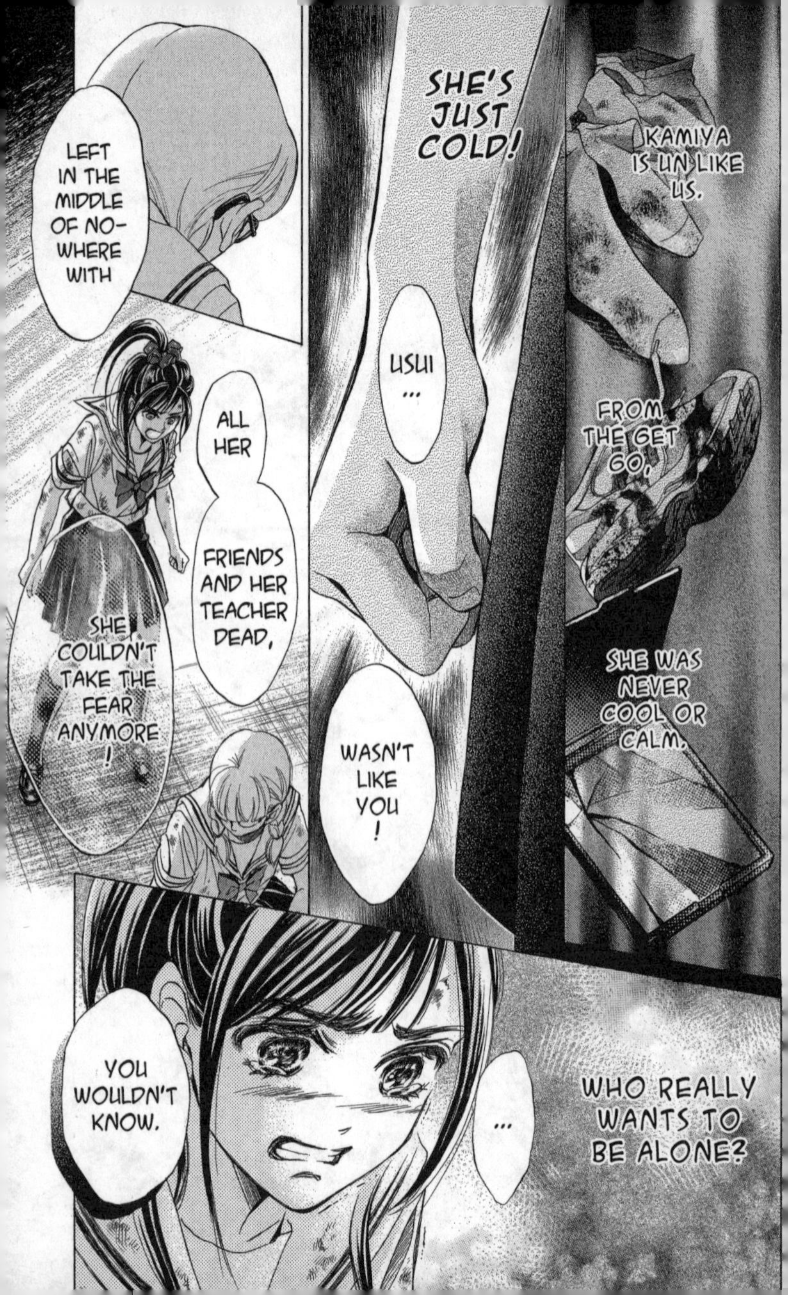
KAMIYA IS UN LIKE US.
FROM THE GET GO,
SHE WAS NEVER COOL OR CALM.
SHE'S JUST COLD!
USUI ...
WASN'T LIKE YOU!
LEFT IN THE MIDDLE OF NO-WHERE WITH
ALL HER FRIENDS AND HER TEACHER DEAD,
SHE COULDN'T TAKE THE FEAR ANYMORE!
WHO REALLY WANTS TO BE ALONE?
...
YOU WOULDN'T KNOW.

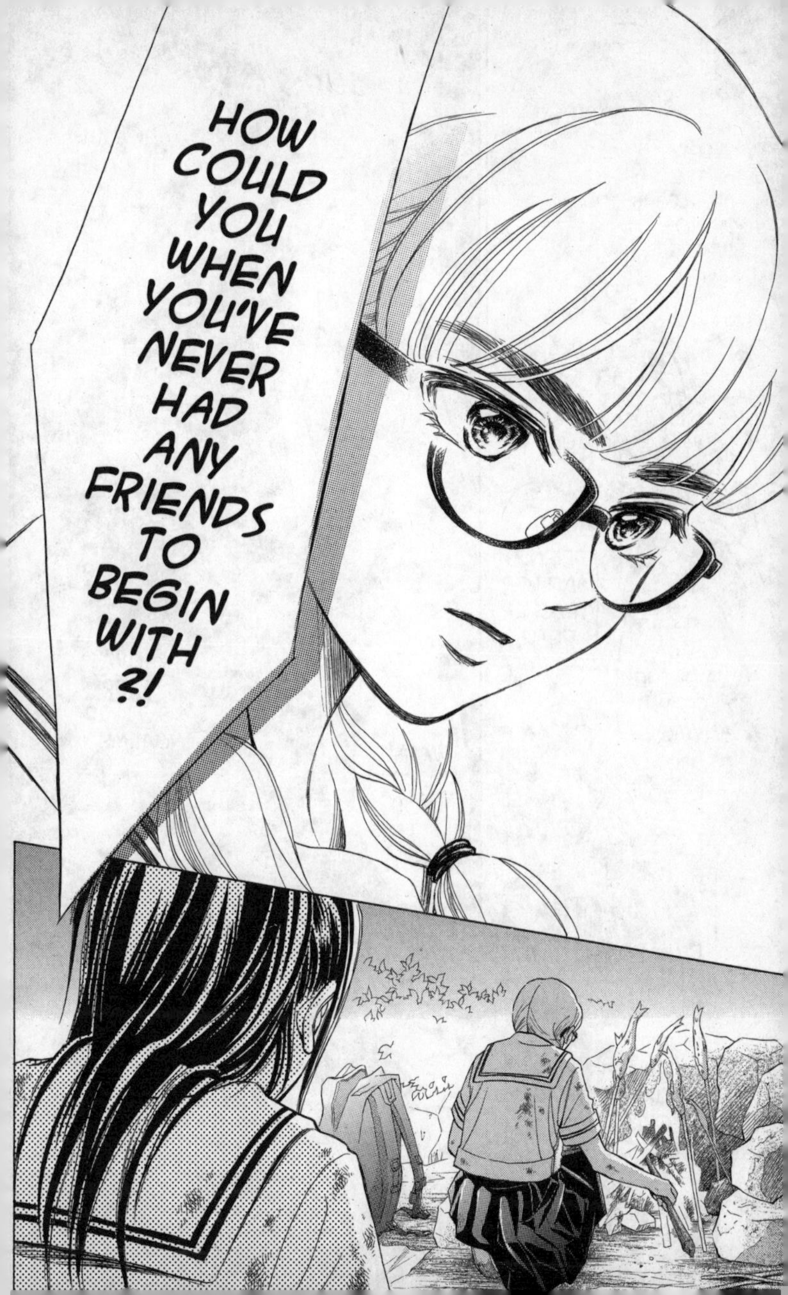
HOW COULD YOU WHEN YOU'VE NEVER HAD ANY FRIENDS TO BEGIN WITH?!

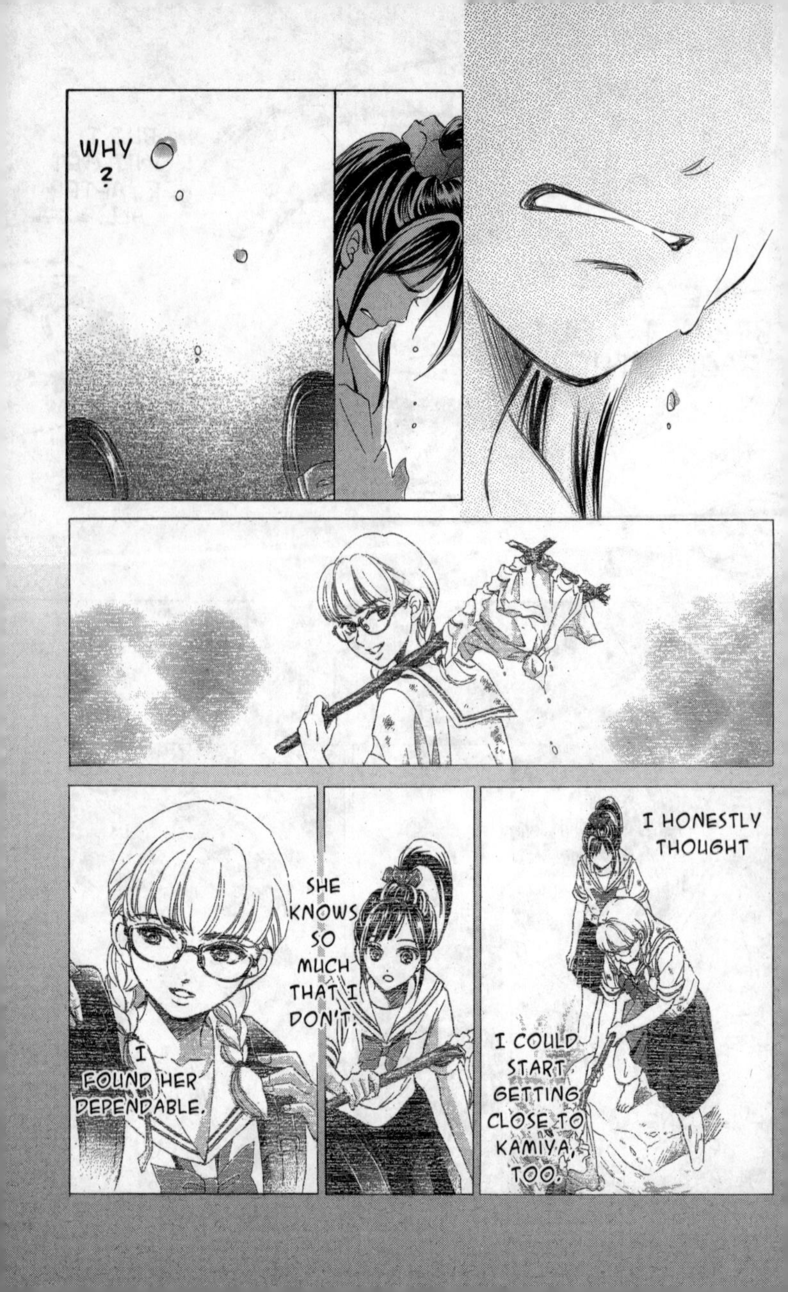
WHY?
I HONESTLY THOUGHT
I COULD START GETTING CLOSE TO KAMIYA, TOO.
SHE KNOWS SO MUCH THAT I DON'T.
I FOUND HER DEPENDABLE.

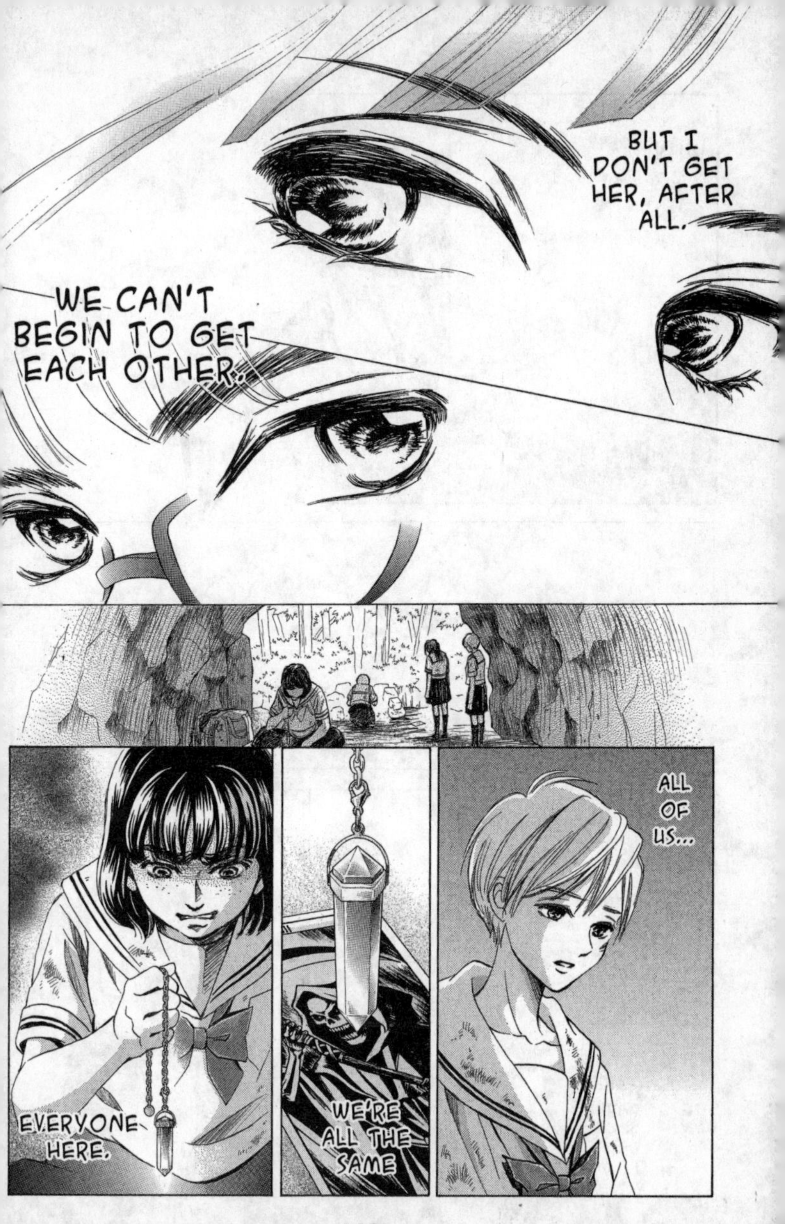
BUT I DON'T GET HER, AFTER ALL.
WE CAN'T BEGIN TO GET EACH OTHER.
ALL OF US...
WE'RE ALL THE SAME
EVERYONE HERE.

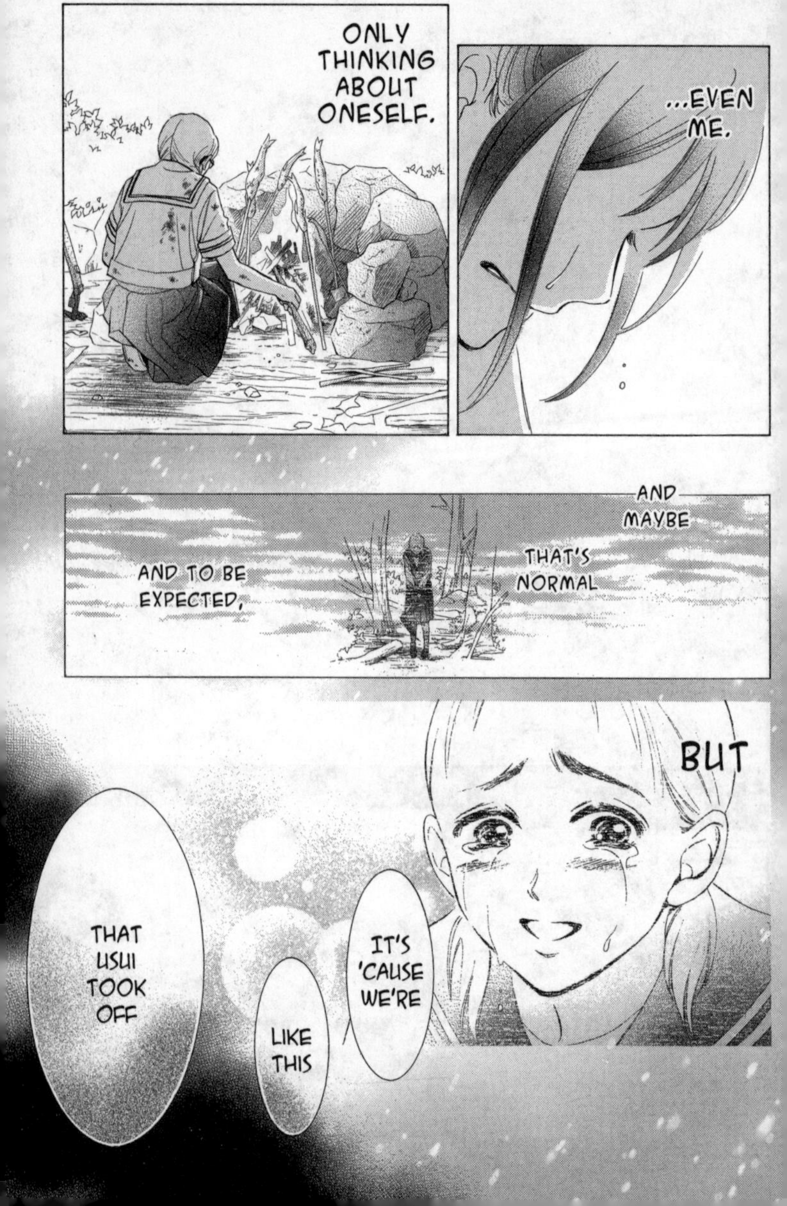
...EVEN ME.
ONLY THINKING ABOUT ONESELF.
AND MAYBE
THAT'S NORMAL
AND TO BE EXPECTED,
BUT
IT'S 'CAUSE WE'RE
LIKE THIS
THAT USUI TOOK OFF

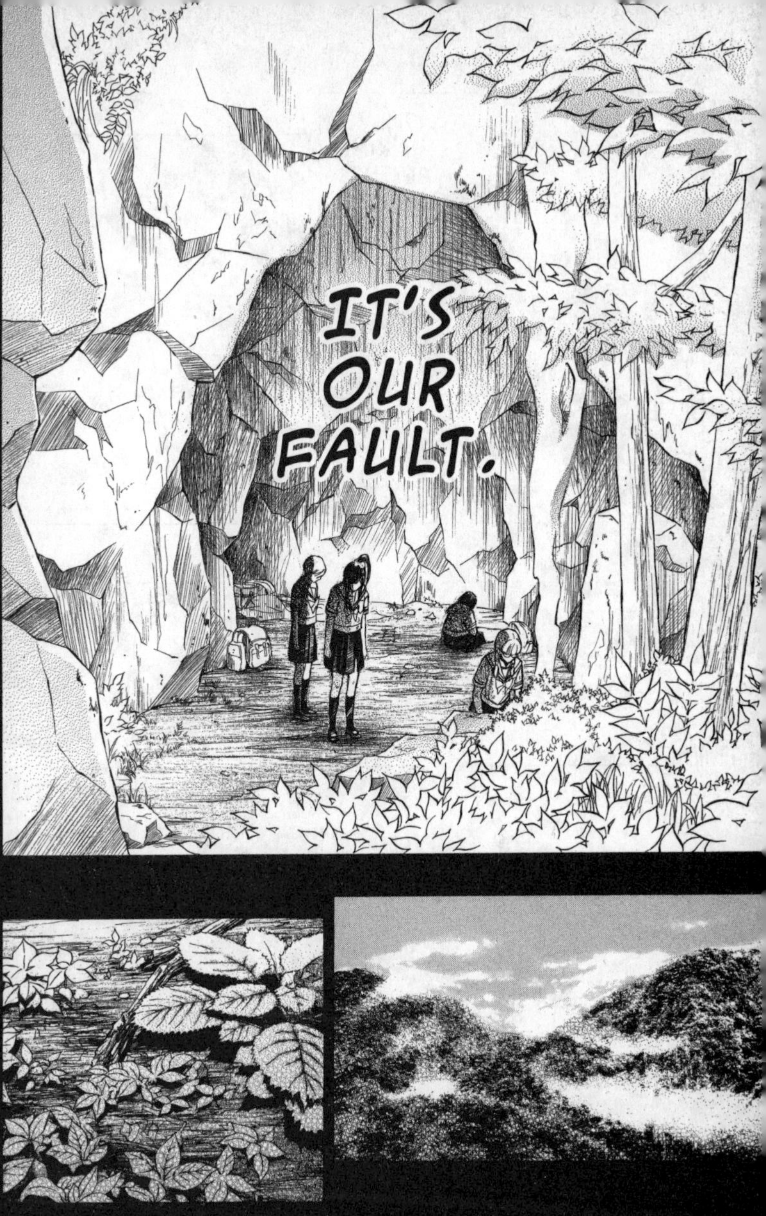
IT'S OUR FAULT.

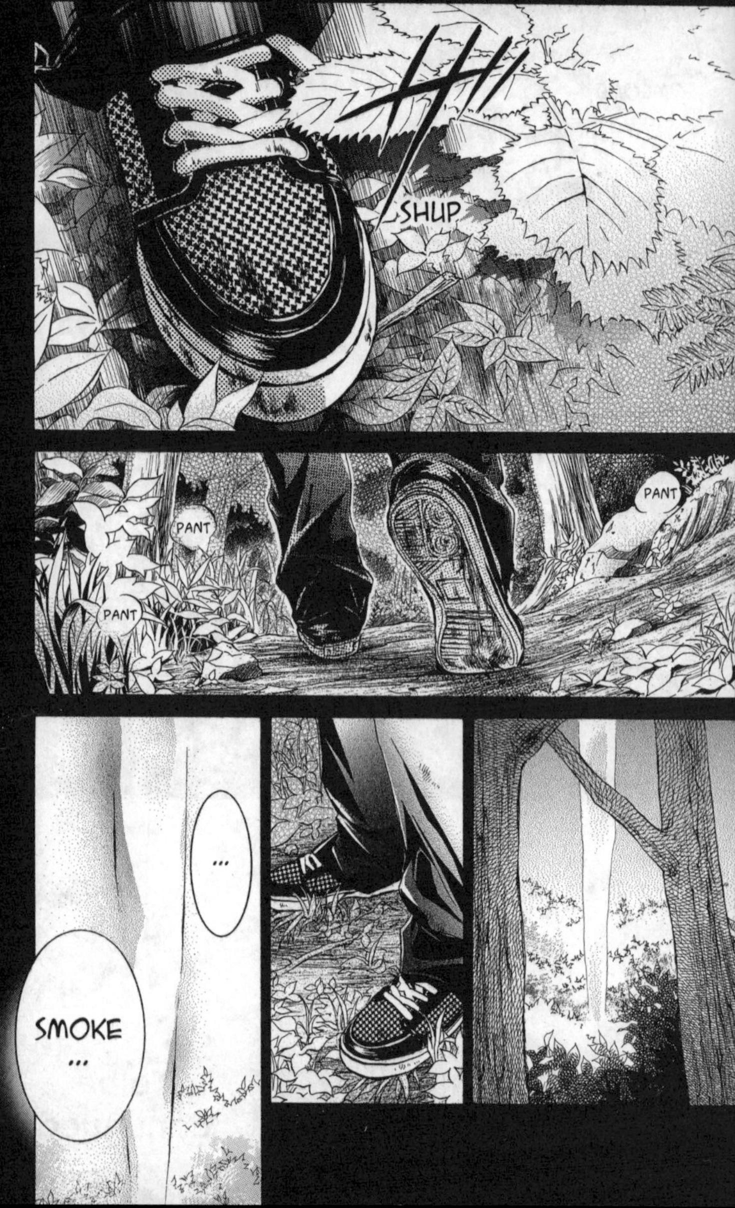
SHUP
PANT
PANT
PANT
...
SMOKE ...

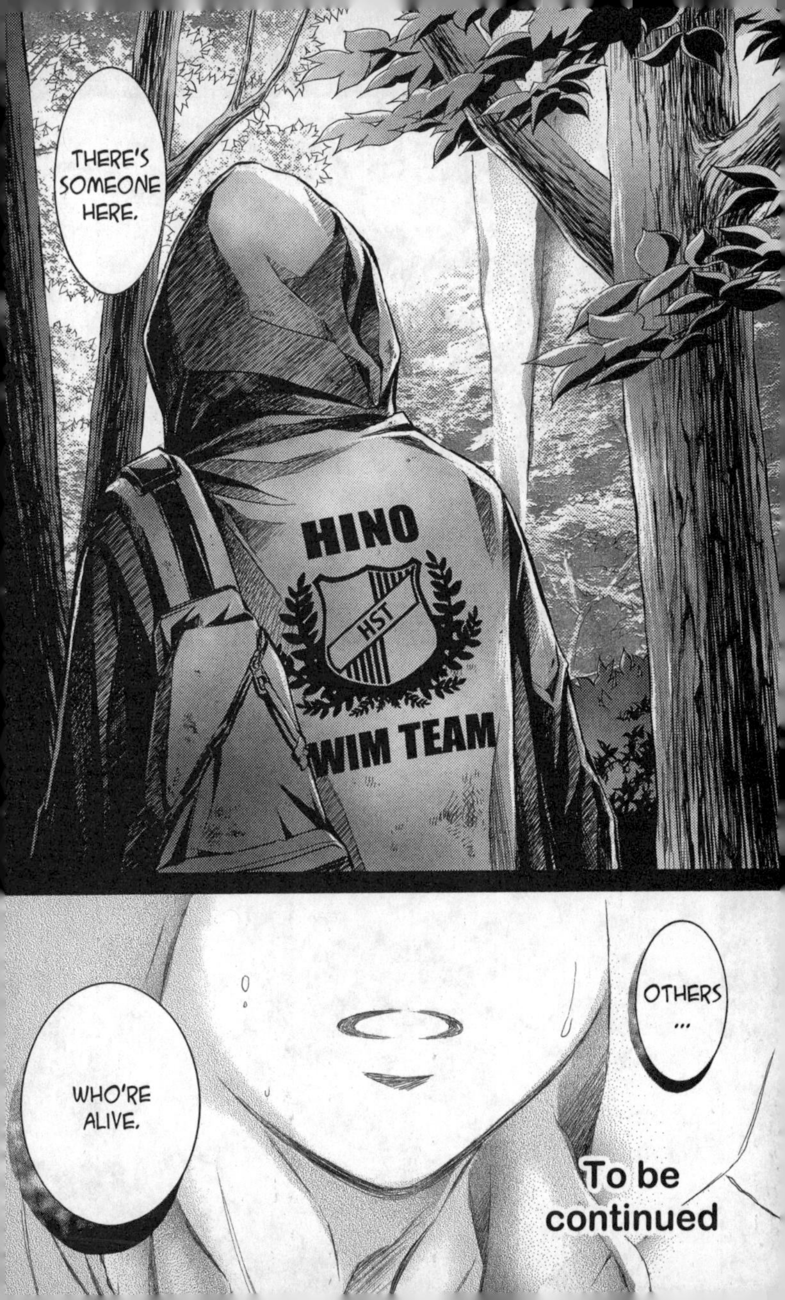
THERE'S SOMEONE HERE.
HINO
HST
WIM TEAM
OTHERS ...
WHO'RE ALIVE.
To be continued

L
I
M
I
T

MY WORKROOM.

THE LIMIT ARCHIVES

~ Things that are helpful when I draw ~

School Sailor suit & **Loafers**

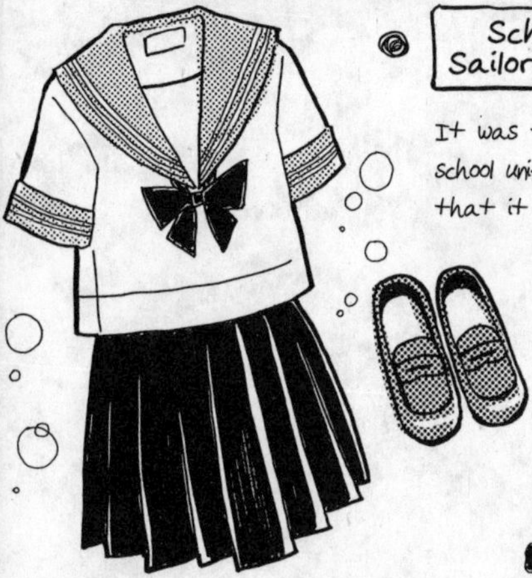

It was the first time I'd ever purchased a school uniform, but it's such a nice visual aid that it really helps!

I occasionally have an assistant put it on and strike a pose, too.

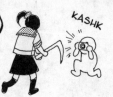

KASHK

A wooden sickle

Apparently used in rites such as groundbreaking ceremonies, even the blade is made of wood so it's safe to touch. Very handy.

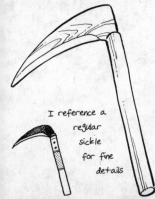

I reference a regular sickle for fine details

Onigiri (Rice balls)

It was very difficult to split them neatly in half.

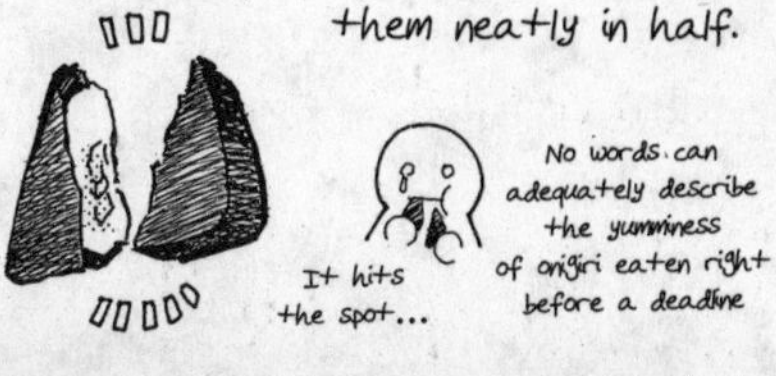

It hits the spot...

No words can adequately describe the yumminess of onigiri eaten right before a deadline

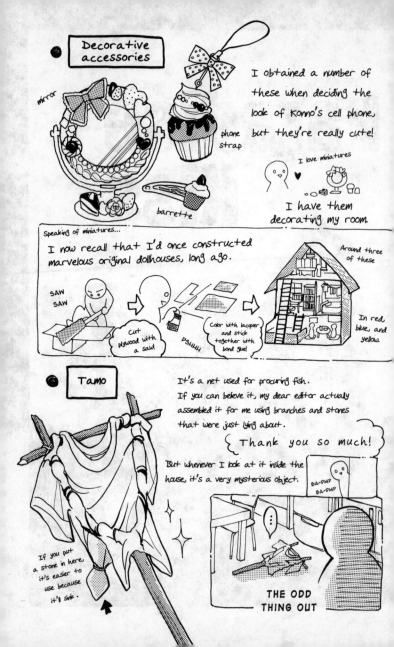

Decorative accessories

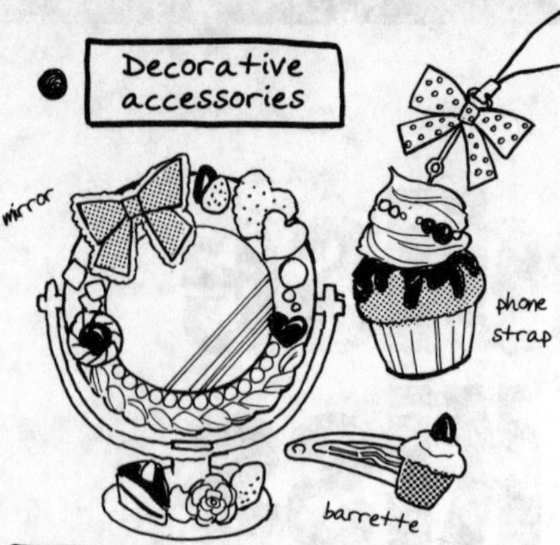
mirror
phone strap
barrette

I obtained a number of these when deciding the look of Konno's cell phone, but they're really cute!

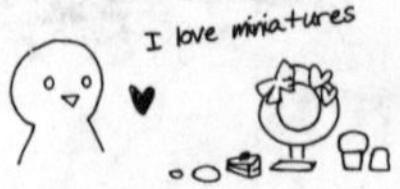
I love miniatures

I have them decorating my room.

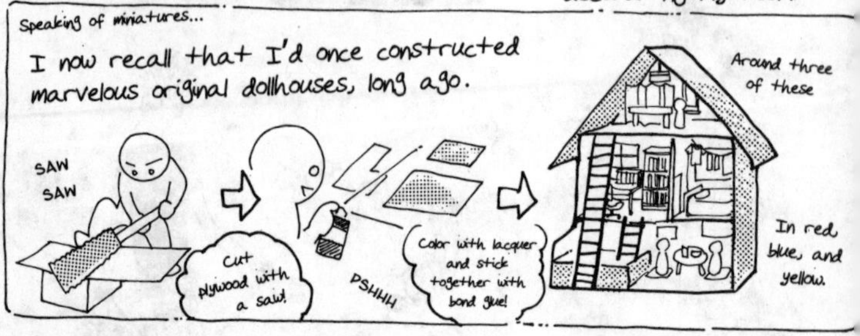
Speaking of miniatures...
I now recall that I'd once constructed marvelous original dollhouses, long ago.
Around three of these
In red, blue, and yellow.
SAW SAW
Cut plywood with a saw!
PSHHH
Color with lacquer and stick together with bond glue!

Tamo

It's a net used for procuring fish.
If you can believe it, my dear editor actually assembled it for me using branches and stones that were just lying about.

Thank you so much!

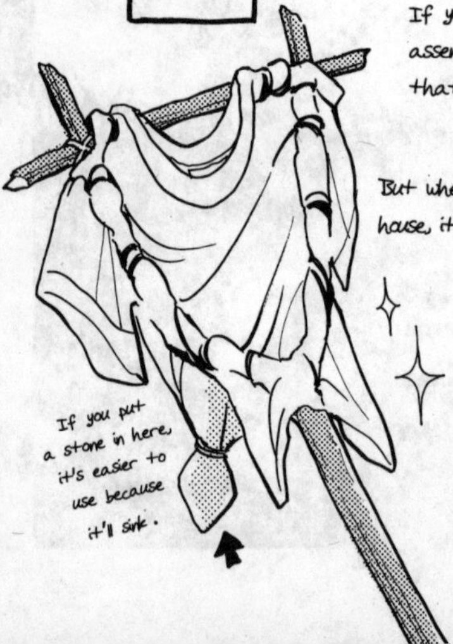
If you put a stone in here, it's easier to use because it'll sink.

But whenever I look at it inside the house, it's a very mysterious object.

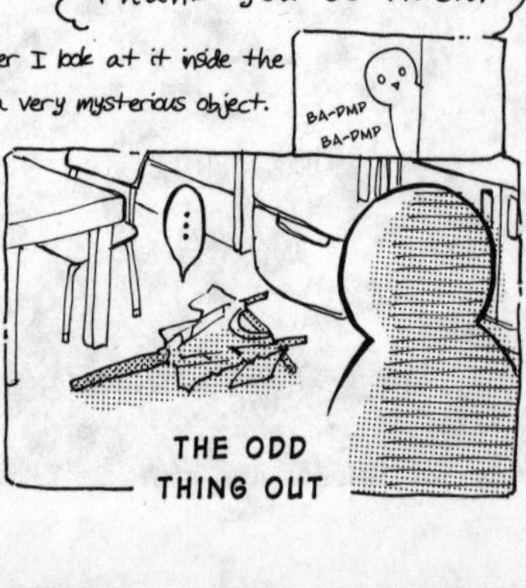
BA-DMP BA-DMP
...
THE ODD THING OUT

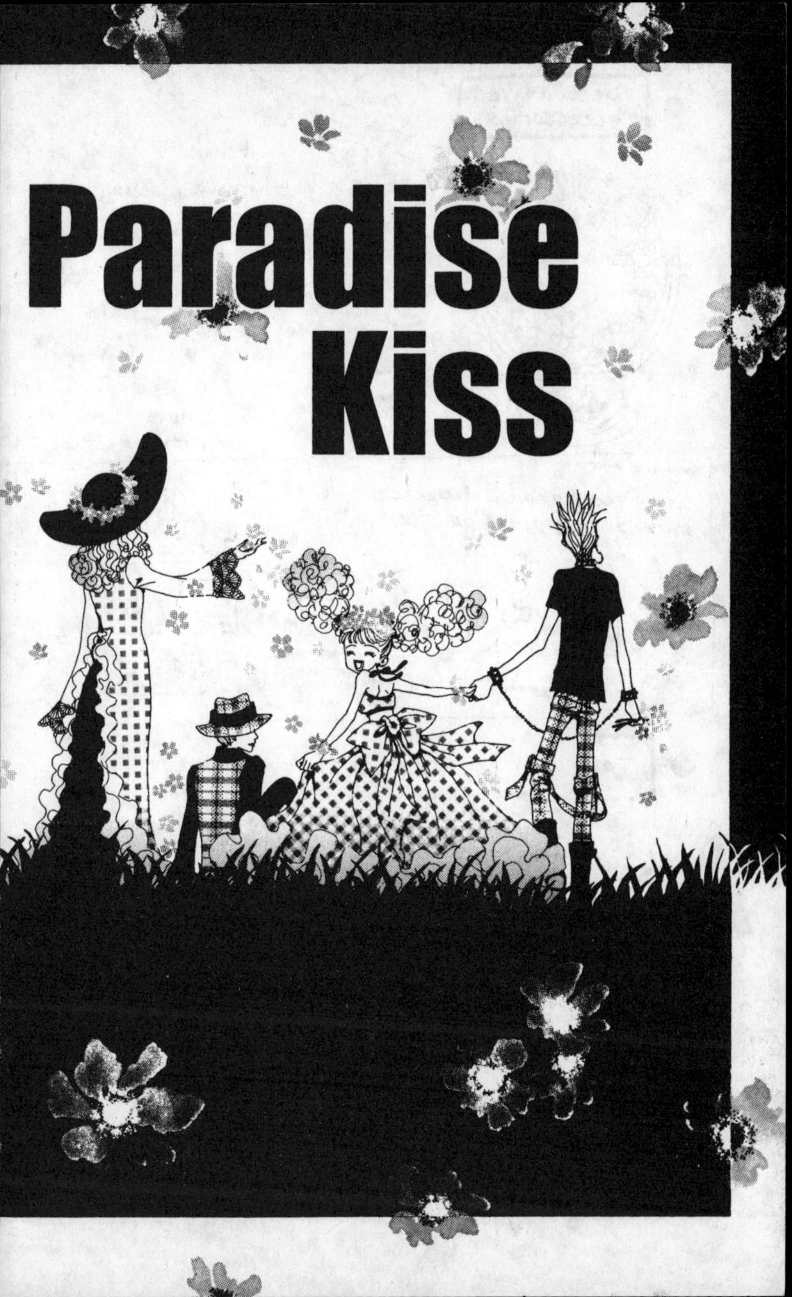
Paradise
Kiss

Fashion Forward

Ai Yazawa's break-through series of fashion and romance returns in a new 3 volume omnibus edition, with a new translation and new gorgeous trim size. Relive this hit all over again, 'cause good manga never goes out of style!

Volumes 1 and 2 available Fall 2012
280 pages each. Color plates, $19.95

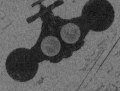

The hit sci-fi
emo-manga by

KEIKO TAKEMIYA

R R A •••

Volume 1
978-1-932234-67-1

Volume 2
978-1-932234-70-1

Volume 3
978-1-932234-71-8

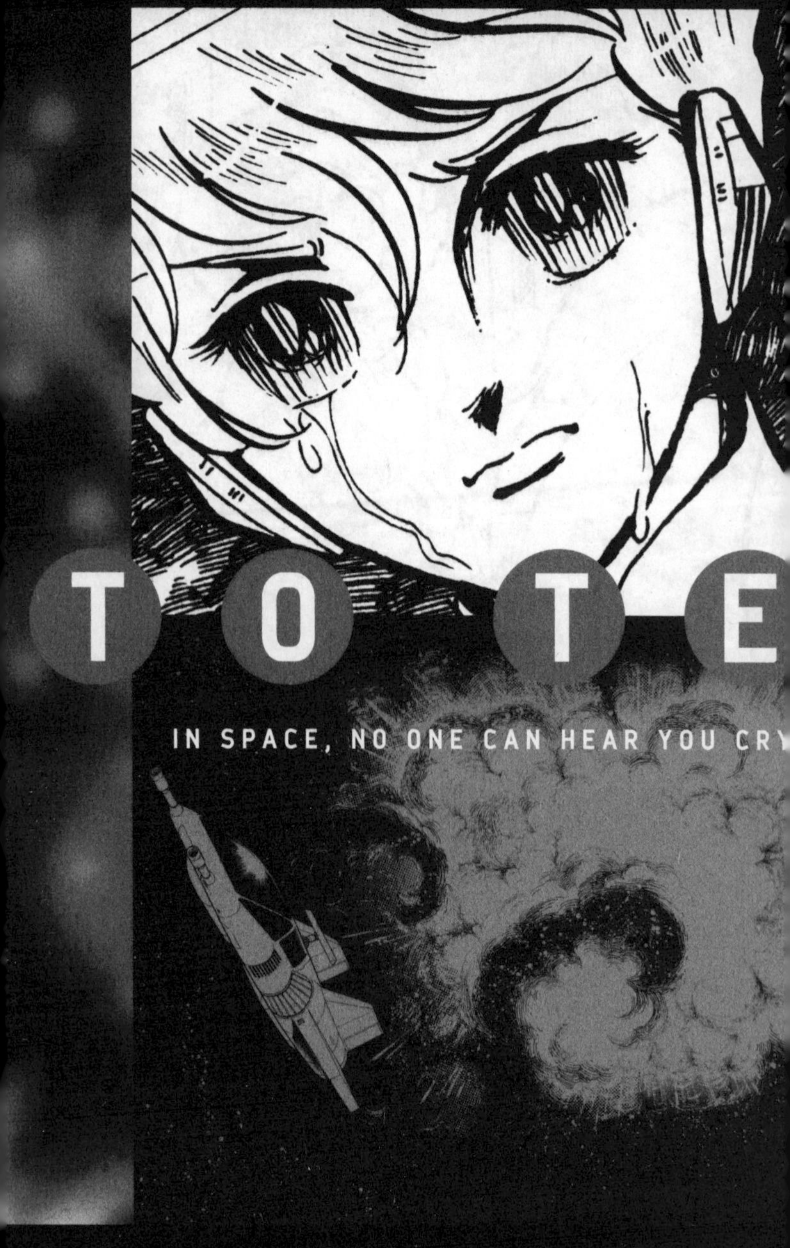
T O T E
IN SPACE, NO ONE CAN HEAR YOU CR

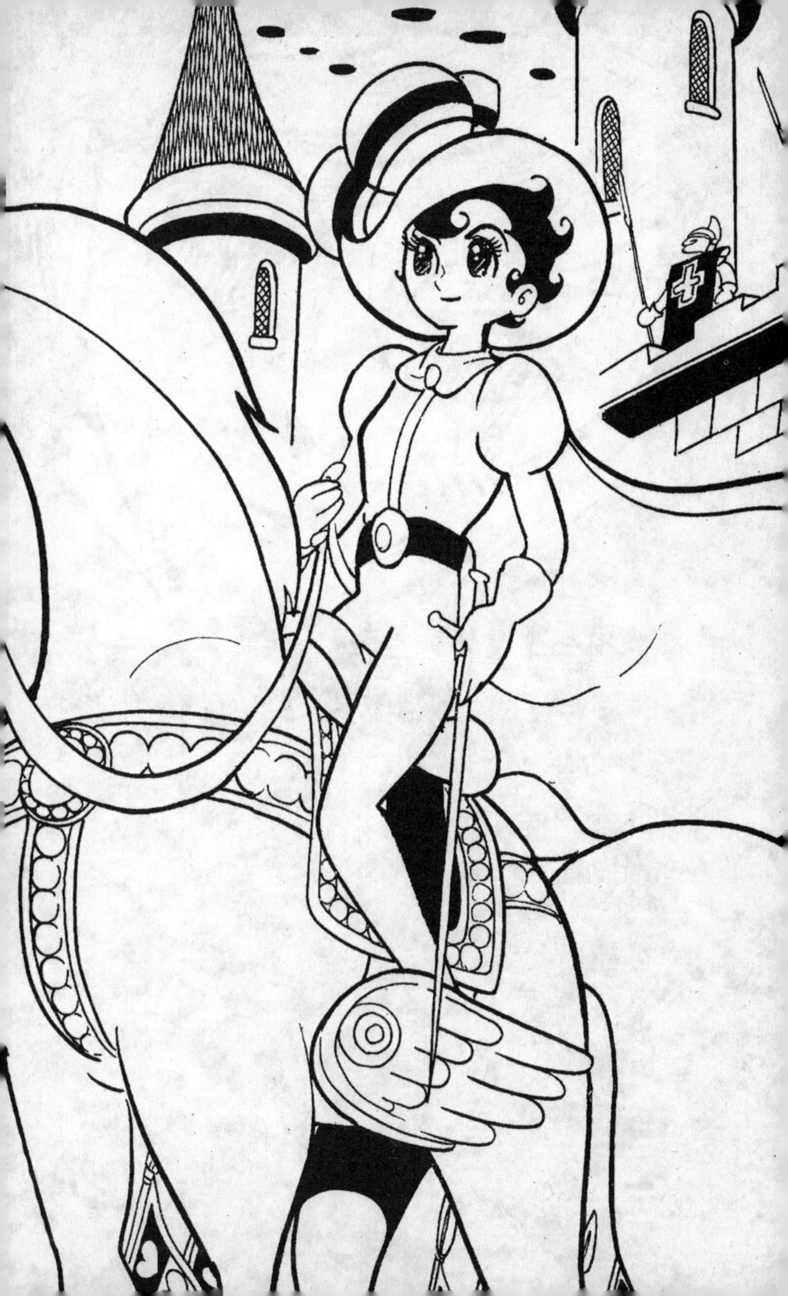

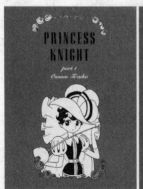
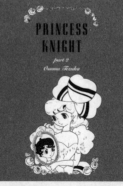

LIMIT

Limit: Volume 2

Translation: Mari Morimoto
Production: Taylor Esposito
Tomoe Tsutsumi
Daniela Yamada

First published in Japan in 2010 by Kodansha, Ltd., Tokyo
Publication for this English edition arranged through Kodansha, Ltd., Tokyo
English language version produced by Vertical, Inc.

Translation provided by Vertical, Inc., 2012
Published by Vertical, Inc., New York

Originally published in Japanese as *Limit 2* by Kodansha, Ltd.
Limit first serialized in *Bessatsu Friend*, Kodansha, Ltd., 2009-2011

ISBN: 978-1-935654-57-5

Manufactured in the United States of America

First Edition

Vertical, Inc.
451 Park Avenue South
7th Floor
New York, NY 10016
www.vertical-inc.com